U0046053

世界童話精選一百段

100 PASSAGES FROM THE WORLD'S BEST CHILDREN'S STORIES

一百叢書 ㉚

英漢對照 English-Chinese

石幼珊 謝山 編譯

世界童話精選
一百段
100 PASSAGES
FROM THE
WORLD'S BEST
CHILDREN'S STORIES

臺灣商務印書館發行

《一百叢書》總序

　　本館出版英漢（或漢英）對照《一百叢書》的目的，是希望憑藉着英、漢兩種語言的對譯，把中國和世界各類著名作品的精華部分介紹給中外讀者。

　　本叢書的涉及面很廣。題材包括了寓言、詩歌、散文、短篇小說、書信、演説、語錄、神話故事、聖經故事、成語故事、名著選段等等。

　　顧名思義，《一百叢書》中的每一種都由一百個單元組成。以一百為單位，主要是讓編譯者在浩瀚的名著的海洋中作挑選時有一個取捨的最低和最高限額。至於取捨的標準，則是見仁見智，各有心得。

　　由於各種書中被選用的篇章節段，都是以原文或已被認定的範本作藍本，而譯文又經專家學者們精雕細琢，千錘百煉，故本叢書除可作為各種題材的精選讀本外，也是研習英漢兩種語言對譯的理想參考書，部分更可用作朗誦教材。外國學者如要研習漢語，本書亦不失為理想工具。

商務印書館（香港）有限公司

編輯部

前　言

　　有的人類學家認為人類各種藝術中，沒有比講故事更為古老的藝術了。早在人們會繪畫、寫字之前，他們已經互相傳述着各種故事。從古代遺物中，我們可以看到大量傳說故事，表達原始部落人們的感情和願望。兒童文學作家Ｇ‧格里菲思和Ｃ‧弗雷說，兒童文學的偉大作品大致形成於1700至1920年之間。世界各地區和國家民族都有自己的童話，帶有各自的特徵，即各個社會的思維方式、習俗和信仰等。但不同地區亦敘有內容相似的童話，這些童話的驚人相似，說明各國家民族之間存在着基本的文化親緣關係。如在本書選用的英格蘭的《諾羅威大黑牛》和匈牙利的《會說話的葡萄、會笑的蘋果和叮噹響的杏子》中就有着明顯的類似之處。讀者還可以在書中找到這種例子。據估計，已發現的《辛德瑞拉（灰姑娘）》的版本就有三百多種。

　　如上述，童話故事最初以口述形式出現，年復一年地傳下來、散播開，匯成文字。後來又出現了夏爾‧佩羅、格林兄弟、漢斯‧安徒生、約瑟夫‧雅各布斯和彼得‧阿斯布約恩森等童話大師。他們和其他童話作家一同為我們留下一座世界兒童文學寶庫。

　　童話是娛樂性的，重要的是，它們寓教育於娛樂之中。但它們從不說教，而只是如拂面的和風，如霏霏的細雨，如甘醇的朝露，滋養着一代又一代人的心靈；它們教人為善，教人真誠。童話的結局**總**是真、善、美戰勝醜惡與虛偽，它們的使命是使失敗者振奮，使怯懦者堅強，使受難者得到慰藉；它們淨化靈魂，使之昇華。不是嗎？在《小美人魚》中，小小的美人魚"願意用三百年的生命換取為人類的一天"，得到不朽的靈魂！這是多麼發人**深**省的一句話！有誰讀完這篇故事之後，能不掩卷**深**思，惕然警悟：小美人魚為了爭得做人的權利，勇敢奮鬥，甘受苦難；那麼已經有幸生而為人的我們，應該如何才無愧於人的稱號呢？應該如何去對待人呢？

雖然童話故事表述的多是想像出來的、實際上不可能的事，但那不是引導我們逃避現實，而是為我們燃起對美好未來的希望。有些童話即使帶有悲劇性的結局，如《快樂王子》和《紅舞鞋》等，但它們仍然有積極的內涵，因此也是樂觀的、正面的。許多天真的兒童讀完《賣火柴的小女孩》之後，央求他們的父母把自己的衣服、書籍甚至玩具送去給可憐的小女孩的事實，就是明證。

在本書中，我們所選的童話，大多數是歐美各國的不朽名篇；為了使讀者接觸到更多不同的文化形態，我們也選了少數雖不為人們熟悉卻自有特色的故事。例如從《被月亮帶走的人》中，可以看到愛斯基摩民族有些習俗和我們相反；他們是以太陽為陰性、以月亮為陽性的，等等。此外，這類童話一般風格純樸可喜，有的充滿幽默機智。

書中所選故事，上自5世紀，下及於今，覆蓋了一千多年。其中有：法國、德國、英國、愛爾蘭、意大利、西班牙、希臘、瑞士（西歐）；俄羅斯、波蘭、匈牙利、布科維納地區（東歐）；芬蘭、挪威、丹麥、冰島（北歐）；美國、墨西哥（南、北美洲）；巴比倫、印度、中國、日本、土耳其及以色列（亞洲）；澳大利亞、非洲；以及猶太民族、愛斯基摩民族、紅印第安部落和北美印第安部落等六個洲二十七個國家或地區、民族，約五十位作家的作品。本書編目大致按作者生年排列，相同國籍的作家編在一起。

遺憾的是，為篇幅所限，本書許多故事都做了刪節。但我們精心保留了原作的特色和精神風貌。我們在必要的地方作了有助於對內容理解的註釋。

本書採用英漢對照的形式。我們還希望它能為青、少年學生和他們的教師提供若干有用的課內、課外學習補充材料。

石幼珊

謝山

一九九八年十二月

PREFACE

Some anthropologists maintained that no human art is older than the art of story-telling. Long before people began to draw or write, they told tales to one another. From the ancient heritage we can read a vast number of traditional tales which express the feelings and aspirations of primitive tribes and races. Great works of children's literature came into being from about 1700 to 1920, according to G. Griffith and C. Frey, writers of children's literature. Various regions and nations of the world have their own folk tales and each tale carries with it the characteristics of the society from which it has come, such as the way of thinking, the customs and the beliefs. However, similar stories are frequently found in different places. These fascinating parallels show that there exists a basic cultural kinship between nations and races of the world. For instance, there are obvious similarities between the English story "The Black Bull of Norroway" and the Hungarian story "The Speaking Grapes, the Smiling Apple and the Tinkling Apricot". You can find some other examples of this kind in the book. It has been estimated that more than three hundred versions of the story of Cinderella have been discovered.

As mentioned above, tales were passed down orally through the years and they travelled far and wide before they took shape in the form of written languages. Later, great masters of children's tales, such as Charles Perrault, the Grimm Brothers, Hans C. Andersen and Peter C. Asbjornsen and many others, emerged and left the world a rich repository of children's literature.

Children's stories are entertaining. What is more important, they are instructive, yet they never preach. They are like the gentle breeze, the soft drizzle and the sweet morning dew, moistening and nourishing the hearts of generation after generation. They teach us to learn to be good and true. In these tales the good, the beautiful and the true always defeat the evil, the ugly and the false in the end. So they fulfil the functions of cheering up the defeated, strengthening the timid and giving comfort to those who suffer. They purify and sublimate the soul. Don't you see that the Little Mermaid "would give all my three hundred years to be a human being for one day" and gain an immortal soul? How enlightening this is! No one who has finished the story and closed the book can help sinking into deep meditation. All of a sudden he may become aware that in order to gain the right of being a human the Little Mermaid has bravely struggled, suffered and endured; then what should we who are fortunately born human beings do to be worthy of that name? And, what attitude should we adopt in dealing with our fellow human beings?

Though children's tales are full of imagination and the impossible, they do not turn us away from the reality, but kindle our hope for a better future. Some of them may have a tragic ending, such as "The Happy Prince", "The Red Shoes" and so on. Still, they are always optimistic and have their own positive meanings. The fact that many innocent children, after reading "The Little Match Girl", have begged their parents to send their favourite clothes, books and toys to the poor little girl may serve as a convincing evidence of such positivity.

In this collection, we have chosen mostly works from European countries and the U. S. that are of lasting appeal. Others are less well known, but they have their own distinctive features, giving the readers a taste of different cultures. For example, in "Carried off by the Moon", we learn that certain Eskimo tribes believe the sun is female and the moon male, contrary to our traditional belief. Moreover, stories of this kind are always written in a simple and pleasant style, full of wit and humour.

This collection covers more than one thousand years, from as early as the fifth century down to the modern times. It includes stories by some fifty authors from France, Germany, England, Ireland, Italy, Spain, Greece and Switzerland (in Western Europe); Russia, Poland, Hungary and the Bukovina region (in Eastern Europe); Finland, Norway, Denmark, Iceland (in Northern Europe); the United States and Mexico (in the Americas); Babylon, India, China, Japan, Turkey and Israel (in Asia); Australia; Africa; as well as from the Eskimo race, the Red Indians and North American Indians, representing all together twenty-seven countries, regions and races on six continents. We have arranged the tales roughly in the chronological order of the birth dates of their authors and grouped them according to the authors' nationalities.

We regret that a number of the stories here have to be abridged because of the limited printing space we have been allowed. Great care, though, has been taken to preserve the spirit, style and special features of the original. We have provided explanatory notes wherever they may aid the readers in understanding the texts.

This anthology is bilingual. We hope it will prove valuable as supplementary reading material to students and their teachers in or outside the classroom.

Shi Youshan
Xie Shan
December, 1998

目　錄
CONTENTS

Prologue 楔子

European Tales 歐洲童話

Northern European Tales 北歐童話

xiv

American Tales 美洲童話

Asian Tales 亞洲童話

Other Tales 其他童話

PROLOGUE

The Golden Key (Germany)

One winter, when a deep snow was lying on the ground, a poor boy had to go out in a sledge to fetch wood. As soon as he had collected together a sufficient quantity, he thought that before he returned home he would make a fire to warm himself, because his limbs were so frozen. So, sweeping the snow away, he made a clear space, and presently found a small gold key. As soon as he picked it up, he began to think that where there was a key there must also be a lock; and, digging in the earth, he found a small iron chest. "I hope the key will fit," thought he to himself; "there are certainly great treasures in this box!" He looked all over it, but could not find any keyhole; but at last he did discover one, which was, however, so small that it could scarcely be seen. He tried the key, and behold! it fitted exactly. Then he turned it once round, and now, if you will wait until he has quite unlocked it, and lifted up the lid, then we shall learn what wonderful treasures were in the chest...

Jakob and Wilhelm Grimm

楔 子

金鑰匙（德國）

　　一個冬天，地上覆蓋着深深的積雪，可一個窮苦的男孩還得乘雪撬出外撿柴。他撿夠了柴，因為手腳都凍僵了，就想回家前先生一堆火暖和暖和。於是，他掃開雪，清出一塊地，這一來發現了一把小小的金鑰匙。他拾起鑰匙，想道：有鑰匙的地方一定有鎖。他挖開泥土找到一個小鐵箱。"但願這把鑰匙能打開它，"他想，"這裏面肯定有大筆財寶！"他上下左右地細看這箱子，卻找不到鑰匙孔。最後他終於找到了一個孔，小得幾乎看不見。他試了試鑰匙。瞧，正好合適。於是他把鑰匙轉動一圈。好啦，如果你耐心等他打開鎖，掀起箱蓋，我們就會知道裏面有些甚麼寶貝了……

　　　　　　　　　　　　雅各布 與 威廉·格林

2

European Tales
歐洲童話

1 The Sleeping Beauty in the Wood (1) (France)

There were formerly a king and a queen, who were sorry they had no children; so sorry that it cannot be expressed. At last, however, the queen had a daughter. There was a very fine christening; and the princess had for her godmothers all the fairies they could find in the whole kingdom — they found seven.

They prepared a great feast for the fairies. There was placed before every one of them a magnificent cover with a case of massive gold, wherein were a spoon, knife and fork, all of pure gold set with diamonds and rubies. But as they were all sitting down at table they saw come into the hall a very old fairy, who had not been invited. The king ordered her a cover, but could not furnish her with a case of gold because seven only had been made for the seven fairies. The old fairy fancied she was slighted and muttered some threats between her teeth. One of the young fairies, who sat by her, overheard how she grumbled, and hid herself behind the hangings, that she might speak last and repair any evil which the old fairy intended.

Meanwhile all the fairies began to give their gifts to the princess. The youngest for her gift said that the princess should be the most beautiful person in the world; the next, that she should have the wit of an angel; the third, that she should have wonderful grace in everything she did; the fourth, that she should dance perfectly; the fifth, that she should sing like a nightingale; and the sixth, that she should play all kinds of music to perfection.

The old fairy's turn coming next, she said that the

一 林中睡美人（一）（法國）

　　從前有一位國王和王后，因為沒有孩子一直悶悶不樂，說不出的煩惱。後來，王后終於生下一個女孩。他們舉行盛大的洗禮儀式，國王和王后從全國將能找到的仙女都請來做公主的教母，一共七位。

　　他們為七位仙女準備好一個盛大的宴會，每個仙女面前擺着一套豪華的餐具：一個實心黃金大托盤上放着純金打成的、鑲滿金剛鑽和紅寶石的匙和刀叉。她們剛要在桌前坐下，大廳裏走進來一位很老的仙女——她沒有受到邀請。國王命人給她放上一套餐具，但沒有金托盤，因為只是專為七仙女打製了七份。年老的仙女覺得受到怠慢，咬着牙發出喃喃的咒罵聲。坐在她旁邊的一位小仙女無意中聽到她在咕噥，便藏到帷幕後面，這樣她就可以排在最後給公主祝福，抵消老年仙女惡毒的咒語了。

　　這時，仙女們開始為公主祝福，最年輕的仙女的禮物是：祝願公主成為世界上最美麗的人；第二位仙女說公主將和天使一樣聰明伶俐；第三位說公主的行為舉止將異常溫雅；第四位則賜給公主最完美的舞姿；第五位說她唱歌將像夜鶯那麼婉轉動聽；第六位說她彈奏諸般音樂能出神入化。

　　輪到年老的仙女時，她說公主將被紡錘尖刺傷手而

princess should have her hand pierced with a spindle and die of the wound. This terrible gift made the whole company tremble, and everybody fell a-crying.

At this very instant the young fairy came out from behind the hangings, and spoke these words aloud: "Assure yourselves, O King and Queen, that your daughter shall not die. The princess shall indeed pierce her hand with a spindle. But she shall only fall into a profound sleep, which shall last a hundred years. After a hundred years a king's son shall come and wake her."

The king, to avoid the misfortune, immediately forbade spinning with a distaff and spindle in the house. About fifteen or sixteen years after, one day the young princess was diverting herself by running up and down the palace. She came into a little room at the top of the tower, where a good old woman was spinning with her spindle. This good woman had never heard of the king's proclamation against spindles.

"What are you doing there, goody?" said the princess.

"I am spinning, my pretty child," said the old woman.

"Ha," said the princess, "this is very pretty. How do you do it? Give it to me so I may see." She had no sooner taken the spindle than it ran into her hand, and she fell down in a swoon.

And now the king who came up at the noise, caused the princess to be carried into the finest apartment in his palace and laid upon a bed all embroidered with gold and silver. One would have taken her for a little angel, she was so very beautiful, for her swooning had not dimmed her complexion: her cheeks were carnation and her lips were coral. The king commanded them not to disturb her, but let her sleep quietly till her hour of awakening was come.

— *Charles Perrault*

6

死。這個惡毒的咒語使所有的人驚駭得顫慄起來，只聽得一片哭聲。

正在這時，那位年輕的仙女從帷幕後走出來，高聲說道："尊敬的國王和王后啊，請放心吧。你們的女兒不會死，公主要被紡錘刺破手，但她只是沉睡一百年罷了。一百年之後，會有一位王子來將她喚醒。"

於是，國王立即下令禁止在宮中使用綫杆和紡錘來紡綫以免發生不幸。十五、六年過去了，一天，小公主一個人在王宮裏跑上跑下地玩。她跑到了塔樓頂的一個小房間，一位慈祥的婆婆正在用紡錘紡綫。這位老婆婆沒有聽說過國王關於紡綞的禁令。

"你在做甚麼哪，老奶奶？"公主問。

"我在紡綫呀，漂亮的孩子。"老婆婆答。

"哈，"公主說，"真好看。您怎麼紡綫的？給我，讓我看看吧。"她一拿過紡錘，手就被刺破了，昏倒在地。

國王聽到嘈雜聲，走上樓來。他命人把公主送到宮內陳設最精緻的一個房間，讓她安臥在繡滿金絲銀綫被褥的牀上。人們看到她，還以為她是個小天使呢。她是那麼美麗。雖然昏睡過去，容顏依然光彩照人，雙頰像粉紅色的石竹花，嘴唇像紅珊瑚。國王禁止人們打擾她，讓她安安靜靜睡到該甦醒的時候。

——*夏爾·佩羅* [1]

---

1. 佩羅：(1628－1703)，法國詩人及評論家，著有《鵝媽媽的故事》，共十八篇。本文及"辛德瑞拉（水晶鞋）"、"小紅帽"等都在其內。這些故事多係作家按古代傳說用法語寫成。

2 The Sleeping Beauty in the Wood (2) (France)

The good fairy, who had saved the life of the princess came immediately. She touched with her wand everything in the palace — except the king and the queen. Immediately upon her touching them they all fell asleep. The very spits at the fire, as full as they could hold of partridges and pheasants, fell asleep also. All this was done in a moment.

And now the king and the queen, having kissed their dear child, went out of the palace, and in a quarter of an hour's time there grew up all round about the park such a vast number of trees, great and small, bushes and brambles, twining one within another, that neither man nor beast could pass through. Nothing could be seen but the very tops of the towers, and those only from a great distance.

When a hundred years were gone and passed the son of the king being gone a-hunting, asked what those towers were which he saw in the middle of a great thick wood. A very aged countryman spoke to him: "May it please Your Royal Highness, there was in this castle a princess, the most beautiful ever seen, who must sleep there a hundred years, and should be awakened by a king's son."

The young prince was all on fire at these words. Believing in this rare adventure, and pushed on by love and honor, he resolved that moment to look into it. Scarce had he advanced toward the wood when all the great trees, the bushes and brambles gave way of themselves to let him pass. The trees closed behind him again as soon as he had passed through. He came into a spacious outward court, where everything he saw might have frozen the most fearless person with horror. There was a frightful silence, and there was nothing to be

二　林中睡美人（二）（法國）

那位救了小公主性命的善良仙女立即趕來了。她用仙杖把宮殿裏的每一樣東西——除了國王和王后——都點了一下。仙杖一點，所有的人和動物都立刻睡着了。就連在火上烤着的、叉滿松雞和野雉的火叉也睡着了。一瞬間，一切都沉沉睡去。

國王和王后吻別了他們親愛的孩子，便走出了宮殿。不過十幾分鐘，花園的周圍便長出了高高矮矮、密密叢叢的樹林，灌木叢和荊棘枝纏藤繞，人獸都進不去。從外面甚麼也看不見了。只在遠處才看得到宮殿塔堡上的頂尖。

一百年過去了。一天，一位王子去打獵，看到一大片密林中的塔尖，便問那是甚麼地方。一位老態龍鍾的農夫對他說："尊敬的殿下，這城堡裏有一位絕色的公主，她要沉睡一百年，才有一位王子來喚醒她。"

年輕的王子聽到這話，激動得熱血沸騰，相信這是一個奇遇。他被愛情和正義感所激勵，決定立即進去看看。他剛走近，所有的大樹、灌木叢和荊棘便立即分開，讓他走過。他一走過，樹木又在他身後合攏了。王子來到一個寬闊的外院，他在那裏見到的情景足以使最勇敢的人也嚇得血液凝固起來：一片駭人的寂靜，到處橫七豎八地躺着

seen but stretched-out bodies of men and animals, all seeming to be dead. He knew, however, by the ruby faces of the beefeaters, that they were only asleep. At last he came into a chamber all gilded with gold, where he saw upon a bed, the curtains of which were open, the finest sight a young prince ever beheld — a princess, who appeared to be about fifteen or sixteen years of age, and whose bright and resplendent beauty had somewhat in it divine. He approached with trembling and admiration and fell down before her upon his knees.

And now, as the enchantment was at an end, the princess awoke, and looking on him with eyes more tender than the first view might seem to admit, "Is it you, my Prince?" said she. "I have waited a long while." The prince, charmed with these words, and much more with the manner in which they were spoken, knew not how to show his joy and gratitude. He assured her he loved her better than he did himself. Their discourse was not well connected, they did weep more than talk — little eloquence, a great deal of love.

Meanwhile all the palace awoke; everyone thought upon their particular business, and as all of them were not in love they were ready to die for hunger. The chief lady of honor, being as sharp set as other folks, grew very impatient and told the princess loudly that supper was served. The prince helped the princess to rise. She was dressed magnificently, but his royal highness took care not to tell her she was dressed like his great-grandmother.

After they had a feast, the whole court assembled in the chapel of the castle where the lord almoner married the princess to the prince. In due course, he brought his bride to his own kingdom where they lived in great happiness ever after.

— *Charles Perrault*

人和動物的軀體，似乎都已死去。但從那些衛士紅噴噴的臉色看，王子知道他們不過是睡着了。最後王子走進一間金碧輝煌的房間，看見一張牀，牀帷掛起，現出連一位王子也是生平僅見的美人 —— 一位看上去十五、六歲的公主。她容貌尊貴，光艷奪目，美若天仙。王子心裏充滿愛慕，微微顫抖着走近公主，跪在她身前。

於是魔術解除了。公主醒過來，用充滿溫柔的眼光看着王子，道：“是你嗎，我的王子？我已經等你好久了。”幾句話，尤其是公主深情的神態，使王子心動神馳，不知怎樣去表達他的喜悅感激之情。他告訴公主，他愛她勝過愛自己。他們斷續傾談，且訴且泣——巧言不多，但情深無限。

這時整個宮殿都甦醒了，人人都記起了自己的職責。因為他們不像王子公主那樣沉浸在戀愛中，所以都快要餓死了。女侍從長官和其他人一樣餓得發昏，她不耐煩了，高聲告訴公主，晚餐已經準備好。王子將公主扶起來，她穿着極其華貴的服裝，王子卻十分小心，不去說出這身打扮竟像他的曾祖母！

盛宴完畢，全宮廷的人都聚集在城堡的小教堂裏，宮廷主管主持了公主與王子的婚禮。之後，王子帶着新娘回到自己的王國，從此過着十分美滿的生活。

—— 夏爾·佩羅

3 The Master Cat (France)

There was a miller who left no more estate to the three sons he had than his mill, his donkey and his cat. The division was soon made. The eldest had the mill, the second the donkey, and the youngest nothing but the cat.

"My brothers," said the poor young fellow, "may get their living handsomely enough by joining their stocks together. But for my part, when I have eaten my cat, and made me a muff of his skin, I must die of hunger."

The cat, who heard all this, said to him with a grave and serious air, "Do not thus afflict yourself, my good master. You need only give me a bag, and have a pair of boots made for me that I may scamper through the brambles. You shall see you have not so bad a portion with me as you imagine."

When the cat had what he asked for, he booted himself very gallantly, and putting his bag about his neck, he went into a warren. He put bran and lettuce into his bag and, stretching out at length as if dead. Scarce had he lain down but he had what he wanted: a rash and foolish young rabbit jumped into his bag. Monsieur Puss[2], immediately drawing close the strings, killed him without pity. Proud of his prey, he went with it to the palace, and asked to speak with his majesty. He said to the king: "I have brought you, sir, a rabbit from the warren, which my noble lord, the Marquis of Carabas[1] has commanded me to present to Your Majesty from him."

---

1. the Marquis of Carabas：貓為抬高其主人身價捏造出來的，實際無此爵位。
2. Puss：源自 pussy-cat，小孩對貓的暱稱。

三　精明的貓（法國）

從前有個磨坊主，死後只給三個兒子留下一座磨坊、一頭毛驢和一隻貓。很快就分好了家，老大得了磨坊，老二要了毛驢，小兒子只得了那隻貓。

這可憐的小伙子說：“我哥哥加上他們原有的家產可以過得很好了，可我呢，吃了貓，用貓皮做副手套，我也就餓死了。”

貓聽了這話，一本正經地對他說：“別這麼苦惱啦，我的好主人，你只要給我一個袋子，再讓人做雙靴子，好讓我在荊棘叢中跑得快，你就會看到，分到我這份家產並不像你想的那麼壞。”

貓得到了要的東西，非常神氣地穿着靴子，把袋子掛在脖子上，去了養兔場，他把穀糠和蒿苣葉放進袋裏，攤手攤腳躺在地上裝死。不出所料，他剛躺下就正中下懷，一隻冒失失、傻乎乎的小兔子跳進了他的袋子裏。貓咪先生立刻抽緊繩子，毫不手軟地殺了兔子。他抓到了獵物很得意，拿着它去王宮要見國王。他對國王說：“王上，我尊貴的主人卡拉巴斯爵爺命我從養兔場拿來一隻兔子代他獻給陛下。”

"Tell your master," said the king, "that I thank him."

The cat continued thus for two or three months to carry to his majesty, from time to time, game of his master's taking. One day in particular, when he knew for certain that the king was to take the air along the riverside with his daughter, the most beautiful princess in the world, he said to his master: "If you will follow my advice your fortune is made. You have nothing to do but wash yourself in the river, and leave the rest to me."

The Marquis of Carabas did what the cat advised him to do. While he was washing, the king passed by, and the cat began to cry out: "Help! Help! My Lord Marquis of Carabas is going to be drowned." At this the king commanded his guards to run immediately to the assistance of his lordship.

The cat came up to the coach and told the king that some rogues went off with his master's clothes. The king immediately commanded the officers to fetch his suits for the Marquis of Carabas.

The fine clothes set off his good mien, for he was well made and very handsome in his person. The Marquis of Carabas had no sooner cast two or three respectful and tender glances upon the king's daughter than she fell in love with him to distraction. The king would needs have[2] him come into the coach and take the air with them. The cat, marched on before, and meeting with some countrymen, who were mowing a meadow, he said to them: "Good people, you who are mowing, if you do not tell the king that the meadow you mow belongs to my Lord Marquis of Carabas, you shall be chopped as small as herbs for the pot."

---

2. would needs have：〔 古 〕 = would have; would oblige (him) to。

"告訴你的主人，"國王說，"我謝謝他。"

貓就這樣在兩、三個月內時不時用他主人的名義給國王送野味。一天，他得到確切消息，說是國王要和女兒——全世界最美的公主——一起去河邊兜風。他便對主人說："你要是聽我的，你就要發迹啦。你別的都不用做，只管在河裏洗澡就行，剩下的我來安排。"

卡拉巴斯侯爵照辦。他正洗澡時，國王走過。貓叫起來："救命！救命！我主人卡拉巴斯侯爵要淹死啦！"聽到喊聲，國王命令衛士立即去救援爵爺。

貓又跑到車前告訴國王，幾個無賴把他主人的衣服拿走了。國王立即命令官員去把他的衣服拿給卡拉巴斯侯爵。

卡拉巴斯配上好衣服顯得風度翩翩，因為他本來就長得魁偉英俊。卡拉巴斯侯爵只是又崇敬又溫柔地瞟了公主兩、三眼，公主已經魂不守舍地愛上了他。國王恭請他上車和他們一起兜兜風。貓雄赳赳地走在車前，看見幾個正在割草的村民，便對他們說："割草的好朋友，你們要不對國王說這片草地屬於我的卡拉巴斯侯爵，你們就要像草一樣被剁碎了放在鍋裏煮。"

The king did not fail to ask the mowers to whom the meadow belonged. Altogether, they answered as what the cat had told them. The Master Cat, who went always before, said the same words to all he met, and the king was astonished at the vast estates of the Marquis of Carabas.

Monsieur Puss came at last to a stately castle, the master of which was an ogre, the richest ever known. The cat asked to speak with him. "I have been informed," said the cat, "that you have the power to take on the shape of the smallest animal; for example, to change yourself into a mouse; but I must own to you I take this to be impossible."

"Impossible!" cried the ogre. "You shall see that presently." At the same time he changed himself into a mouse and began to run about the floor. Puss no sooner perceived this than he fell upon him and ate him up.

Meanwhile the king saw this fine castle and had a mind to go into it. Puss ran out, and said to the king: "Your Majesty is welcome to this castle of my Lord Marquis of Carabas." "What, my Lord Marquis!" cried the king. "And does this castle also belong to you?"

The marquis gave his hand to the princess and followed the king, who went first. They passed into a spacious hall, where they found a magnificent collation. His majesty was charmed with the good qualities of the Lord Marquis of Carabas, as was his daughter, and seeing the vast estate he possessed, decided to make him his son-in-law. So the marquis married the princess that very same day. Puss became a great lord, and never ran after mice any more.

— *Charles Perrault*

國王果然問這些割草人牧場是誰的。他們異口同聲照着貓教的話回答了。這精明的貓一直走在前面，對所有遇到的人都說了同樣的話，國王對卡拉巴斯侯爵擁有的巨大產業驚嘆不已。

貓咪先生最後來到一座雄偉的城堡前，城堡的主人是個富甲天下的巨魔。貓求見他，說："聽說你有魔力能把自己變成最小的動物，比方說，變成一隻老鼠。可我得承認我覺得不可能。"

"不可能？！"巨魔喊起來，"現在就變給你看看。"說話間，他變成一隻老鼠，滿地亂跑。貓一見，馬上撲上去把他吃了。

就在這時，國王看到這座堂皇的城堡，想進去看看。貓跑出去對國王說："歡迎陛下來到我主人卡拉巴斯侯爵的城堡。""甚麼？侯爵大人！"國王喊道，"這座城堡也是你的？"

國王先進去，侯爵挽着公主跟在後面。他們進入一個寬敞的大廳，廳裏擺着一桌極精美的茶點。國王陛下和女兒一樣傾心於卡拉巴斯侯爵的高雅品格，又看到他擁有的巨大財產，決定招他為婿。於是這位侯爵當天就娶了公主，貓也成為一位大爵爺，再也不用整天捉老鼠吃了。

———— *夏爾·佩羅*

4 Cinderella or the Little Glass Slipper (1) (France)

Once there was a gentleman who married, for his second wife, the proudest and most haughty woman that was ever seen. She had, by a former husband, two daughters of her own humor, who were, indeed, exactly like her in all things. He had likewise a young daughter, but of unparalleled goodness and sweetness of temper.

The stepmother could not bear the good qualities of this pretty girl, and all the less because they made her own daughters appear the more odious. She employed her in the meanest work of the house. The girl slept in a sorry garret, upon a wretched straw bed, while her sisters lay in fine rooms.

The poor girl bore all patiently. When she had done her work, she used to go into the chimney corner and sit down among cinders and ashes, which caused her to be called Cinderwench[1]. But afterwards they called her Cinderella. However, Cinderella, notwithstanding her mean apparel, was a hundred times handsomer than her sisters.

It happened that the king's son gave a ball and invited all persons of fashion to it. The two sisters were also invited. They were delighted at this invitation and wonderfully busy in choosing such gowns, petticoats and headdresses as might become them. This was a new trouble to Cinderella, for it was she who ironed her sisters' linen and plaited their ruffles. As she was doing this, they said to her: "Cinderella, would you not like to go to the ball?" "Alas," she said, "you only

---

1. Cinderwench：cinder 意為煤渣，wench 意為村女。Cinderella 的 "ella" 為女子名後綴，故稱灰姑娘。

四　灰姑娘或水晶鞋（一）（法國）

　　從前有一位紳士，再婚娶了位最傲慢、最驕悍的女人。她帶來兩個前夫的女兒，這兩個女兒的心地和她一樣，處處都｜足像她。那位紳士自己也有一個小女兒，她的溫柔善良，舉世無匹。

　　後娘不能容忍這個品德又好、容貌又美的女孩，而且因為相形之下，自己的女兒顯得更令人討厭，這尤其使她受不了。她讓女孩做最粗賤的家務。女孩睡在破舊頂樓骯髒的稻草鋪上，而兩個姐姐卻睡在陳設精美的房間裏。

　　可憐的小姑娘默默地忍受着這一切。每當幹完活兒，她就走到煙囱角落裏，坐在煤渣和爐灰上，因此人們叫她灰丫頭。後來又叫她辛德瑞拉。但是，破舊的衣衫遮掩不住辛德瑞拉的美貌，她比她的姐姐漂亮千百倍。

　　一天，王子舉辦舞會，邀請所有上流社會人士參加，兩位姐姐也在被邀請之列。她們興高采烈，為挑選合適的禮服、裙子和頭飾忙個不停。這給辛德瑞拉又添了麻煩，她得為她們熨衣衫、鑲褶邊。辛德瑞拉幹着活的時候，她們說：＂辛德瑞拉，你不想參加舞會嗎？＂＂唉，你們這不

jeer at me. It is not for such as I to go thither." "You are in the right of it," replied they. "It would certainly make people laugh to see a cinderwench at a palace ball."

At last the happy day came. They went to court, and Cinderella followed them with her eyes as long as she could, and when she had lost sight of them, she fell a-crying. Her godmother, who was a fairy, said to her, "You wish to go to the ball. Is it not so?" "Yes," cried Cinderella, with a great sigh. "Well," said her godmother, "run into the garden and bring me a pumpkin."

Cinderella went immediately to gather the finest one and brought it to her godmother. Her godmother scooped out all the inside of it, leaving nothing but the rind; which done, she struck it with her wand, and the pumpkin was instantly turned into a fine coach, gilded all over with gold. She then went to look into her mousetrap, where she found six mice, all alive. She gave each mouse a little tap with her wand, the mouse was that moment turned into a fine horse. Being at a loss for a coachman, Cinderella said, "I will go and see if there is a rat in the rat-trap." She brought the trap to her, and in it there were three huge rats. The fairy made choice of the one which had the largest beard, and having touched him with her wand, he was turned into a fat, jolly coachman, who had the smartest whiskers eyes ever beheld. After that, the godmother touched Cinderella with her wand, and at the same instant her clothes were turned into cloth of gold and silver, all beset with jewels. This done, she gave her a pair of glass slippers, the prettiest in the whole world. Being thus decked out, Cinderella climbed into her coach, but her godmother, above all things, commanded her not to stay till after midnight, telling her, at the same time, that if she stayed one moment longer, everything would become just as it was before.

是笑話我嗎？那可不是我這樣的人去的地方呀。""你真算説對了，"她們説，"在宮廷舞會上看到個灰丫頭，才會讓人笑掉大牙呢。"

好日子終於到了，兩個姐姐去了宮廷，辛德瑞拉眼巴巴一直望到看不見她們了，才哭了起來。她的教母是個仙女，她對辛德瑞拉説："你想參加舞會，是吧？""是的，"辛德瑞拉長長地嘆了一口氣，哭着説。"好，"教母道，"到園子裏去給我摘個南瓜來。"

辛德瑞拉立刻去摘了個最好的南瓜交給教母，教母將南瓜瓤全部掏空，只剩下皮，又用仙杖點了一下，南瓜立刻變成了一輛精美的四輪馬車，車身全部鍍金。教母又去看了一下她的捕鼠器，找到六隻小鼠，全是活的。她用仙杖把每隻輕輕一點，小鼠們立刻變成了一匹匹駿馬。就缺一個車夫了。辛德瑞拉説："我去看看大捕鼠夾上有沒有大老鼠。"她拿來一個大鼠夾，上有三隻大老鼠。仙女選了一隻鬍子最多的，又用仙杖點了一下，大鼠立刻變成了一個胖乎乎、笑呵呵的車夫，長有最漂亮的兩撇髭鬍。然後，教母又用仙杖點了辛德瑞拉一下，一瞬間，她的衣服變成是金絲銀綫織成的，而且還綴滿珠寶。然後教母又給了她一雙全世界最漂亮的水晶鞋。這樣裝備齊全後，辛德瑞拉便上了馬車。但教母又千叮萬囑，叫她不能在宮裏呆到半夜十二點鐘，告訴她只要超過一分鐘，一切就會原形畢露。

Cinderella promised her and then away she drove, scarce[2] able to contain herself for joy. The king's son, who was told that a great princess, whom nobody knew, had come, ran out to receive her. He gave her his hand as she alighted from the coach and led her into the hall. There was immediately a profound silence. They left off dancing, and the violins ceased to play, so attentive was everyone to contemplate the singular beauties of the unknown newcomer. Nothing was then heard but a confused noise of: "Ha! How handsome she is! Ha! How handsome she is!"

— *Charles Perrault*

2.　scarce ：＝ scarcely。

辛德瑞拉答應了，掩蓋不了心中喜悅，就坐車走了。王子聽說有一位非常尊貴、但沒有人認識的公主駕到，趕快跑出去迎接。他把她扶下馬車，帶她進了大廳。大廳立即肅靜下來，人們停下舞步，琴師也忘了演奏，都屏息凝神地打量着這位不知姓名的公主那絕世的美艷，其廳都聽不見了，只聽到一陣陣讚歎聲：“她真美呀！她真美啊！”

——夏爾·佩羅

5 Cinderella or the Little Glass Slipper (2)
(France)

The king's son conducted her to the most honorable seat, and afterward took her out to dance with him, and she danced so gracefully that all more and more admired her. Suddenly, she heard the clock strike eleven and three-quarters, whereupon she immediately made a curtsy to the company and hastened away as fast as she could.

Reaching home, she ran to seek out her godmother and was eagerly telling her godmother whatever had passed at the ball, when her two sisters knocked at the door, which Cinderella ran and opened. "How long you have stayed!" cried she, rubbing her eyes and stretching herself as if she had been just waked out of her sleep. One of her sisters told her how there had come thither the finest princess, and how she showed them a thousand civilities.

The next day the two sisters were at the ball, and so was Cinderella, but dressed more magnificently than before. The king's son was always by her and never ceased his compliments and kind speeches to her. All this was so far from being tiresome that she quite forgot what her godmother had commanded her. At last, she counted the clock striking twelve when she took it to be no more than eleven. She then rose up and fled. The prince followed but could not overtake her. She left behind one of her glass slippers, which the prince took up most carefully.

The guards at the palace gate were asked if they had not seen a princess go out. They had seen nobody but a young girl, very meanly dressed, and who had more the air of a poor country wench than a gentlewoman.

五 灰姑娘或水晶鞋(二)（法國）

王子將辛德瑞拉引到貴賓席首座。之後，又請她一起跳舞。她跳得優雅極了，所有的人都越來越傾慕她。忽然間，她聽到時鐘敲響十一點三刻，她立刻向人羣行了個屈膝禮，急匆匆地離開了。

回到家後，她跑去找教母。她正興奮地向教母描述舞會的情景時，兩個姐姐敲門了。辛德瑞拉跑去開門。"你們去的時間真久呀！"她喊道，一邊揉着眼睛，伸着懶腰，好像剛睡醒。一個姐姐告訴她，怎樣來了一位最尊貴的公主，她怎樣對她們萬分客氣。

第二天，兩位姐姐又去參加舞會，辛德瑞拉也去了，而且比前一天穿得更華麗。王子和她寸步不離，不住地傾訴對她的稱讚、愛慕。這使得她十分愜意，以至於幾乎把教母的囑咐忘在腦後。最後，十二點鐘敲響了，她還以為頂多不過十一點鐘呢。她馬上站起身，飛快地跑了。王子跟着，但沒有追上她。辛德瑞拉掉下一隻水晶鞋，王子小心翼翼地拾起來。

被問及有沒有見到一位公主離去時，宮殿大門的守衛説，只看見一位小姑娘出去了。衣著很破舊，氣度不像貴族小姐，倒像個村裏的窮丫頭。

A few days afterward the king's son caused it to be proclaimed, by sound of trumpet, that he would marry her whose foot the glass slipper would just fit. They whom he employed began to try it upon the princesses, then the duchesses, and all the court, but in vain. It was brought to the two sisters, who each did all she possibly could to thrust her foot into the slipper. But they could not effect it. Cinderella, who saw all this, and knew her slipper, said to them, laughing: "Let me see if it will not fit me."

Her sisters burst out laughing and began to banter her. The gentleman who was sent to try the slipper looked earnestly at Cinderella and, finding her very handsome, said it was but just she should try, and that he had orders to let everyone make trial. He obliged Cinderella to sit down, and putting the slipper to her foot, he found it went on easily and fitted her. The astonishment of her two sisters was great, but still greater when Cinderella pulled out of her pocket the other slipper and put it on her foot. There upon, in came her godmother who, having touched Cinderella's clothes with her wand, made them richer and more magnificent than any she had worn before.

And now her two sisters found her to be that fine, beautiful lady they had seen at the ball. They threw themselves at her feet to beg pardon for all the ill-treatment they had made her undergo. Cinderella raised them up and embraced them.

She was conducted to the young prince. He thought her more charming than ever and, a few days after, married her. Cinderella, who was no less good than beautiful, gave her two sisters lodgings in the palace, and that very same day matched them with two great lords of the court.

— *Charles Perrault*

數天後，王子命人吹着喇叭宣佈，哪個姑娘的腳正好穿上水晶鞋子，他就娶她為妻。侍從們先讓公主們試穿，然後讓公爵小姐，再讓整個宮廷的貴族小姐試穿，但都不合適。侍從們拿鞋來讓兩個姐姐試穿。她們想盡辦法要把腳塞進鞋裏，但怎麼也穿不上。辛德瑞拉看到了這一切，認得這是她的鞋，便笑着說：「讓我試試看穿得上不。」

她的姐姐哈哈大笑，說各種話奚落她。王子派來的人仔細打量辛德瑞拉，發現她長得十分漂亮，便說要公平地讓她試試，因為他奉命讓每個姑娘都試一試的。他請辛德瑞拉坐下，把鞋給她穿，很容易便穿進去了，正好貼腳。兩個姐姐看得瞠目結舌，但是當辛德瑞拉從衣袋裏拿出另一隻水晶鞋來穿在腳上的時候，她們更吃驚了。這時教母進來了，用仙杖一點辛德瑞拉的衣服，她的衣裙變得比上兩次的更為華麗。

這時，兩個姐姐才認出她就是舞會上她們見到的那位高貴、美麗的公主。她們跪倒在她腳下，請求她寬恕她們從前對她的種種虐待。辛德瑞拉扶起她們，擁抱她們。

辛德瑞拉去見了王子，王子覺得她比先前更美艷動人。數天後，他們成了婚。辛德瑞拉不僅美麗，而且善良，她把兩位姐姐接到宮廷裏住，當天，又把她們許配給了宮裏的一兩個大臣。

——夏爾·佩羅

6 Toads and Diamonds (France)

There was once upon a time a widow who had two daughters. The elder was so much like her in face and humor that whosoever looked upon the daughter saw the mother. They were both disagreeable and proud. The younger, who was the very picture of her father for courtesy and sweetness of temper, was withal one of the most beautiful girls ever seen. As people naturally love their own likeness, this mother doted on her elder daughter, and at the same time had a horrible aversion for the younger.

Among the other things, this poor child was forced twice a day to draw water above a mile and a half from the house and bring home a pitcher full of it. One day, as she was at this fountain, there came to her a poor woman, who begged of her to let her drink. She, immediately rinsing the pitcher, took up some water from the clearest place of the fountain, and gave it to her. The good woman having drunk, said to her, "You are so very pretty, my dear, so good and so mannerly, I cannot help giving you a gift." For this was a fairy. The fairy continued, "At every word you speak, there shall come out of your mouth either a flower or a jewel."

When this pretty girl came home her mother scolded her for staying so long at the fountain. "I beg your pardon, mamma," said the poor girl, "for not making more haste." And in speaking these words out of her mouth there came two roses, two pearls and two diamonds.

"What is it I see there?" said her mother, astonished. "How happens this, child?" The poor girl told her frankly all that had happened, not without dropping infinite numbers of diamonds.

六　癩蛤蟆與鑽石 （法國）

　　從前一位寡婦有兩個女兒。大女兒相貌性情都十分像母親，無論是誰看見女兒，就知道母親是甚麼樣子的了。兩個人都很傲慢，難與人相處。小女兒卻是父親的模子，謙恭有禮，性情溫和，且相貌絕美。當然啦，人都是喜歡氣味相投的人，這母親便十分寵愛驕縱大女兒，對小女兒卻百般嫌棄厭惡。

　　這可憐的孩子每天幹活，其中一項是從離家一哩半還要遠的泉水汲兩次水，裝滿大水罐，提回家。一天，她正在泉邊，一個窮女人向她走來，請她給點兒水喝。她立刻沖洗乾淨水罐，從泉水最清澈潔淨的地方打了些水，遞給那女人。好心的女人喝完水，對她說："你長得真漂亮，好孩子。又這麼善良、彬彬有禮。我一定要送件禮物給你。"這人其實是個仙女，仙女接着說："你開口說話，說每個字都會有一朵鮮花或是一塊寶石從你嘴裏落下來。"

　　這美麗的小姑娘回到家，母親罵她不該在泉水邊呆那麼長時間，可憐的姑娘說："媽媽，請您原諒我沒有趕快回來。"說着，嘴裏冒出兩朵玫瑰，兩顆珍珠和兩塊鑽石。

　　"這是怎麼回事兒？"母親目瞪口呆地說，"怎麼會這樣的，孩子？"可憐的姑娘將發生的事情一五一十地全告訴了她，嘴裏不停地滾出數不清的鑽石。

"In good faith," cried the mother, "I must send my elder child thither." Then she said to her elder daughter, "you have nothing to do but draw water out of the fountain, and when a certain poor woman asks you to let her drink, to give it her very civilly."

"It would be a very fine sight indeed," said this ill-bred minx, "to see me draw water." "You shall go, hussy," said the mother, "and this minute."

So she went, but grumbling all the way, taking with her the best silver tankard in the house. She was no sooner at the fountain than she saw coming out of the wood a lady most gloriously dressed, who came up to her and asked to drink. This was the very fairy who appeared to her sister, but had now taken the air and dress of a princess. "Am I come hither," said the proud, saucy girl, "to serve you with water, pray? I suppose the silver tankard was brought for your ladyship? However, you may drink out of it, if you have a fancy." So the fairy gave her for gift that at every word she spoke there should come out of her mouth a snake or a toad.

So soon as her mother saw her coming she cried out, "Well, daughter?" "Well, mother?" answered the pert hussy, throwing out of her mouth two vipers and two toads.

"Oh, mercy!" cried the mother. "Oh, it is that wretch your sister who has occasioned all this, but she shall pay for it." And immediately she ran to beat her. The poor child fled away from her and went to hide herself in the forest, not far thence.

The king's son, then on his return from hunting, met her, and seeing her so pretty, asked what she did there alone and why she cried. "Alas, sir, my mother has turned me out of doors." The king's son, who saw five or six pearls and as many diamonds come out of her mouth, desired her to tell him how that happened. She thereupon told him the whole

"説真的，"母親喊起來，"我得讓我的大女兒去！"她對大女兒説："不用做別的，只要從泉裏打水就成了。有個窮婦人跟你要水喝，你就客客氣氣地給她。"

"讓我打水！樣子倒真好看！"這沒有教養的壞女孩説。"去吧，丫頭，這就去，"母親説。

她去了。一路上嘟嘟囔囔，拿了個家裏最好的大銀杯。她剛到泉邊，就看見一位衣著華麗的夫人從樹林裏走出來。她走到她面前，請她給點兒水喝。這正是她妹妹見到的那位仙女，可現在卻是王妃的裝束和氣度。傲慢的姑娘莽撞地説："請問，我到這兒來是為侍候你喝水的嗎？這銀杯帶來是為你這貴夫人的？算了吧，要是你喜歡，就用它喝吧。"於是，仙女給了她一份禮物，這禮物是她每説一個字，嘴裏就爬出一條蛇或跳出一隻癩蛤蟆。

母親一見她回來，便叫道："怎麼樣，女兒？""嗯，媽？"這蠻橫的丫頭回答，嘴裏竄出兩條毒蛇和兩隻癩蛤蟆。

"哎喲，老天保佑！"母親叫喊起來，"這都怪你妹妹那壞丫頭，都是她幹出來的好事，我得叫她吃點苦頭。"她立刻跑去打她。那可憐的孩子逃出家門，藏進不遠的一片樹林裏。

恰巧王子打獵回來，碰到她。見她這樣美麗，便問她獨自一人在這兒做甚麼，為甚麼哭泣。"唉，先生呀，我媽媽把我趕出家門了。"王子見有五、六顆珍珠和五、六顆鑽石從她嘴裏滾出來，便請她告訴他怎麼回事。她對他

story. The king's son fell in love with her, and considering with himself that such a gift was worth more than any marriage portion, conducted her to the palace of the king his father, and there married her.

As for the proud elder sister, she soon made herself so much hated that her own mother turned her off.

— *Charles Perrault*

講了整個經過。這王子愛上了她，又暗自思忖：這份禮物可沒有別的嫁妝比得上啊，便領她回父王的王宮，在宮中和她成了婚。

至於她那傲慢的姐姐，很快她便招得天怒人怨，連自己的母親都把她趕出了家門。

——夏爾·佩羅

7 The Shepherdess (France)

Once upon a time there lived a king who had two daughters. When they grew up, he made up his mind he would give his kingdom to whichever best proved her devotion. So he called the elder princess and said to her: "How much do you love me?" "As the apple of my eye!" answered she. "Ah," exclaimed the king, "you are indeed a good daughter." Then he sent for the younger and asked her how much she loved him. "I look upon you, my Father," she answered, "as I look upon salt in my food." The king did not like her words and ordered her to quit the court and never again appear before him.

The poor princess sadly left the castle where she was born, carrying her jewels and her best dresses in a bundle. As she was afraid no housewife would want to engage a girl with such a pretty face, she determined to make herself as ugly as she could. She therefore put on some clothes belonging to a beggar. After that she smeared ashes over her hands and face and shook her hair into a great tangle. Having thus changed her appearance, she went about offering herself as a goosegirl or shepherdess. After walking for many days, she came to a large farm where they were in want of a shepherdess and engaged her gladly.

One day, when she was keeping her sheep in a lonely tract of land, she washed herself carefully in the stream, and as she always carried her bundle with her, it was easy to shake off her rags and transform herself into a great lady. The king's son, who had lost his way out hunting, perceived this lovely damsel a long way off. As soon as the girl saw him she fled into the wood. The prince ran after her, but as

七 牧羊女 (法國)

　　從前有位國王有兩個女兒。女兒長大成人後,他決定要把王國傳給最愛他的女兒。於是,他喚來大公主對她說:"你愛我有多深?"她答:"就像愛我的珍寶一樣!""嗯,"國王說:"你真是個好女兒。"他又喚來小女兒問她愛他有多深,小女兒答:"父王,我把您看作我食物中的鹽。"國王不喜歡這回答,命她出宮,再也不要見到她。

　　可憐的公主傷心地離開了她出生的城堡,攜着一包她的珠寶和最漂亮的衣裳。她擔心哪家的主婦也不願意僱用一個臉蛋這麼漂亮的姑娘,便要把自己打扮得盡量醜一些。於是她穿上乞丐的衣服,又把爐灰抹在手上臉上,把頭髮弄得亂蓬蓬的。這樣改頭換面之後,她便四處尋找放鵝牧羊的活計。走了許多天,她來到一個大農場,那裏正需要個牧羊女,便高興地僱用了她。

　　一天,她到一片荒涼的地裏放羊時,在小溪裏好好地洗了個澡。因為她總隨身帶着衣包,脫掉渾身破爛,便不難變回一位高貴公主了。有個王子打獵迷了路,遠遠便望見了這可愛的姑娘。可是姑娘一見他,便趕緊逃進樹林裏。王子在後面緊追不捨,但腳絆在樹根上摔倒了,等到

he was running he caught his foot in the root of a tree and fell. When he was up again, she was nowhere to be seen. When she was quite safe, she put on her rags again and smeared her face and hands. However, the young prince found his way to the farm to ask for a drink of cider, and he inquired the name of the beautiful lady who kept the sheep. At this everyone began to laugh, for they said the shepherdess was one of the ugliest creatures under the sun.

But the king's son thought often of the lovely maiden he had seen only for a moment. At last he dreamed of nothing else, and grew thinner day by day, till his parents inquired what was the matter. He dared not tell them, so he only said he would like some bread baked by the shepherdess at the distant farm. They hastened to fulfill it. The girl merely asked for some flour, salt and water, and also that she might be left alone in a little room adjoining the oven, where the kneading trough stood. Before beginning her work she washed herself carefully and even put on her rings. While she was baking, one of her rings slid into the dough. When she had finished she again made herself as ugly as before.

The loaf was brought to the king's son. But in cutting it he found the ring of the princess and declared to his parents he would marry the girl whom the ring fitted. So the king made a proclamation through his whole kingdom, and ladies came from afar to lay claim to the honor. But the ring was so tiny that even those who had the smallest hands could only get it on their little fingers. In a short time all the maidens of the kingdom had tried on the ring. The prince observed he had not yet seen the shepherdess. They sent for her, and she arrived covered with rags, but with her hands clean and she easily slipped on the ring.

The king's son declared he would fulfill his promise. When his parents mildly remarked that the girl was only a

他爬起來，姑娘已不見蹤影。到了無人之處，姑娘又穿上破衣爛衫，塗污了手、臉。但是小王子找到路到了農場，討點蘋果汁喝，他還問起那美麗的牧羊小姐的名字。眾人聽見笑了起來，都說那牧羊女是天底下最醜的丫頭。

但是，王子雖然只見過一眼，卻時常想起那可愛的姑娘。他眠思夢想，日漸消瘦，直到有一天他父母問起緣由，他不敢相告，只說他喜歡吃遠處農場裏牧羊女烤的麵包。他們馬上想法滿足他的要求。那姑娘只要了些麵粉、鹽和水，還要求獨自留在有個揉麵缽的小房間裏，房間旁邊有個烤爐。開始工作前，她仔細梳洗乾淨，還戴上戒指。烤麵包時，一個戒指掉到麵團裏。麵包烤完後，她又把自己打扮得像原來那樣醜。

麵包送了去給王子。切麵包時，王子發現了公主的戒指，便對他父母說，他要娶能戴上這戒指的姑娘。國王向全國宣佈了這個消息，名門淑女不遠千里而來，爭取這個榮譽。可這戒指十分纖小，即使有最纖細手指的人也只能戴在小指上。一時間，王國裏所有的姑娘都試過了。王子冷眼旁觀卻仍未見到那牧羊姑娘。人們叫來牧羊女，她穿着那身襤褸衣衫，可兩手潔淨。她輕輕地便戴上了戒指。

王子宣稱要履行諾言。他的父母委婉地提醒他，這姑

keeper of sheep, and a very ugly one too, the maiden boldly said that she was born a princess and asked to be given some water and leave her for a few minutes. They did what she asked, and when she entered in a magnificent dress, the king's son recognized the charming damsel of whom he had once caught a glimpse and, flinging himself at her feet, asked if she would marry him. The princess then told her story and said it would be necessary to send an ambassador to her father to ask his consent and invite him to the wedding.

The princess' father, who had never ceased to repent his harshness toward his daughter, had sought her through the land. Therefore it was with great joy he heard she was living and that a king's son asked her in marriage. He quitted his kingdom to be present at the ceremony.

By orders of the bride, at the wedding breakfast they served her father bread without salt and meat without seasoning. Seeing him make faces and eat very little, his daughter, who sat beside him, inquired if his dinner was not to his taste. "No," he replied, "the dishes are carefully cooked and sent up, but they are all so tasteless." "Did not I tell you, my Father, that salt was the best thing in life?"

— *Paul Sébillot*

娘只是個牧羊女，況且還非常醜。小姑娘卻大膽地説自己原本生在王家，貴為公主，又請人給她一些水，離開她一會兒。他們照辦了。當她穿着華麗的衣裳走進來時，王子認出了這迷人的女郎正是他見過一眼的那位姑娘。他跪倒在她腳下，向她求婚。公主這時説出自己的身世，並説須得派個大使去見她父親，求得他的同意，並請他參加婚禮。

公主的父親一直懊悔苛待了小女兒，曾在全國各地尋找她。因此，聽到她還活着，又有位王子向她求婚，大喜過望。他離開他的王國去參加婚禮。

新娘吩咐，在婚禮的早餐上，把沒有鹽的麵包和沒有調料的肉給她父親吃。坐在父親身旁的公主見他食難下嚥，便問飯食是否不合口味。"是的，"他回答，"這些菜雖然都是精心烹調送上來的，但就這麼一點味道也沒有。""父王，我不是告訴過你嗎？鹽是生活中最好的東西呀。"

—— 保羅·塞比洛

8 Fairy Gifts (France)

The Flower Fairy lived in a lovely palace, with the most delightful garden, full of flowers and trees and fountains and fishponds and everything nice. The fairy herself was so kind and charming everybody loved her. All the young princes and princesses who formed her court lived happily with her. They came to her when they were quite tiny and never left until they were grown up and had to go away into the great world. When that time came she gave to each whatever gift was asked of her.

The fairy loved the Princess Sylvia with all her heart. She had nearly reached the age when the gifts were bestowed. However, the fairy had a great wish to know how the other princesses, who had left her, were prospering. Before the time came for Sylvia to go away, she resolved to send her to some of them. So one day her chariot drawn by butterflies was made ready, and she sent Sylvia to the court of Iris.

When two months were over she stepped joyfully into the butterfly chariot and got back quickly to the Flower Fairy and said, "You sent me, madam, to the court of Iris, on whom you had bestowed the gift of beauty. It seemed her loveliness had caused her to forget her other gifts or graces. Unfortunately, she became seriously ill and though she presently recovered, her beauty is entirely gone. She hates the very sight of herself and is in despair. She entreated me to tell you what had happened and to beg you, in pity, to restore her beauty."

"You have told me what I wanted to know," cried the fairy, "but alas! I cannot help her. My gifts can be given but once."

八 仙子的禮物（法國）

花仙子住在一座美麗的宮殿裏，裏面有個令人心曠神怡的花園；花木茂盛、泉水潺潺、魚塘點點，景色宜人。花仙子本人巾和藹可親，人人都愛她。所有住在宮裏的小王子小公主們都跟她一起快樂地生活。他們年紀很小時便來到她身邊，到長大成人，要進入更廣闊的世界時才離開。這時，不管他們要甚麼禮物她都贈送給他們。

花仙子最疼愛西爾維婭公主，她快到接受禮物的年齡了。可花仙子有個宏願，想知道那些離開她的公主們生活怎樣，是不是事事遂意。在西爾維婭離開前，她決定讓她去探望她們中的幾位。一天，她那輛由蝴蝶駕駛的彩車備好，她要派西爾維婭到艾里斯的宮殿去。

兩個月後，西爾維婭高高興興跨上彩車，很快便回到了花仙子的家。她說：“夫人，您讓我去艾里斯的宮殿，您給她的禮物是美貌。看來美貌使她忘卻了其他稟賦或美德。不幸她得了重病，現在雖已康復，卻已紅顏枯槁。她怕見自己的容貌，沮喪絕望。她求我告訴您這情況，求您發善心恢復她的花容月貌。”

“你把我想知道的告訴了我，”花仙子說，“但可惜得很！我幫不了她，我的禮物只能給一次。”

Some time passed, she sent for Sylvia again and told her she was to stay for a while with the Princess Daphne. Before very long she returned to the Flower Fairy's palace. "How was Daphne?" asked the fairy. "She was one of the princesses who asked for the gift of eloquence."

"And very ill the gift of eloquence becomes a woman," replied Sylvia. "It is true she speaks well and her expressions are well chosen, but she never leaves off talking. And, though at first one may be amused, one ends by being wearied to death. Oh, I cannot tell you how glad I was to come away."

After allowing her a little time to recover the fairy sent Sylvia to the court of the Princess Cynthia. The fairy had given Cynthia the gift of pleasing.

"I thought at first," said Sylvia when she came back, "that she must be the happiest princess in the world. She had a thousand suitors who vied with one another in their efforts to please and gratify her. The longer I stayed the more I saw Cynthia was not really happy. In her desire to please everyone she ceased to be sincere and degenerated into a mere coquette. So in the end her suitors went away disdainfully."

Sylvia went to Phyllida and returned to report to the fairy: "She received me with much kindness and immediately began to exercise that brilliant wit you had bestowed upon her. I was fascinated by it. But like the gift of pleasing, it cannot really give satisfaction. I perceived more and more plainly it is impossible to be constantly smart and amusing without being frequently ill-natured and too apt to turn all things into mere occasions for a brilliant jest."

Now the time came for Sylvia to receive her gift and all her companions were assembled. The fairy asked what she would take with her into the great world. Sylvia paused for a

過了一段時間，她又把西爾維婭找來，讓她去和達夫妮公主相處一段時間。不久她回到花仙子的宮殿，"達夫妮好嗎？"花仙子問，"這位公主要的禮物是口才。"

"能說會道這種禮物對女人真不合適，"西爾維婭回答，"她的確口才出眾，說起話來選辭擇句恰到好處。可她總是滔滔不絕、口若懸河。最初人們還喜歡聽，到後來卻煩死了人。哎呀，離開她回到這裏，我真有說不出的高興。"

西爾維婭休息了一段時間，花仙子又送她去辛西婭公主的宮殿。花仙子送給辛西婭的禮物是討人歡喜的才能。

西爾維婭回來時說："開始我還以為她一定是世上最快樂的公主了，她有上千個求婚者，他們費盡心機爭相取悅於她。可我住的時間越長，越看出辛西婭並不真正幸福快活。她為想使人人都喜歡，便失去真誠，把自己貶低成了搔首弄姿的女郎。所以到了最後，她的求婚者都鄙視她，離她而去。"

後來西爾維婭又去了費麗達公主那兒，回來向花仙子報告："她十分友善地接待了我，馬上就開始使用起您送給她的機智風趣來。我簡直着迷了。但也像討人喜歡的能力一樣，機智並不能使人真正滿足。我越來越清楚地看到，要永遠顯得聰明風趣，總不免常常使性，而且容易對一切事情都逢場作戲。"

這時，西爾維婭接受禮物的時候到了，她的同伴歡聚一堂。花仙子問她進入大千世界時想要甚麼。西爾維婭躊

moment, and then answered, "A quiet spirit." And the fairy granted her request. This lovely gift makes life a constant happiness to its possessor and to all who are brought in contact with her.

— Comte de Caylus

躇片刻然後答道：“平靜的心靈。”花仙子滿足了她的要求。這件美好的禮物使擁有它的人和周圍所有的人都終生幸福。

—— 凱呂斯伯爵 [1]

---

1. 凱呂斯（1692 — 1765），法國考古學家和文學家。

9 The Frog Prince (Germany)

In the olden days when wishing was still of some use, there lived a King whose youngest daughter was so fair that even the sun, who sees so many wonders, could not help marveling every time he looked into her face. Near the King's palace lay a large dark forest and there, under an old linden tree, was a well. When the day was very warm, the little Princess would go off into this forest and sit at the rim of the cool well. There she would play with her golden ball, tossing it up and catching it deftly in her little hands.

Now it happened one day that, as the Princess tossed her golden ball into the air, it did not fall into her uplifted hands as usual. Instead, it fell to the ground and rolled into the water. The well was deep. So she cried and cried and could not stop. "What is the matter, little Princess?" said a voice behind her. "You are crying so that even a hard stone would have pity on you." The little girl looked around and there she saw a frog. He was in the well and was stretching his fat ugly head out of the water.

"Oh, it's you — you old water-splasher!" said the girl. "I'm crying over my golden ball. It has fallen into the well." "Oh, as to that," said the frog, "I can bring your ball back to you. But what will you give me if I do?" "Whatever you wish, dear old frog," said the Princess. The frog answered: "If you can find it in your heart to like me and take me for your playfellow, if you will let me sit beside you at the table, eat from your little golden plate and drink from your little golden cup, and sleep in your own little bed: if you promise me all this, then I will gladly go down to the bottom of the well and bring back your golden ball." "Oh yes," said the

九　青蛙王子 (德國)

　　在那只要發個心願也許就會實現的古時候，一位國王有個非常美麗的小女兒，連見多識廣的太陽每次照到她的臉兒都情不自禁要驚嘆她的美貌。土宮不遠處有一片黑沉沉的大森林，森林裏有棵菩提古樹，樹下有一口水井。每當天氣很熱時，小公主便到森林裏，坐在清涼的水井邊玩她的金球。她把它拋到空中，再靈巧地用小手接住。

　　這天，公主拋球後，舉起小手，卻沒有像平常那樣接住金球，球落到地上滾入水井。水井很深，公主哭起來，哭個不休。這時聽見身後有人說：“小公主，怎麼啦？你哭得頑石都要為你難過了。”小女孩轉頭看看，見到一隻青蛙在井裏，正把肥胖醜怪的頭伸出水面。

　　“噢，是你這在水裏啪噠亂跳的老傢伙呀！”她說，“我哭我的金球呢，它掉到井裏了。”青蛙說：“這件事麼，我能給你把金球撈上來，可你拿甚麼謝我？”公主說：“親愛的老青蛙，你想要甚麼我給你甚麼。”青蛙答道：“只要你心裏喜歡我，讓我和你作伴玩耍，坐在你身邊，用你桌上的小金碟子吃飯，小金杯喝水，還睡在你的小牀上。你答應我這些，我就願意到井底去把金球給你撈上來。”“好吧，我都答應你，”公主說。但又暗暗思忖：

Princess, "I'll promise anything you say." But to herself she thought: "What is the silly frog chattering about? He can only live in the water and croak with the other frogs; he could never be a playmate to a human being."

As soon as the frog had heard her promise, he disappeared into the well. But he soon came up again, holding the golden ball in his mouth. He dropped it on the grass at the feet of the Princess who was wild with joy when she saw her favorite plaything once more. She picked up the ball and skipped away with it, thinking no more about the little creature.

The next evening, the Princess was eating her dinner at the royal table when — plitch plotch, plitch plotch — something came climbing up the stairs. When it reached the door, it knocked at the door and cried: "Youngest daughter of the King, open the door for me!" The Princess opened the door, there sat the frog, wet and green and cold! Quickly she slammed the door and sat down at the table again, her heart beating loud and fast. The King could see well enough that she was frightened and worried, and he said, "My child, what are you afraid of? Is there a giant out there who wants to carry you away?" "Oh no," said the Princess, "It's not a giant, but a horrid old frog!" "And what does he want of you?" asked the King. The princess was telling her father what had happened in the forest, when the frog knocked at the door once more and said:

> *"Youngest daughter of the King,*
> *Open the door for me.*
> *Mind your words at the old well spring;*
> *Open the door for me!"*

At that the King said, "If we make promises, daughter, we must keep them; so you had better go and open the door." The Princess still did not want to do it but she had to obey. When she opened the door, the frog hopped in and followed

48

"這青蛙盡說傻話！它只能呆在水裏和別的青蛙一起呱呱叫，哪能做人的玩伴啊。"

青蛙得到公主的許諾，潛入水裏不見了，但很快便含着金球出來，把球放在草地上公主的腳旁。公主看到心愛的金球，興高采烈，拾起金球蹦蹦跳跳走了，把可憐的青蛙忘在腦後。

第二天黃昏，公主正在王宮餐桌前進餐，啪噠啪噠，甚麼東西爬上台階，到了門口，敲門叫道："小公主，給我開門！"公主跑去開了門，看到正是那隻濕淋淋、冷冰冰的青蛙坐在門前！她慌忙把門砰地關上，回到飯桌邊坐下，心怦怦地跳。國王早看出她又害怕又煩惱，便說："孩子，你害怕甚麼？莫非外面有個巨人要把你拐走？""不，不是巨人，是隻怕人的老青蛙！""這青蛙要你做甚麼？"國王問。公主正告訴她父親森林裏發生的事，青蛙又敲門了。他說：

> "小公主，給我開門吧，
>
> 　記住在古井邊說過的話，
>
> 　給我開門呀！"

國王聽了，說："女兒，答應了就要守信用。你還是去開門吧。"公主勉強地去開了門。青蛙跳進來跟着她跳

her until she reached her chair. Then he wanted to be put on the table.

The frog enjoyed the meal and ate heartily, but the poor girl could not swallow a single bite. At last the frog said, "Now I've eaten enough and I feel tired. Carry me to your room so I can go to sleep." The Princess began to cry, for she was afraid of the cold frog and she did not like to touch him. But the King said, "He helped you in your trouble. Is it fair to scorn him now?" There was nothing for her to do but to pick up the creature — she did it with two fingers — and to carry him up into her room and put him at the foot-end of her bed.

When the night was over and the morning sunlight burst in at the window, the frog crept out from under her pillow and hopped off the bed. But as soon as his feet touched the floor he was no longer a cold, fat, goggle-eyed frog, but a young Prince with handsome friendly eyes! Then he told her that he had been bewitched by a wicked woman and no one but she could break the spell.

"And will you let me be your playmate now?" said the Prince, laughing. "Mind your words at the old well spring!" At this the Princess laughed too, and they both ran out to play with the golden ball. For years they were the best of friends and the happiest of playmates, and it is not hard to guess that when they were grown up they were married and lived happily ever after.

— *Jakob and Wilhelm Grimm*

到椅子邊，又要她把他放上桌子。

　　他吃得很有滋味，可憐的公主卻一口也嚥不下。最後，青蛙說："我吃飽了，我累了，帶我到你房間睡覺吧。"公主哭起來，她害怕這隻冷冰冰的青蛙，連碰都不願碰他。但是國王說："他在你困難的時候幫助過你，你現在卻看不起他，那公平嗎？"公主只好用兩個指頭捏起青蛙走上樓來到她的房間，把他放在牀腳。

　　黑夜過去，早晨的陽光射進窗子，青蛙從公主的枕頭下爬出來跳下牀。但他的腳一踏上地板，便再不是一隻臃腫冰冷、眼睛鼓出的青蛙了，變成了一個小王子，長着一雙美麗友善的眼睛。他告訴她他是被一個邪惡的女人變成青蛙的，除了公主沒有別人能把巫術破去。

　　王子笑着說："你現在讓我陪你玩了吧？別忘了古井邊的話呀！"公主也笑了。他們一起跑去玩金球。許多年他們一直是最好的朋友和最快樂的玩伴。你不難猜出，等到他們長大，便結了婚，快樂地生活在一起。

　　　　　　　　　　　　　　—— 雅各布 與 威廉·格林 [1]

1.　雅各布（1785 — 1863）、威廉·格林（1786 — 1859），德國民間文學研究者，他們將收集到的民間歌謠和故事匯編成《兒童與家庭童話集》（*Children's and Household Tales*），現已譯成近百種文字。本書各篇皆選自其英譯本。格林兄弟曾任普魯士皇家科學院院士，提出並參加編纂《德語大辭典》。

10 Dr. Know-it-all (Germany)

Once a poor peasant by the name of Crabbe hauled a cord of wood to town in a wagon drawn by two oxen, and sold his wood to a doctor for two talers[1]. When he came in to get his money, the doctor was sitting at the table. The peasant saw what lovely things he had to eat and drink, and he longed to be a doctor. After standing there awhile, he asked: "Is there any way of my getting to be a doctor?" "Why not?" said the doctor. "It's easy." "What would I have to do?" asked the peasant. "First, buy yourself an ABC book, the kind with a rooster in it; second, sell your wagon and your two oxen, take the money and buy clothes and the other things a doctor needs; third, have the words 'I am Dr. Know-it-all' painted on a sign, and hang it over the door of your house."

The peasant did everything he had been told. When he had doctored awhile but not for so very long, some money was stolen from a rich nobleman. Someone told him about Dr. Know-it-all. So the nobleman went to the peasant's house and asked: "Are you Dr. Know-it-all?" "That's me." "Then come with me and find the money that was stolen from me." "All right. But my wife Greta must come along." The nobleman had no objection. He seated them in his carriage, and away they drove together. When they got to the manor, dinner was on the table, and the peasant was asked to sit down. "Gladly," he said, "but my wife Greta must sit with us." So they sat down, and when the first servant came in with a platter of fine food, the peasant nudged his wife and

---

1. talers：德國舊銀幣名。

十　萬事知博士（德國）

　　從前，一位窮苦的農夫克拉比趕着一輛兩條牛拉的車，送一車木柴進城。他將柴賣給了一位博士，抨得兩個泰勒。他進屋拿錢時，博士正坐在餐桌前。農夫見他吃好的、喝香的，便心想也當個博士。他站了一會兒，問道："有沒有法子讓我也當個博士呢？""怎麼沒有？"博士說。"容易得很。""我該怎麼辦呀？"農夫問。"第一，買本初學啟蒙的書——裏面畫着一隻大公雞的那種；第二，把你的車和兩條牛賣掉，用這錢買一身衣服和當博士用的什物；第三，造個寫着'萬事知博士'的招牌，掛在你家大門上就行了。"

　　農夫一一照辦。他開業了一陣子，但也不算太久，就有個有錢的貴族丟了錢。有人告訴他有個萬事知博士。於是這個貴族來到農夫的家，問："你是萬事知博士嗎？""是我。""那你跟我來，給我找我丟了的錢吧。""好的。可我太太格麗塔也得一起去。"貴族不反對。他讓他們坐上他的馬車，就一起走了。到達莊園時桌上已擺好正餐。農夫獲請坐下，他說："謝謝，可我太太格麗塔得跟我們坐在一起。"於是他們坐下。第一個僕人端着一盤美味佳餚走進來，農夫用臂肘捅捅他的太太，說："格麗塔，那

said: "Greta, that's the first," meaning the servant with the first course. But the servant thought he had meant to say: "That's the first thief." And since that's just what he was, he took fright and said to his comrades in the kitchen: "The doctor knows it all, we're in trouble. He said I was the first." The second didn't even want to go in, but he had to. When he appeared with his platter, the peasant nudged his wife: "Greta," he said, "that's the second," and the second servant hurried out of the room, as frightened as the first. The third fared no better. The fourth brought in a covered dish, and the nobleman said: "Now show your skill. Tell me what's under the cover." It was a crab. The peasant looked at the dish. He hadn't the faintest idea what was in it. "Poor Crabbe[2]!" he cried out. When the nobleman heard that, he said: "If he knows that, he must know who has the money."

The servant was frightened to death. He signaled to the doctor to come outside for a minute. When he met them outside, all four servants confessed they had stolen the money. They offered to hand it over and give him a tidy sum in addition, if only he didn't tell anyone who had taken it, for if he did they would be hanged. Then they led him to the place where the money was hidden, and that was good enough for the doctor. He went back in, sat down at the table, and said: "Your lordship, now I will look in my book and find out where the money is." At that, the fifth servant crawled into the stove, wanting to find out how much the doctor actually knew. The doctor opened his ABC book and leafed backward and forward, looking for the rooster. When he couldn't find it, he said: "I know you're there, so what's the good of hiding?" The servant in the stove thought the doctor was

---

2. Crabbe："克拉比"和 crab（螃蟹）在德文中同音。

是第一個。"意思指那端第一道菜的僕人。可僕人以為他說的是:"那是第一個賊。"他正是那個賊,便大吃一驚,回到廚房對他的同夥說:"那博士甚麼都知道,我們要壞事了。他說我是第一個。"第二個便不敢進去,但他不去又不行。他端盤進去時,農夫捅捅他太太説:"格麗塔,那是第二個。"第二個僕人和第一個一樣,嚇得倉惶退出房間。第三個也好不了多少。第四個僕人端來一個帶蓋的盤子。貴族説:"給我們顯顯本事看,告訴我蓋子下是甚麼。"那是隻螃蟹。農夫看着盤子,哪裏知道裏面是甚麼?"可憐的克拉比!"他叫喊起來。貴族聽了,説:"他既然看穿這道菜,一定知道誰拿了我的錢。"

那僕人嚇得要死,他打手勢請博士到外面去一會兒。農夫在外面會見他們,四個僕人都向他承認是他們偷了錢。他們答應把錢交出來,外加一點小好處給他,只求他不説出他們來。因為如果他説了,他們就要被弔死。之後,他們帶他去看藏錢的地方,博士真是喜從天降。他回到房間,坐在桌前,説:"爵爺,現在我要翻翻書,看看錢在哪兒了。"這時第五個僕人爬進爐子想聽聽博士到底確實知道多少。博士打開初學啟蒙書,把書頁來回地翻,找那隻大公雞,但找來找去都找不到,就説:"我知道你就是在那裏的呀,藏起來有甚麼用?"爐子裏的僕人以為

speaking of him and popped out in a fright, shouting: "He knows it all! He knows it all!" Then Dr. Know-it-all showed the nobleman where the money was, but didn't tell him who had stolen it. He was richly rewarded by both parties and became a famous man.

— *Jakob and Wilhelm Grimm*

博士是在説他呢，嚇得跳了出去，喊道："他甚麽都知道！他甚麽都知道！"接着，萬事知博士指給貴族藏錢之處，但沒有告訴他誰偷了錢。貴族和賊兩方都重重地酬謝了他，他也成了一位名人。

—— 雅各布 與 威廉 · 格林

11 The Riddle (Germany)

A king's son once had a great desire to travel through the world, so he started off, taking no one with him but one trusty servant. One day he came to a great forest, and as evening drew on and he could find no shelter he could not think where to spend the night. All of a sudden he saw a pretty girl going toward a little house. He spoke to her, and said: "Dear child, could I spend the night in this house?" "Oh, yes," said the girl in a sad tone, "but I should not advise you to do so. Better not go in." "Why not?" asked the king's son. The girl sighed, and answered, "My stepmother deals in black arts, and she is not friendly to strangers." But the prince was not at all afraid and he stepped in with his groom. The old woman pretended to be quite friendly. She was cooking something in a little pot. But her daughter had warned the travelers to be careful not to eat or drink anything, as the old woman's brews were likely to be dangerous.

They went to bed and slept soundly till morning. When they were ready to start, and the king's son had already mounted his horse, the old woman said, "Wait a minute. I must give you a stirrup cup." While she went to fetch it the king's son rode off, and the groom who had waited to tighten his saddle girths was alone when the witch returned. "Take that to your master," she said. But as she spoke the glass cracked and the poison spurted over the horse. It was so powerful the poor creature sank down dead. The servant ran after his master and told him what had happened, and then, not wishing to lose the saddle as well as the horse, he went back to fetch it. When he reached the spot he saw a raven had perched on the carcass and was pecking at it. The man

十一 一個謎（德國）

　　從前有位王子極想周遊世界，於是他出發旅行，隨身只帶了一個忠僕。一日，他來到一片大森林中，天色漸晚，他找不到歇宿之處。忽然，他看到一個漂亮的姑娘正向一間小屋走去。他對她說：“好姑娘，我可以在屋裏過夜嗎？”姑娘憂鬱地道：“當然可以啦，但我勸你還是別進去的好！”“為甚麼呢？”王子問。姑娘嘆着氣說：“我的後娘是煉邪術的，對過路人不懷好意。”但是王子一點不害怕，和僕人走進了小屋。那老太婆顯得很殷勤，她正在用個小鍋煮東西。女兒事先警告客人小心，別吃別喝，因為老太婆很可能在酒裏下了毒。

　　他們上牀熟睡，一覺到早晨。他們收拾好要上路了，王子已經跨上馬。這時候老太婆說：“等一下，我要給你們喝杯送行酒。”她去拿酒時，王子騎馬走了。等到老太婆拿着飲料回來，只有僕人還在繫緊馬鞍。她說：“把這送給你的主人去。”正說着，杯子突然爆裂，毒液灑在馬身上。毒性猛烈，可憐那馬倒地而斃。僕人追上主人，將發生的事稟告給他。僕人不願丟掉馬鞍和馬，又掉頭回去取。僕人回到那地方時，看見一隻烏鴉正停在死馬身上啄

shot the raven and carried it off. At nightfall they reached an inn. The servant made the landlord a present of the raven. Now, as it happened, this inn was the resort of a band of robbers, and the old witch, too, was in the habit of frequenting it. As soon as it was dark twelve thieves arrived, with the full intention of killing and robbing the strangers. However, they sat down first to table, where the landlord and the old witch joined them, and they all ate some broth in which the flesh of the raven had been boiled. They had hardly taken a couple of spoonfuls when they all fell down dead. And the prince rode on with his servant.

After traveling about for some time they reached a town where lived a lovely but arrogant princess. She had announced that anyone who asked her a riddle which she was unable to guess should be her husband, but should she guess it he must forfeit his head. She claimed three days in which to think over the riddles. The king's son dazzled by her beauty, determined to risk his life. He came before her and propounded his riddle. "What is this?" he asked. "One slew none and yet killed twelve." She thought and thought and looked through all her books of riddles and puzzles. She found nothing to help her and could not guess. In fact, she was at her wits' end. As she could think of no way to guess the riddle, for two successive nights, she respectively ordered her maid and lady-in-waiting to steal at night into the prince's bedroom and listen to his dreams. But the clever servant had taken his master's place, and when they came, he tore off their cloaks and chased them off. On the third night the king's son thought he really might feel safe, so he went to bed. But in the middle of the night the princess came herself, wrapped in a misty gray mantle, and sat down near him. When she thought he was fast asleep, she asked, "One slew none — what is that?" And he answered: "A raven which fed on the

食死馬的肉，他用槍打死了烏鴉，帶着死鴉上路。夜色降臨時分，他們來到一家客棧。僕人將烏鴉送給了店主。不料，這是一夥強盜的賊窩，那個老巫婆也是一夥的，常到這裏來。天一黑，十二個賊就來了，滿心想殺掉旅客。但他們先在桌前坐下，店主、女巫也湊在一起。他們一起喝煮好的烏鴉肉湯，沒吃幾匙，就都倒地死去。王子也就騎上馬和僕人走了。

他們到處旅行了一段時間，來到一座城市。那裏有一位美麗卻極傲慢的公主。她宣佈誰能出一個謎把她難倒，她便嫁給他。但如果她猜到了，這個男子也就要人頭落地。她要求用三天時間來猜謎語。王子被公主的美艷所眩惑，決定拿生命作賭。他被引見給公主，說出他的謎語："有樣東西，沒殺一個，卻殺了十二個。這是甚麼？"公主冥思苦想；又翻遍所有謎語書，但都無助於她，還是猜不到。她智竭計窮，別無他法，只好連續兩夜分別命她的侍婢和宮女悄悄溜進王子的臥室偷聽他的夢話。可是聰明的僕人躺在王子牀上，每次侍女進來，他都撕下她們的外衣，把她們趕了出去。第三夜，王子覺得應該安全了，便睡到牀上。但到了半夜，公主親自來了，披着一件淺灰色的紗斗篷，在王子身邊坐下。她以為他已睡熟，便問："有樣東西，沒殺一個，這是甚麼？"王子答："吃了被毒

carcass of a poisoned horse." "And yet killed twelve — what is that?" "Those are twelve robbers who ate the raven and died of it." As soon as she knew the riddle she tried to slip away, but he held her mantle so tightly she was obliged to leave it behind. Next morning the princess announced she had guessed the riddle and sent for the twelve judges, before whom she declared it. But the young man begged to be heard, too, and said: "She came by night to question me." The judges said, "Bring us some proof." So the servant brought out the three cloaks. When the judges saw the gray one, which the princess was in the habit of wearing, they said: "Let it be embroidered with gold and silver. It shall be your wedding mantle."

— *Jakob and Wilhelm Grimm*

死的馬屍體的烏鴉。""卻殺了十二個，這是甚麼？""那是吃了烏鴉肉死去的十二個強盜。"公主知道了謎底，就想悄悄走掉，可王子緊抓她的斗篷，她只好把它丟下。第二天早上，公主宣佈猜出了謎語，派人請來十二位法官，當着他們的面說出謎底。可王子要求申辯，說："她半夜來我的房間問了我。"法官說："把證據給我們拿來。"於是僕人拿來三件斗篷。當法官看到那件公主常穿的淺灰色斗篷時，就說："把這件斗篷繡上金絲銀綫，當作你的婚紗吧。"

——雅各布 與 威廉·格林

12 The Clever Tailor (Germany)

Once upon a time there lived an exceedingly proud princess. If any suitor for her hand ventured to present himself, she would give him some riddle or conundrum to guess. When he failed, he was hunted out of town with scorn and derision. She made a proclamation that all comers were welcome to try their skill and that whosoever could solve her riddle should be her husband. Now it happened three tailors had met together. The two elder thought that, having successfully put in so many fine and strong stitches with never a wrong one amongst them, they were certain to do the right thing here too. The third tailor was a lazy young scamp. He did not even know his own trade properly but thought surely luck would stand by him now.

The three tailors arrived at court, where they had themselves duly presented to the princess, and begged she would propound her riddles. Then said the princess, "I have on my head two different kinds of hair. Of what colors are they?"

"If that's all," said the first tailor, "they are most likely black and white." "Wrong," said the princess.

"Then," said the second tailor, "if they are not black and white, no doubt they are red and brown." "Wrong again," said the princess.

Then the young tailor stepped **boldly** forward, and said, "The princess has one silver and one golden hair on her head." When the princess heard this she turned pale and almost fainted with fear. The little tailor had hit the mark. When she had recovered herself she said, "Don't fancy you have won me yet, there is something else you must do first. Below in

十二　聰明的裁縫（德國）

從前有個極端傲慢的公主，哪個求婚者敢於毛遂自薦，她便給幾個謎讓他猜。要是猜不出來，他就會被百般嘲弄辱罵，然後趕出城去。公主宣稱歡迎所有來訪者顯示他們的才智技巧，誰能解開謎底，誰就可做她丈夫。這天，三個裁縫湊巧碰在一起，兩個年紀大些的想：做過這麼多細密結實的針綫活，從沒有縫錯一針，這事肯定也會幹得漂亮。第三個裁縫是個好吃懶做的調皮鬼，手藝不精卻認定自己會走運。

三個裁縫進了宮，按規矩謁見了公主，請她說出謎語。公主說：“我頭上有兩種不同的頭髮，這兩種頭髮是甚麼顏色？”

第一個裁縫說：“就這謎語？那一定是黑白兩色的了。”“錯了，”公主說。

第二個裁縫說：“如果不是黑色和白色，毫無疑問，一定是紅色和棕色。”“又錯了，”公主說。

接着小裁縫大膽地走上前，說：“公主頭上長着銀色和金色的頭髮。”公主聽到這話面色蒼白，幾乎暈倒，小裁縫一語中的。她定了定神說：“別以為你已經得到了我，你還得先做點事兒呢。下面馬廄裏有一頭熊，你得和

the stable is a bear with whom you must spend the night. If I find you still alive in the morning you shall marry me."

She expected to rid herself of the tailor in this way. The tailor, however, had no notion of being scared, but said cheerily, "Bravely dared is half won."

When evening came on he was taken to the stable. The bear tried to get at him at once and to give him a warm welcome with his great paws. "Gently, gently," said the tailor, "I'll soon teach you to be quiet." He coolly took out a fiddle and began playing on it. When the bear heard the music he could not help dancing.

After he had danced for some time he was so pleased he said to the tailor, "I say, is fiddling difficult?" "Mere child's play," replied the tailor. "Look here! You press the strings with the fingers of the left hand, and with the right you draw the bow across them, so — then it goes as easily as possible, up and down, tra la la la la—"

"Oh," cried the bear, "I do wish I could play like that. Would you give me some lessons?" "With all my heart," said the tailor, "if you are sharp about it. But just let me look at your paws. Dear me, your nails are terribly long. I must really cut them first." Then he fetched a pair of stocks[1], the bear laid his paws on them, and the tailor screwed them up tight. "Now just wait while I fetch my scissors," said he. But he left the bear growling away, while he lay down in a corner and fell fast asleep.

When the princess heard the bear growling so loud that night, she felt sure he was roaring with delight as he worried[2] the tailor. Next morning she rose, feeling quite cheerful and

---

1. stocks：樹幹，木頭。
2. worried：撕咬。

66

它在一起過一個晚上，明天早上你還活着的話，我就嫁給你。"

她想用這法子把小裁縫甩掉，可小裁縫不懂得害怕，興沖沖地說："勇敢地面對危險便成功了一半。"

到了晚上，他被帶到馬廄，熊立刻向他撲來，用大熊爪來熱烈歡迎他。小裁縫道："輕一點、輕一點。我馬上來教你怎麼安靜點兒。"他冷靜地拿出一把小提琴開始拉奏。熊聽到音樂，情不自禁跳起舞來。

熊跳得興起，便對裁縫道："我說，奏小提琴難嗎？""小孩子的玩藝兒罷了，"裁縫說，"瞧這兒！用左手手指按弦，右手在弦上拉弓，再容易不過了，上上、下下、特拉拉拉——"

"噢！"熊叫道，"我真想學會拉得這樣好，你能教我嗎？""太願意啦，要是你有這份聰明的話。可得先讓我看看你的爪子。啊呀，你的指甲太長了，我得先把你的指甲剪短。"他拿來兩根木頭，熊把爪子放在上面，裁縫把它們綑緊，說："好啦。等着，我拿剪刀去。"他讓熊在一邊咆哮，自己在一個角落躺下，沉沉睡熟。

夜間公主聽到熊吼聲如雷，心想他肯定是已經把裁縫撕爛，嚼碎享用，快活得大叫呢。第二天早上她起牀時，

free from care, but when she looked toward the stables, there stood the tailor before the door, as fresh and lively as a fish in the water. After this it was impossible to break the promise she had made so publicly, and the king ordered out the state coach to take her and the tailor to be married.

— *Jakob and Wilhelm Grimm*

輕鬆愉快，向馬廄一望，只見裁縫正站在門前，像條水中游魚一樣活生生的。這回她再也不能違背她當眾作出的諾言了。國王便命御車載她和裁縫去結婚。

—— 雅各布 與 威廉·格林

13 Snow-White (1) (Germany)

One wintry afternoon — and snow was falling — a Queen sat at her window. Its frame was of the dark wood called ebony. And as she sewed with her needle she pricked her finger, and a drop of blood welled up on the fair skin. She raised her eyes, looked out of the window, and sighed within herself: "Oh that I had a daughter, as white as snow, her cheeks red as blood, and her hair black as ebony!" By-and-by her wish came true, and she called the child Snow-White.

Some years afterwards this Queen died, and the King took another wife. She, too, was of a rare dark beauty, but vain and cold and proud. Night and morning she would look into her magic looking-glass and would cry softly:

"Looking-glass, looking-glass on the wall,
Who is the fairest of women all?"

And a voice would answer her out of the looking-glass: "Thou, O Queen."

But as the years went by, Snow-White grew ever more lovely, and the Queen more jealous. And one day, when the Queen looked yet again into her looking-glass and asked it as usual. The looking-glass answered:

"Fair, in sooth¹, art thou², O Queen;
But fairer than Snow-White is nowhere seen."

At this, the Queen was beside herself with rage and hatred; and in secret she sent for a huntsman, and bade him

---

1. in sooth：〔古〕 = in truth。
2. art thou：〔古〕 = are you。

70

十三 白雪公主（一）（德國）

　　一個冬日的下午，大雪紛飛。有位王后坐在窗前，窗框是烏檀木做的。王后做着針綫，不留神針刺了手指。一滴血冒出在細嫩的皮膚上。她抬眼望着窗外，心中嘆息："但願我有個女兒，像雪一樣白，兩頰像血一樣紅，頭髮像烏檀木一樣黑就好了！"後來，她果然如願以償。她給孩子取名白雪公主。

　　幾年後，王后去世了。國王另娶。她也是個絕色的黑髮美人，但卻自負、冷酷和驕傲。她每天早晚照看她的魔鏡，輕輕地喊道：

　　　"牆上的鏡子啊、鏡子，

　　　　天下女人誰最美？"

　　魔鏡出聲回答："啊，王后，是您。"

　　可是，年復一年，白雪公主長得越來越美麗，王后也更嫉妒了。一天，當王后又照鏡，像往常一樣問鏡子時，鏡子答道：

　　　"王后，王后，您確實很美，

　　　　可白雪公主世間無人比。"

　　王后聽後氣得發狂，惱恨交加，她偷偷叫來一個獵

take Snow-White into the forest and do away with her. But he had not the heart to do the Queen's bidding, so he speared a wild boar, and dabbling Snow-White's kerchief in its blood, returned to the Queen.

Snow-White, left alone in the forest, hastened on in terror. She came at last to a little house and went in. In the middle of the room stood a table with seven little stools around it; while on the table itself lay seven platters and seven bowls, with seven spoons beside them, and seven tiny loaves of bread, and seven little glasses for wine. For it was the Seven Dwarfs' house. Snow-White was hungry, so she broke off a mouthful from each tiny loaf in turn, and sipped a sip of wine from one of the glasses. Then she went upstairs, and came into a room with seven little beds. She sat down on one of the beds to rest herself; but from sitting slipped into lying, and then fell fast asleep.

Towards evening, the Seven Dwarfs came home and found their door ajar. They went in, and climbed up the stairs, and found Snow-White on one of the beds. The dwarfs clustered together round the bed on which Snow-White was lying and looked at her. In all their wanderings they had never seen a lovelier face. When Snow-White woke up she told them her story. The dwarfs said, "Hide with us here, and you are safe." So Snow-White became the housekeeper of the dwarfs while they went out all day long to seek for gold and silver in the mountains. She was happy with the Seven Dwarfs.

Now one day the Queen looked into her magic glass and whispered:

> *"Looking-glass, looking-glass on the wall,*
> *Who is the fairest of women all?"*

And the voice from within replied:

> *"Fair in sooth, art thou, O Queen;*

人，讓他把白雪公主帶到森林裏殺死。但獵人不忍服從王后，便刺死一頭野熊，用熊血蘸在白雪公主的手帕上去回覆王后。

白雪公主獨自被留在森林裏，驚恐萬分地向前跑。最後，她來到一座小屋前，走了進去。房間中央有張桌子，周圍有七把小凳；桌子上擺着七個碟子和七個碗，旁邊放着七把匙子，還有小小七塊麵包和小小七杯酒。原來這是七個小矮人的家。白雪公主餓了，便從每塊麵包咬下一小口，又從一個杯子裏喝一小口酒。之後，她上樓來到一個房間，裏面有七張小牀。她在一張小牀上坐下歇歇，但漸漸躺倒睡着了。

黃昏時分，七個小矮人回家來，發現門開着。他們走進屋，來到樓上，發現白雪公主躺在其中一張牀上。小矮人擠在她的牀邊看着她。他們走遍各地，從未見過這樣可愛的臉龐。白雪公主醒來後，講了自己的身世遭遇。小矮人說：「躲在我們這裏吧，你會平安無事的。」於是，白雪公主留在家裏為他們料理家務，而他們每日早出晚歸，在大山裏尋找金礦銀礦。她和七個小矮人在一起過得很快樂。

一天，王后又來照魔鏡，輕聲問：

　　「牆上的鏡子啊、鏡子，

　　　天下女人誰最美？」

有聲音從魔鏡裏傳出來，回答：

　　「王后，王后，您確實很美，

But fairer than Snow-White is nowhere seen.
Happy she lives, beyond words to tell,
Where the dwarfs of the mountains of copper dwell."

At this, the face looking back out of the glass at the Queen became so black and crooked with rage that she hardly knew herself. She stole down to a little secret closet and made a poisonous apple, rosy red on the one side, green on the other. The very sight of it made her mouth water, and she smiled to herself as she looked at it and thought: "This is the end."

— *Jakob and Wilhelm Grimm*

可白雪公主世間無人比；

她過得快樂、幸福、如意，

和銅礦山中的小矮人住在一起。"

鏡子中照出的王后氣得臉色鐵青，歪扭變形，連自己都不認識了。她偷偷走進一間小密室做了一個毒蘋果，一半紅，一半青，令她看了饞涎欲滴。她看着蘋果暗暗發笑，想道："這下成了。"

—— 雅各布 與 威廉·格林

14 Snow-White (2) (Germany)

The Queen dressed up and disguised herself as a very old woman, hunched and ragged. When a little before sunset she came to the house of the dwarfs. The Queen spied Snow-White up there peering down from the window, and cackled softly: "Ripe apples, ripe apples! Who'll buy my ripe apples?" Snow-White shook her head, but the Queen cut the apple in half, and threw the rosy half up to the window. And Snow-White, thinking what pleasure such fruits as these would give the dwarfs, caught the piece of apple, and lifted it to her nose to smell its sweetness. Then she took a bite, but before she could swallow it she fell down on the floor, seemingly dead.

That midnight the Queen stole catlike to her looking-glass and whispered the same question. The voice within cried hollowly: "Thou, O Queen!"

When the Seven Dwarfs came home that evening, their hearts were sad and dismal indeed. Nothing they could do brought any tinge of colour back into Snow-White's cheeks, or warmth to her fingers. Yet they could not bear to think of hiding her away in the dark, cold ground, so, working all of them together, they made a coffin of glass, and put up a wooden bench not far from the house, and rested the glass coffin on it, mantling it with garlands of green leaves and flowers. The birds that Snow-White used to feed with her crumbs and scraps sang beside the coffin.

One fresh morning, when early summer was in the forest again, a Prince came riding with his huntsmen, and seeing this glass coffin on the bench, dismounted from his horse, and, pushing the green garlands aside, looked in at Snow-White lying there. His heart misgave him at the sight of her,

十四 白雪公主（二）（德國）

　　王后把自己裝扮成一個很老的駝背老太婆，衣衫破爛。日將落時來到小矮人的屋前。王后偷眼看見白雪公主正從上面窗戶探頭往下看，便格格地發出刺耳的聲音，低聲喊道：“熟蘋果囉，熟蘋果囉！誰買我的熟蘋果啊？”白雪公主搖搖頭。但王后把蘋果切成兩半，把紅的一半拋上窗子。白雪公主想，把這麼好的蘋果給小矮人，他們該多高興啊，便接住那塊蘋果拿到鼻子下聞聞香味，然後又咬了一口；還沒嚥下，就栽倒在地，看上去像死了。

　　半夜裏，王后偷偷摸摸來到魔鏡前，輕聲問的還是那句話。魔鏡發出空洞的回聲道：“王后，您最美。”

　　當晚，小矮人回到家，心裏非常難過。他們沒有辦法使白雪公主的兩頰紅潤起來，沒有辦法使她的手指溫暖，又不忍心將她葬在漆黑冰冷的地下，於是便一起做了一個玻璃棺材，把它停放在屋子近處一張木凳上，覆蓋着綠葉和鮮花製成的花環。過去她常用麵包屑餵的鳥兒在棺材旁歌唱。

　　初夏又降臨到森林，在一個天朗氣清的早晨，有位王子和他的獵人騎馬經過，看見木凳上的玻璃棺材，便下馬，撥開綠色的花環，看到裏面躺着的白雪公主。他滿腹

for he had never seen a face so lovely or so wan. Then he told the dwarfs: "My father, the King, has a leech who is wondrously skilled in magic herbs. Give me leave to carry off this coffin, and I promise you that, your Snow-White, shall come back to you alive and well, or sleeping on as she sleeps now." The dwarfs talked together in grief and dismay at the thought of losing Snow-White, even though only for a few days. But they agreed at last that this should be so.

It was dark night when the huntsmen were drawing near the palace of the King, and one of them stumbled over the jutting root of a tree. By this sudden jarring of her glass coffin, the morsel of poisonous apple that was stuck in Snow-White's throat became dislodged. She lifted her head, coughed out the morsel, and cried: "God help me!" The Prince, hearing her cry, took off the lid of the coffin. Then Snow-White sat up, and gazed at him. The Prince rejoiced with all his heart, and sent back two of his huntsmen to give the dwarfs the glad news that Snow-White had come alive again; and that their master, the Prince, had bidden them all to the King's palace.

The King and Queen, having heard Snow-White's story, rejoiced with their son the Prince, and gave a banquet to welcome her; and the Seven Dwarfs sat at a table on stools of ebony, their napkins white as snow, and their wine red as blood. And Snow-White herself poured out wine for them just as she used to do.

As for the murderous Queen, she had become lean and haggard and dreaded even the thought of her magic looking-glass. In time she fell mortally sick. At last, in the dead of night she summoned one of her waiting-women and bade her take down the looking-glass from the wall, and bring it to her bedside. Then she drew close the curtains round her bed, and whispered:

驚疑，因為他從未見到過這樣美麗、這樣蒼白的臉。於是他告訴小矮人："我父王宮中有個食客，身具神奇醫術，請讓我把棺材抬走。我答應你們，如果不能把你們的白雪公主救活醫好送回來，也會讓她像現在這樣安臥在棺材裏。"小矮人商量了一下，雖然只不過和白雪公主分別幾天，也使他們悲傷沮喪不已。但最後還是同意了，覺得理應如此。

　　這羣打獵的人到達王宮附近時已是深夜。一個人被露出地面的樹根絆了一下。這樣一來震動了玻璃棺材，堵在白雪公主喉嚨裏的那塊毒蘋果鬆動了。她抬起頭，把那塊蘋果咳了出來，叫道："上帝保佑我！"王子聽到聲音，揭開了棺材蓋。白雪公主坐起來，痴痴地看着他。王子滿心歡喜，差遣兩個獵人將白雪公主復活的喜訊告訴小矮人，並請他們都到王宮來。

　　國王和王后聽到白雪公主的遭遇後，分享了王子的喜悅，舉行盛宴為她洗塵。七個小矮人坐在桌旁的烏檀木凳子上，餐巾白得像雪，葡萄酒紅得像血。白雪公主像往常一樣為他們斟酒。

　　說到那兇殘的王后，此時已變得消瘦憔悴，連想也不敢想她的魔鏡了。不久她病重垂危，最後，在一個死一般寂靜的深夜，她叫來宮女，把魔鏡從牆上拿下到她的牀邊。她把四周牀帷拉下，悄聲問道：

> *"Looking-glass, looking-glass on the wall,*
> *Who is the fairest of women all?"*

And the voice within replied:

> *"Fair, in sooth, wert thou[1], I ween[2],*
> *But Snow-White too is now a Queen.*
> *Fairer than she is none[3], I vow.*
> *Look at thyself! Make answer! Thou!"*

At this, the looking-glass slipped out of her hand, and was dashed to pieces on the floor. Her blood seemed to curdle to ice in her body, and she fell back upon her pillows and died.

— *Jakob and Wilhelm Grimm*

---

1. wert thou：〔古〕 = were you。
2. ween：〔古〕 = think。
3. Fairer than she is none： = None / No one is fairer than she (is)。

"牆上的鏡子啊、鏡子，

　　　天下女人誰最美？"

鏡子裏傳出聲音答道：

　　"說實話，我認為您過去確實美，

　　　可現在有個王后白雪公主，

　　　我發誓她的美艷世上無人比。

　　　照照鏡子吧，您的樣子會回答您！"

　　說着，鏡子從她手中掉到地上，摔成碎片。她全身血液仿佛凝結在體內，倒在枕上死了。

　　　　　　　　　　——*雅各布* 與 *威廉·格林*

15 Clever Grethel (Germany)

There was once a cook, and her name was Grethel. Now one day her master said to her: "I have a guest coming this evening, Grethel, and I want you to roast us a pair of fowls for supper."

Grethel said: "Why, yes, master. They shall taste so good you won't know what you're eating." So she killed two fowls, stuffed them with stuffing, and towards evening put them down to a clear, red fire to roast. And when they were done to a turn[1] and smelt sweet as Arabia[2], Grethel called out to her master: "If that guest of yours don't come soon, master, I shall have to take the fowls away from the fire. And I warn you, they will be utterly spoilt, for they are just at their juiciest." Her master said: "So, so! I will run out and see if he is coming."

As soon as her master had turned his back, Grethel thought to herself she would have a little sip of wine. Having had one sip, she took another sip, and then another. Then she looked out of the window; and when she saw that nobody was coming, she said to herself: "There! one of the wings is burning." So she cut off the wing and holding it between her finger and thumb, ate every scrap of it up, to the very bone. Then, "Dear me," she sighed to herself, looking at the chicken, "that one wing left looks like another wing missing!" So she ate up the other.

---

1. to a turn：食物煮熟，恰到好處。
2. Arabia：阿拉伯半島，以生產香料著名。

十五　聰明的格列希爾（德國）

　　從前，有個廚子名叫格列希爾。一天，她的主人吩咐她：“格列希爾，今晚我有個客人要來，你給我們烤兩隻雞做晚餐。”

　　格列希爾說：“噯，好的，老爺，我會把雞烤得味道好到你都嚐不出是甚麼來。”她殺了兩隻雞，填好配料，傍晚時放在明火上烤。等雞烤得恰到好處，香味四溢，格列希爾就叫她的主人：“老爺，如果你那客人不是很快就到，我得把雞從火上拿下來了。我還得告訴你，這時雞汁正多呢！不吃可就糟蹋了。”她的主人說：“哦！哦！我趕緊出去看他來了沒有。”

　　她的主人剛轉過背，格列希爾便暗自思忖：得來一小口酒。她呷了一口，再呷一口，又一口，然後向窗外張望一下，見沒有人來，便自言自語道：“啊！一隻翅膀烤焦了。”於是她切下翅膀，用拇指和食指捏着，吃得乾乾淨淨只剩下骨頭。“天呀，”她嘆口氣，看着雞，“留着這翅膀倒顯得少了另一隻！”她就又把另一隻翅膀吃個精光。

Then she said, "Once those two poor hens were sisters, and you couldn't tell 'em apart. But now one whole and the other nowt[3] but legs!" So she gobbled up the wings of the other chicken to make the pair look more alike. And still her master did not come. Then said she to herself:

"Lor', Grethel, my dear, why worry? There won't be any guest to-night. He has forgotten all about it. And master can have some nice dry bread and cheese." With that she ate up completely one of the chickens, and then, seeing how sad and lonely the other looked all by itself with its legs sticking up in the air and both its wings gone, she finished off that too.

She was picking the very last sweet morsel off its wishbone when her master came running into the kitchen, and cried: "Quick, Grethel! Dish up! dish up! Our guest has just turned the corner." But he at once rushed out to see if the table was ready, and the wine on it; snatched up the great carving-knife, and began to sharpen it on the doorstep.

Pretty soon after, the guest came to the door and knocked. Grethel ran softly out, caught him by the sleeve, pushed him out of the porch, pressed her finger on her lips, and whispered: "Ssh! Ssh! on your life! Listen, now, and be off, I beseech you! My poor master has gone clean out of his senses at your being so late. If he catches you, he will cut your ears off. Hark now! He is sharpening his knife on the doorstep!"

At this the guest turned pale as ashes, and hearing the steady rasping of the knife on the stone, ran off down the street as fast as his legs could carry him. As soon as he was out of sight, Grethel hastened back to her master. "La, master!" she said, "*you've* asked a nice fine guest to supper!"

---

3. nowt：即 nought 或 nothing。

接着她又説："這兩隻可憐的母雞原是姐妹倆，你都分不出誰是誰。可現在一隻有手有腳，那傢伙卻只剩下了兩條腿！"於是她狼吞虎嚥地吃下了另一隻雞的翅膀，好讓這兩隻雞樣子更像。這時她的主人還是沒有來，她又嘀嘀咕咕説：

"老天爺，格列希爾好寶貝兒，發甚麼愁呀？今兒晚上不會有客人來了，他早把這事忘得一乾二淨啦。老爺呢，吃點兒乾麵包和奶酪就得了。"這樣想着，她把一整隻雞都吃光了。這時她看到另外那隻雞兩條腿直挺挺向上伸着，兩隻翅膀都沒了。沒個伴兒，多麼孤獨多麼難過呀。她又把這隻雞也吃了。

她正從雞胸骨上撕下最後一片香噴噴的雞肉時，她的主人跑進廚房，喊道："快，格列希爾！上菜！上菜！客人拐過牆角啦。"但他立刻又衝出去看看桌子擺好沒有，酒有沒有上桌。然後，抓過那把大切肉刀在門口台階上磨了起來。

不一會兒，客人來到門前敲門了。格列希爾輕輕溜出去，抓住他的袖子，把他往門廊外推，又把手指按在嘴唇上，悄悄説："噓！噓！要命就聽着！走吧！求求你了！為你來得這麼晚，我家可憐的老爺氣得得了失心瘋。要是他逮住你，非把你的耳朵割下來不可！聽！他正在台階上磨刀呢！"

聽了這話，客人嚇得面如死灰，又聽到一下接一下霍霍的磨刀聲，便順着大街沒命地跑走了。等他跑得沒了影兒，格列希爾趕快回到主人那裏。"唉呀，老爺！"她説，"你可真是請了個好客人來吃晚餐啊！"

"What's wrong with him?"

"Wrong!" says she. "Why, he had scarce put his nose in at the door, when he gives a sniff. 'What! chicken!' says he. And away he rushed into the kitchen, snatched up my two poor *beeootiful*[4] birds, and ran off with them down the street."

"Heaven save us!" said her master. "Then I shall have nothing for supper!" And off he ran in chase of his guest, crying out as he did so: "Hi, there! Stop! Stop! Hi! Just one! Just one! Only one!" But the guest, hearing these words, and supposing that the madman behind him with his long knife meant one of his ears, ran on faster than ever into the darkness of the night. And Grethel sat down, happy and satisfied.

— *Jakob and Wilhelm Grimm*

---

4. *beeootiful*：beautiful 拉長聲。

“他怎麼啦？”

“怎麼啦！哼！他把鼻子伸到門口，就使勁一吸氣兒：‘哦！雞！’說着他就衝進廚房，抓起我那兩隻可憐又可愛的雞，順着大街跑了。”

“老天爺保佑吧！”她主人說，“那我晚飯沒吃的了！”說着就跑去追他的客人，一邊跑一邊喊：“嗨！喂！站住！站住！嗨！只要一隻！只要一隻！我只要一隻啊！”那客人聽到這話，以為追在後面手拿長刀的瘋子要的是他的一隻耳朵，跑得更快了，一會兒便消失在漆黑的夜色中。格列希爾坐了下來，高高興興，心滿意足。

—— 雅各布 與 威廉·格林

16 The Shreds (Germany)

Once upon a time there was a maiden who was very pretty, but lazy and careless. When she used to spin, she was so impatient that, if there chanced to be a little knot in the thread, she snapped off a long bit with it and threw the pieces down on the ground near her. Now she had a servant girl, who was industrious, and used to gather together the shreds of thread, clean them, and weave them, till she made herself a dress with them. A certain young man had fallen in love with this lazy maiden; and their wedding-day was appointed. On the evening before, the industrious servant girl kept dancing about in her fine dress, till the bride exclaimed:

"Ah! how the girl does jump about,
Dressed in my shreds and leavings!"

When the bridegroom heard this, he asked the bride what she meant, and she told him that the maid had worked herself a dress with the shreds of thread which she had thrown away. As soon as the bridegroom heard this, and saw the difference between the laziness of his intended and the industry of her servant, he gave up the mistress and chose the maid for his wife.

— *Jakob and Wilhelm Grimm*

十六　斷　頭（德國）

　　從前有個姑娘，長得非常漂亮，但是又懶又粗心。她常常紡綫，卻很不耐煩幹，只要綫上打了個小結，她就把小結連着一段長綫掐斷，扔在旁邊地上。她有個很勤快的婢女，這個婢女總是把她丟掉的綫頭收拾起來，清洗乾淨，織成布，後來給自己做成一件衣裳。有個年輕人愛上了這懶姑娘，並訂下婚期。結婚前夕，勤快的婢女穿上她製作精美的衣裳不斷地跳舞，一直跳到新娘叫喊道：

　　　"哎！這丫頭跳來跳去跳得歡，

　　　　穿的卻是我的綫頭織成的衣裳！"

　　新郎聽到了，就問新娘這話甚麼意思。新娘告訴他，她的婢女用她扔掉的綫頭給自己織布做了件衣裳。新郎一聽，又看到意中人的懶惰和婢女的勤快之間的差別，便和新娘退了婚約，選擇婢女做妻子。

——雅各布 與 威廉·格林

17 The Little Shepherd Boy (Germany)

Once upon a time there was a little shepherd boy who was famed far and wide for the wise answers which he gave to all questions. Now the king of the country heard of this lad, but he would not believe what was said about him, so the boy was ordered to come to court. When he arrived the king said to him: "If you can give me answers to each of the three questions which I will now put to you, I will bring you up as my own child, and you shall live here with me in my palace."

"What are these three questions?" asked the boy.

"The first is: How many drops of water are there in the sea?"

"My lord king," replied the shepherd boy, "let all the waters be stopped up on the earth, so that not one drop shall run into the sea before I count it, and then I will tell you how many drops there are in the sea!"

"The second question," said the king, "is: How many stars are there in the sky?"

"Give me a large sheet of paper," said the boy; and then he made in it with a pin so many minute holes that they were far too numerous to see or to count, and dazzled the eyes of whomsoever looked at them. This done, he said: "So many stars are there in the sky as there are holes in this paper; now count them." But nobody was able. Thereupon the king said: "The third question is: How many seconds are there in eternity?"

十七　小牧童（德國）

　　從前有個小牧童，以聰明睿智，能回答別人提出的所有問題而聲名遠播。這個國家的國王聽説了，可他不相信關於孩子的傳言，便命孩子進宮。孩子來了，國王對他説：“我現在要對你提三個問題，如果你都能回答，我就把你當作親生孩子撫養，讓你住在我的宮內。”

　　“三個甚麼問題呢？”男孩子問。

　　“第一個問題是：海裏有多少滴水？”

　　“國王陛下，”牧童答，“您先把所有的水都堵住在地面上，不讓一滴流入海中，然後我來數水滴，告訴你海裏有多少滴水。”

　　“第二個問題是，”國王説，“天上有多少顆星星？”

　　“給我一大張紙，”孩子説；然後他用針在紙上刺了無數針眼，多得看不清、數不盡，誰看着都會眼花。刺完了，他説：“紙上有多少孔，天上就有多少星星，請數吧。”可沒有人能數。因此國王説：“第三個問題是：永恆裏面一共有多少秒？”

"In Lower Pomerania[1] is situated the adamantine mountain, one mile in height, one mile in breadth, and one mile deep; and thither comes a bird once in every thousand years which rubs its beak against the hill, and, when the whole shall be rubbed away, then will the first second of eternity be gone by."

"You have answered the three questions like a sage," said the king, "and from henceforward you shall live with me in my palace, and I will treat you as my own child."

— Jakob and Wilhelm Grimm

---

1. Lower Pomerania：歐洲東北部歷史地區，今大部分屬波蘭，最西部屬德國。

"在下波美拉尼亞有座金剛石山，高一英里，縱橫各一英里，每一千年有一隻鳥兒飛過去，用鳥喙在山石上磨擦。等到整座山都磨掉，永恆的第一秒就過去了。"

　　"你的回答精妙，有似聖哲之言，"國王說，"自此以後，你就仕在我宮內，我要把你當親生孩子對待。"

——*雅各布* 與 *威廉*·格林

18 The Four Musicians[1] (Germany)

There was once a donkey, a dog, a cat and a cock who had worked for their masters faithfully many years, but their strength at last began to fail, and became more and more unfit for work. Finally their masters concluded it was no longer worthwhile to keep them and were thinking of putting an end to them. They saw that mischief was brewing and ran away. The four went on together. They were going to the city and wanted to be musicians because they thought each of them had a good voice.

The city was, however, too far away for them to reach it on the first day of their travelling, and when, toward night, they came to a thick wood, they decided to pass the night among the trees. Before they went to sleep the rooster flew up to the top of a great oak to look around making sure that everything was all right. In so doing he saw in the distance a little light shining, and he called out to his companions, "There must be a house no great way off, for I can see a light."

At length they drew near the place, and found it was a robber's house. Then they consulted together and at last hit on a plan. The donkey stood on his hind legs with his forefeet on the window-sill, the dog got on the donkey's shoulders, the cat mounted the back of the dog, and the rooster flew up and perched on the back of the cat. When all was ready they began their music.

---

1. The Four Musicians：原名 "The Musicians of Bremen" （"不來梅的音樂家"）。

94

十八 四個音樂家（德國）

從前有一頭毛驢、一條狗、一隻貓和一隻公雞。他們經年累月忠心耿耿地為他們的主人工作，到頭來年老體衰，越來越不中用。最後主人認為不值得留下他們，決定把他們殺掉。他們眼見大禍臨頭，只好逃命。他們走在一起，要進城去當音樂家，因為他們都覺得自己有一副好嗓子。

可是進城太遠，一天走不到。夜色降臨時，他們來到一片密林裏，決定在林中過夜。入睡前，公雞飛到一棵大橡樹樹頂，看看周圍是否平靜無事。他看見遠處閃爍着一點亮光，便招呼夥伴們說，"不遠處一定有人家，因為我看見了燈火。"

他們終於走近那地方，發現是個強盜窩。他們經過商量，定下一條妙計。毛驢前腿踏着窗框，後腿站在地上；狗爬上毛驢的肩膀；貓騎到狗背上；公雞飛起站上貓背。一切就緒，他們就開始了大合唱。

"Hehaw! hehaw! hehaw!" brayed the donkey.

"Bow-wow! bow-wow!" barked the dog.

"Meow! meow!" said the cat.

"Cock-a-doodle-doo!" crowed the rooster.

Then they all burst through the window into the room, breaking the glass with a frightful clatter. The robbers, not doubting that some hideous hobgoblin was about to devour them, fled to the woods in great terror.

The donkey and his comrades now sat down at the table and made free with the food the robbers had left, and feasted as if they had been hungry for a month. When they had finished they put out the lights and each sought a sleeping-place to his own liking. They were all tired and soon fell fast asleep.

About midnight the robbers came creeping back to the house. They saw that no lights were burning and everything seemed quiet. So the robber captain stepped softly along to the house and entered the kitchen. There he groped about until he found a candle and some matches on the mantel over the fireplace. The cat had now waked up and stood on the hearth watching the robber with shining eyes. He mistook those eyes for two live coals and reached down to get a light by touching a match to them. The cat did not fancy that sort of thing and flew into his face, spitting[1] and scratching. Then he cried out in fright and ran toward the door, and the dog, who was lying there, bit the robber's leg. He managed, however, to get out in the yard, and there the donkey struck out with a hind foot and gave him a kick that knocked him down, and Chanticleer who had been roused by the noise, cried out "Cock-a-doodle-doo! Cock-a-doodle-doo!"

---

1. spitting：貓狗等動物動怒時發出的呼嚕呼嚕聲。

“哞——噢！哞——噢！”驢鳴。

“汪——汪！汪——汪！”狗吠。

“咪——嗚！咪——嗚！”貓叫。

“喔——喔！喔——喔！”雞啼。

　　緊接着他們一齊破窗而入，窗玻璃嘩地粉碎。強盜們以為有甚麼可怕的妖怪要吃掉他們，嚇得魂飛魄散，跳窗逃到樹林去了。

　　毛驢和夥伴們坐在桌前，狼吞虎嚥吃下強盜留在桌上的食物，就像餓了整整一個月。飯後，他們熄了燈各自找一塊自己喜歡的睡覺的地方。因為已經精疲力竭，很快就沉沉睡去。

　　夜半時分，強盜又潛回這座房子。他們看到房子裏一片漆黑，一切平靜如常。於是強盜頭兒躡手躡腳走向房子進入廚房。他在廚房摸摸索索，從壁爐架上摸到一枝蠟燭和幾根火柴。這時貓已醒來，站在爐邊目光灼灼地盯着那強盜。強盜以為貓眼睛是兩個燒紅的煤炭，就彎下身用火柴頭去碰煤炭，想點着火柴。貓惱了，一下子撲到強盜臉上，又啐又抓。強盜嚇得大叫着向門口跑去。躺在門邊的狗一口咬住他的腿。他好不容易才逃跑到院子裏，毛驢卻在院子舉起後腿，一腳把他踢倒。公雞先生被吵醒，“喔喔喔！喔喔喔！”地啼起來。

The robber captain had barely strength to crawl away to the other robbers. He told them that witches lived in the house.

So the robbers went away and never came back, and the four musicians found themselves so well pleased with their new quarters that they did not go to the city, but stayed where they were; and I dare say you would find them there at this very day.

— Jakob and Wilhelm Grimm

強盜頭兒用盡氣力連爬帶滾才會合了其他強盜。他告訴他們有許多妖婆住在屋子裏。

於是強盜們跑了，再也沒有回來。四個歌唱家很喜歡他們的新居。他們不進城了，就在這裏住下來。我敢說直到今天你還會在那裏找到他們。

—— 雅各布 與 威廉·格林

19 The Elves and the Shoemaker (Germany)

There was once a shoemaker who, through no fault of his own, had become so poor that at last he had only leather enough left for one pair of shoes. At evening he cut out the shoes which he intended to begin upon the next morning and since he had a good conscience, he lay down quietly, said his prayers, and fell asleep.

In the morning when he had prayed, as usual, and was preparing to sit down to work, he found the pair of shoes standing finished on his table. He was amazed, and could not understand it in the least. He took the shoes in his hand to examine them more closely. They were so neatly sewn that not a stitch was out of place, and were as good as the work of a master-hand.

Soon after a purchaser came in, and as he was much pleased with the shoes, he paid more than the ordinary price for them, so that the shoemaker was able to buy leather for more pairs with the money. The same happened in the evening and the following morning and this continued until he was soon again in comfortable circumstances, and became a well-to-do man.

Now it happened one evening, not long before Christmas, when he had cut out shoes as usual, that he said to his wife: "How would it be if we were to sit up to-night to see who it is that lends us such a helping hand?" The wife agreed, lighted a candle, and they hid themselves in the corner of the room.

At midnight came two little naked men, who sat down at the shoemaker's table, took up the cut-out work, and began with their tiny fingers to stitch, sew, and hammer so neatly

十九　小精靈與鞋匠（德國）

從前有個鞋匠，不懶不笨，卻不知怎的窮得精光，最後只剩下夠做一雙鞋的皮子。這天晚上，他剪裁好鞋料，打算明天一早就開始做鞋。因為他心境平和，躺下、做過祈禱，就安然入睡了。

早上他如常禱告完畢，正準備坐下開始工作，卻看見那雙鞋已經做好放在工作台上。他很驚訝，一點也不明白是怎麼回事。他拿起鞋子就近端詳。這鞋子針腳細密均勻，做工精良，像是出於技藝高超的工匠之手。

不久就來了一位顧客，對這雙鞋愛不釋手，用高於平常的價錢買走了。鞋匠用這錢買了夠做更多雙鞋的皮料。當天晚上及第二天早晨，同樣的事情發生了，這樣持續下去，很快他就過上了好日子，不久成了個富裕的人。

聖誕節快到了。一天晚上，鞋匠如常裁好皮料，對他妻子說："要不咱們今晚不睡覺，看看到底是誰這樣幫咱們一把。"妻子同意了，點了根蠟燭，他們便藏在屋角裏。

夜半時分，兩個光着身子的小人兒進來了，坐在工作台邊，拿起裁好的皮料，用他們的小手又快又巧地敲敲縫

and quickly, that the shoemaker could not believe his eyes. They did not stop till everything was quite finished, and stood complete on the table; then they ran swiftly away.

The next day the wife said: "The little men have made us rich, and we ought to show our gratitude. They run about with nothing on, and must freeze with cold. Now I will make them little shirts, coats, waistcoats, hose, and stockings, and you shall make them each a pair of shoes." The husband agreed.

At midnight the little men came skipping in, and were about to set to work; but, instead of the leather ready cut out, they found the charming little clothes. At first they were surprised, then excessively delighted. With the greatest speed they put on and smoothed down the pretty clothes, singing:

> *"Now we're dressed so fine and neat,*
> *Why cobble more for others' feet?"*

Then they hopped and danced about, and leaped over chairs and tables and out at the door. Henceforward, they came back no more, but the shoemaker fared well as long as he lived, and had good luck in all his undertakings.

— *Jakob and Wilhelm Grimm*

縫起來，鞋匠簡直不相信自己的眼睛。他們一刻不停地幹，直到把鞋做好放在工作台上。然後飛快地跑了。

第二天早上，鞋匠的妻子說：“這兩個小人兒幫助咱們致富，咱們應該表示感謝才好。他們這樣赤身露体地跑來跑去，一定很冷。我來為他們做些小襯衫、外套、馬甲、褲子和長襪。你呢，給他們一人做雙鞋吧。”鞋匠很同意。

半夜，兩個小人兒蹦蹦跳跳走進屋，剛要幹活，沒看到裁好的皮子，卻有漂亮的小衣服。他們開始愣了一下，後來高興極了，他們飛快地穿好衣服，撫平拉好，唱道：

　“現在我們穿好又着暖囉，

　　哪去管別人的鞋子破不破！”

他們又蹦蹉又跳舞，躍過桌椅出了門。從此以後，他們再也不來了。可是鞋匠在有生之年一直生意興隆，事事遂意。

──*雅各布 與 威廉*·格林

20 Rapunzel (Germany)

Once a man and wife had long wished in vain for a child. In the back of their house there was a little window that looked out over a wonderful garden, full of beautiful flowers and vegetables. But there was a high wall around the garden, and no one dared enter it because it belonged to a witch. One day the wife stood at this window, looking down into the garden, and her eyes lit on a bed of the finest rapunzel[1]. And it looked so fresh and green that she longed for it and her mouth watered. Her craving for it grew from day to day, and she began to waste away because she knew she would never get any. Seeing her so pale and wretched, her husband took fright and asked: "What's the matter with you, dear wife?" "Oh," she said, "I shall die unless I get some rapunzel to eat from the garden behind our house." Her husband, who loved her, thought: "I shall get her some of that rapunzel, cost what it may."

As night was falling, he climbed the wall into the witch's garden, took a handful of rapunzel, and brought it to his wife. She ate it hungrily right away. But it tasted so good, so very good, that the next day her craving for it was three times as great. So at nightfall the husband climbed the wall again, but when he came down on the other side he had an awful fright, for there was the witch right in front of him.

"Oh, please," he said, "my wife saw your rapunzel. She felt such a craving for it that she would have died if I hadn't got her some." At that the witch's anger died down and she

---

1. rapunzel：萵苣的一種。

二十 萵苣女（德國）

　　從前，一對夫婦很久就想要個孩子，卻不能如願。他們家後牆上有扇小窗，從那兒可以望見一個長滿鮮花和蔬菜的美麗花園。但花園被一道高牆圍住，沒有人敢進去，因為它是一個巫婆的。一天，那妻子站在窗旁望着下面的花園，眼光落在一畦茂盛的萵苣上，萵苣長得新鮮碧綠，這女人看了饞涎欲滴。她天天看着這畦萵苣，越來越想吃，因為知道吃不到，人也漸漸消瘦了。丈夫見到她那樣憔悴痛苦，十分吃驚，問道：“好太太，你怎麼啦？”“哎，”她說，“要是吃不到屋後花園裏的萵苣，我就要死了。”丈夫很愛她，想：“無論付出甚麼代價，我也要給她弄些萵苣來。”

　　夜色降臨，他翻過牆頭進了巫婆的花園，採了一把萵苣拿給太太。她馬上三口兩口吃了。可這味道實在太好，第二天，她比原來更想吃三倍。她丈夫只好天黑時又翻牆過去，可是當他從牆那邊跳下來時，嚇得半死，因為那巫婆正站在他面前。

　　“哎呀，發發好心吧，”他說，“我太太看到您的萵苣特別想吃，我要是不給她拿點兒，她就會死了。”巫婆聽

said: "If that's how it is, you may take as much rapunzel as you wish, but on one condition: that you give me the child your wife will bear." In his fright, the man agreed to everything, and the moment his wife was delivered, the witch appeared, gave the child the name of Rapunzel, and took her away.

Rapunzel grew to be the loveliest child under the sun. When she was twelve years old, the witch took her to the middle of the forest and shut her up in a tower that had neither stairs nor door, but only a little window at the very top. When the witch wanted to come in, she stood down below and called out: "Rapunzel, Rapunzel, let down your hair for me." Rapunzel had beautiful long hair, as fine as spun gold. When she heard the witch's voice, she undid her braids and fastened them to the window latch. They fell to the ground twenty ells[2] down, and the witch climbed up on them.

A few years later it so happened that the king's son was passing through the forest. When he came to the tower, he heard someone singing. And he saw a witch come to the foot of the tower and heard her call out something. Whereupon Rapunzel let down her braids, and the witch climbed up to her. The next day, when it was beginning to get dark, he went to the tower and called out as the witch did. A moment later her hair fell to the ground and the prince climbed up.

At first Rapunzel was dreadfully frightened, for she had never seen a man before, but the prince gently told her how he had been so moved by her singing that he couldn't rest easy until he had seen her. At that Rapunzel lost her fear, and when he asked if she would have him as her husband and she said yes. And they agreed he would come every

---

2.　twenty ells：形容頭髮很長。ell 為舊長度單位，相當於 45 英寸。

到這話息了怒，說："既然如此，這萵苣你想拿多少便拿多少好了。可是有個條件：你太太會懷個孩子，你得把那孩子給我。"這人在慌亂中甚麼都答應了。到了他妻子臨盆時，巫婆來了，給孩子起名叫萵苣女，便把她帶走了。

萵苣女慢慢長成一個天下最美的姑娘。她十二歲時，巫婆把她帶到森林深處，鎖在一座既無梯子也沒有門，只在頂部有個小窗的塔裏。巫婆想進去時，就站在下面叫："萵苣女，萵苣女，把你的頭髮放下來讓我上去。"萵苣女長有一頭長長的、金絲般的秀髮，她聽到巫婆的聲音，便解開髮辮把頭髮拴在窗門上，金瀑似的長髮便垂落到地面上，巫婆就順着長髮爬上塔去。

數年後，一位王子偶然路過林中，來到塔前，聽到有人唱歌；又看見一個巫婆來到塔下叫喚，萵苣女放下辮子她便爬了上去。第二天，天剛轉黑，王子來到塔下，也像巫婆那樣叫。不一會兒，姑娘的頭髮垂落下來，王子便爬了上去。

開始萵苣女非常害怕，因為她從未見過一個男人。但王子溫柔地告訴她他怎樣被她的歌聲深深感動，見不到她不能安寧。聽到這些，萵苣女的懼怕消失了。王子問她是否願意嫁給他，她同意了。他們又商量好他每天晚上來，

evening and bring a skein of silk every time to make a ladder for her to climb down. The witch noticed nothing until one day Rapunzel said to her: "Tell me, Godmother, how is it that you're so much harder to pull up than the young prince?" "Wicked child!" cried the witch, "You've deceived me." In her fury she picked up a pair of scissors and cut her lovely long hair. She then sent poor Rapunzel to a desert place, where she lived in misery and want.

At dusk the witch fastened Rapunzel's severed braids to the window latch, and when the prince climbed up, she was waiting for him with angry, poisonous looks. "Aha!" she cried. "You've come to take your darling wife away, but the bird is gone from the nest, she won't be singing any more; you'll never see her again." The prince was beside himself with grief, and in his despair he jumped from the tower. It didn't kill him, but the brambles he fell into scratched his eyes out and he was blind. He wandered through the forest, weeping and wailing over the loss of his dearest wife.

At last he came to the desert place where Rapunzel was living in misery with the twins she had borne — a boy and a girl. When he approached Rapunzel recognized him, fell on his neck and wept. Two of her tears dropped on his eyes, which were made clear again, so that he could see as well as ever. He took her to his kingdom, where she was welcomed with rejoicing, and they lived happy and contented for many years to come.

— *Jakob and Wilhelm Grimm*

每次帶一束絲來做梯子，好讓她爬下去。老巫婆毫無察覺，直到有一天萵苣女對她說：「告訴我吧，教母，為甚麼拉你上來要比拉那小王子上來費力得多呢？」「你這壞孩子！」老巫婆喊道，「你騙了我。」盛怒中，她拾起剪刀，剪斷了她美麗的長髮。之後她把可憐的萵苣女送到一個荒漠中，讓她在傷心和飢渴中煎熬。

那天黃昏，她把從萵苣女頭上剪下的長髮拴在窗閂上，王子爬上了塔樓，兇惡的、滿面狠毒的巫婆正等着他。「啊哈！」她叫道，「你到這兒來想把你的寶貝太太帶走是不是？可那小鳥兒已經不在巢裏了，再也不會唱歌了，你永遠也見不到她了。」王子滿腔悲憤，失魂喪魄，絕望中跳下高塔。但他沒有摔死，卻掉在荊棘叢中傷了眼珠，瞎了。他在森林中摸索、漂泊，為失去心愛的妻子悲泣、痛哭。

最後，他來到一片荒漠，在這裏萵苣女正帶着生下的一男一女雙胞胎在痛苦中生活。他一走近，萵苣女便認出他來。她摟着他傷心哭泣，兩滴眼淚滴進他的眼睛，洗清了眼窩。他又重見光明了。他帶她回到王國，她受到熱烈的歡迎。此後他們的生活美滿幸福，白頭到老。

—— 雅各布 與 威廉·格林

21 The Three Lazy Sons (Germany)

A king had three sons whom he loved equally, and he didn't know which of them he should choose to be king after his death. When it came time for him to die, he called them to his bedside and said: "Dear children, I've come to a decision which I will now reveal to you: whichever one of you is the laziest shall become king after me." The eldest said: "Father, then the kingdom is mine, because I'm so lazy that when I'm lying on my back all ready to fall asleep and the rain starts falling in my eyes, I'd sooner stay awake than close them." The second said: "Father, the kingdom is mine, because I'm so lazy that when I sit warming myself by the fire, I'd sooner burn my heels than pull my legs in." The third said: "Father, the kingdom is mine, because I'm so lazy that if I were going to be hanged and the noose were already around my neck, and somebody handed me a sharp knife and said I could cut the rope with it, I'd sooner let them hang me than raise my hand to the rope." When the father heard that, he said: "You're the laziest of all. You shall be king."

— Jakob and Wilhelm Grimm

二十一 三個懶兒子 (德國)

一位國王有三個兒子。他對他們不偏不倚一樣疼愛，拿不定主意死後把王位傳給哪一個。臨終時，他把他們叫到牀邊，說："好孩子，我已經做出決定了，現在我來告訴你們：我要選你們當中最懶的一個在我死後繼位為國王。"老大說："父王，那麼這王國是我的了，因為我懶到仰面朝天準備睡覺時，要是下雨，我情願醒着讓雨滴進眼睛也懶得閉上眼。"老二說："父王，王國是我的，因為我懶到坐在爐邊烤火，情願燒了腳跟也懶得把腿縮回來。"老三說："父王，王國是我的，因為我懶到要是我去受絞刑，絞索已經套上脖子，有人遞給我一把快刀，說我可以割斷繩索。我寧願弔死，也懶得抬手去割那繩子。"國王一聽這話，便說："你是三個人中最懶的，王位就傳給你啦。"

—— 雅各布 與 威廉·格林

111

22 Tyll Ulenspiegel's Merry Prank (Germany)

When Tyll was in Poland, King Casimir[1] ruled, and a merry monarch he was. He had two court jester, and when he heard Tyll was in the land he invited him also to his palace.

Now, the king was proud of his jesters and knew a trick or three himself. Often they argued, and Tyll was always ready with a quick answer, particularly when it came to answering the jesters. So one day the king decided to test which was the cleverest of the three.

There was a great gathering of nobles in the court when the king offered twenty gold pieces and a fine new coat to the one of the three who could make the greatest wish. All the court applauded the generosity of their ruler.

"And," added he, "the wish must be made right now before me and all the court."

Said the first jester, "I wish the heaven above us were nothing but paper and the sea nothing but ink so that I could write the figures of how much money should be mine."

Spoke the second, "I want as many towers and castles as there are stars in heaven so that I might keep all the money that my fellow court jesters here would have."

It was now Tyll's turn. He opened his mouth and spoke, "I would want the two here to make out their wills, leaving their money to me, and then you, your Majesty, would order them to the gallows right after."

---

1. King Casimir：可能是卡齊米爾三世（1310—1370），號稱“和平君主”的波蘭國王。

二十二　梯爾‧烏連斯派格爾的俏皮話
（德國）

梯爾在波蘭時，正當卡齊米爾國王在位，他是個快活瀟灑的國王，有兩個弄臣。他聽説梯爾在波蘭，便也邀請他進宮。

國王對他的弄臣是頗感自豪的，他自己也會一兩手花招。他們常常爭辯，而梯爾每每對答如流，特別是對那兩個弄臣，更是有問必答。於是有一天，國王決定考考他們，看三個裏面到底誰的腦子最快。

宮廷裏官紳顯貴齊集，國王拿出二十塊金幣和一件華麗的新外衣，三個人當中誰能説出最宏大的願望，就賞給誰。滿朝都為國王的慷慨大度歡呼喝采。

國王又説：“這個願望必須現在當着我和滿朝大臣説出來。”

第一個弄臣説：“我願藍天作紙大海當墨，讓我寫得下我該擁有的錢財的數字。”

第二個説：“我願有像天上繁星那麼多的樓塔城堡，用來裝我的弄臣同僚們擁有的錢。”

輪到梯爾了，他張嘴説道：“我願他們倆都立下遺囑，把錢留給我。然後尊敬的陛下，您命令人馬上把他們吊上絞刑架。”

The king and all his court laughed merrily at this, and Tyll won the coat and the money.

Now you know how a quick and merry answer can bring one fame and fortune.

— M. A. Jagendorf

國王和滿朝大臣聽了都開懷大笑，梯爾贏得了外衣和錢。

　　現在你知道了，一句機智俏皮的回答可以使人既得名又得利呢。

——M・A・傑根道夫

23 A Reply of a Boy to Cardinal Angelotto (Italy)

The Roman cardinal Angelotto, a sarcastic and quarrelsome man, was long on words but short on common sense. At the time when Pope Eugenius[1] was in Florence, a very clever ten-year-old boy came to visit Angelotto and in a few words made him a brilliant speech. Angelotto wondered at the maturity and polish of the boy's diction and asked him some questions, which he answered cleverly. Turning to the bystanders Angelotto said: "Those who display such intelligence and learning in their childhood decrease in wit as they increase in age, and finally turn out to be stupid." Then the boy retorted: "Then you must indeed have been extraordinarily learned and wise when you were young." The Cardinal was staggered at this impromptu witty reply, for he had been rebuked for his foolishness by what he thought was a mere child.

— *Poggio Bracciolini*

---

1. Pope Eugenius：可能是指教皇猶金四世（1383 — 1447）。

二十三　機敏的應對[1]（義大利）

　　羅馬紅衣主教安傑洛托是個尖酸刻薄，喜歡爭辯的人，他長於語言而不諳人情。羅馬教皇猶金駐蹕在佛羅倫斯之時，一個極為聰穎的十歲男孩去謁見安傑洛托，語出成章。安傑洛托驚嘆孩子思想成熟和談吐不凡，便問了他幾個問題，孩子應對精妙。安傑洛托轉身向周圍的人說："有些人小時聰明有學識，長大後聰明學識反而減退，最後變得愚魯蠢鈍。"男孩反駁說："那您小時候一定是非常有學識和聰明伶俐的了。"紅衣主教對這脫口而出的機智應對竟訥訥不能置答，因為他說了蠢話，竟被一個他認為不過是個小小的孩子反罵了他。

—— 波焦·布拉喬利尼[2]

---

1. 我國漢末時文學家孔融（153—208），少異悟，年十歲時，到當時名重一時的李膺家，出語驚人。有陳韙者，説他"小時了了，大未必佳"。孔融應聲説："想君小時，必當了了。"上文十歲男孩的應對，與孔融所説幾乎一字不差。驚異於古今中外的文化竟如此相通，故錄譯此篇。值得注意的是孔融的時代比篇中男孩早了約 1,200 年。
2. 波焦·布拉喬利尼（1380—1459），義大利人文主義者，文藝復興時期最著名的學者之一。

24 Pinocchio (excerpt) (Italy)

Everyone, at one time or another, has found some surprise awaiting him. Of the kind which Pinocchio had on that eventful morning of his life, there are but few. On awakening, Pinocchio put his hand up to his head and there he found —

Guess!

He found that, during the night, his ears had grown at least ten full inches!

He went in search of a mirror, but not finding any, he just filled a basin with water and looked at himself. There he saw what he never could have wished to see. His manly figure was adorned and enriched by a beautiful pair of donkey's ears.

I leave you to think of the terrible grief, the shame, the despair of the poor Marionette[1].

He began to cry, to scream, to knock his head against the wall, but the more he shrieked, the longer and the more hairy grew his ears. A fat, little Dormouse came into the room and asked what was wrong.

"Oh, what have I done? What have I done?" cried Pinocchio, grasping his two long ears in his hands and pulling and tugging at them angrily.

"My dear boy," answered the Dormouse to cheer him up a bit, "why worry now? What is done cannot be undone. Fate has decreed that all lazy boys who come to hate books and schools and teachers and spend all their days with toys and games must sooner or later turn into donkeys."

---

1. Marionette：意大利語，小木偶。

二十四 木偶奇遇記（選段）（義大利）

　　人生在世總會有時碰到那麼一點意外之事。但是像匹諾曹在那終身難忘的一個早上的遭遇卻極為罕見。一覺醒來，匹諾曹抬手摸摸腦袋，摸到了——

　　猜猜看，摸到了甚麼？

　　他發現一夜之間，他的耳朵至少長了足足十英寸！

　　他想找面鏡子，可哪兒也找不到，就打了一臉盆水當鏡子照了照。竟照到了一副他決不想見到的怪模樣，他那堂堂男子漢的容貌居然裝上了一對漂亮的驢耳朵！

　　你們想像一下吧，可憐的小木偶是多麼傷心欲絕，羞愧難當，多麼絕望哪！

　　他哭起來，尖聲喊叫，又用頭碰牆。但是他越叫喊，耳朵就越長，而且越發毛茸茸的了。這時一隻胖胖的小睡鼠走進房間，問出了甚麼事。

　　"嗚，我幹甚麼壞事了？我幹甚麼壞事了？"匹諾曹哭道。他用手抓住兩隻長耳朵，生氣地又拽又扯。

　　睡鼠勸道："親愛的孩子，現在哭已經晚啦。事情做過，後悔莫及了。那些懶孩子不愛上學唸書，不喜歡老師，整天只知道玩玩具、做遊戲，命裏注定早晚要變成毛驢的。"

"But the fault is not mine. The fault is all Lamp-Wick's, a classmate of mine."

Pinocchio went to find Lamp-Wick who was in much the same plight. Both had to cover up their heads with a cotton bag to conceal their strange and shameful appearance.

When the Marionette and his friend Lamp-Wick saw each other both stricken by the same misfortune, instead of feeling sorrowful and ashamed, began to poke fun at each other, and after much nonsense, they ended by bursting out into hearty laughter.

But all of a sudden Lamp-Wick stopped laughing. He tottered and almost fell. Pale as a ghost, he turned to Pinocchio and said: "Help, help, Pinocchio!"

"What is the matter?"

"Oh, help me! I can no longer stand up."

"I can't either," cried Pinocchio; and his laughter turned to tears as he stumbled about helplessly.

They had hardly finished speaking, when both of them fell on all fours and began running and jumping around the room. As they ran, their arms turned into legs, their faces lengthened into snouts, and their backs became covered with long gray hairs.

This was humiliating enough, but the most horrible moment was the one in which the two poor creatures felt their tails appear. Overcome with shame and grief, they tried to cry and bemoan their fate.

But what is done can't be undone! Instead of moans and cries, they burst forth into loud donkey brays, which sounded very much like, "Haw! Haw! Haw!"

— *Carlo Lorenzini*

"可這不能怪我呀，這都怪我的同學小燈蕊兒。"

於是他出去找小燈蕊兒。他也正和他一樣倒霉呢。兩人都得用個棉布口袋套在頭上，蓋住那醜怪的、丟人的模樣。

當小木偶和小燈蕊兒看到彼此的倒霉相之後，居然不覺得難過，也沒有不好意思，反而你取笑我，我揶揄你。胡說了一陣，最後還哈哈大笑起來。

突然間，小燈蕊兒不笑了。他一踉蹌幾乎摔倒，臉色白得像個鬼，向匹諾曹叫道："救命啊，救命啊，匹諾曹！"

"怎麼回事？"

"哎，救命，救命！我站不住了。"

"我也站不住了呀，"匹諾曹喊道。他的笑聲變成了哭腔，在地上跌跌撞撞，無法控制自己。

他們的話還沒有說完，已經四肢着地滿屋子亂跑亂跳起來。他們跑着，胳膊變成了腿，臉也拉長變成驢臉，背上生滿灰色的長毛。

這就夠丟臉的了，更可怕的是，這兩個可憐的傢伙竟感覺到自己長出了尾巴。他們羞愧萬分，悲傷欲絕，為他們的不幸痛哭。

但是，壞事做過，後悔已遲！他們的哭聲變成驢叫。聽起來很像"哞！哞！哞！"

—— 卡羅·羅蘭西尼[1]

---

1. 羅蘭西尼（1826—1890），筆名科羅狄（Coilodi），意大利記者，《木偶奇遇記》為其所著長篇童話故事。

25 King Canute on the Seashore (England)

A hundred years or more after the time of Alfred the Great[1] there was a king of England named Canute[2]. King Canute was a Dane. The great men and officers who were around King Canute were always praising him. "You are the greatest man that ever lived," one would say. Then another would say, "O king! there can never be another man so mighty as you." And another would say, "Great Canute, there is nothing in the world that dares to disobey you."

The king was a man of sense, and he grew very tired of hearing such foolish speeches.

One day he was by the seashore, and his officers were with him. They were praising him, as they were in the habit of doing. He thought that now he would teach them a lesson, and so he bade them set his chair on the beach close by the edge of the water.

"Am I the greatest man in the world?" he asked. "O king!" they cried, "there is no one so mighty as you."

"Do all things obey me?" he asked. "There is nothing that dares to disobey you, O king!" they said. "The world bows before you, and gives you honour."

"Will the sea obey me?" he asked; and he looked down at the little waves which were lapping the sand at his feet.

---

1. Alfred the Great：英國歷史上稱為 Alfred, the Great of Wessex（849 — 899），英格蘭西南部撒克遜人的西撒克斯王朝國王，在位時文修武治，有很盛的功業。

2. Canute：克努特大帝（994?—1035），英格蘭和丹麥國王，1016—1035 在位為英格蘭國王，1018—1035 兼丹麥國王。英國歷史上的名王。這篇是關於他的傳說。

二十五　克努特大帝在海邊(英國)

　　阿爾弗烈德大帝時代之後一百多年，英格蘭的國王名叫克努特，是丹麥人。克努特大帝周圍的王公大臣們對他阿諛奉承，"您真偉大啊，前無古人！"一個人說。於是另一個人就會說："國王陛下，您真偉大啊！後無來者！"又一個人說："偉大的克努特啊，世上甚麼東西都不敢不服從您。"

　　克努特大帝是個有理智的人，愈來愈厭聞這種無聊的吹捧。

　　一天，他剛好在海邊，他的官員們跟隨左右。他們按照老規矩，又對他極盡讚美之能事。克努特想，這回得給他們一點教訓，於是吩咐他們把他的御座放在沙灘上海水邊。

　　"我是世上最偉大的人嗎？"他問。"陛下啊！"他們說，"再沒有人像您有那樣大的權能了。"

　　"一切事物都服從我嗎？"他又問。"國王陛下啊！沒有甚麼敢違背您的意願。"他們回答："全世界都向您頂禮膜拜，都向您致敬。"

　　"大海會服從我嗎？"他看着腳下輕輕拍打着沙灘的細

The foolish officers were puzzled, but they did not dare to say "No." "Command it, O king! and it will obey," said one.

"Sea," cried Canute, "I command you to come no farther! Waves, stop your rolling, and do not dare to touch my feet!"

But the tide came in, just as it always did. The water rose higher and higher. It came up around the king's chair, and wet not only his feet, but also his robe. His officers stood about him, alarmed, and wondering whether he was not mad.

Then Canute took off his crown, and threw it down upon the sand.

"I shall never wear it again," he said. "And do you, my men, learn a lesson from what you have seen[3]. There is only one King who is all-powerful; and it is he who rules the sea, and holds the ocean in the hollow of his hand. It is he whom you ought to praise and serve above all others."

— edited by James Baldwin

---

3. And do you...from what you have seen：這是個修辭疑問句，不用問號，讀出時不用升調。

浪，問道。那些愚蠢的官員愕然了，可又不敢説個"不"字。有個人説："陛下，下命令吧！大海會服從的。"

於是克努特喝令："大海，我命令你不要湧過來！海浪，停止翻滾，不要碰我的腳！"

然而浪潮湧過來了，就像常日一樣。海水越湧越高，到了國王御座周圍，不僅浸濕了他的腳，連王袍也打濕了。官員們站在左右，驚恐不安，懷疑國王是不是瘋了。

這時，國王摘下王冠扔在沙灘上。

"我再也不戴王冠了，"他説，"我的大臣們啊，你們要從眼前的情景得到一個教訓。只有一位全能的王，只有他能夠統治大海，能將大洋握在掌中。你們應該讚美的是他，應該把他置於萬民之上頂禮膜拜。"

—— 傑姆斯·鮑德溫 編

26 Three Wise Men of Gotham (England)

There is a town in England called Gotham[1], and many merry stories are told of the queer people who used to live there.

One day two men of Gotham met on a bridge. Hodge was coming from the market, and Peter was going to the market. "Where are you going?" said Hodge. "I am going to the market to buy sheep," said Peter. "Buy sheep?" said Hodge. "And which way will you bring them home?" "I shall bring them over this bridge," said Peter. "No, you shall not," said Hodge; "Yes, but I will," said Peter. "You shall not." "I will."

Then they beat with their sticks on the ground as though there had been a hundred sheep between them. "Take care!" cried Peter. "Look out that my sheep don't jump on the bridge." "I care not where they jump," said Hodge; "But they shall not go over it." "But they shall," said Peter. "Have a care," said Hodge; "for if you say too much, I will put my fingers in your mouth." "Will you?" said Peter.

Just then another man of Gotham came from the market with a sack of meal on his horse. He heard his neighbours quarrelling about sheep; but he could see no sheep between them, and so he stopped and spoke to them. "Ah, you foolish fellows! It is strange that you will never learn wisdom.— Come here, Peter, and help me lay my sack on my shoulder."

Peter did so, and the man carried his meal to the side of

---

1. Gotham：傳說中英格蘭諾丁漢郡的一個村莊。

二十六　愚人村中的三個聰明人 (英國)

　　英格蘭有個鎮子叫愚人村，住着一些行為怪誕的人，關於他們，流傳着許多聽了令人忍俊不禁的故事。

　　一天，愚人村兩個聰明人在橋上相遇，霍奇剛從集市來，彼得要到集市去。“你上哪兒去啊？”霍奇問。“我去集市買綿羊，”彼得説。“買綿羊？”霍奇問，“那你從哪條路趕羊回家？”“我趕羊從這橋上過，”彼得説。“不行，你不能從橋上走，”霍奇説。“行，我就要從橋上過，”彼得説。“你不能。”“我偏要。”

　　於是他們用手杖頓地吵了起來，好像他們身邊已經有了上百隻羊似的。“小心了！”彼得叫道，“留神別讓我的羊在橋上跳。”“我才不管它們在哪兒跳呢，”霍奇説，“反正不許它們從橋上過。”“可它們要過，”彼得説。“小心，”霍奇説，“你要是話説得太多，我會堵住你的嘴的。”“是嗎？你倒試試看！”彼得説。

　　正在這時，愚人村裏另外一個人從集市回來了，他的馬馱着一袋糧食。他聽到鄰人正為羊爭吵，可又見不到他們身邊有羊，便停下腳步對他們説：“哎，你們這些傻子！真是怪事，你們怎麼總也學不到聰明一點兒——彼得，過來幫我把麻袋放在我肩膀上。”

　　彼得照辦了，那人將糧食扛到橋邊，“看着我，”他

the bridge. "Now look at me," he said, "and learn a lesson." And he opened the mouth of the sack, and poured all the meal into the river. "Now, neighbours," he said, "can you tell how much meal is in my sack?"

"There is none at all!" cried Hodge and Peter together. "You are right," said the man; "and you that stand here and quarrel about nothing, have no more sense in your heads than I have meal in my sack!"

Which was the wisest of these three? Judge for yourself.

— *edited by James Baldwin*

説，"汲取點兒教訓。"說着便解開袋口，把糧食統統倒進河裏。"好啦，街坊，"他說，"你們能告訴我麻袋裏還有多少糧食嗎？"

"一點都沒有了啊！"霍奇和彼得齊聲叫道。"對啦，"那人說，"你們站在這兒為根本沒有的東西瞎吵，你們那腦袋裏懂得的東西還沒有我麻袋裏的糧食多呢！"

這三個人當中誰最聰明，還是請您自己去判斷吧。

——*傑姆斯·鮑德溫 編*

27 Catskin (England)

Once upon a time there lived a gentleman who owned fine lands and houses, and he very much wanted to have a son to be heir to them. So when his wife brought him a daughter, though she was bonny[1] as bonny could be, he cared nought for her. So she grew up to be a beautiful maiden, though her father never set eyes on her till she was fifteen years old and was ready to be married. Then her father said roughly, "She shall marry the first that comes for her."

Now when this became known, who should come along and be first but a nasty, horrid, old man. So she didn't know what to do, and went to the hen-wife[2] and asked her advice. The hen-wife suggested she should not marry him unless she was given a coat of silver cloth, then a coat of beaten gold, and then a coat of catskin. These demands were fulfilled. But still she would not take the nasty, horrid, old man.

So she put on the coat of catskin tied up her other coats into a bundle, and when it was night-time, ran away with it into the woods. Now she went along, and went along, till she saw a fine castle. Then she hid her fine dresses by a crystal waterfall and went up to the castle-gates and asked for work. The lady of the castle hired her to be their scullion. They called her Catskin. But the cook was very cruel to her.

One day, the young lord of the castle came home, and there was to be a grand ball in honour of the occasion. Catskin asked to be allowed to go to the ball, but the cook only dashed

---

1. bonny：漂亮的，主要用於蘇格蘭語中。
2. hen-wife：古用法，現已廢。

二十七　貓皮(英國)

　　從前有位紳士擁有華廈良田，渴望有個兒子來繼承產業。後來他的妻子生了個女兒，雖然這女孩長得要多健康美麗有多健康美麗，他卻一點不把她放在心上。這個被父親厭惡，連一眼也不看的女孩還是長成了一個美麗的少女。到了十五歲，可以出嫁了，父親粗暴地說："把她嫁給第一個來求婚的算了。"

　　人們都得到了消息。誰想第一個來到的竟是個粗鄙可厭的邋遢老頭子。她不知怎麼辦，就去請教養雞婆。養雞婆讓她向那人要一件銀的外衣，又要一件金箔做的外衣，還要一件貓皮外衣，他都一一滿足了她。但她還是不願嫁給這老頭子。

　　她穿上貓皮外衣，把其他外衣打成一綑，拿着它趁黑夜逃進森林。她走啊走，最後看到一座美麗的城堡。於是她將好衣服藏在清澈的瀑布後，走到城門口要找一份工作。城堡的夫人僱她在廚房洗碗。人們叫她"貓皮"，廚子對她非常狠毒。

　　一天，城堡的小爵爺回家來，要舉辦一個盛大的舞會為他接風。貓皮請求讓她也參加舞會，廚子卻把一盆水潑

a basin of water into her face. Now when the day of the ball arrived, Catskin slipped out of the house and went to the edge of the forest where she had hidden her dresses, and put on her coat of silver cloth, and hastened away to the ball. As soon as she entered all were overcome by her beauty and grace, while the young lord at once lost his heart to her, and he would dance with none other. When it came to parting time, the young lord asked where she lived. But Catskin curtsied and said:

"Kind sir, if the truth I must tell,
At the sign of the 'Basin of Water' I dwell,"

Then she flew from the castle and donned her catskin robe again, and slipped into the scullery.

The young lord went the very next day and searched for the sign of the "Basin of Water"; but he could not find it. So another ball was soon arranged in hopes that the beautiful maid would appear again. This time when Catskin asked to be allowed to go to the ball, the cook broke a ladle across Catskin's back. Catskin again ran off to the forest and put on her coat of beaten gold, and off she went to the ballroom. As soon as she entered, the young lord at once recognized her as the lady of the "Basin of Water," claimed her hand for the first dance, and did not leave her till the last. When that came, he again asked her where she lived. But all that she would say was:

"Kind sir, if the truth I must tell,
At the sign of the 'Broken Ladle' I dwell";

and with that she curtsied and flew from the ball, off with her golden robe, on with her catskin, and into the scullery without the cook's knowing.

But this time the young lord followed her, and watched her change her fine dress for her catskin dress, and then he knew her for his own scullery-maid. Next day he went to his

132

在她臉上。開舞會的日子到了，貓皮悄悄溜出房子，來到森林邊她藏衣服的地方，穿上銀外衣，趕去參加舞會。她一進去，所有的人都被她的美貌和高雅的儀態攝住了。年青的爵爺對她一見傾心，再也沒有和別人跳舞。曲終筵散時，小爵爺問她住在哪裏，貓皮行個屈膝禮答道：

> "好心的少爺，要我説真話，
> 　　我就住在'水盆街'。"

說完她跑出城堡，又穿上貓皮，悄悄回到洗碗間。

小爵爺第二天立刻四處尋找"水盆街"，可找不到。因此不久他又安排了一個舞會希望那美麗女郎再次出現。這回貓皮請求去參加舞會時，廚子用長柄勺打她後背，把勺柄都打斷了。貓皮又跑到森林，穿上金箔外衣去參加舞會。她一進去，小爵爺立刻認出她就是那"水盆街"小姐。從第一支舞曲到最後一支，他都請她跳舞。跳最後一次時，他又問她住在哪裏，可她只回答：

> "好心的少爺，要我説真話，
> 　　我就住在'斷勺路'。"

她行個屈膝禮便跑出舞廳，脫下金箔衣，換上貓皮，趁廚師不知不覺時悄悄回到洗碗間。

可是這次小爵爺跟在她後面，看着她脫下金外衣換上貓皮，知道了她就是他的洗碗女傭。第二天他去找母親說

mother, and told her that he wished to marry the scullery-maid, Catskin.

"Never," said the lady of the Castle, "never so long as I live." Well, the young lord was so grieved, that he took to his bed and was very ill indeed. The doctor tried to cure him, but he would not take any medicine unless from the hands of Catskin. At last the doctor went to the mother, and said that her son would die if she did not consent to his marriage with Catskin; so she had to give way. Then she summoned Catskin to her, and Catskin put on her coat of beaten gold before she went to see the lady; and she, of course was overcome at once, and was only too glad to wed her son to so beautiful a maid. So they were married, and she told her husband all about her father, and begged he would go and find out what had become of her parents.

Now her father had never had any other child, and his wife had died; so he was all alone in the world, and sate[3] moping and miserable. When the young lord came in he hardly looked up. Then Catskin's husband asked him, "Pray, sir, had you not once a young daughter whom you would never never see or own?" And the miserable man said with tears, "It is true; I am a hardened sinner. But I would give all my worldly goods if I could but see her once before I die." Then the young lord told him what had happened to Catskin, and brought him to his own castle, where they lived happily ever afterwards.

— *Flora Annie Steel*

---

3. sate：sat 的古體。

他要娶那洗碗女貓皮。

"不行！"夫人說，"只要我活着你就別指望！"這下小爵爺傷心欲絕，病得臥牀不起。醫生給他治病，但他説除了貓皮，誰給他藥他都不吃。最後醫生找到他母親，説她再不同意兒子娶貓皮，他就要死了。母親只好讓步。她叫貓皮來見她，貓皮穿上了金箔衣才來。當然啦，她一下子就得到了夫人的歡心，她兒子能娶到這樣美麗的少女，她高興還來不及呢。他們結了婚。貓皮對她丈夫講了她父親的事情，請求他去看看她雙親的近況。

這時，她父親膝下無兒無女，妻子也已去世，世上只剩下他孤零零一個人，終日獨坐，心境愁苦。小爵爺走進屋時他頭都不抬。貓皮的丈夫問道："請問先生，您有過一個您不願見也不願認的女兒嗎？"這個傷心人含淚道："是的，我是個狠心的罪人。但是我願意用我世上的財富換來死前見她一面。"小爵爺告訴了他貓皮的遭遇，又把他接到自己的城堡，他們幸福地生活在一起。

—— 弗勞拉·安妮·斯梯爾[1]

---

1. 斯梯爾（1847 — 1929），英國小説家，曾在印度教學，著有 *Tales of the Punjab* 等。

28 Little Red Riding Hood (European Folk Tale)

Once upon a time there lived a little country girl, the prettiest creature ever seen. Her mother was very fond of her, and her grandmother doted on her still more. This good woman had made a little red riding hood for her, which became the girl so well that everybody called her Little Red Riding Hood.

One day her mother said to her, "Go, my dear, and see how your grandmamma is, for I hear she has been very ill. Carry her a custard and this little pot of butter." Little Red Riding Hood set out immediately to go to her grandmother who lived in another village. As she was going through the woods, she met Gaffer[1] Wolf, who had a very great mind to eat her up, but he dared not, because some faggot makers were hard by[2] in the forest. He asked her whither[3] she was going. The poor child, who did not know it was dangerous to stay and hear a wolf talk, told him.

"Well," said the wolf, "I'll go and see her too. I will go this way and you go that, and we shall see who will be there soonest."

Then the wolf began to run as fast as he could, taking the nearest way, and the little girl went by that farthest about, diverting herself in gathering nuts, running after butterflies, and making nosegays of such little flowers as she found. It was not long before the wolf reached the old woman's house. He knocked at the door — tap, tap.

---

1. Gaffer：老漢，鄉下老頭兒。
2. hard by：在近處。
3. whither：〔古〕= where。

二十八　小紅帽[1]（歐洲民間故事）

　　從前，有個鄉下小姑娘，長得可愛極了。她媽媽非常喜愛她，外婆更把她當心肝兒。好外婆給她做了一頂小小的紅風帽，她戴上去那麼合適好看，於是人人都叫她小紅帽。

　　一天，她媽媽對她說："好孩子，去看看你外婆怎麼樣了，聽說她病得很厲害呢。把奶蛋糕和這小罐奶油帶給她吧。"小紅帽立即動身去外婆家，她住在另一個村子裏。小紅帽穿過樹林時，碰到了老狼。老狼恨不得一口吃掉她，但又不敢，因為樹林裏有些樵夫就在近處。老狼問她上哪兒去，可憐的孩子不知和狼在一起、聽它說話有多麼危險，便對他說了。

　　老狼說："讓我也去探望她吧。我走這條路，你走那條路，看誰到得快。"

　　之後，狼拼命地跑起來，抄最近的路。小姑娘卻走了一條最遠的路，一路上摘果子，追蝴蝶，還採來小花編花球。狼很快便到了老太太家。他敲敲門——嗒，嗒。

1.　此文有多種版本，本篇由兩種版本合編而成。

"Who is there?"

"Your grandchild, Little Red Riding Hood," replied the wolf, imitating her voice.

The good grandmother, who was in bed because she was ill, cried out, "Pull the bobbin, and the latch will go up." The wolf pulled the bobbin, and the door opened. Then he fell upon the good woman and ate her up in a moment. He then shut the door and went into the grandmother's bed, expecting Little Red Riding Hood, who came sometime afterward and knocked at the door — tap, tap.

"Who is there?" Little Red Riding Hood, hearing the big voice of the wolf, was at first afraid; but believing her grandmother had a cold and was hoarse, answered: " 'Tis your grandchild, Little Red Riding Hood."

The wolf cried out to her, softening his voice as much as he could, "Pull the bobbin, and the latch will go up." Little Red Riding Hood pulled the bobbin, and the door opened. The wolf, seeing her come in, said to her, hiding himself under the bedclothes: "Come and lie down with me."

Little Red Riding Hood climbed into the bed and where, being greatly amazed to see how her grandmother looked in her nightclothes, she said to her:

"Grandmamma, what great arms you have!"

"That is the better to hug you, my dear."

"Grandmamma, what great legs you have!"

"That is to run the better, my child."

"Grandmamma, what great ears you have!"

"That is to hear the better, my child."

"Grandmamma, what great eyes you have!"

"It is to see the better, my child."

"Grandmamma, what great teeth you have!"

"That is to eat you up." And saying these words, this

"誰呀？"

"你的外孫女兒小紅帽啊，"狼裝出小紅帽的聲音答道。

好外婆正臥病在牀。她大聲說："拉拉門扣上的吊帶把手，閂閂就扯起來了。"狼扯了吊帶把手，門打開了。他撲向好婆婆，一會兒就把她吃下肚。接着，他關上門，躺到外婆牀上等着小紅帽。過了一會兒，小紅帽來了。她敲敲門——嗒，嗒。

"誰呀？"小紅帽聽到狼的大嗓門，開始有些害怕。可又想是外婆害了感冒，嗓子啞了，便回答："是你的外孫女兒小紅帽。"

狼盡量把聲音放柔和，對她叫："拉拉吊帶把手，閂閂就扯起來了。"小紅帽拉起吊帶把手，門開了。狼看見她走進來，便藏在被裏，說："躺到我被窩裏來吧。"

小紅帽爬上牀，看到穿着睡袍的外婆的樣子，十分驚訝，說：

"外婆，你的胳膊真粗呀！"

"好抱你啊，好孩子。"

"外婆，你的腿真長啊！"

"孩子，這樣跑得快呀。"

"外婆，你的耳朵好大呀！"

"好聽得清楚啊，孩子。"

"外婆，你的眼睛多大啊！"

"這樣看得清呀，孩子。"

"外婆，你的牙很尖啊！"

"那正好吃你呀！"一邊說着，惡狼撲到小紅帽身上，

wicked wolf fell upon Little Red Riding Hood, and ate her up, too.

Then the wolf got back into bed, fell asleep, and began to snore very very loud. A faggot maker was just passing and hearing the snore, he stepped into the house and saw the wolf was in it. "You old sinner!" he said, "I've found you at last. It's been a long time."

He leveled his muster and was just about to fire when it occurred to him that the wolf might have swallowed the grandmother and that there might still be a chance of saving her. So he took a pair of scissors and started cutting the sleeping wolf's belly open. After two snips, he saw the little red cap, and after another few snips the little girl jumped out, crying: "Oh, I've been so afraid! It was so dark inside the wolf!" And then the old grandmother came out, and she too was still alive, though she could hardly breathe.

Little Red Riding Hood ran outside and brought big stones, and they filled the wolf's belly with them. When he woke up, he wanted to run away, but the stones were so heavy that his legs wouldn't carry him and he fell dead.

— retold by F. A. Steel

把她也吃進肚裏。

接着狼又上牀睡熟了，呼呼地大聲打鼾。一個樵夫正好路過，聽到鼾聲便走進屋，看到了老狼。"你這個老壞蛋！"他説，"我一直在找你，這下可找到了。"

他舉起獵槍正要打，忽然想到狼可能把婆婆吃了，也許還能救活她。他就拿了一把剪刀，把睡着的狼肚皮剪開。才剪了兩下，就看到一頂小紅帽，再剪幾下，這小姑娘就跳了出來，叫道："哎呀，嚇死我了，狼肚子裏這麽黑！"接着外婆也出來了。她還活着，但已憋得透不過氣來。

小紅帽跑到外面拿來些大石塊，他們把石塊塞到狼肚裏。老狼醒來要跑，可石頭太重，他跑不動，倒下來死了。

——F·A·斯梯爾 述

29 The Black Bull of Norroway (1) (England)

Long ago in Norroway there lived a lady who had three daughters. One night they fell a-talking of whom they meant to marry. The third, the prettiest and the merriest, said playfully, with a twinkle in her eye, "As for me I would be content with the Black Bull of Norroway."

Then one morning a terrible bellowing was heard at the door, and there was a great big Black Bull waiting for his bride, the youngest sister. She wept and she wailed, and ran away and hid herself in the cellar for fear, but there the Bull stood waiting, and at last the girl came up and said: "I must keep my word. Farewell, mother."

Then she mounted on the Black Bull's back, and it walked away with her. And ever it chose the smoothest paths and the easiest roads, so that at last the girl grew less afraid. But she became very hungry and was nigh[1] to faint when the Black Bull said to her, in quite a soft voice:

> *"Eat out of my left ear,*
> *Drink out of my right,*
> *And set by what you leave*
> *To serve the morrow's night."*

So she did as she was bid, and lo and behold, the left ear was full of delicious things to eat, and the right was full of the most delicious drinks, and there was plenty left over for several days. Thus they journeyed on and they journeyed on, and she slept soft and warm on his broad back.

---

1. nigh：〔古〕 = near。

142

二十九 諾羅威大黑牛[1] (一)(英國)

　　從前，諾羅威的一位夫人有三個女兒。一天晚上，她們談論起心目中的夫婿。最漂亮、最開朗的小妹妹眨眨眼睛，開玩笑道："我呀，找個諾羅威大黑牛也就心滿意足啦。"

　　後來，一天早上，聽得門口一聲可怕的牛吼，一頭大黑牛正在那兒等着他的新娘子 —— 最小的妹妹呢。小妹妹流淚痛哭，嚇得跑到地窖裏藏起來。可黑牛站在那兒等着。最後，小姑娘跑上來說："我說過的就要做到。再見了，媽媽。"

　　她騎上牛背，牛負着她走了。黑牛總是挑最平坦好走的路走，小姑娘最後逐漸減少了懼意，可卻餓得快昏過去了。這時黑牛柔聲對她說：

>　"在我左耳找吃的，
>　　在我右耳找喝的，
>　　吃不了的放一邊，
>　　留着明晚吃。"

　　她照着做了，啊，你瞧，左耳果然有許多好吃的，右耳有許多好喝的，還剩有足夠吃喝好幾天的。就這樣，他們走啊走的，她睡在他那又暖和又柔軟的寬闊背脊上。

---

1. 蘇格蘭古老傳說中諾羅威大黑牛是一隻可怕的大怪物。

So it came to pass[2] that he grew tired and was limping with one foot when just as the sun was setting they came to a beautiful palace where Princes and Princesses were disporting themselves with ball on the green grass. They asked the girl to join them, and ordered the grooms to lead away the Black Bull to a field. But she, remembering all he had done for her, said, "Not so! He will stay with me!" Then seeing a large thorn in the foot with which he had been limping, she stooped down and pulled it out.

And lo and behold! in an instant, there appeared, not a frightful monstrous bull, but one of the most beautiful Princes ever beheld, who fell at his deliverer's feet, thanking her for having broken his cruel enchantment. A wicked witch-woman who wanted to marry him had, he said, spelled him until a beautiful maiden of her own free will should do him a favour. "But," he said, "the danger is not all over. You have broken the enchantment by night; that by day has yet to be overcome."

So the next morning the Prince had to resume the form of a bull, and they set out together; and they rode, and they rode, and they rode, till they came to a dark and ugsome[3] glen. And here he bade her dismount, and sit on a great rock. "Here you must stay," he said, "while I go yonder and fight the Old One. And mind! move neither hand nor foot whilst[4] I am away, else I shall never find you again. If everything around you turns blue, I shall have beaten the Old One." And with that, he set off to find his foe.

Well! she sate[5] as still as a mouse, moving neither hand

---

2. came to pass：＝happened。
3. ugsome：蘇格蘭語，即horrible。
4. whilst：〔古〕＝while。
5. sate：〔古〕＝sat。

到後來太陽下山時，黑牛走累了，一隻腳一瘸一拐的。他們來到一座美麗的宮殿前，王子公主們正在青草坪上玩球。他們請小姑娘和他們一起玩，又讓馬夫將黑牛牽到田裏去。可小姑娘想起他對她的溫柔體貼，便說：「別這樣！我要他跟着我！」看到他腳上扎了一根大刺，所以走路一瘸一拐，她就彎腰替他把刺拔了出來。

嗨，就在這時，眼前出現一個最漂亮的王子，不是怪嚇人的大黑牛了。他跪在恩人腳下，感謝她破了兇殘的妖術，把他解救出來。他說，一個狠毒的妖女想嫁給他，便在他身上施了妖術；只有一位美麗少女出於真心才能救他。他又說：「可是危險還未完全過去，你只破了夜間的妖術，白天的還得破呢。」

第二天早上，王子又變成了牛，他們又一同出發了；走啊走的，來到一個陰森險惡的峽谷。他讓她下來坐在一塊大石上，說：「我到那邊去和那妖精撕殺的時候，你必須在這裏呆着。記住，我不在時，你只要動一下手腳，我就再也找不到你了。要是你周圍的東西都變成藍色，就是我打敗了妖精。」說完，他就動身找他的仇人去了。

好啦，她像隻小老鼠般靜靜地坐着，不動手也不動

nor foot, nor even her eyes, and waited, and waited. Then at last everything turned blue. But she was so overcome with joy to think that her lover was victorious that she forgot to keep still, and lifting one of her feet, crossed it over the other! So she waited, and waited, and waited. Long she sate, and aye[6] she wearied; and all the time he was seeking for her but he never found her. At last she rose and determined to seek for her lover through the whole wide world.

One day in a dark wood she came to a little hut where lived an old, old woman who gave her food and shelter, and bid her God-speed[7] on her errand, giving her three nuts: a walnut, a filbert, and a hazel nut, with these words:

"When your heart is like to break,
And once again is like to break,
Crack a nut and in its shell
That will be that suits you well."

— *Robert Chambers*

---

6. aye：〔古〕用於詩文，即 forever。

7. God-speed：= May God prosper you，指幸運、成功。

146

腳，連眼皮都不眨一下地等着，等着，終於周圍的東西都變成藍色了。想到心上人已得勝，她激動萬分，忘記不能動，便抬起了一隻腳，放在另一隻腳上！這下，她等了又等，坐了又坐；她疲乏，她心焦。這時王子一一直在找她，可再也找不到了。最後，她站起身來，決心走遍茫茫世界也要找到她的心上人。

一天，在一座黑森林裏，她來到一間小茅屋前。這裏住着一位很老很老的婆婆。老婆婆給她飯吃，留她住宿，祝福她辦事如意，又給了她三個硬殼果：一個胡桃、一個大榛子和一個小榛子，說道：

> "若逢心欲碎，
> 心碎不自已，
> 敲破硬果殼，
> 心願自得遂。"

——*羅伯特‧錢伯斯*[2]

---

2. 錢伯斯（1802－1871），英國作家、出版家，著有《愛丁堡的傳說》，極受文豪司各脱（Sir Walter Scott）讚賞，本文採自此書。

30 The Black Bull of Norroway (2) (England)

Now she went on her way and had not gone far before she came to a palace castle. She heard the horns of hunters and cries of "Room! Room for the Duke of Norroway and his bride!" And who should ride past but the beautiful Prince she had but half unspelled[1], and by his side was the witch-woman who was determined to marry him that very day. Well! at the sight she felt that her heart was indeed like to break, and over again was like to break. So she broke the walnut, and out of it came a wonderful wee[2] woman carding wool as fast as ever she could card.

Now when the witch-woman saw this wonderful thing she offered the girl her choice of anything in the castle for it. "If you will put off your wedding with the Duke for a day, and let me watch in his room to-night," said the girl, "you shall have it."

She consented; but before the Duke went to rest she gave him, with her own hands, a posset[3] so made that any one who drank it would sleep till morning. Thus though the girl was allowed alone into the Duke's chamber, and though she spent the livelong night sighing and singing:

"Far have I sought for thee,
Long have I wrought[4] for thee,
Near am I brought to thee,

---

1. unspelled：spell 指妖法，前綴 un- 表示破除。
2. wee：極小的。
3. posset：飲料，牛奶甜酒。
4. wrought：〔古、詩〕work 的過去式和過去分詞。此外，同行的 thee 是 thou (you) 的賓格。

148

三十　諾羅威大黑牛（二）（英國）

　　她繼續趕路，沒走多遠，來到一座宮殿前。只聽到獵人吹着號角喊道：〝讓路！讓路！諾羅威公爵和新夫人駕到！〞騎馬過的，不是別人，正是那身上妖術只被她破了一半的英俊王子。他身旁是那個妖女，就在今天，她要嫁給他。哎呀，看到這情景，她真覺得心像要碎了，心碎不已了。於是，她剝開胡桃。咦，胡桃裏出現了一個可愛的小小的女人，飛快地梳着羊毛。

　　妖女看到這麼奇妙的東西，就要和姑娘交換，讓她任選宮中的東西。〝只要把你和公爵的婚期推遲一天，讓我今晚守在他房間裏，我就給你。〞姑娘説。

　　妖女同意了。但公爵臨睡前，她親手給他喝了一杯牛奶甜酒，誰喝了都會一覺睡到天亮。這樣，雖然小姑娘得到准許單獨在公爵的寢室裏，漫漫長夜都在嘆息、歌唱：

　　　〝我苦苦尋你到天邊，

　　　　我為你辛勞不計年，

　　　　如今我守在你身旁，

> *Dear Duke o'[5] Norroway,*
> *Wilt[6] thou say naught[7] to me —"*

the Duke never wakened, but slept on. So when day came the girl had to leave him without his ever knowing she had been there.

Then once again her heart was like to break, and over and over again like to break, and she cracked the filbert nut. And out of it came a wonderful, wee, wee woman spinning away as fast as ever she could spin. Now when the witch-bride saw this wonderful thing she once again put off her wedding so that she might possess it. And once again the girl spent the livelong night in the Duke's chamber sighing and singing just as she had done the night before. But the Duke, who had drunk the sleeping-draught, never stirred, and when dawn came the girl had to leave him without his ever knowing she had been there.

Then, indeed, the girl's heart was like to break, so she cracked the last nut — the hazel nut — and out of it came the most wonderful, wee, wee, wee-est woman reeling away at yarn as fast as she could reel. And this marvel so delighted the witch-bride that once again she consented to put off her wedding for a day.

Now it so happened that when the Duke was dressing that morning he heard his pages talking amongst themselves of the strange sighing and singing they had heard in the night; and he said to his faithful old valet, "What do the pages mean?" And the old valet, who hated the witch-bride, said:

5.　o'：= of。

6.　Wilt：will 的第二人稱單數。

7.　naught：〔古〕= nothing。

親愛的諾羅威公爵啊，

你怎沒有一句話兒對我講——"

公爵卻一直昏睡不醒。天亮了，她只好離開，而他一點兒也不知道她來過。

她的心又像要碎了，心碎不已。於是她敲碎大榛子，出現了一個可愛的、小小的、小小的女人，飛快地在紡紗。妖女見了這麼奇妙的東西，又推遲了婚期把它換到手。漫漫長夜，姑娘又像昨夜那樣在公爵的寢室裏嘆息、唱歌。可是公爵喝了催眠劑，沉沉熟睡，動也不動；黎明時分，姑娘只好離開，公爵一點兒也不知道她來過。

這下，姑娘的心真的要碎了。所以她打碎了最後一個硬殼果小榛子，走出一個最可愛、最小最小的小女人，在飛快地繞綫。這東西太神奇了。妖女又將婚期推遲一天。

事有湊巧，公爵早上梳洗穿衣時，聽到他的侍從在議論晚間他們聽到的奇怪的嘆息聲和歌聲，便問他忠心的貼身老僕："侍從們説甚麼呢？"老僕心恨妖女新娘，説：

"If the master[8] will take no sleeping-draught to-night, mayhap[9] he may also hear what for two nights has kept me awake."

At this the Duke marvelled greatly, and when the witch-bride brought him his evening posset, he made excuse it was not sweet enough, and while she went away to get honey to sweeten it withal[10], he poured away the posset and made believe he had swallowed it.

So that night when dark had come, and the girl stole in to his chamber with a heavy heart, thinking it would be the very last time she would ever see him, the Duke was really broad awake. And when she sate down by his bedside and began to sing: "Far have I sought for thee —" he knew her voice at once, and clasped her in his arms.

Then he told her how he had been in the power of the witch-woman and had forgotten everything, but that now he remembered all and that the spell was broken for ever and aye. So the wedding feast served for their marriage, since the witch-bride, seeing her power was gone, quickly fled the country and was never heard of again.

— *Robert Chambers*

---

8. the master：不用you是對對方的尊敬用語。後面 he may中的he亦是同樣用法。

9. mayhap：〔古〕= perhaps。

10. withal：〔古〕= with。

"要是少爺今晚不喝那催眠劑，您也許會聽到這兩晚吵得我睡不着的聲音。"

公爵聽了十分驚訝。妖女新娘給他睡前飲料時，他借口不夠甜。待妖女去拿蜜加甜時，他乘機將甜酒倒掉，讓她以為他喝了。

當晚天黑後，姑娘悄悄來到他的寢室，心情沉重，想到這是她最後一次見他了。這時公爵全無睡意。她坐到他牀邊，唱道："我苦苦尋你到天邊，……"他立刻聽出是她的聲音，把她緊緊抱在懷裏。

他告訴她他受了女妖的魔法，失去記憶，但現在甚麼都記起來了，妖術永遠永遠地破除了。於是，原來準備的婚禮喜筵成為他們結褵的酒宴。女妖見她妖術已破，匆匆逃離，不知所終。

——*羅伯特·錢伯斯*

31 Lazy Jack (England)

Once upon a time there was a boy whose name was Jack, and he lived with his mother on a common[1]. They were very poor, and the old woman got her living by spinning, but Jack was so lazy that he would do nothing. So they called him Lazy Jack. At last his mother told him that if he did not begin to work for his porridge she would turn him out to get his living as he could.

This roused Jack, and he went out and hired himself for the next day to a neighbouring farmer for a penny; but as he was coming home, he lost it in passing over a brook. "You stupid boy," said his mother, "you should have put it in your pocket." "I'll do so another time," replied Jack.

The next day, Jack went out again and hired himself to a cowkeeper, who gave him a jar of milk for his day's work. Jack put the jar into the large pocket of his jacket, spilling it all, long before he got home. "Dear me," said his mother, "you should have carried it very carefully in your hands." "I'll do so another time," replied Jack.

Now the next day, Lazy Jack hired himself to a baker, who would give him for his work a large tom-cat. Jack took and carried it very carefully in his hands, but in a short time pussy scratched him so much that he was compelled to let it go. When he got home, his mother said to him, "You silly fellow, you should have tied it with a string, and dragged it along after you." "I'll do so another time," said Jack.

---

1. common：英國用法，指村中或村外公用的草地或荒地。

154

三十一 懶漢傑克[1]（英國）

　　從前有個小伙子名叫傑克，和母親住在村子公用荒地的小破屋裏。他們非常窮，全靠老母親紡綫過活。但傑克卻懶得甚麼也不做。所以人們叫他懶漢傑克。最後母親跟他說如果他還不開始自食其力，她就要把他趕出家門讓他自謀生路了。

　　這一來激發了傑克的志氣。第二天他出門為鄰近一個農人幹活兒，掙了一個便士。可是在回家路上過河時，他把錢掉到小河裏了。"你這傻小子，"母親說，"你該把錢放在口袋裏呀。""下次我放吧。"傑克答。

　　第二天傑克出門去給一個養奶牛的幹活兒。這人給他一瓶牛奶當一天的工錢。傑克把瓶子放在外衣的大口袋裏，還沒到家早就把牛奶全灑了。"天啊，"母親說，"你該用兩隻手小心地捧着啊。""下次我捧着吧。"傑克答。

　　好，第二天傑克給一個麵包師幹活。麵包師給他一隻大公貓為報酬。傑克拿了貓小心翼翼地用雙手捧着，可不久這貓咪又抓又撓，沒辦法，他只好把貓放走了。他到了家，母親說，"你這傻東西，你該用根繩子拴住它，牽在身後走呀。""下回我牽着吧。"傑克答。

---

1. 本文選自 *Popular Rhymes and Nursery Tales of England*。但這故事在英國甚至歐洲極為普遍，有多種版本。

So on the following day, Jack hired himself to a butcher, who rewarded him by the handsome present of a shoulder of mutton. Jack took the mutton, tied it to a string, and trailed it along after him in the dirt, so that by the time he had got home the meat was completely spoilt. "You ninney-hammer," said his mother; "you should have carried it on your shoulder." "I'll do so another time," replied Jack.

Well, on the next day, Lazy Jack hired himself to a cattle-keeper, who gave him a donkey for his trouble. Now though Jack was strong he found it hard to hoist the donkey on his shoulders, but at last he did it, and began walking home slowly with his prize. Now it so happened that in the course of his journey he passed a house where a rich man lived with his only daughter, a beautiful girl, who was deaf and dumb. And she had never laughed in her life, and the doctors said she would never speak till somebody made her laugh. So the father had given out that any man who made her laugh would receive her hand in marriage. Now this young lady happened to be looking out of the window when Jack was passing by with the donkey on his shoulders; and the poor beast with its legs sticking up in the air was kicking violently and heehawing with all its might. Well, the sight was so comical that she burst out into a great fit of laughter, and immediately recovered her speech and hearing. Her father was overjoyed, and fulfilled his promise by marrying her to Lazy Jack, who was thus made a rich gentleman.

— *James Orchard Halliwell*

第二天傑克又僱給一個屠夫，他給的報酬挺豐厚，是一隻羊前肘。傑克拿來羊肉，用根繩子拴上，在泥路上一直拖在身後。等到了家，這塊肉已經完全不成樣子了。"你這笨蛋，"母親說，"你該扛在肩膀上的呀。""下次我扛吧。"傑克答。

　　好啦，第二天，懶漢傑克去給一個養牛的人幹活。他給傑克一頭毛驢做辛苦錢。雖然傑克身強體壯，但把一頭毛驢扛在肩膀上還是太吃力。他好不容易扛上了，帶着這份酬勞慢慢地走回家。路上他恰巧走過一家人家，這裏住着一個有錢人和他的獨生女兒。女兒是個美麗的姑娘，可惜又聾又啞。她生下來就沒有開口笑過。醫生說若非有人讓她笑出來，她這輩子也不會開口說話。因此她父親傳出話去：哪個男人把她逗笑就可以娶她為妻。傑克肩扛毛驢走過時，姑娘碰巧望着窗外。被傑克扛在肩上的可憐牲畜四腳朝天地亂踢，一面還拼命"咔，咔"地嘶叫。啊，這樣子太滑稽了，她忍不住哈哈大笑不止，立即恢復了聽力，也會說話了。她父親歡喜若狂，遵守諾言將女兒嫁給了懶漢傑克，傑克也就成了有錢有體面的人啦。

　　——詹姆斯·奧查德·哈利韋爾

32 The Three Little Pigs (England)

Once upon a time there was an old sow who had three little pigs, and as she had not enough for them to eat, she said they had better go out into the world and seek their fortunes.

Now the eldest pig went first, he met a man carrying a bundle of straw. So he said very politely: "If you please, sir, could you give me that straw to build me a house?" And the man, seeing what good manners the little pig had, gave him the straw, and the little pig set to work and built a beautiful house with it. Now, when it was finished, a wolf happened to pass that way; and he saw the house, and he smelt the pig inside. So he knocked at the door and said: "Little pig! Little pig! Let me in! Let me in!"

But the little pig saw the wolf's big paws through the keyhole, so he answered back: "No! No! No! by the hair of my chinny chin chin[1]!"

Then the wolf showed his teeth and said: "Then I'll huff and I'll puff and I'll blow your house in."

So he huffed and he puffed and he blew the house in. Then he ate up little piggy.

Now, the next piggy, when he started, met a man carrying a bundle of furze, and, being very polite, he asked him to

---

1. by the hair of my chinny chin chin：此句直譯為："憑我下巴頦兒的小鬍子起誓"。by 在此處用於表達強烈的感情或誓言，如 by God、by Heaven 等。chinny, chin chin 都是小兒用語。chinny 表示"小小的下巴"，chin chin 是小兒常用的單字重疊。

三十二　三隻小豬的故事（英國）

　　從前有隻老母豬生了三隻小豬。母豬養不起小豬了，就說不如放他們自己謀生去吧。

　　最大的小豬先走了，他碰見一個人揹着一綑稻草，就對他很客氣地説："先生，能把那綑稻草給我用來蓋間屋子嗎？"那人見小豬這樣有禮貌，便給了他。小豬動手用稻草蓋了間美麗的屋子。屋子蓋好時，一條狼剛好路過，看見屋子，嗅到裏面小豬的味道，便敲門説："小豬！小豬！讓我進去！讓我進去！"

　　小豬從鑰匙孔裏看見狼的大爪子，回答："不讓！不讓！不讓！説甚麼也不能讓你進來！"

　　狼呲着牙説："那我就呼呼地吹，噗噗地吹，吹倒房子好進去。"

　　於是狼呼呼地吹，噗噗地吹，吹倒房子進去把小豬仔吃掉了。

　　第二隻豬仔上路遇到一個人揹着一綑荊豆枝。他很有禮貌地請那人把荊豆枝給他蓋間屋子，那人給了他。小豬用荊豆枝蓋了一間美麗的屋子。屋子一蓋好，狼又走過，

give him that furze to build him a house, which the man consented. And the little pig built himself a beautiful house. Now it so happened that when the house was finished the wolf passed that way, and he saw the house, and he smelt the pig inside. The poor little pig met his fate just as the first one did.

Now the third little piggy, when he started, met a man carrying a load of bricks. And the man gave him the bricks at his request, and the little pig built himself a beautiful house. And once again it happened that when it was finished the wolf chanced to come that way; and he saw the house and he smelt the pig inside.

Well! He huffed and he puffed. He puffed and he huffed. And he huffed, huffed, and he puffed, puffed; but he could not blow the house down. Then he said: "Little pig! I know where there is ever such a nice field of turnips in Farmer Smith's garden. If you will be ready at six o'clock to-morrow morning, I will call round for you, and we can go together and get turnips for dinner."

"Thank you kindly," said the little piggy, "I will be ready at six o'clock sharp." But he got up at five, trotted off to Farmer Smith's field, rooted up the turnips, and was home eating them for breakfast when the wolf clattered at the door and cried:

"Little pig! Little pig! Aren't you ready?"

The little piggy said, "Why! I've been to the field and come back again, and I'm having a nice potful of turnips for breakfast." Then the wolf grew red with rage; but he was determined to eat little piggy.

He went next day to the little piggy's house and called through the door, as mild as milk: "Little pig! Little pig! Will you come with me to the fair this afternoon?" "Thank you kindly," said little piggy, "what time shall we start?"

看見了屋子，聞到裏面小豬的味道，可憐的小豬和第一隻小豬遭到了同樣的厄運。

第三隻豬仔上路，碰到一個人挑着一擔磚。那人答應小豬的要求把磚給了他，小豬用磚蓋了一間美麗的屋子。屋了蓋好，狼又恰巧過路來了。他看到屋子，嗅到裏面的小豬。

哼，他呼呼地吹、噗噗地吹，吹了又吹，吹個沒完，但是吹不倒這間屋子。他就説："小豬，我知道種地的史密斯家園子裏有一塊挺好的蘿蔔地。你要是明天早上六點鐘準備好，我過來叫你一起去挖點蘿蔔當正餐。"

"太謝謝你啦，"小豬仔説，"我六點鐘整準備好。"可是小豬五點就起牀了。一路小跑到農夫史密斯的園子裏拔起蘿蔔就回家。老狼來敲門時他已經在吃蘿蔔當早餐了。

老狼説："小豬！小豬！準備好了嗎？"

小豬仔説："哈，我都去過回來啦。拿來一大鍋蘿蔔當早餐呢。"老狼氣得發瘋，但他決心非吃掉這豬仔不可。

第二天狼又到豬仔家來了，柔聲細氣隔門對小豬説："小豬！小豬！今天下午你和我趕集市去好嗎？""太謝謝

"At three o'clock sharp," said the wolf.

The little piggy started early in the morning and went to the fair, and rode in a swing, and enjoyed himself ever so much, and bought himself a butter-churn as a fairing, and trotted away towards home long before three o'clock. But what should he see but the wolf coming up, all panting and red with rage!

Well, there was no place to hide in but the butter-churn; so be crept into it, and was just pulling down the cover when the churn started to roll down the hill. The wolf was so frightened that he turned tail and ran away. He went again next day to the house and told the little pig what had happened and how frightened he had been.

"Dear me!" says the little piggy, "that must have been me! I hid inside the butter-churn when I saw you coming and it started to roll! I am sorry I frightened you!"

But this was too much. The wolf danced about with rage and swore he would come down the chimney and eat up the little pig for his supper. But while he was climbing on to the roof the little pig made up a blazing fire and put on a big pot full of water to boil. Then, just as the wolf was coming down the chimney, the little piggy off with the lid, and plump! in fell the wolf into the scalding water. So the little piggy put on the cover again, boiled the wolf up, and ate him for supper.

— *edited by Joseph Jacobs*

你啦，"豬仔説，"咱們幾點走呀？""準三點吧，"狼道。

　　豬仔清早就到了集市，打了一會鞦韆，玩了個夠，又買了一個奶油攪拌器，離三點還早呢，就一路小跑回家。可一眼望見，不是別個，正是惡狼怒沖沖喘吁吁地跑來！

　　唉，除了攪拌器沒有別的地方可藏了。他一頭鑽進去，把蓋子拉下時攪拌器便滾下山。老狼嚇得掉頭就跑。第二天他又來到小豬家門前，告訴小豬這件事，還説把他嚇得半死。

　　"哎呀！"豬仔説："那就是我呀！我看到你來，便藏在攪拌器裏，它便滾起來！把你嚇着了！真對不起！"

　　太過份了。狼氣得直跳，發狠説要從煙囱爬下去把小豬當晚餐吃掉。當他爬上屋頂，小豬就生了個大火放上裝滿水的大鍋燒水。老狼從煙囱往下跳時，小豬仔揭開鍋蓋。噗通！狼一下子掉進滾燙的水裏。小豬仔又蓋上蓋，把老狼煮熟，狼倒成了小豬的晚餐了。

—— *約瑟夫·雅各布斯*[1] *編*

---

1. 雅各布斯(1854—1916)，英國民俗學家、童話作家、歷史學家、人類學家。著有《英國神話集》及《伊索寓言通俗本》等。

33 Connla and the Fairy Maiden (England)

Connla of the Fiery Hair was son of Conn[1] of the Hundred Fights. One day as he stood by the side of his father on the height of Usna, he saw a maiden clad in strange attire towards him coming. "Whence comest thou[2], maiden?" said Connla.

"I come from the Plains of the Ever Living," she said, "there where is neither death nor sin. And we have no strife. And because we have our homes in the round green hills, men call us the Hill Folk."

The king and all with him wondered much to hear a voice when they saw no one. For save Connla alone, none saw the Fairy Maiden.

"To whom art thou talking, my son?" said Conn the king. Then the maiden answered, "Connla speaks to a young, fair maid, whom neither death nor old age awaits. I love Connla, and now I call him away to the Plain of Pleasure, Moy Mell, where Boadag is king for aye, nor has there been sorrow or complaint in that land since he held the kingship. Oh, come with me, Connla of the Fiery Hair, ruddy as the dawn, with thy tawny skin. Come, and never shall thy comeliness fade, nor thy youth, till the last awful day of judgment."

The king, in fear at what the maiden said, which he heard though he could not see her, called aloud to his Druid[3], Coran by name. "O Coran of the many spells," he said, "I call upon

---

1. Conn：即 Conn Cétchathach，在愛爾蘭傳說中，是愛爾蘭第一代 國王，但亦有史學家認為他只是詩歌中的虛構人物。

2. Whence comest thou：〔古〕= Where do you come from。

3. Druid：凱爾特人（Celt）的祭司。

三十三　康拉和神仙女[1]（英國）

　　紅髮康拉是身經百戰的康恩的兒子。一天，在烏斯那高地，他站在父親身旁，看到一個身穿奇裝異服的少女向他走來，"姑娘，你從哪裏來？"康拉問。

　　"我從長生平原來，"她說，"那裏沒有死亡，沒有罪惡，也沒有爭鬥。因為我們住在圓圓的青山翠嶺中，人們叫我們做山裏人。"

　　國王和所有隨從看不到人，卻聽到聲音，都十分詫異，只有康拉一個人看到了這神仙女。

　　"你和誰談話呀，我兒？"國王康恩問。那姑娘答道，"康拉在和一位年輕美麗、長生不老的姑娘說話。我愛康拉，現在把他召去莫伊梅爾歡樂平原。在那兒，博達格永在王位。從他即位以後，那個國度就再未有過悲傷怨恨。啊，跟我來吧，臉似朝陽，褐色皮膚的紅髮康拉。來吧，你將美貌永駐、青春長在，直到那可怕的世界末日來臨。"

　　國王聽到聲音卻看不到人，對姑娘的話感到恐懼。他大聲叫喚他的祭司柯立恩："掌握許多魔法符咒的柯立恩

---

1. 選自《古凱爾特童話》，是史前時期凱爾特人（Celts）流傳下來的故事。凱爾特人的最早史料產生於公元前 3 世紀，他們居住在今英、法、比利時、德國西部及意大利北部一帶。

thy aid. A maiden unseen has met us, and by her power would take from me my dear, my comely son."

Then Coran the Druid stood forth and chanted his spells towards the spot where the maiden's voice had been heard. And none heard her voice again, nor could Connla see her longer. Only as she vanished before the Druid's mighty spell, she threw an apple to Connla.

For a whole month from that day Connla would take nothing, either to eat or to drink, save only from that apple. But as he ate, it grew again and always kept whole. And all the while there grew within him a mighty yearning and longing after the maiden he had seen. But when the last day of the month of waiting came, Connla saw the maiden come towards him, and again she spoke to him. "The folk of life, the ever-living ones, beg and bid thee come to Moy Mell, the Plain of Pleasure, for they have learnt to know thee."

When Conn the king heard the maiden's voice, he called his men to summon his Druid. Then the maiden said: "O mighty Conn, Fighter of a Hundred Fights, the Druid's power is little loved; it has little honour in the mighty land, peopled with so many of the upright. When the Law comes, it will do away with the Druid's magic spells."

Then Conn the king observed that since the coming of the maiden Connla his son spoke to none that spake[4] to him. So Conn of the Hundred Fights said to him, "Is it to thy mind what the woman says, my son?"

"'Tis[5] hard upon me," said Connla, "I love my own folk above all things; but yet a longing seizes me for the maiden."

---

4. spake：〔古〕speak 的過去式。
5. 'Tis：〔古〕= It is。

啊，"他說："我求您的幫助。一個隱身少女來見我們，要用她的魔力奪走我親愛的、英俊的兒子。"

於是，祭司柯立恩走上前，對着少女發出聲音的地方念咒。沒有人再聽到她的聲音，康拉也看不見她了。但她在祭司威力巨大的法術下消失之時，向康拉扔去一個蘋果。

從那天起整整一個月，康拉不吃不喝，只吃那個蘋果。蘋果隨吃隨長，吃過後還是一整個。康拉吃過蘋果，逐漸對他見到的少女產生了強大思念渴望。他等了一個月，最後的一天，康拉見到那姑娘向他走來，又對他說："我們長生不老的人請您、求您到莫伊梅爾歡樂平原去，因為他們已經聽說到您。"

國王康恩聽到姑娘的聲音，馬上呼喚他的士兵隨從傳召他的祭司。那姑娘說："偉大的身經百戰的康恩啊，祭司的法力在我們住着許多正直人民的偉大國度裏是不受歡迎、不受尊敬的。大律到來之時，便是祭司魔法破除之日。"

康恩王看到：從那姑娘來後，誰對他兒子康拉說話，他也不答。身經百戰的康恩對他說："我兒，那女人的話你聽進心裏去了嗎？"

"我心裏很痛苦，"康拉說，"我愛我的同胞勝於一切，可又解脫不開對那姑娘的渴慕。"

When the maiden heard this, she answered and said: "The ocean is not so strong as the waves of thy longing. Come with me in my curragh[6], the gleaming, straight-gliding crystal canoe. Soon can we reach Boadag's realm."

When the maiden ceased to speak, Connla of the Fiery Hair rushed away from his kinsmen and sprang into the curragh, the gleaming, straight-gliding crystal canoe. And then they all, king and court, saw it glide away over the bright sea towards the setting sun, away and away, till eye could see it no longer. So Connla and the Fairy Maiden went forth on the sea, and were no more seen, nor did any know whither[7] they came.

— edited by Joseph Jacobs

6.　curragh：〔愛爾蘭語〕即 coracle ，小艇。

7.　whither：〔古〕to which place 。

姑娘聽到這些，便回答：「你的渴念思慕比大海的波濤還要猛烈。跟我來吧，登上我的柳條艇，我那亮閃閃的、筆直滑行的水晶小舟，我們很快便會到達博達格的國土。」

她的話音剛落，紅髮康拉便從族人中跑出來，跳進那柳條艇——那亮閃閃、筆直滑行的水晶小舟。於是，國土和他的臣子們看着它在陽光燦爛的大海上向着西沉的太陽輕盈地駛去，越駛越遠，直到再也看不見了。康拉和神仙女一起駛向大海，從此再沒有人見過他們，也沒有人知道他們的下落。

——約瑟夫·雅各布斯 編

34 A Son of Adam (England)

A man was working one day. It was very hot, and he was digging. By and by he stopped to rest and wipe his face; and he grew very angry to think he had to work so hard just because of Adam's sin[1]. So he complained bitterly, and said some very hard words about Adam.

It happened that his master heard him, and he asked: "Why do you blame Adam? You'd ha' done[2] just like Adam, if you'd a-been[3] in his place."

"No, I shouldn't," says the man. "I should ha' know'd[4] better."

"Well, I'll try you," says his master. "Come to me at dinner-time."

So come dinner-time, the man came, and his master took him into a room where the table was a-set[5] with good things of all sorts. And he said: "Now, you can eat as much as ever you like from any of the dishes on the table; but don't touch the covered dish in the middle till I come back." And with that the master went out of the room and left the man there all by himself. So the man began to taste some o' this dish

---

1. Adam's sin：《聖經》載：上帝創造亞當、夏娃，使之居伊甸園，但誡以不得食善惡樹上禁果。亞當和夏娃受到誘惑，偷食禁果，能辨善惡、識羞恥。但上帝震怒，將他們逐出伊甸園，打發他們去種地。二人成為人類始祖。
2. You'd ha' done：＝ You would have done。
3. if you'd a-been：＝ if you had been。
4. should ha' know'd：＝ should have known。
5. a-set：〔古〕＝ set。

三十四　亞當的子孫 (英國)

　　一天有個人在幹活兒，天氣非常熱，他在鋤地。過了一會兒，他停下歇口氣，擦把臉。他想到只因亞當當年犯了罪，害得他要幹這樣累的活兒，十分惱火。他滿腹牢騷，怨聲不絕，大罵亞當。

　　正好主人聽見了。主人問："你怎麼怪到亞當身上去了呢？如果你和亞當易地而處，你也會像他那樣做的。"

　　"不會的，"那人說，"我會比他懂事些。"

　　"好吧，讓我考驗考驗你，"主人說，"午餐時候你到我那裏來一下。"

　　午餐時這人去了。主人把他帶進一個房間，桌上擺滿山珍海錯，他說："吃吧，桌上所有的菜餚你能吃多少就吃多少，可中央那碟蓋着的菜在我回來之前你不要碰。"說着主人出去了，房間只留下那人一個人。於是這人這道

and some o' that, and enjoyed himself finely. But after a while, as his master didn't come back, he began to look at the covered dish, and to wonder whatever was in it. And he wondered more and more, and he says to himself: "It must be something very nice. Why shouldn't I just look at it? I won't touch it. There can't be any harm in just peeping." So at last he could hold back no longer, and he lifted up the cover a tiny bit; but he couldn't see anything. Then he lifted it up a bit more, and out popped a mouse. The man tried to catch it; but it ran away and jumped off the table and he ran after it. It ran first into one corner, and then, just as he thought he'd got it, into another, and under the table, and all about the room. And the man made such a clatter, jumping and banging and running round after the mouse, a-trying to catch it, that at last his master came in.

"Ah!" he said, "never you blame Adam again, my man!"

— *English Folk Tale*

菜嚐嚐，那道菜嚐嚐，吃得津津有味。但是過了一會兒，
因為主人還未回來，他開始去看那蓋着的碟子，心裏想不
知那裏面是甚麼。他愈來愈好奇，自言自語說：「一定是
特別好吃的東西。我只看一眼有何不可呢？我又不碰它，
看一眼該沒有甚麼害處。」最後他實在忍不住了，揭開那
蓋子一條縫。可是他甚麼也看不見。他又開大一點。噗地
跳出來一隻老鼠。那人趕忙捉老鼠。可是老鼠跑開，跳下
桌子，他便在後面追。老鼠先是逃到屋角裏，他剛以為可
以捉住了，它又逃到另一個角落。後來又跑到桌子底下，
又滿屋亂跑。那人追在後面，也滿屋亂跑，把東西碰得乒
乒乓乓響，又是跳，又是撲，要抓住它。最後主人進來
了。

　「哈！」他說，「老弟，你再也不罵亞當了吧！」

—— 英國民間故事

35 Peter Pan in Kensington Gardens (abridged)
(England)

The only people awake in Kensington Gardens at night are the fairies — and Peter Pan. In the daytime, of course, the fairies are there, just the same, only they are almost invisible, because they pretend to be flowers. Indeed, fairies are very tricky people. This is because they are not quite exactly real themselves. They are just bits of a baby's laugh. When the first baby laughed for the first time, his laugh broke up into thousands and thousands of little pieces, which went slithering and twinkling all over the world, and turned by and by into fairies. It is plain that they are not the same as you and I, and they can't be expected to know much. They can dance, of course. And they have parties, but you wouldn't think much of the refreshments. Too small, too few, and with not enough taste. Anyhow, that is what Peter thought. The cowslip wine wasn't sweet, the cakes were so small there were no crumbs to them, and the ices—well, there were no ices.

For this poor-refreshments reason, and for other reasons too, Peter found himself growing rather tired of the fairies. So, one night, when he had been piping extra well, and wishing extra hard that there was something really eatable on the fairy table-cloth, he was much pleased to hear the Fairy Queen call him to her side. She said, "Kneel down, Peter. I am going to reward you for playing so beautifully. I will give you the wish of your heart."

三十五　潘彼得[1] 在肯辛頓花園（節選）（英國）

　　肯辛頓花園裏不睡覺的夜貓子只是那些仙女 —— 還有潘彼得。當然啦，仙女白天也在花園裏，只不過因為她們都變成了花兒，所以幾乎就看不見她們了。仙女實在都是些很會玩花招的人，這是因為她們也不完全真是她們自己，她們只是小娃娃的笑聲。當第一個小娃娃第一次笑出聲來時，他的笑聲便裂成千萬片碎片，這些碎片在世界上到處飄蕩閃爍，慢慢地變成了一個個小仙子。當然啦，她們不像你和我，你也不能指望她們懂得許多事。她們自然會跳舞，也開晚會。但你別想着有許多好吃的，吃的東西太小，又少，沒甚麼味兒。不管怎麼説，至少潘彼得是這樣想的吧。黃花酒不甜，蛋糕小得連渣兒也沒有。冰飲料呢，哎，壓根兒就沒有。

　　就因為沒甚麼好吃的，還有些別的原因，潘彼得越來越厭煩那些小仙子了。所以，一天晚上，彼得的笛吹得特別好，又格外希望仙子餐桌上有點真正可吃的東西，一聽仙后喚他到身邊，就非常高興。她説：“彼得，跪下。你吹得這麼動聽，我得獎給你點東西。你心裏想要甚麼，我就給你甚麼。”

---

1. 潘彼得：《潘彼得》（*Peter Pan*）1904 年在倫敦第一次出版，出版後立刻獲得極大成功，膾炙人口。其後續作品及各種版本受到一代又一代兒童的喜愛，書中的潘彼得是個不想長大的男孩，會飛，和同伴一起經歷無數驚險，構成一個個有趣的故事。《潘彼得在肯辛頓公園》為《潘彼得》後續作品之一。

"I hope it will be nice food," thought Peter. He said aloud, rather doubtfully, "Thank you," but he was such a long time trying to remember what was the wish of his heart (in case there was no new food), that, by the time his knees were getting cramped, the Queen had nearly forgotten all about her promise. At last he asked, "If I said, I wish to go back to my mother, could you give me that?" Everyone was startled, and rather vexed: for they had never dreamed of Peter wanting to go away, and of course he would take his pipe with him: they would have to dance without his music, which would be dull indeed.

The Queen said scornfully, "Why don't you have a bigger wish than that? Such a skimpy little wish to ask for!" Peter answered, "How big would a big wish be, then?" The Queen spread out her skirt as wide as it would go, and said, "Well, something about that size." "Oh!" said Peter, surprised. "Well, then — I would rather have two small skimpy wishes than one big one. I wish, first, to be able to fly back to my mother, and to be able to come back again if I don't care for it when I get there."

The fairies did not like this any better, but they had to pretend it was all right. Still, the Queen tried to make it sound very difficult. She told him, "I can make you able to fly, but I can't unfasten the door when you get there. It will be tight shut." Peter replied, "O, Mother always keeps the window open, the window where I flew out, in case I may come back to her." So his first wish had to be granted: the second one, he kept a secret, thinking he might want it later on. The fairies now were ordered by the Queen to give him the power to fly: they came crowding round and tickled him on the shoulder-

"我想有點好吃的，"他心裏想。可又遲遲疑疑地大聲說："謝謝您啦。"他費了半天去想甚麼是他心裏的願望（萬一沒有甚麼新的食物呢），等到他膝蓋都跪得痠麻了的時候，仙后也差不多忘了答應他的事了。最後，他問："要是我說我想回去找我媽，您能答應嗎？"所有人都吃了一驚，又有些不高興，因為她們做夢也沒想到彼得想走，而且當然還會帶走他的笛，跳舞沒有他的伴奏那可太沒勁啦。

　　仙后輕蔑地説："你怎麼就沒一個大點兒的願望呢？這麼點兒大的小願望也值得提出來？"彼得答道："多大才算大呀？"仙后把裙子展開到最闊限度，説："嗐，就是這樣大。""啊！"彼得吃驚地説："好吧，那我寧願要兩個小願望不要一個大的。第一個，我希望能飛回我媽的身邊，要是我到了那裏不喜歡，還能再回來。"

　　仙子們對這個也不喜歡，可她們得裝出"好吧"的樣子。仙后還是想把這事説得很難辦，她對他説："我能讓你飛，可你到了那兒我不能打開門，門會關得緊緊的。"彼得答："啊，我媽經常開着窗戶的，就是那扇我飛出來的窗戶，她想着也許我會回到她那裏去的。"這樣，仙后得滿足他第一個願望。第二個願望，他沒説出來，想着以後再提。這會兒，仙后吩咐仙子們賜給彼得飛的能力。仙子們一擁而上，將彼得團團圍住，撓他的肩胛骨。彼得一

blades. Then he felt that he could fly once more. And he flew right away over the Gardens and the roofs and turned homeward to his mother's window.

— *James M. Barrie*

下子覺得又會飛了。他馬上飛過了花園和房頂，向家裏媽媽的窗口飛去。

—— 詹姆斯·M·巴瑞[2]

2. 巴瑞 (1860 — 1937)，英國記者，小説家，著有《潘彼得》等一系列
著作。

36 The Happy Prince (1) (Ireland)

High above the city, on a tall column, stood the statue of the Happy Prince. He was gilded all over with thin leaves of fine gold, for eyes he had two bright sapphires, and a large red ruby glowed on his sword-hilt.

One night there flew over the city a little Swallow. His friends had gone away to Egypt six weeks before, but he had stayed behind, for he was in love with the most beautiful Reed. "Will you come away with me?" he said finally to her, but the Reed shook her head, she was so attached to her home. "You have been trifling with me," he cried. "I am off to the Pyramids. Good-bye!" All day long he flew, and at night-time he arrived at the city. Then he saw the statue on the tall column. So he alighted just between the feet of the Happy Prince and he prepared to go to sleep; but just as he was putting his head under his wing a large drop of water fell on him.

"What a curious thing!" he cried; "there is not a single cloud in the sky, the stars are quite clear and bright, and yet it is raining." Then another drop fell, and a third. He looked up, and saw — Ah! what did he see?

The eyes of the Happy Prince were filled with tears and tears were running down his golden cheeks. "Who are you?" he said. "I am the Happy Prince." "Why are you weeping then?" "When I was alive and had a human heart," answered the statue, "I did not know what tears were, for I lived in the Palace of Sans-Souci[1], where sorrow is not allowed to enter.

---

1. Sans-Souci：法語，即without care。Palace of Sans-Souci，無憂宮，亦有譯作桑索西宮的。

三十六 快樂王子（一）（愛爾蘭）

在一座高高的圓柱上，立着快樂王子的雕像，俯瞰全城。他全身鑲着純金金箔，眼睛是兩顆亮晶晶的藍寶石，一粒碩大的紅寶石在他的劍柄上熠熠發光。

一天夜裏，一隻小燕飛到這座城市上空。他的朋友們六個星期前已去了埃及，可他因為愛戀那棵最美麗的蘆葦，遲遲沒有成行。最後，他對她說：“你能跟我一起走嗎？”蘆葦搖搖頭，她實在難捨故土。“原來你一直在戲弄我，”燕子叫起來，“我要到金字塔那裏去了，再見吧。”他飛了整整一天，入夜到了這座城市，便看到了高柱頂上的雕像。他停落在快樂王子的兩腳之間，正準備睡覺，剛把頭放到翅膀下，一大滴水珠落到他身上。

“多奇怪！”他叫道，“天上沒有一絲雲，星星也清澈明亮，可卻在下雨。”又一滴、再一滴水珠落下來。他抬眼望去，只見——啊，他看到了甚麼？

快樂王子滿眼淚水，眼淚順着他金色的面頰簌簌落下。“你是誰？”燕子問。“我是快樂王子。”“那你為甚麼哭泣？”雕像說，“我活着的時候，有一顆常人的心，卻不知眼淚為何物，因為我住在無憂宮裏，甚麼憂愁煩惱

In day time I played with my companions in the garden, and in the evening I led the dance in the Great Hall. My courtiers called me the Happy Prince. And now that I am dead they have set me up here so high that I can see all the ugliness and all the misery of my city, and though my heart is made of lead yet I cannot choose but weep."

"Far away," continued the statue in a low musical voice, "far away in a little street there is a poor house. I can see a woman seated at a table. Her face is thin and worn. She is embroidering passion-flowers on a satin gown for the loveliest of the Queen's maids-of-honour to wear at the next Court-ball. In a bed in the corner of the room her little boy is lying ill. He has a fever, and is asking for oranges. Swallow, Swallow, little Swallow, will you not bring her the ruby out of my sword-hilt?" "I am waited for in Egypt," said the Swallow. "My friends are flying up and down the Nile." "Swallow, Swallow, little Swallow," said the Prince, "will you not stay with me for one night, and be my messenger? The boy is so thirsty, and the mother so sad."

So the Swallow picked out the great ruby from the Prince's sword, and flew away with it in his beak over the roofs of the town. At last he came to the poor house and looked in. The boy was tossing feverishly on his bed, and the mother had fallen asleep, she was so tired. In he hopped, and laid the great ruby on the table beside the woman's thimble. Then he flew gently round the bed, fanning the boy's forehead with his wings. "How cool I feel!" said the boy, " I must be getting better"; and he sank into a delicious slumber.

When day broke the Swallow flew down to the river and had a bath. When the moon rose he flew back to the Happy Prince. "Have you any commissions for Egypt?" he cried, "I am just starting." "Swallow, Swallow, little Swallow," said the Prince, "will you not stay with me one night longer?" "I

都進不了宮。白天我和同伴在花園裏遊玩，晚上我在大廳堂領着眾人跳舞。宮中大臣稱我快樂王子。現在我死了，他們把我高高地豎立在這兒，我便看到了我的城市中所有的醜惡和苦難。縱然我的心是鉛鑄的，我仍禁不住流淚哭泣。"

"離這裏很遠很遠的地方，"雕像繼續用那低低的、音樂般的聲音說，"一條小巷裏有間破屋。我看到一個女人坐在桌旁，她瘦削蒼老，正為王后最美麗的女侍從官參加下次宮廷舞會要穿的緞袍繡上西番蓮花。她的小兒子躺在屋角的牀上，生病發着燒，要吃桔子。燕子，燕子，小燕子，你難道不願把我劍柄上的紅寶石送去給她嗎？""朋友們在埃及等着我呢，他們正在尼羅河上空飛翔，"燕子說。"燕子，燕子，小燕子，"王子說，"你難道不能陪我一個晚上，替我送點東西嗎？孩子那麼口渴，母親那麼憂傷。"

於是，燕子從王子的寶劍上啄下那大塊紅寶石，含在嘴裏，掠過城市鱗次櫛比的屋頂，最後到了那舊房子前，向裏望去。男孩發着燒，在牀上輾轉反側；母親太疲倦，已睡着了。燕子跳進去，將紅寶石放在桌上母親的頂針旁，然後又輕輕地繞着牀飛，用翅膀搧着男孩的前額。"好涼快啊！"男孩說，"我肯定是好些了，"說着便酣然睡去。

第二天拂曉，燕子飛到河裏洗了個澡。等到月亮升起時，他飛回到快樂王子身旁，"你有甚麼信息要帶到埃及嗎？"他喊道，"我就要動身啦。""燕子，燕子，小燕子，"王子說，"你不能再陪我一夜嗎？""朋友們在埃及

am waited for in Egypt." "Swallow, Swallow, little Swallow," said the Prince, "far away across the city I see a young man in a garret. He is leaning over a desk covered with papers. He is trying to finish a play, but he is too cold to write any more. There is no fire in the grate, and hunger has made him faint."

— *Oscar Wilde*

等着我呢。"　"燕子，燕子，小燕子，"王子說，"我看見城市遠處那邊有間閣樓，裏面有個年青人，他伏在堆滿紙張稿件的桌上，正寫一個劇本，可是他冷得寫不下去了，爐中沒有生火，飢餓使他頭昏眼花。"

—— *奧斯卡·王爾德* [1]

1. 王爾德 (1854 — 1900)，愛爾蘭作者，詩人。19世紀末英國唯美主義運動主要代表，名著有 *The Happy Prince*（《快樂王子》）、戲劇 *Lady Windermere's Fan*（《少奶奶的扇子》）及 *The Importance of Being Earnest*（《誠實的重要》）等。

37 The Happy Prince (2) (Ireland)

"I will wait with you one night longer," said the Swallow, who really had a good heart. "Shall I take him another ruby?" "Alas! I have no ruby now," said the Prince, "my eyes are all that I have left. They are made of rare sapphires. Pluck out one of them and take it to him. He will sell it to the jeweller and buy firewood and finish his play." "Dear Prince," said the Swallow, "I cannot do that"; and he began to weep. "Swallow, Swallow, little Swallow," said the Prince, "do as I command you." So the Swallow plucked out the Prince's eye, and flew away to the student's garret.

The next day when the moon rose he flew back to the Happy Prince. "I am come[1] to bid you good-bye," he cried. "Swallow, Swallow, little Swallow," said the Prince, "will you not stay with me one night longer?" "It is winter," answered the Swallow, "and the chill snow will soon be here. In Egypt the sun is warm on the green palm-trees. Dear Prince, I must leave you, but I will never forget you. And next spring I will bring you back two beautiful jewels in place of those you have given away. The ruby shall be redder than a red rose, and the sapphire shall be as blue as the great sea."

"In the square below," said the Happy Prince, "there stands a little match-girl. She has let her matches fall in the gutter, and they are all spoiled. Her father will beat her if she does not bring home some money, and she is crying. She has no shoes or stockings, and her little head is bare. Pluck

---

1. I am come：舊用法，come 為過去分詞，作表語。最普通的如 He is gone、I am tired 等，現在還通用。

186

三十七　快樂王子(二)(愛爾蘭)

　　"那我就等等，再陪你一晚吧，"燕子説，他確實有一顆善良的心，"我再給他送去一塊紅寶石嗎？""可惜，我沒有紅寶石了，只剩下一雙眼睛，是用珍貴的藍寶石做的。摘一顆下來送給他吧。那他就可以賣給珠寶商，買回來柴火，寫完他的劇本了。""親愛的王子，我不能摘啊，"燕子説着哭了起來。"燕子，燕了，小燕子，"王子説，"照我説的去做吧。"於是，燕子啄下王子的一隻眼睛，飛到那學生的閣樓。

　　第二天月亮升起的時候，燕子飛回快樂王子身邊，叫道："我來向你告別啦。""燕子，燕子，小燕子，"王子説，"你不能再陪我一晚嗎？""冬天到了，"燕子答，"這裏很快就會漫天飛雪。在埃及，太陽正暖洋洋地照在鬱鬱蔥蔥的棕櫚樹上呢。親愛的王子，我一定要離開你了，可是我永遠也忘不了你。明年春天我要給你帶回來兩顆美麗的寶石，補上你送給人的兩顆。紅寶石會比紅玫瑰還要紅，藍寶石會比大海還要蔚藍清澈。"

　　"下面的廣場上，"王子説，"站着一個賣火柴的小女孩。她的火柴掉進了水溝，都浸壞了。如果她沒有錢空手回家，她父親要打她的。她正在哭呢。她腳上沒有鞋襪，

out my other eye, and give it to her, and her father will not beat her." "I will stay with you one night longer," said the Swallow, "but I cannot pluck out your eye. You would be quite blind then." "Swallow, Swallow, little Swallow," said the Prince, "do as I command you."

So he plucked out the Prince's other eye, and darted down with it. He swooped past the match-girl, and slipped the jewel into the palm of her hand. She ran home, laughing. Then the Swallow came back to the Prince. "You are blind now," he said, "so I will stay with you always." "No, little Swallow," said the poor prince, "you must go away to Egypt."

"I will stay with you always," said the swallow, and he slept at the Prince's feet.

All the next day he sat on the Prince's shoulder, and told him stories of what he had seen in strange lands. "Dear little Swallow," said the Prince, "fly over my city, little Swallow, and tell me what you see there." So the Swallow flew over the great city, and saw the rich making merry in their beautiful houses, while the beggars were sitting at the gates. He flew into dark lanes, and saw the white faces of starving children. Then he flew back and told the Prince what he had seen.

"I am covered with fine gold," said the Prince, "you must take it off, leaf by leaf, and give it to my poor." Leaf after leaf of the fine gold the Swallow picked off, till the Happy Prince looked quite dull and grey. Leaf after leaf of fine gold he brought to the poor, and the children's faces grew rosier.

Then the snow came, and after the snow came the frost. The poor little Swallow grew colder and colder, but he would not leave the Prince, he loved him too well. At last he knew that he was going to die. He had just enough strength to fly up to the Prince's shoulder once more. "Good-bye, dear Prince!" he murmured, "will you let me kiss your hand?" "I am glad that you are going to Egypt at last," said the Prince,

頭上沒有戴帽子。摘下我另一隻眼睛給那女孩吧，她父親就不會打她了。""我再陪你一夜吧，"燕子説，"可我不能摘下你的眼睛，那樣你就全瞎了。""燕子，燕子，小燕子，"王子道，"照我説的去做吧。"

於是燕子啄下王子另一隻眼睛，含着它飛了下去。他掠過賣火柴的女孩，將寶石掉落在她手心裏。小女孩笑着跑回家去。燕子回到王子身旁，"你現在瞎了，"他説，"我要永遠陪伴你。""別這樣，小燕子，"可憐的王子説，"你一定得到埃及去。"

"我要永遠陪伴着你了，"小燕子説。他睡在王子的腳旁。

第二天整整一天，燕子坐在王子的肩膀上給他講他在異國他鄉的見聞。"親愛的小燕子，"王子説，"在我的城市上空飛過，告訴我你看到的東西吧。"燕子飛到這大都市的上空，見到富人在豪華宅邸裏尋歡作樂，乞丐卻坐在大門外。他飛進陰暗的小巷，看見飢餓的孩子面有菜色。燕子飛回去，將見到的告訴了王子。

"我全身貼滿純金箔，"王子説，"你一片片揭下送給我的窮人吧。"燕子揭下一片一片的金葉送給窮人，最後快樂王子看上去黯淡淡、灰濛濛的，孩子們的面孔卻紅潤起來了。

下雪了。雪後便是霜。可憐的小燕子感到越來越冷，但他不願離開王子，他太愛他了。最後，他知道自己快要死了，他用最後一點力氣飛上王子的肩膀。"再見了，親愛的王子！"他喃喃地説，"能讓我親吻一下你的手嗎？""我真高興你終於要去埃及了，你在這裏已經呆得太久

"you have stayed too long here; but you must kiss me on the lips, for I love you." And he kissed the Happy Prince on the lips, and fell down dead at his feet.

At that moment a curious crack sounded inside the statue, as if something had broken. The fact is that the leaden heart had snapped right in two. It certainly was a dreadfully hard frost.

As the statue now looked very shabby, people pulled it down and melted it in a furnace. But its broken lead heart would not melt. So they threw it on a dust-heap where the dead Swallow was also lying.

"Bring me the two most precious things in the city," said God to one of His Angels; and the Angel brought Him the leaden heart and the dead bird.

"You have rightly chosen," said God.

— Oscar Wilde

了，"王子說，"你吻我的嘴唇吧，因為我愛你。"小燕子吻了王子的嘴唇，便跌落在他腳下死去。

就在這時，塑像裏發出一種奇怪的聲音，就像甚麼東西破裂了似的。那是快樂王子那鉛做的心凍裂成了兩半。真是天寒地凍啊。

因為雕像變得寒酸難看了，人們將它推倒，放到火爐裏熔化。但是那顆鉛心總也燒不化，人們便把它扔到垃圾堆裏。死了的小燕子也躺在那裏。

上帝對一位天使說，"把這城裏最寶貴的兩件東西給我拿來。"天使把鉛心和死鳥拿去給他。

上帝說："你選得對。"

—— 奧斯卡·王爾德

38 The Selfish Giant (Ireland)

Every afternoon, as they were coming from school, the children used to go and play in the Giant's garden. It was a large lovely garden, with soft green grass. Here and there over the grass stood beautiful flowers like stars, and there were twelve peach-trees that in the spring-time broke out into delicate blossoms of pink and pearl, and in the autumn bore rich fruit. The birds sat on the trees and sang so sweetly that the children used to stop their games in order to listen to them. "How happy we are here!" they cried to each other.

One day the Giant came back. When he arrived he saw the children playing in the garden.

"What are you doing here?" he cried in a very gruff voice, and the children ran away. "My own garden is my own garden," said the Giant, "and I will allow nobody to play in it but myself." So he built a high wall all round it, and put up a notice-board: *"Trespassers will be Prosecuted"*.

The poor children had now nowhere to play. They tried to play on the road.

Then the Spring came, and all over the country there were little blossoms and little birds. Only in the garden of the Selfish Giant it was still winter. The birds did not care to sing in it as there were no children, and the trees forgot to blossom. "I cannot understand why the Spring is so late in coming," said the Selfish Giant, "I hope there will be a change in the weather." But the Spring never came, nor the Summer. The Autumn gave golden fruit to every garden, but to the Giant's garden she gave none.

One morning the Giant was lying awake in bed when he heard some lovely music. It was a little linnet singing outside

三十八　自私的巨人（愛爾蘭）

　　每天下午孩子們放學後，總是到巨人的花園去玩耍。那是一個景色怡人的大花園，有柔軟的青草，草地上點綴着繁星般的美麗花朵，還有十二棵桃樹。春天，桃樹綻出粉紅色和珍珠色的鮮嫩的花朵；秋天又結出纍纍的果實。鳥兒在樹枝上囀鳴，歌聲悅耳，孩子們常常停下遊戲，側耳傾聽。"我們在這兒多快活啊！"他們喊道。

　　一天，巨人回來了。他一到家，就看見孩子們在花園裏玩耍。

　　"你們在這兒幹甚麼？"他惡狠狠地叫道，孩子們嚇得一哄而散。"我的花園就是我的花園，"巨人說，"除了我自己，誰也不許在裏面玩。"他築一道高牆把花園圍住，又樹起一塊告示牌："閒人莫入，違者法辦"。

　　這下，可憐的孩子們沒有地方玩啦，他們只好在街道上玩耍。

　　春天來了，遍地是小花，處處是小鳥，只有自私的巨人的花園裏還是蕭殺的嚴冬。因為沒有孩子，鳥兒不願在裏面歌唱，桃樹也忘記了開花。"我真不明白春天為甚麼這樣姍姍來遲，"自私的巨人說，"但願很快就會冬去春來。"可是春天還是不來，夏天也不到。秋天給每個花園掛滿金色的果實，而巨人的花園空空如也。

　　一天早上，巨人醒來躺在牀上，隱約聽到悅耳的音樂聲，那是隻小紅雀在他窗外唱歌。一陣花的芬芳從敞開的

his window. And a delicious perfume came to him through the open casement. "I believe the Spring has come at last," said the Giant; and he jumped out of bed and looked out. What did he see? He saw a most wonderful sight. Through a little hole in the wall the children had crept in, and they were sitting in the branches of the trees. In every tree that he could see there was a little child. And the trees were so glad to have the children back again that they had covered themselves with blossoms. The birds were flying about and twittering with delight. It was a lovely scene, only in one corner it was still winter, and in it was standing a little boy. He was so small that he could not reach up to the branches of the tree, and he was wandering all round it, crying bitterly. The poor tree was still covered with frost and snow, and the North Wind was blowing and roaring above it.

And the Giant's heart melted as he looked out. "How selfish I have been!" he said; "now I know why Spring would not come here." He was really very sorry for what he had done. So he crept downstairs and opened the front door quite softly, and went out into the garden. But when the children saw him they were so frightened that they all ran away, and the garden became winter again. Only the little boy did not run, for his eyes were so full of tears that he did not see the Giant coming. And the Giant stole up behind him and took him gently in his hand, and put him up into the tree. And the tree broke at once into blossom, and the birds came and sang on it, and the little boy stretched out his two arms and flung them round the Giant's neck, and kissed him. And the other children, when they saw that the Giant was not wicked any longer, came running back, and with them came the Spring. "It is your garden now, little children," said the Giant, and he took a great axe and knocked down the wall.

— *Oscar Wilde*

窗戶吹送過來。"我想春天終於來啦。"巨人從牀上一躍而起，向窗外望去。他看到了甚麼？他看到了一幅最美的畫景：孩子們從牆上的一個小洞爬進來，都坐到了樹枝上。他看得到的每棵樹上都有個小孩，樹木為孩子們回來高興得綻開滿樹鮮花。鳥兒飛來飛去，高興得嘰嘰喳喳叫。多麼可愛的畫面啊，只有一個角落依舊是嚴冬。那裏正站着一個小男孩，他太小了，夠不着樹枝，正在樹旁轉來轉去，傷心地哭泣着。這棵可憐的樹仍然掛滿霜雪，北風在樹頂怒吼。

巨人向外看到這情景，他的心融化了。"我太自私了！"他說，"這下我知道春天為何不到這裏來了。"他為自己的所為感到非常歉疚。於是他悄悄走下樓梯，輕手輕腳打開前門，走進花園。但孩子們一見他，全都嚇跑了，花園又回到冬天。只有那個小男孩沒有跑，因為他淚水滿眶，沒有看見巨人走來。巨人悄悄走到他身後，輕輕地把他抱起放到樹上。樹立刻鮮花盛開，鳥兒也飛來了，在樹上唱着歌。男孩仲開雙臂摟住巨人的脖子，親吻他。其他孩子見巨人不再那麼兇，都跑回來。春天也和他們一起回來了。"小朋友，現在這是你們的花園啦，"巨人說着拿起巨斧拆掉了圍牆。

—— *奧斯卡·王爾德*

39 William Tell (Switzerland)

William Tell was the most famous crossbowman[1] of Switzerland. He lived in a little mountain cottage and loved the freedom and peace of the life there. He spent many days hunting the deer; often too he went fishing on the storm-swept lake of Uri and none could surpass his skill in managing a boat.

Now one day there was a fair in the little market town of Altdorf. Thither went William with his little son. But the Austrians had conquered the Swiss, and the tyrant Gessler was ordering all who entered Altdorf to pay homage to the Duke of Austria's cap, which was set up on a pole in the market square. William Tell hated this sign of bondage, and, though threatened with death, he refused to bend his knee in submission to those who had destroyed the liberty of the Swiss people.

Gessler then seized William's son and ordered the soldiers to bind him to the trunk of a linden tree some distance away and place an apple on his head. Then, turning to the lad's father, he said, "All praise is given you for your skill as a crossbowman. I have a mind to test you. You must shoot an arrow so as to split the apple on your son's head. If you can do this, your life will be spared; if not, or if you injure the child, your life will be forfeited."

William saw the crafty smile on Gessler's lips and thrust two arrows into his girdle. With an anxious heart, yet steady

---

1. crossbowman：crossbow，石弓，一種中世紀的武器。

三十九　威廉‧特爾[1]（瑞士）

威廉‧特爾是瑞士一位最著名的石弓射手。他住在山間一座小屋裏，他熱愛那裏自由而平靜的生活。他常常出外獵鹿，也常到風狂雨暴的烏里湖捕魚。他駕船的本領無人能及。

一天，小市鎮阿爾特道夫舉辦一個集市，威廉‧特爾帶着他的小兒子去趕集。但當時瑞士已被奧地利人征服，殘暴的格斯勒下令，所有進入阿爾特道夫鎮的人，都必須向奧地利公爵的帽子行禮致敬，這頂帽子放在集市廣場一根柱子頂上。威廉‧特爾憎恨這種屈辱的表示，雖然受到不執行者將被處死刑的威脅，仍然拒絕向那些使瑞士人民失去自由的人俯首屈膝。

格斯勒於是抓住威廉的兒子，命士兵將孩子縛到一棵有一定距離的椴樹樹幹上，頭上放一個蘋果。然後他轉身對孩子的父親說："都說你的石弓技術高明，百發百中。我想考一考你。你得用一枝箭就把你兒子頭上的蘋果射中、裂開。要是你做到了，就饒你不死；如果射不中，或是傷了這孩子，你就沒命了。"

威廉看到格斯勒一臉奸笑，便把兩支箭插在腰帶上，

---

1. 威廉‧特爾是十三至十四世紀間瑞士烏里郡的農民、傳奇英雄。文中故事據說發生於1307年11月，而瑞士從奧地利人統治下獲得自由是在 1308 年元旦。其他民族在此之前已有多種內容類似的故事。

hand, he fitted one arrow to his bow string. Slowly he took aim, then swiftly sped the arrow through the air, and, splitting the apple in half, it buried itself in the tree beyond, leaving the child untouched.

Gessler's anger knew no bounds, yet must he grant William his life. Noting the other arrow in William's belt, however, he asked why it had been placed there. With fearless words William replied: "Had I hurt my child, this arrow would have entered your heart."

— edited by F. H. Lee

他心焦，但手穩。他把一枝箭搭上弓弦，慢慢地瞄準，然後飛快地射出；箭嗖的一聲把蘋果射得裂成兩半，餘力未盡插入樹幹。孩子未損一絲毛髮。

格斯勒怒氣衝天，但不得不赦免威廉。可是他注意到威廉腰帶上另外那枝箭，便問為甚麼他把箭插在那裏，威廉面無懼色，直言不諱：“萬一我射傷孩了，這枝箭就送到你心臟裏了。”

——*F·H·*李 編

40 The Jokes of Single-toe (Spain)

The Padre[1] asked Single-Toe (so named because he had only one on his left front foot) if the chestnuts were riping. The squirrel put his paw beside his nose as though he were trying to think up an answer to a riddle. "I'll try to let you know in three days," he mumbled, "but don't do anything about chestnuts until you see me again."

But the Padre was suspicious and sent somebody to see what the squirrel family is up to that morning. The report was: the squirrels were throwing down the chestnuts for dear life. Single-Toe is making them work all the harder, and giggling at something he seemed to think very funny.

"Oh, the rascal," chuckled the Padre. "The sly little one-toed sinner!" He took three of the oatmeal sacks from the cupboard and trotted off, pushing his wheelbarrow.

Up among the leaves, busy pulling the polished nuts out of the burrs, Single-Toe and his relatives did not hear the Padre arrive. Patter, plop, plop, plop, patter—the brown nuts were falling down.

The Padre beamed as he tried the chestnuts. He made little piles of the biggest ones, and began filling his sacks. Finally he had all the wheelbarrow would carry. He called out in his silkiest voice, "Many thanks, Single-Toe. You will see that I have taken only the big ones."

---

1. Padre：指 Padre Porko——波爾科老爹，是西班牙民間傳説中一個獨特的角色，一隻頗有紳士派頭的豬。他聰明機智又溫文爾雅，輕描淡寫地就解決了自己和鄰居的種種難題。Padre，西班牙語，即 Father：父親、神甫、牧師。本篇選自《波爾科老爹》一書。

四十 愛惡作劇的獨趾松鼠（西班牙）

波爾科老爹問獨趾松鼠（因左前足只有一個腳趾而得名）栗子熟了沒有。這松鼠把爪子放在鼻子邊，做出一付絞盡腦汁要解開個謎語的樣子，"我爭取三天之內告訴你吧。"他嘟噥道，"可你在見到我之前別去打栗子的主意。"

老爹陡然生疑，找了個人去看看松鼠一家子這天上午在幹甚麼。得到的回報是，他們正拚命摘栗子呢。獨趾在監工，還格格地笑，好像有點甚麼滑稽可笑的事情。

"哈，這壞傢伙，"老爹呵呵一笑，"這狡猾的一趾小壞蛋！"他從食櫥裏拿了三個燕麥袋，推起手推車急急地走了。

獨趾一家大小連同親戚在樹枝上正忙着把油光烏亮的栗子剝出外殼，沒有聽見老爹來。啪啦啪，啪啦啪——褐色的栗子紛紛落地。

老爹嚐嚐栗子，笑逐顏開。他把個兒最大的栗子堆成幾堆，往燕麥袋裏裝，最後裝到手推車險些推不動。這時他才用最柔和悅耳的聲音叫道："多謝啦，獨趾。你瞧我只拿了些個兒大的。"

There was a sudden calm in the chestnut grove. The squirrels came leaping down to a low bough, from where they could send sour looks after the Padre, trundling his barrow along toward the bridge.

One day three or four weeks later the Padre was doing a little carpentering under the umbrella pine, when something behind him sniffed. He jumped. There, under the table, tears running down their noses, were Mrs. Single-Toe and the four children. Padre exclaimed, "What can be as wrong as all that?" "It's Papa," said the oldest boy. "He's been in a hole by the old oak for four days, and is almost starved. The fox won't let him out. He's mad because of Papa's jokes."

The Padre's mouth opened in a wide grin. "More of the jokes that other people don't find funny, eh? Well, I'll have a talk with the fox."

The fox was lying with his muzzle just an inch from the hole. "I've got him this time," he snarled. "My mother brings my meals and keeps guard while I eat. He'll not get away this time!"

"He is a nuisance with his jokes," said the Padre peaceably, "but he doesn't do any real harm. Don't you think a good scare would be enough for him?"

"No, I don't," snapped the fox. "And don't you mix in this business, Padre."

The Padre walked away, deep in thought. There must be some way to save him. Suddenly he saw some crows gossiping in a dead pine. "Will one of you black boys do me a favor, in a great hurry?" he called. "Fly low through the woods, and tell every rabbit you see that I want their road commissioner to come to my house for dinner."

The Padre's guest was promptness itself. "Now for serious business," said the Padre, leading the way to the garden, when they had finished their second glass of

剎那間栗子林靜了下來，松鼠們跳下到低枝上，氣惱地看着老爹推車向小橋走去。

過了三、四個星期，有一天，老爹正在那棵傘形松樹下做零碎木匠活兒，聽見身後有抽泣聲。他跳將起來，獨趾太太和四個孩子在桌子下面呢，哭哭啼啼的。老爹喊道："甚麼事至於這麼哭呀？""爸爸出事了。"大兒子說，"他困在老橡樹旁的洞裏四天啦，快餓死了。狐狸不讓他出來。爸爸的惡作劇把他氣瘋了。"

老爹咧開嘴笑起來："玩笑開多了，別人就不覺得好玩了，是吧？好啦，我去跟狐狸談談。"

狐狸在洞口躺着，嘴巴離洞口只有一英寸。"這回我可逮住他了，"他咆哮道，"我媽給我送飯，我吃飯時她守着。這次他可跑不了啦！"

"他這愛開玩笑的毛病是惹人煩，"老爹息事寧人地說，"可倒也沒害人，嚇唬他一下也就夠了吧？"

"不，不夠，"狐狸怒氣沖沖地打斷他的話，說："老爹，這事你別摻和進來。"

老爹走了，心裏在想主意。總得想個法子救救他呀。忽然他看到幾隻烏鴉在一棵枯松樹上聊天。"你們這些黑小子有誰能幫我個忙嗎？還得快。"他喊，"低低地飛進樹林去，看見兔子就傳我的話，請他們的道路管理專員來我家吃晚餐。"

老爹的客人挺爽快。喝完第二杯蒲公英酒後，老爹領着客人來到園子，說道："現在來談正事。咱們畫張地

dandelion wine. "We will draw a map." He made a cross in the soft earth with a stick. "Here is the oak that the lightning split. And here in front of it is a rabbit hole that was begun, but never finished." The road commissioner nodded.

"Now," continued the Padre, "how far is the bottom of this unfinished hole from one of your regular tunnels, and how long would it take to dig up to it?" The road commissioner replied, "I should say it would take two hours to join the hole." The Padre gave the road commissioner ten carrots, saying, "Mr. Commissioner, will you do this little job of digging for me? You will find a friend of mine in the unfinished hole. Don't let him make a noise, but bring him here the moment you can get him free."

Daylight was fading when the rabbit returned. He was supporting a hoarse, hungry, and grimy red squirrel. The Padre welcomed them, pointing to the cupboard. "Sh-h-h-sh, go and see what's inside, Single-Toe."

Safe, fed, and warmed, the red squirrel became his own gay self again. He began to chuckle, then to shake with merriment. "Ha, ha, ha! That silly old fox is still there, watching an empty hole! Won't it be a priceless joke, if I climb the oak and drop a rotten egg on his nose?"

At the word "joke", Mrs. Single-Toe, the four little squirrels, and the good Padre, all stiffened. "Don't you ever say that word again," said his wife. "Do you hear, no more jokes, never, never."

— *Robert Davis*

圖。"他在鬆軟的地上用樹枝畫個十字，"這兒，雷劈了的橡樹前就是那動了工而沒有挖好的兔子洞。"專員點點頭。

"好，"老爹接着說，"從你們常用的通道到這個沒完工的洞底有多遠？挖通了要多少時間？"專員答："估計兩個小時可以挖通吧。"老爹給了道路專員一根胡蘿蔔，說："專員先生，你能幫我幹這點兒挖土活兒嗎？你會看到我有個朋友在那沒完工的洞裏，讓他別出聲，他一脫身你就把他帶來。"

兔子回來時天色已漸暗。他扶着那隻聲音沙啞、飢腸轆轆、滿身污垢的紅松鼠。老爹迎着他們，指着食櫥說："噓，別做聲，獨趾，去看看裏面有甚麼。"

平安脫險，酒足飯飽，渾身暖和過來的紅松鼠又原形畢露，快活起來，他呵呵笑得渾身發顫。"哈，哈，哈！那個笨蛋老狐狸還守着個空洞哪！要是我爬上橡樹往他鼻子上扔個臭雞蛋，這個玩笑不是怪有趣的嗎？"

一聽"玩笑"二字，獨趾太太、四隻小松鼠和好心的老爹都收起了笑容。他的太太道："再也不許提這兩個字！聽見了嗎，別鬧惡作劇了，再也別鬧了。"

—— 羅伯特·戴維斯

205

41 The Wise Little Girl (Russia)

Two brothers were traveling together: one was poor and the other was rich, and each had a horse, the poor one a mare, and the rich one a gelding. They stopped for the night, one beside the other. The poor man's mare bore a foal during the night, and the foal rolled under the rich man's cart. In the morning the rich man roused his poor brother, saying, "Get up, brother. During the night my cart bore a foal." The brother rose and said. "How is it possible for a cart to give birth to a foal? It was my mare who bore the foal!" The rich brother said, "If your mare were his mother, he would have been found lying beside her."

To settle their quarrel they went to the authorities. The rich man gave the judges money and the poor man presented his case in words. Finally word of this affair reached the tsar himself. He summoned both brothers before him and proposed to them four riddles: "What is the strongest and swiftest thing in the world? What is the fattest thing in the world? What is the softest thing? And what is the loveliest thing?" He gave them three days' time and said, "On the fourth day come back with your answers."

The rich man thought and thought, remembered his godmother and went to ask her advice. "What are the riddles? Tell me." He told her the first riddle. "That's not difficult! My husband has a bare mare; nothing in the world is swifter than she is." As for the second riddle, his godmother said, "My spotted boar has become so fat that he can barely stand on his legs." "The third riddle is: 'What is the softest thing in the world?'" "That's well known. Eider down." "The fourth riddle is: 'What is the loveliest thing in the world?'" "The

四十一 聰明的小女孩 (俄羅斯)

　　兩兄弟一起出門旅行：一個窮酸，一個闊綽。兩人都騎了馬，窮的騎匹牝馬，闊的騎匹閹馬。晚上他們歇宿，並排睡在一起。窮兄弟的牝馬夜間下了小馬駒，馬駒卻滾到了闊兄弟的車下。早上，闊兄弟叫醒窮的，說：“兄弟，起來吧，夜裏我的車下了匹馬駒！”窮兄弟起身道：“車怎麼可能下馬駒呢？是我的牝馬生的！”闊兄弟說：“要是你那牝馬是小馬駒的媽，它就應該躺在她身邊。”

　　他們去找官府讓官府判斷是非。闊兄弟用錢賄賂了法官，窮兄弟只能說理。最後，沙皇聽到這件事。他喚來兩兄弟，給他們出了四個謎語：“世上甚麼東西最強最快？甚麼最肥？甚麼最軟？甚麼最稱心可愛？”他給他們三天時間，說：“第四天帶着你們的答案來。”

　　闊兄弟冥思苦想，想起他的教母，便去請教她。“告訴我謎語是甚麼吧。”他說了第一個謎語。“這不難！我當家的有一匹不用鞍的牝馬，世上再沒有比她跑得更快的了。”說到第二個謎語，他的教母說，“我那頭花點子公豬肥得站都站不住了。”“第三個謎語是：甚麼是世上最軟的？”“這誰不知道？鴨絨唄。”“第四個：甚麼是世上最

loveliest thing in the world is my grandson."

As for the poor brother, he shed bitter tears and went home. His seven-year-old daughter said, "Why are you sighing and shedding tears, Father?" "The tsar has proposed four riddles to me, and I shall never be able to solve them." "Tell me, what are these riddles?" And he told her.

"Father, go to the tsar and tell him that the strongest and fastest thing in the world is the wind; the fattest is the earth, for she feeds everything that grows and lives; the softest of all is the hand, for whatever a man may lie on, he puts his hand under his head; and there is nothing lovelier in the world than sleep."

The two brothers came to the tsar. The tsar heard their answers to the riddles, and asked the poor man, "Did you solve these riddles yourself, or did someone solve them for you?" The poor man answered, "Your Majesty, I have a seven-year-old daughter, and she gave me the answers." The tsar listened to him and gave him a hundred and fifty eggs, saying, "Give these eggs to your daughter; let her hatch one hundred and fifty chicks by tomorrow."

The peasant returned home. "Ah, my daughter," he said, "we are barely out of one trouble before another is upon us." "Grieve not, Father," answered the seven-year-old girl. "Tell him that one-day grain is needed to feed the chicks. In one day let a field be plowed and the millet sown, harvested, and threshed; our chickens refuse to peck any other grain."

The tsar listened to this and said, "Since your daughter is so wise, let her appear before me tomorrow morning— and I want her to come neither on foot nor on horseback, neither naked nor dressed, neither with a present nor without a gift."

The seven-year-old girl said to her father, "Go to the hunters and buy me a live hare and a live quail." The father

稱心可愛的？”“世上最稱心可愛的就是我的孫子了。”

窮兄弟呢，他流着氣苦的眼淚回到家。他七歲的女兒說：“爸爸，你幹嗎又嘆氣又流淚的呀？”“沙皇給了四個謎語，可我一輩子也猜不出來。”“告訴我是甚麼謎語吧。”他告訴了她。

“爸爸，去見沙皇吧，告訴他世上最強最快的是風；最肥的是大地，因為她供養萬物生長；最軟的是手，因為誰要是躺着，都要用手墊在頭下；世上再沒有比睡覺更稱心愜意的啦。”

兩兄弟去見沙皇，沙皇聽了答案後，問窮兄弟：“是你自己猜到的，還是甚麼人幫你猜的？”窮兄弟答：“陛下，我有個七歲的女兒，是她教給我的答案。”沙皇聽後，給了他一百五十個雞蛋，說：“把這些雞蛋給你女兒，讓她明天孵出一百五十隻小雞來。”

農夫轉回家，說：“哎，女兒啊，我們一個麻煩沒完又來一個啦。”“爸爸，別難受，”七歲的女兒答，“告訴陛下，我要一天就長出來的糧食餵小雞。要有塊地一天之內就得做完耕耘，播種，收割，打穀。我們的小雞只吃這種糧食，別的不吃。”

沙皇聽了說：“既然你女兒這麼聰明，讓她明早來見我——我要她不能走着來也不能騎馬來；不能光着身子也不能穿衣服；不能帶禮物又不能不帶禮物。”

七歲的女孩對父親說：“去獵人那裏買隻活野兔和活

bought her a hare and a quail.

Next morning the seven-year-old girl took off her clothes, donned a net, took the quail in her hand, sat upon the hare, and went to the palace. The tsar met her at the gate. She bowed to him, saying, "Here is a little gift for you, Your Majesty," and handed him the quail. The tsar stretched out his hand, but the quail shook her wings and—flap, flap!—was gone.

"Very well," said the tsar, "you have done as I ordered you to do. Now tell me—since your father is so poor, what do you live on?"

"My father catches fish on the shore, and I make fish soup in my skirt."

"You are stupid! Fish never live on the shore, fish live in the water."

"And you—are you wise? Who ever saw a cart bear foals?"

The tsar awarded the foal to the poor peasant.

— Aleksander Afanasyev

鵪鶉來。"父親照辦了。

第二天早上，七歲的女孩脫去衣服，披上一張網，手拿鵪鶉騎在野兔背上，去了王宮。沙皇在大門迎接她，她向沙皇鞠躬行禮，說："陛下，這是一點小禮物。"說着遞上那隻鵪鶉。沙皇伸出手，可是鵪鶉搧搧翅膀——啪！啪！——飛走了。

"很好，"沙皇說，"我吩咐的你都做到了，那麼你告訴我，既然你父親這樣窮，你們是怎麼生活的。"

"我父親在岸上抓魚，我就在我裙子裏煮魚湯。"

"你太笨了！魚生在水裏，哪能活在岸上？"

"那您就聰明了嗎？有誰見過車生馬駒的？"

於是沙皇把馬駒判給了窮農夫。

—— 亞歷山大·阿法納謝夫 [1]

---

1. 阿法納謝夫（1826—1871），俄國歷史學家，民間文學家，編有《俄國民間童話集》，收錄六百多篇童話。

42 The Bad Wife (Russia)

There was once a bad wife who made life impossible for her husband and disobeyed him in everything. If he told her to rise early, she slept for three days; if he told her to sleep, she did not sleep at all. If her husband asked her to make pancakes, she said, "You don't deserve pancakes, you scoundrel!" If her husband said, "Don't make pancakes, wife, since I don't deserve them," she made an enormous panful, two whole gallons of pancakes, and said, "Now eat, scoundrel, and be sure that all of them are eaten!" If he said, "Wife, do not wash the clothes nor go out to cut hay — it is too much for you," she answered, "No, you scoundrel, I will go and you shall come with me."

One day, after a quarrel with her, he went in distress to the woods to pick berries, found a currant bush, and saw a bottomless pit in the middle of it. As he looked at it, he thought to himself, "Why do I go on living with a bad wife and struggling with her? Could I not put her in that pit and teach her a lesson?" He went back home and said, "Wife, do not go to the woods for berries." "I shall go, you fool!" "I found a currant bush, don't pick it!" "I shall go and pick it clean — and what is more, I won't give you any currants!" The husband went out and his wife followed him. He came to the currant bush and his wife jumped toward it and yelled, "Don't go into that bush, you scoundrel, or I'll kill you!" She herself went into the middle of it, and fell plop! — into the bottomless pit.

The husband went home happily and lived there in peace for three days. On the fourth day, he went to see how his wife was getting along. He took a long towrope, let it down

四十二　惡婆娘（俄羅斯）

　　從前有個惡婆娘，鬧得她丈夫天天不得安寧，事事都和他作對。要是他要她早起，她就大睡三天；要她去睡，她偏通夜不眠。丈夫請她做些煎餅，她就說：“你這流氓，你不配吃煎餅！”若是丈夫說：“老婆，別做煎餅啦，我也不配吃。”她卻做一大鍋，整整兩加侖煎餅，說：“吃吧，壞蛋，都給我吃光！”要是他說：“老婆，別洗衣也別割草，怕累着你。”她就答：“我偏要做，你這惡棍，你得跟我來幹。”

　　一天，和她吵了一架之後，他心煩意亂到樹林採草莓，找到一叢醋栗，又看見醋栗叢中央有一個深不見底的坑。他望着坑想：“我幹嘛要和一個惡婆娘一起過日子，天天和她吵個不休呢？不如把她扔在這坑裏教訓她一下？”他轉回家去，說：“老婆，可別到林子裏採莓子啊。”“笨蛋，我偏要去！”“我找到一叢醋栗，別去摘！”“偏要摘，摘個乾淨！── 還一個也不給你！”丈夫出門走在前，老婆跟在後。到了醋栗叢老婆就跳了進去，嚷道：“你這無賴，不許進來，進來就宰了你！”她一頭鑽到樹叢中央，撲通一聲，掉進深不見底的坑裏。

　　丈夫高高興興地回家，安安靜靜過了三天。第四天，他去看看老婆怎麼樣了。他拿了一根長繩吊到坑裏，卻拉

into the pit, and dragged out a little imp. He was frightened and was about to drop him back into the pit, when the imp began to shriek and then said imploringly, "Peasant, do not put me back, let me out into the world. A bad wife has come into our pit — she torments, bites, and pinches all of us, we are sick to death of her. If you let me out, I will do you a good turn!" So the peasant let him go free in holy Russia. The imp said, "Well, peasant, let us go to the town of Vologda[1]. I will make people sick and you shall cure them."

Now the imp set to work on merchants' wives and daughters; he would enter into them and they would go mad and fall ill. Our peasant would go to the house of the sick woman; the imp would leave, a blessing would come on the house; everyone thought that the peasant was a doctor, gave him money, and fed him pies. The peasant thus amassed an uncountable sum of money. Then the imp said to him, "You now have plenty, peasant. Are you satisfied? Next I shall enter a boyar's daughter, and mind you do not come to cure her, else I shall eat you."

The boyar sent for the peasant, the famous "doctor". He came to the boyar's beautiful house and told him to have all the townspeople and all the carriages and coachmen gather in the street in front of the house; he gave orders that all the coachmen should crack their whips and cry aloud, "The bad wife has come, the bad wife has come!" Then he went into the sick maiden's room. When he came in, the imp was enraged at him and said, "Why have you come here, Russian man? Now I will eat you!" He said, "What do you mean? I have not come to drive you out, but to warn you that the bad wife is here!" The imp jumped on the windowsill, stared

---

1. Vologda：俄羅斯西北部一古城。

上來一個小鬼。他很害拍，剛要把它扔回坑裏，小鬼尖叫起來，又苦苦哀求：「農夫，別放我回去，讓我到這世上來吧，有個惡婆娘進了我們的坑——她折磨我們，又咬又擰，我們煩死了。要是你讓我出來，我會報答你的！」於是，農夫放他出來到了神聖的俄羅斯。小鬼說：「好啦農夫，咱們去沃伏洛達吧，我讓人得病，而你來把他們醫好。」

小鬼在有些富商的太太女兒身上施展鬼技，他附到她們身體裏，她們便精神錯亂，一一病倒。咱們這農夫就來到病人家；小鬼一走，這家子便逢凶化吉了。人人都以為農夫是個醫生，給他錢，給他好吃的。農夫因此積聚了無數錢財。後來小鬼對他說：「農夫，現在你發財啦，滿足了嗎？下回我要附到一個大貴族的小姐體內，你不許給她醫治，不然我就吃了你。」

大貴族派人來喚農夫這著名的「醫生」。他來到貴族豪華的府第，讓貴族叫鎮上所有的人、馬車和車夫都到他府前的街上來。他吩咐所有的車夫都抽着鞭子齊聲高叫「惡婆娘來啦！惡婆娘來啦！」然後他走進生病的小姐的房間。他一進去，小鬼就對他大發脾氣，道：「俄國佬，你幹嗎來了？我馬上就吃了你！」農夫說：「你這是甚麼意思？我不是來趕你走的，我是來給你送個信息：惡婆娘來

fixedly, and listened intently. He heard all the crowd in the street cry in one voice, "The bad wife has come!" "Peasant," said the imp, "where shall I hide?" "Return to the pit. She won't go there again!" The imp went there and joined the bad wife. The boyar rewarded the peasant by giving him half his possessions and his daughter in marriage; but the bad wife to this day sits in the pit in nether darkness.

— *Aleksander Afanasyev*

啦！"小鬼跳上窗台，瞪着眼看，側着耳聽。只聽街上的人羣都在同聲喊："惡婆娘來啦！"小鬼道："農夫，我該藏到哪兒好呢？""回那坑裏去，她不會再去了！"小鬼回到坑裏，和惡婆娘作伴去了。大貴族重重賞了農夫，把一半家產給了他，又把女兒嫁給他。可到今天，那惡婆娘還坐在地獄般漆黑的坑裏呢。

—— 亞歷山大·阿法納謝夫

43 Dividing the Goose (Russia)

Once there was a poor peasant who had many children, but no possessions except one goose. He saved this goose for a long time; but hunger is nothing to be trifled with—and things had reached such a point that he had nothing to eat. So the peasant killed the goose, roasted it, and put it on the table. So far, so good; but he had no bread and not a grain of salt. He said to his wife, "How can we eat the goose without bread or salt? Perhaps I should take the goose to the baron as a gift and ask him for bread." "Well, go with God," said his wife.

The peasant came to the baron and said, "I have brought you a goose as a gift. You are welcome to all I have. Do not disdain it, little father[1]." "Thanks, peasant, thanks. Now divide the goose among us, without doing wrong to anyone."

Now this baron had a wife, two sons and two daughters— all in all there were six in his family. The peasant was given a knife and he began to carve and divide the goose. He cut off the head and gave it to the baron. "You are the head of the house," he said, "so it is fitting that you should have the head." He cut off the pope's nose and gave it to the baron's wife, saying. "Your business is to sit in the house and take care of it, so here is the pope's nose for you." He cut off the legs and gave them to the sons. Saying, "Here is a leg for

---

1. little father：俄語中人名或有些名詞的詞尾可變化以表示小稱或暱稱。如此文中的 little father 亦即 dear father。father 在俄語中可作 "老爺子" 解，即對長者的尊稱，故譯為 "好老爺"。

四十三　分鵝（俄羅斯）

　　從前一個窮苦的農夫有許多孩子，卻除去一隻鵝以外別無家產，這隻鵝他餵養了很長時間捨不得殺，可餓肚子不是鬧着玩兒的——而且事情已經到了山窮水盡的地步，沒有吃的了。農夫只好宰了鵝，烤好，擺上桌子。暫時一切順利；可是他沒有麵包，連一粒鹽也沒有。他對太太說："沒有麵包沒有鹽，咱們怎麼吃鵝啊？要不然我把這鵝送給爵爺，向他要些麵包來吧。""去吧，願上帝與你同在，"太太說。

　　農夫去見爵爺，說："好老爺，我給你送來一隻鵝，這是我所有的一切了，請笑納吧，不要嫌棄。""多謝，農夫，多謝了。咱們把這鵝平分了吧，誰也別虧了誰。"

　　這爵爺有個夫人，有兩個兒子和兩個女兒——滿打滿算家裏有六口人，農夫接過一把刀便切起鵝來。他切下頭遞給爵爺，說："您是一家之主，所以您應該吃頭。"他切下鵝屁股遞給爵爺夫人，說："您是坐管全家的，鵝屁股給您。"他切下腿遞給兩個兒子說："這腿你們一人一隻，

each of you, to trample your father's paths with." And to each daughter he gave a wing. "You won't stay long with your father and mother; when you grow up, off you will fly. And I," he said, "I'm just a stupid peasant, so I'll take what is left." Thus he got most of the goose. The baron laughed, gave the peasant wine to drink, rewarded him with bread, and sent him home.

A rich peasant heard about this, envied the poor one, roasted five geese, and took them to the baron. "What do you want, peasant?" asked the baron. "I have brought Your Grace five geese as a gift."

"Thanks, brother! Now apportion them among us without doing wrong to anyone." The peasant tried this and that, but saw no way of dividing the geese equally. He just stood there scratching his head.

The baron sent for the poor peasant and told him to divide the geese. He took one goose, gave it to the baron and his wife, and said, "Now you are three." He gave another goose to the two sons and a third one to the two daughters, saying, "Now you also are threes." The last pair of geese he took for himself, saying, "Now I and the geese are another three." The baron said, "You are a clever fellow; you have managed to give everyone an equal share and you have not forgotten yourself either." He rewarded the poor peasant with money and drove out the rich one.

— *Aleksander Afanasyev*

好踏着你爹的路走。"他給了兩個女兒每人一隻翅膀，"你們不能總守着爹媽，長大成人就會飛走。至於我呢，"他説，"我只是個蠢鈍的種田人，剩下的我就拿了吧。"這樣他得了差不多整隻鵝。爵爺哈哈大笑，給農夫喝了酒，又給他麵包，便打發他回家了。

一個富裕的農夫聽到此事，又嫉妒又羨慕，烤了五隻鵝拿着去見爵爺。"你想要甚麼啊，農夫？"爵爺問。"我送給閣下五隻鵝。"

"兄弟，多謝！那咱們分了吧，別虧了誰。"農夫這樣分那樣分就是找不到平分鵝的辦法，只好站在那裏直搔頭。

爵爺派人去叫窮農夫來分鵝。他拿起一隻鵝遞給爵爺和夫人，説："這下你們合起來是三個。"又把一隻鵝遞給兩個兒子，一隻給了兩個女兒，説："這下你們也都是三個。"他把最後兩隻鵝留給自己，説："我和這兩隻鵝也是三個。"爵爺説："你真是個聰明人，對誰都不偏不倚，也沒忘了自己。"他賞錢給窮農夫，把富農夫趕跑了。

——　*亞歷山大·阿法納謝夫*

44 The Speaking Grapes, the Smiling Apple, and the Tinkling Apricot (Hungary)

There was once, I don't know where, beyond seven times seven countries, a king who had three daughters. One day the king was going to the market, and thus inquired of his daughters: "What shall I bring you from the market, my dear daughters?"

The eldest said, "A golden dress, my dear royal father"; the second said, "A silver dress for me"; the third said, "Speaking grapes, a smiling apple, and a tinkling apricot for me."

"Very well, my daughters," said the king, and went. He bought the dresses for his two elder daughters in the market, as soon as he arrived; but, in spite of all exertions and inquiries, he could not find the speaking grapes, the smiling apple, and tinkling apricot. He was very sad that he could not get what his youngest daughter wished, for she was his favourite; and he went home. It happened, however, that the royal carriage stuck fast on the way home, although his horses were of the best breed, for they were such high steppers that they kicked the stars. So he at once sent for extra horses to drag out the carriage; but all in vain, the horses couldn't move either way. He gave up all hope, at last, of getting out of the position, when a dirty, filthy pig came that way, and grunted, "Grumph! grumph! grumph! King, give me your youngest daughter, and I will help you out of the mud." The king, never thinking what he was promising, and over-anxious to get away, consented, and the pig gave the carriage a push with its nose, so that the carriage and horses at once moved

四十四　會說話的葡萄、會笑的蘋果和　叮噹響的杏子（匈牙利）

從前，我也不知道是哪兒，大概是越禍十七十四十九個國家的地方吧，一個國王有三個女兒。一天，國王去趕集，問三個女兒：“親愛的女兒，你們要我從集市帶點甚麼回來呀？”

大女兒說：“親愛的父王，我要件黃金衣”；二女兒說：“我要件白銀的”；三女兒說：“我要會說話的葡萄、會笑的蘋果和叮噹響的杏子。”

“好的，好的。”國王說着就走了。一到集市他就給大女兒、二女兒買了她們要的衣服。但是找來找去、問來問去都買不到會說話的葡萄、會笑的蘋果和叮噹響的杏子。他買不到小女兒要的東西，心裏很煩悶，因為他最疼愛這小女兒。無奈只好回家。國王的御馬神駿非凡，跑起來騰雲駕霧，腳踢星斗。可是不巧，在半路上馬車輪子牢牢地陷入泥濘裏。他立刻派人去牽備用的馬來拉馬車，但是沒有用，左拉右拉拉不出。最後他覺得沒有希望了，馬車出不來了。這時來了一隻又骯髒又邋遢的豬，嘟噥着說：“咕噥噥！咕噥噥！咕噥噥！國王呀，把你的小女兒給我，我就把你從泥潭裏拉出來。”國王急於脫困，沒有深想便答應了。豬用鼻子把馬車一拱，就把馬和車立即拱出泥

out of the mud. Having arrived at home the king handed the dresses to his two daughters, and was now sadder than ever that he had brought nothing for his favourite daughter; the thought also troubled him that he had promised her to an unclean animal.

After a short time the pig arrived in the courtyard of the palace, dragging a wheelbarrow after it, and grunted, "Grumph! grumph! grumph! King, I've come for your daughter."

The king was terrified, and, in order to save his daughter, he sent her down, as promised, but dressed in ragged, dirty tatters, thinking that she would not please the pig; but the animal grunted in great joy, seized the girl, placed her in the wheelbarrow.

The pig went on and on with the sobbing girl, till, after a long journey, it stopped before a dirty pig-sty and grunted, "Grumph! grumph! grumph! Girl, get out of the wheelbarrow." The girl did as she was told. "Grumph! grumph! grumph!" grunted the pig again; "go into your new home."

The girl, whose tears, now, were streaming like a brook, obeyed; the pig then offered her some Indian corn[1] that it had in a trough, and also its litter which consisted of some old straw, for a resting-place. The girl had not a wink of sleep for a long time, till at last, quite worn out with mental torture, she fell asleep.

Being completely exhausted with all her trials, she slept so soundly that she did not wake till next day at noon. On awakening, she looked round, and was very much astonished to find herself in a beautiful fairy-like palace, her bed being of white silk with rich purple curtains and golden fringes. At

---

1. Indian corn：〔英〕玉米。

潭。到家後，國王把衣服給了兩個女兒，但因為沒有東西給最疼愛的小女兒，心裏更難過了。想到還把她許了給一隻骯髒的豬，更是懊惱。

過了不久，那隻豬來到王宮內院，還拖着一輛手推車，哼着說：「咕嚕嚕！咕嚕嚕！咕嚕嚕！國王，我接你的女兒來了。」

國王驚駭萬分，但為了實踐諾言，只好送小女兒出去。但他為了救下女兒，便讓她穿上又髒又破的衣服，想着這樣一來豬就不喜歡她了。可是那隻豬高興得又咕嚕又哼哼，一把拉住姑娘，讓她坐上了手推車。

這豬走啊走，姑娘哭啊哭，走了很長的路之後，豬在一個豬圈前停下，哼着道：「咕嚕嚕！咕嚕嚕！咕嚕嚕！姑娘，下車吧。」姑娘下了車。「咕嚕嚕！咕嚕嚕！咕嚕嚕！」豬又哼哼：「進你的新家去。」

姑娘淚如雨下，聽話地進去了；豬盛一木槽玉米給她吃，讓她在他的舊稻草窩裏休息。姑娘躺下半天不能闔眼，後來因為心靈受到折磨，實在太倦了，才沉沉睡去。

經歷了這些磨難，她筋疲力竭，酣睡到次日午間才醒來。她看看四周，驚異地發現自己竟是在一座美如仙境的宮殿裏。牀上鋪的是雪白的絲綢，掛着華麗的紫色帷幕和金色的流蘇。她一醒來，就有侍女送上貴重的衣裙，然後

the first sign of her waking, maids appeared, bringing her costly dresses. They accompanied her to her breakfast in a splendid hall, where a young man received her with great affection. After breakfast he led her into a beautiful garden and came to that part of the garden which was laid out as an orchard, and the bunches of grapes began to speak, "Our beautiful queen, pluck some of us." The apples smiled at her continuously, and the apricots tinkled a beautiful silvery tune. "You see, my love," said the handsome youth, "here you have what you wished for. You may know now, that once I was a monarch but I was bewitched into a pig and I had to remain in that state till a girl wished for speaking grapes, a smiling apple, and a tinkling apricot. You are the girl and I have been delivered; and if I please you you can be mine forever." The girl was enchanted with the handsome youth and the royal splendour, and consented. They went with great joy to carry the news to their father, and to tell him of their happiness.

— *Rev. W.H. Jones*

陪侍她到一個豪華的大廳裏用早餐。那裏有個年青人熱情
地迎接她。飯後他帶着她進入一個美麗的花園，走到花園
中的一個果園裏。這時一串串葡萄開始説話了：“美麗的
王后，請把我們摘下幾串來吧。”蘋果不斷對她微笑，杏
子叮叮噹噹地發出銀鈴似的音調。那英俊的青年説：“親
愛的，你看，你想要的東西就在這裏。現在可以告訴你
了：我原來是個君王，被妖法變成豬。除非有個姑娘發出
願望，想要會説話的葡萄、會笑的蘋果和叮噹響的杏子，
我才能變回人形。你就是這位姑娘，你解救了我。要是你
願意的話，你就永遠是我的人了。”姑娘看到青年人又英
俊，王家一切富麗堂皇，便答應了。他們興高采烈把喜訊
送給她父親，並告訴他他們非常幸福。

——*W·H·*瓊斯神父

45 The Crow (Poland)

Once upon a time there were three princesses who were all young and beautiful; but the youngest, was the most lovable of them all. About half a mile from the palace in which they lived stood a castle. It was uninhabited and almost a ruin, but the garden was a mass of blooming flowers, and in this garden the youngest princess used often to walk.

One day, when she was pacing to and fro under the lime trees, a black crow hopped out of a rosebush in front of her. It was torn and bleeding, and the kind little princess was quite unhappy about it. When the crow saw this it turned to her and said: "I am an enchanted prince. If you only liked, Princess, you could save me. But you would have to say good-bye to all your own people and be my constant companion in this ruined castle. There is one habitable room in it. You will have to live all by yourself and, whatever you may see or hear in the night, you must not scream out, for if you do so my sufferings will be doubled." The good-natured princess at once left her home and her family and hurried to the ruined castle and took possession of the room with a golden bed.

At midnight she heard to her great horror someone coming along the passage, and in a moment her door was flung wide open and a troop of strange beings entered the room. They at once proceeded to light a fire in the huge fireplace; then they placed a great caldron of boiling water on it. When they had done this, they approached the bed on which the trembling girl lay and, screaming and yelling, they dragged her toward the caldron. She nearly died with fright,

四十五　烏鴉[1]（波蘭）

從前，有三位公主，個個年輕貌美，其中小公主最可愛。離她們住的宮殿半里路有一座城堡，裏面無人居住，幾乎是一片廢墟，但花園卻鮮花盛開。小公主常到園裏散步。

一天，她正在椴樹下漫步，一隻黑烏鴉從她面前的玫瑰花叢中跳出來，渾身是傷，鮮血淋漓。小公主心地善良，見到這樣子心生惻隱。烏鴉見她如此，便轉身對她說：“我是個被施了妖術的王子。公主，只要你願意就可以救我。但是你得告別所有親人，在這廢城堡裏和我長相廝守。城堡裏有一間可以住的房間，你要一個人住在裏面。夜裏不管看到聽到甚麼，都一定不能叫喊。一出聲，我受的苦難就要加倍了。”好心的公主立刻離開家園和親人，趕快回到廢城堡，住進了那鋪有一張金牀的房間。

夜半時分，她聽到有人沿着走廊走來，她十分驚恐。不一會兒，房門被大力推開，一羣怪物進了房間。他們立刻在巨大的壁爐裏生上火，然後在火上放了一大鍋滾開的水。之後，他們走近那張牀鋪，小姑娘正躺在上面嚇得簌簌發抖。他們尖聲嘶叫，把她拖向大鍋。她嚇得半死，卻

---

1. 本篇選自《童話與民間故事》（*Klethe*）。

but she never uttered a sound. Then of a sudden the cock crew, and all the evil spirits vanished. At the same moment the crow appeared and hopped round the room with joy. It thanked the princess most heartily for her goodness and said that its sufferings had already been greatly lessened.

So she lived in solitude all the daytime, and at night she would have been frightened had she not been so brave. But every day the crow came and thanked her for her endurance and assured her that his sufferings were far less than they had been. And so two years passed away, when one day the crow came to the princess and said: "In another year I shall be freed from the spell I am under. But before I can resume my natural form and take possession of the belongings of my forefathers, you must go out into the world and take service as a maidservant."

The young princess consented at once, and for a whole year she served as a maid. One evening, when she was spinning flax and had worked until her little hands were weary, she heard a rustling beside her and a cry of joy. Then she saw a handsome youth standing beside her, who knelt down at her feet and kissed the little weary hands. "I am the prince," he said, "whom in your goodness you freed from the most awful torments. Come now to my castle with me, and let us live there happily together."

So they went to the castle where they had both endured so much. But when they reached it, it had all been magnificently rebuilt. And there they lived for a hundred years of joy and happiness.

— Polish Folk Tale

始終不出一聲。突然間雄雞高唱，所有的鬼怪頓時消失。這時，烏鴉來了，它高興地在房間裏跳來跳去，由衷地感謝公主的好心幫助，說它的痛苦已經大大減輕了。

就這樣，白天她形單影隻地生活；夜晚，要是她不是那麼勇敢的話，就要被嚇壞了。但烏鴉每天都來感謝她表現出的堅忍毅力，而且說他的苦痛已日漸減輕。兩年過去了。一天，烏鴉來對公主說：“再有一年我就要脫離魔障了，可是在我恢復原身，繼承祖業之前，你要出去做個婢女。”

小公主馬上同意了。她做了整整一年的婢女。一天傍晚，她在紡麻紗，兩隻小手都已疲累不堪。這時，她聽到身旁沙沙作響，又有一聲快樂的叫聲。之後，她看到一位英俊的年輕人站在她身旁。他在她腳前跪下，吻着那痠痛的小手。“我就是那個王子，”他說，“就是因你的善良而從最可怕的痛苦中解救出來的人。跟我到我的城堡去，一起快樂幸福地住在那兒吧。”

於是，他們去到那個他們倆共同受過如許苦難的城堡。但他們來到時，整座城堡都重建得富麗堂皇了。他們在那裏幸福美滿地生活了一百年。

———— *波蘭民間故事*

46 The Heavy Sword (Poland)

There was once upon a time a witch, who in the shape of a hawk would every night break the windows of a certain village church. In the same village there lived three brothers, who determined to kill the mischievous hawk. But in vain did the two eldest mount guard. As soon as the bird appeared high above their heads, sleep overpowered them, and they only awoke to hear the windows crashing in. Then the youngest brother took his turn at guarding the windows, and to prevent sleep he placed a lot of thorns under his chin. The moon was already risen, and it was as light as day, when suddenly he heard a fearful noise, and at the same time his eyelids closed, and his head sank on his shoulders. But the thorns were so painful that he awoke at once. He saw the hawk swooping down upon the church, and in a moment he seized his gun and shot at the bird. The hawk fell heavily upon a big stone, severely wounded. The youth ran to look at it and saw that a huge abyss had opened below the stone.

He went at once to fetch his brothers, and determined to explore the abyss and, letting himself down by a rope, soon reached the bottom. Here he found a lovely meadow full of green trees and exquisite flowers. In the middle of the meadow stood a huge stone castle, with its iron gate wide open. A lovely girl was combing her golden hair. The youth looked at her more closely and saw that her skin was smooth and fair, her blue eyes bright and sparkling and her hair as golden as the sun. He fell in love with her on the spot and, kneeling at her feet, implored her to become his wife.

The lovely girl accepted him gladly but warned him she could never come up to the world above till the old witch

四十六　沉重的劍（波蘭）

　　從前有個巫婆，每天夜裏化作一隻鷹把村裏教堂的窗戶打破。這村裏住着兄弟三人，決心殺死這隻為非作歹的鷹。可是老大、老二守夜都不成功，鷹一飛到頭頂，他們便沉沉熟睡。醒來時已聽到窗戶嘩啦啦地被撞碎了。後來輪到小弟弟來守護窗戶。為了不打瞌睡，他在下頦下面放了一大把荊棘。當月上中天，照得如同白晝之時，他突然聽見一種駭人的聲音，雙眼同時也就闔上了，頭垂落到肩膀上。但荊棘刺得劇痛，他立刻醒過來，只見惡鷹向教堂猛撲。他馬上舉槍向鷹射擊。鷹沉重地摔落到一塊大石上，受了重傷。年青人跑過去看，只見石頭下面裂開一條深淵。

　　他立即把兩個哥哥找來，同時決定下去看看。他拉着一根繩子下去，很快就到了深淵底。下面有一片美麗的草地，樹木青翠、百花爭妍。草地中央聳立着一座巨大的石砌城堡，鐵門洞開。有位可愛的姑娘正梳理她的金髮。年青人仔細端詳，只見她皮膚光潔細膩，碧眼明亮晶瑩，頭髮金光燦爛。年青人立時愛上了她，向她跪下求婚。

　　可愛的姑娘樂意地答應了，可是告誡他說，要是女巫不死，她永遠不能去到地面的世界上；而只有用懸在城堡

was dead. The only way the witch could be killed was with the sword hanging in the castle; but the sword was so heavy no one could lift it. Then the youth found a room where another beautiful girl, the sister of his bride, handed him the sword. But though he tried with all his strength he could not lift it. At last a third sister came to him and gave him something to drink. After he had drunk three drops of it, he was able to swing the sword over his head.

Then he hid himself in the castle and awaited the old witch's arrival. At last, as it was beginning to grow dark, she swooped down upon a big apple tree and pounced down upon the earth. When her feet touched the ground she turned from a hawk into a woman. The youth swung his mighty sword with all his strength and the witch's head fell off.

He packed up all the treasures of the castle in a great chest, and gave his brothers a signal to pull them up out of the abyss. First the treasures were attached to the rope and then the three lovely girls. Now everything was up above and only he remained below. As he was a little suspicious of his brothers, he fastened a heavy stone to the rope and let them pull it up. When the stone was halfway up they let it drop suddenly, and it fell to the bottom and broke into a hundred pieces. "So that's what would have happened to my bones had I trusted myself to them," said the youth sadly.

For a long time he wandered sadly through the underworld, and one day he met a magician and told him all that had befallen him, and the magician said, "Do not grieve, young man! Hide yourself here, and at midnight you will see our enemy."

At midnight the youth beheld a long thick serpent crawling towards them. Then he swung his mighty sword in the air and with one blow cut off the serpent's head. The magician was so delighted that he carried him up to the world above.

裏的那把劍才能殺死女巫。但那劍十分沉重，無人能舉起。於是年青人找到了一個房間，裏面又有一位美麗的姑娘，是他未婚妻的姐妹。她遞給他一把劍。但他用盡全身氣力也拿不起來。最後，第三個姐妹來到，給他喝了點東西，他喝下三滴，就能揮劍過頭頂了。

於是他藏在城堡裏等着老女巫來。天漸轉黑，巫婆便飛撲在一棵大蘋果樹上，又跳落地下；雙腳一觸地，便從鷹變成一個女人。年青人用盡全力，重劍一揮，女巫的頭顱應聲落地。

年青人將城堡裏的財寶全部裝進一個大箱裏，向兄弟發出信號，讓他們把他們拉上去。他先用繩子吊起財寶，然後又吊起三位美麗的姑娘。這時人和物都到了地面，只有他留在地下。他對兄弟存了點戒心，便將一塊沉重的石頭縛在繩子上讓他們拉上去。他們拉到一半，突然鬆手，石頭掉到溝底，摔得粉碎。年青人傷心地説："假如我信任了他們，恐怕我此時已粉身碎骨。"

他憂傷地在地下世界徬徨徘徊，過了很久。一天他遇到一位魔術師並告訴了他自己的全部遭遇。魔術師説："年青人，別難過！你藏身在這地方，半夜就會見到我們的仇人。"

到了半夜，年青人看見一條又長又粗的蟒蛇向他們爬過來。年青人揮起重劍，只一下便砍斷蛇頭。魔術師十分高興，便把年青人送上了地面。

With what joy did he hurry now to his brothers' house! He burst into a room where they were all assembled, but no one knew who he was. Only his bride recognized him at once. His brothers, who had quite believed he was dead, flew into the woods in terror. But the good youth forgave them all they had done. At last he lived happily with his golden-haired wife till the end of their lives.

— *Polish Folk Tale*

他向兄弟的家跑去，這時他是多麼高興啊！他衝進屋去，他們正聚在一起呢，可都不知道他是誰。只有他的未婚妻一眼便認出了他。他的兄弟原以為他已經摔死，嚇得逃進樹林。但好心的年青人對他們不究既往。最後，他和他的金髮愛妻幸福地過了一輩子。

—— *波蘭民間故事*

47 The Hazelnut Child (Bukovina)

There was once upon a time a couple who had no children, and they prayed every day for a child, though it were no bigger than a hazelnut. At last their prayer was heard and they had a child exactly the size of a hazelnut, who never grew an inch. The parents were devoted to the little creature and nursed and tended it carefully. Their tiny son was as clever as could be, and sensible.

When the hazelnut child was fifteen years old, he was sitting one day in an eggshell on the table beside his mother. She turned to him, and said, "You are now fifteen years old. What do you intend to be?"

"A messenger," answered the hazelnut child.

Then his mother burst out laughing, and said, "What an idea! Why, your little feet would take an hour to go the distance an ordinary person could do in a minute!"

But the hazelnut child replied, "Just send me with a message and you'll see that I shall be back in next to no time[1]."

So his mother said, "Very well, go to your aunt in the neighboring village, and fetch me a comb."

The hazelnut child jumped quickly out of the eggshell and ran out into the street. Here he found a man on horseback who was just setting out for the neighboring village. He crept up the horse's leg, sat down under the saddle, and then began to pinch the horse. The horse set off at a hard gallop, in spite of its rider's efforts to stop it. When they reached the village,

---

1. next to no time：幾乎不用甚麼時間。

四十七 榛子大的小人兒[1] （布科維納）

　　從前，有一對夫婦沒有孩子，他們天天祈禱上天賜給他們一個孩子，哪怕只有榛子那麼一點大也好。最後上天聽到他們的祈禱，他們真的有了一個恰好就像榛子那麼大的孩子，一吋也不長。兩口子百般呵護這小傢伙，無微不至地撫養照料他。這小小的兒子要聰明有多聰明，又明白事理。

　　榛子大小人兒長到十五歲，一天，坐在媽媽身旁桌上的一個蛋殼裏。媽媽轉身對他説：“你十五歲啦，打算做個甚麼呀？”

　　“當個送信的吧。”小人兒答。

　　媽媽忍不住哈哈大笑，説：“想得倒好！咳，普通人走一分鐘的路你那雙小腳得走上一個鐘頭！”

　　可是小人兒回答：“給我個差事試試，你看只要一眨眼工夫我就回來啦。”

　　媽媽説：“好吧，到鄰村你姨媽家去，給我拿把梳子來。”

　　榛子大小人兒一跳跳出蛋殼，跑到街上去了。他看到一個人騎在馬上，正朝鄰村方向去，便順着馬腿輕輕爬上去，坐在馬鞍下。他不斷地搯那馬，馬飛跑起來，騎馬人怎麼也勒不住它。等他們到了那村子，榛子大小人兒便住

---

1. 選自《布科維納故事與傳説》。布科維納（Bukovina）為東歐一地區，今在羅馬尼亞及烏克蘭一帶。

the hazelnut child left off pinching the horse, and the poor tired creature pursued its way at a snail's pace. The hazelnut child took advantage of this and crept down the horse's leg. Then he ran to his aunt and asked her for a comb. On the way home he met another rider and did the return journey in exactly the same way.

He handed his mother the comb and said, "Ah, Mother, you see I was quite right."

One day, his father told him to look after his horse in the field. A robber passed by and saw the horse grazing without anyone watching it. He mounted the horse and rode away. But the hazelnut child climbed up the horse's tail and talked to it. So it paid no attention to the robber but galloped straight home. The father was astonished when he saw a stranger riding his horse, but the hazelnut child climbed down quickly and told him all that had happened, and his father had the robber arrested.

One autumn when the hazelnut child was twenty years old he said to his parents, "Farewell, my dear Father and Mother. I am going out into the world, and as soon as I have become rich I will return home to you."

In the evening the hazelnut child crept on to the roof, where some storks had built their nest. The storks were fast asleep and he climbed onto the back of the father stork and bound himself by a silk cord to one of its wings. Then he crept among its soft down feathers and fell asleep.

Next morning the storks flew toward the south, for winter was approaching. The hazelnut child flew through the air on the stork's back. In this way he reached the country of the black people. When the people saw the hazelnut child they were much astonished, and took him with the stork to the king of the country. The king was delighted with the little creature and kept him always beside him and soon grew so

手不掐。可憐那馬跑累了，繼續趕路，慢得像蝸牛。小人兒趁馬走得慢，順着馬腿溜了下來，然後跑去姨媽家，向她要了一把梳子。回家的路上，他又碰見另一個騎馬的人，如法炮制走完了歸程。

他把梳子遞給媽媽，説："哈，媽媽，我説對了吧。"

一天，他父親吩咐他看管在田野裏的馬兒，一個強盜路過，看見這馬正吃草，沒人看管，便騎上走了。可是小人兒爬上馬尾，對馬説了幾句話，馬便不聽強盜的，一直奔回家去。父親見一個陌生人騎在他的馬上，很奇怪。但小人兒快快地爬下來，告訴了他怎麼一回事，父親便把強盜抓了起來。

小人兒二十歲那年的秋天，他對父母説："再見了，親愛的爸爸媽媽，我要出去闖世界了。等發了財，我會回家的。"

晚上，小人兒爬到房頂上，那兒有個鸛巢，幾隻鸛鳥正熟睡着。他爬上雄鸛背，用絲索把自己**縛**在鸛的翅膀上，然後就輕輕爬到柔軟的絨毛中睡着了。

第二天早晨，因為冬季將臨，鸛鳥向南飛去。小人兒騎在鸛背上穿雲破霧，就這樣到了一個黑人的國家。人們見到小人兒都很驚異，將他和鸛一起帶去見國王。國王很

fond of him that he gave him a diamond four times as big as himself.

The hazelnut child fastened the diamond firmly under his stork's neck with a ribbon. When he saw the storks were getting ready for their northern flight he mounted the bird and away they went. At length the hazelnut child came to his native village. He undid the ribbon from the stork's neck and the diamond fell to the ground. He covered it first with sand and stones and then ran to get his parents. He himself was not able to lift the great diamond.

So the hazelnut child and his parents lived together in happiness and prosperity.

— Von Wliolocki

喜歡這小人兒，常常把他帶在身邊，很快便更寵愛他，賜給他一塊比他本人還大四倍的金剛鑽。

　　小人兒用絲帶把這塊鑽石緊緊縛在鸛鳥頸下。當他見到鸛鳥準備北飛時，便爬上鸛背一起飛走了。最後，小人兒到了故鄉，他鬆開鸛頸上絲帶，鑽石落到地上。他先用沙土石子埋上鑽石，然後跑去找他的父母。他自己可抬不動這塊大鑽石啊。

　　從此，小人兒和父母住在一起，過着幸福富足的生活。

—— 馮·符里奧洛斯基

48 The Death of the Sun-Hero (Bukovina)

Many, many thousands of years ago there lived a mighty king whom Heaven had blessed with a clever and beautiful son. When he was only ten years old the boy was more clever than all the king's counselors, and when he was twenty he was thought the greatest hero in the whole kingdom. All the people in the land loved him dearly, and called him the Sun-Hero.

Now it happened one night that both his parents had the same extraordinary dream that a girl all dressed in red come to them and said, "If you wish that your son might really become the Sun-Hero in deed and not only in name, let him go out into the world and search for the Tree of the Sun, and let him pluck a golden apple from it and bring it home." They at once bade their son set forth in search of the Tree of the Sun. The prince was delighted and set out on his travels that very day.

For a long time he wandered all through the world, and at last he arrived at a golden castle, which stood in the middle of a vast wilderness. Finding no one about, the prince rode on and came to a great meadow, where the Tree of the Sun grew. He put out his hand to pick a golden apple. But all of a sudden the tree grew higher so he could not reach its fruit. Then he heard someone behind him laughing. Turning round he saw a girl in red walking toward him.

"Do you really imagine, brave son of the earth, that you can pluck an apple so easily from the Tree of the Sun?" she said. "Before you can do that, you must guard the tree for nine days and nine nights from the ravages of two wild black wolves. If you do not succeed, the Sun will kill you." With

四十八 太陽勇士之死（布科維納）

多少萬年以前，有一位偉大的國王，上天賜給他一個
又聰明又英俊的兒子。這孩子長到十歲，聰明才智便勝過
了國王所有的大臣，二十歲的時候，人們都認為他是全王
國最偉大的英雄了。國中所有的臣民衷心愛戴他，稱他為
太陽勇士。

一天夜裏，他的父母做了同樣的怪夢，夢中一位全身
穿着紅衣的少女走來對他們説：“如果你們想使自己的兒
子成為真正的太陽勇士而不是徒有虛名，就讓他走遍世
界，尋找太陽之樹吧，讓他從樹上摘個金蘋果帶回家來。”
他們立即讓兒子出發去找太陽之樹，王子十分高興，當天
便動身了。

他走遍世界，尋找了很長時間，最後來到莽莽荒原中
的一座金色城堡前。王子見四周無人，縱馬前行，走到一
片廣闊的草地上，那裏生長着那棵太陽之樹。他伸手剛要
去摘金蘋果，但樹卻陡然長高，他搆不到蘋果了。接着他
又聽到身後傳來笑聲，轉過身去，見是一個紅衣少女向他
走來。

“勇敢的大地之子啊，你難道真的以為這麼輕而易舉就
能從太陽樹上摘下蘋果嗎？”她説，“你必須守護着這株
樹九日九夜，不讓兩頭黑色野狼把樹毀掉，才能摘到蘋
果。假如你做不到的話，太陽神會殺了你。”説着，紅衣

these words the Red Girl went back into the golden castle. She had hardly left him when the two black wolves appeared. The Sun-Hero beat them off with his sword, and they retired, only to reappear in a very short time. This went on for seven days and nights, when the white horse that his mother had given him turned to the Sun-Hero and said:

"Listen to what I am going to say. A fairy gave me to your mother that I might be of service to you. The fairy also put everyone in the world under a spell, to prevent their obeying the Sun's command to take your life. But she forgot one person, who will certainly kill you if you fall asleep and let the wolves damage the tree!"

Then the Sun-Hero strove with all his might and kept the black wolves at bay and conquered his desire to sleep. But on the eighth night his strength failed him, and he fell fast asleep. When he awoke a woman in black stood beside him, who said, "You have let the two black wolves damage the Tree of the Sun. I am the mother of the Sun, and I command you to ride away from here at once. I pronounce sentence of death upon you, for you proudly let yourself be called the Sun-Hero without having done anything to deserve the name." The youth mounted his horse sadly and rode home.

After a time the prince forgot all about his adventure, and married a beautiful princess, with whom he lived very happily. But one day, when he was out hunting, he felt very thirsty, and coming to a stream he stooped down to drink from it. This caused his death, for a crab came swimming up, and with its claws tore out his tongue. He was carried home, and as he lay on his deathbed the black woman appeared and said:

少女轉身走回金色城堡。她剛離開，兩頭黑狼便來了。太陽勇士用寶劍將它們擊退，可一轉眼它們又來了，這樣鏖戰了七日七夜。這時母親送給太陽勇士的白馬向他說：

"聽着我說的話，我是一位仙子送給你母親供您驅使的，這位仙子還對世上所有人都施了魔法，不讓他們遵從太陽神的旨意去殺您，可她卻漏掉了一個人。如果您睡着，讓狼毀了這樹，那個人肯定會殺了你的。"

於是太陽勇士鼓足全力，不讓黑狼越雷池半步，同時勉強壓下昏昏睡意。可到了第八個夜晚，他精疲力竭，沉沉睡去。等到他醒來時，一個黑衣女人站在他身旁說："你已經讓兩頭黑狼毀了這太陽樹。我是太陽神的母親，我命令你立刻騎馬離開這裏，並宣判你的死刑。因為你竟敢驕傲地稱為太陽勇士，卻毫無勞績，徒有其名。"年青人垂頭喪氣上馬回家去了。

過了一段時間，王子將這番遭遇忘得一乾二淨，娶了一位美麗的公主，生活得很幸福。可是一天，他出外打獵時，覺得十分口渴，便來到一條小溪旁，彎身喝水。這就帶來殺身之禍，一隻螃蟹游上來用蟹鉗撕下他的舌頭。人們把他抬回家，臨終時，黑衣女人出現了，說：

"So the Sun has, after all, found someone who was not under the fairy's spell. A similar fate will overtake everyone who wrongfully assumes a title to which he has no right."

— Von Wliolocki

"你看太陽神終於找到了沒有被仙子施過魔法的一位。凡是錯誤地給自己加上不符其實的虛名的人都會有同樣的下場。"

—— 馮·符甲奧洛斯基

Northern European Tales
北歐童話

49 The Golden Ship (Finland)

In olden[1] days, there lived in Finland a woodsman whose name was Toivo. He got a golden ship from the Gnomes of the mountain when the latter had a quarrel among themselves over their wealth. Afterwards, Toivo got on the golden ship loaded with gold and the ship leaped down the steep mountain and far out across the sea. Soon after Toivo brought it to a perfect landing before the King's castle.

It happened that the King's daughter was on the castle steps at that very moment. All at once she saw the golden ship. "This must surely be a prince from some wonderful country," she said to herself. So she asked if Toivo would marry her. But he was so humble and not worthy. Yet the Princess begged and begged for seven days. At last he consented and let the Princess step into the ship and asked where she would like to go. "To the very middle of the sea. I've heard that there is an island where the berry bushes are loaded with red and purple fruit."

The golden ship flew over land and sea. Soon it dived from the sky right down to the center of an island. Toivo jumped out and ran to look for the purple and red berries.

The first berries that he found were yellow. Toivo tasted them, and he fell to the ground in a deep sleep. The Princess waited for three days and decided that he had deserted her, and she grew very angry and flew back to the castle on the ship.

---

1. olden：〔古〕古昔的。

四十九　金船[1]（芬蘭）

　　古時候，芬蘭有個名叫托伊沃的樵夫。他乘着山精們為財富發生爭吵時，他從他們手裏奪到一艘金船。他跳上滿載金子的船，將船駛下陡壁，跨海而去。不久，托伊沃駕船在一座王宮前穩穩地着陸了。

　　這時正巧公主在宮殿的台階上，她一眼看見了金船。"這一定是從哪個富饒國家來的王子，"她自言自語説。因此她便問托伊沃是否願意娶她。但托伊沃自慚形穢，覺得配不上。公主苦苦求了七天，最後，他同意了，請公主上了金船，問她要去哪裏。"咱們到大海的正中央去吧。傳説中那裏有個島，上面長滿了草莓樹，結着紅色和紫色的果子。"

　　金船飛過陸地，飛過海洋，很快便從天上落到一個海島的中央。托伊沃跳下船，跑去找那紫色和紅色的草莓。

　　他找到的第一種草莓是黃色的，剛嚐了嚐，便一頭栽到地上昏睡不醒。公主等了三天，斷定他拋棄了她，非常生氣，便乘船飛回城堡。

---

1. 本篇選自 *Tales from a Finnish Tupa*。

253

At the end of another day, Toivo woke up. He searched everywhere, but he could not find the golden ship nor the Princess. He hunted high and low and found a bush laden with purple berries. Toivo filled his left pocket with the fruit and thrust a berry into his mouth. All at once he felt horns growing out from his head, monstrous pronged horns like the antlers of a wild moose. They were heavy and they hurt terribly. Then he saw a bush with red berries on it. He filled his right pocket this time, and crunched one of the red berries between his teeth. No sooner had he done so than the heavy horns fell by magic from his head and he became the most handsome man in the world.

Next day a ship appeared over the edge of the sea. The sailors gladly took Toivo and set him down before the King's castle. There he walked through the garden and met the King's Butler. He took a shining red berry from his right pocket and gave it to the Butler who crunched the berry between his teeth, and at once became the handsomest man in the kingdom, next of course to Toivo himself. He was so delighted that he hid Toivo in a corner of the pantry.

At dinner time the Princess saw how wonderfully changed the Butler was in his looks, and it made her very curious and asked him what had happened. He told her everything. The Princess told the Butler to fetch Toivo. When the Princess saw Toivo, he was so handsome that she did not know him at all. She said, "If you can make me as beautiful as you are handsome, I'll be your bride." Toivo became hot with anger. "Very well," he said, "Eat this berry." He took a purple berry from his left pocket, and as the Princess crunched the berry between her teeth a pair of monstrous pronged horns grew out from her head.

Toivo ran off to hide. The King sent soldiers into every part of his kingdom with this message: "Whoever will cure

第二天黃昏，托伊沃醒來，他找遍全島也不見金船和公主的蹤影。他攀高爬低地尋找，找到一叢草莓樹，上面掛滿了紫草莓。托伊沃把紫草莓裝滿了左邊口袋，又把一個草莓放進嘴裏。他立刻覺得頭上長出了碩大無朋的、開叉的角，就像野鹿角那樣。角很重，而且長在頭上伸他痛徹心肺。後來，他又看到一叢長着紅草莓的樹，這回他裝滿了右邊口袋。他用牙咬一口一個紅草莓，不一會兒，沉重的角奇蹟般從頭上落下來，他變成了世上最英俊的男人。

　　第二天，一條船出現在天際，船上的水手們熱情地讓他上船，把他載到王宮前。他穿過花園，碰到了國王的司膳官。他從右邊口袋拿出一顆亮晶晶的紅草莓給那司膳官，那人咬了一口，馬上就變成了全王國最英俊的人——當然啦，僅次於托伊沃。他高興極了，把托伊沃藏在廚房的角落裏。

　　吃晚飯時，公主見司膳官的儀表變得這樣英俊，覺得很奇怪，便問他怎麼回事？他把一切和盤托出。公主吩咐司膳官把托伊沃帶來，因為他變得那麼瀟灑英俊，公主見到他一點也認不出了。她說：「你要是把我變得和你一樣漂亮，我就嫁給你。」托伊沃怒火中燒，便說：「很好，吃了這顆草莓吧。」他從左邊口袋拿出了一個紫草莓。公主剛咬了一口，頭上便長出了一對其大無比的、有叉的角。

　　托伊沃跑開藏了起來。國王派士兵走遍全國傳令：有誰能去掉公主的怪角，便可以娶公主為妻。醫生、巫師、

the King's daughter by removing her monstrous horns shall receive the hand of the King's daughter in marriage." From every part of the kingdom came doctors and healers and magicians. They tried all their medicines and potions, all their spells and wonders. But the horns still remained.

At last, after many days, Toivo came forward from the crowd and knelt before the King, saying: "O King, I am the only one who knows the right charm." Then he asked the page boy to fetch him three long straight willow twigs and called for the Princess. He shut the door, set the Princess on a bench, and began to beat her soundly with the willow twigs. "I'll teach you to run away with my golden ship and leave me to die in the middle of the sea!" he shouted between the strokes. "I am Toivo, the man you promised to marry!"

The Princess's shoulders were soon red and welted from the blows of the willow twigs. She cried: "Stop beating me, stop beating me and I'll explain everything. For three long days and nights I waited for you. I can't tell you how lonely it seemed. I felt sure you had deserted me." When Toivo heard this he drew a shining red berry from his right pocket. The Princess crunched it between her teeth; at once the ugly horns fell from her head and her face became as fair as a new-blown rose.

Toivo married his Princess and they lived happily ever after.

— *J.C. Bowman and M. Bianco*

術士從全國各地紛至沓來，試盡各種藥方，施盡各種法術，但那角仍在頭上。

過了許多天，托伊沃才從人羣中走出，跪在國王面前，說："陛下，只有我才有醫治的符咒。"他讓一個書僮去拿二根又長又直的柳枝來，又叫來公主，把門關上，把公主按在長凳上，用柳枝使勁把她抽打起來。"我要好好教訓你，叫你偷走我的金船把我扔在大海中等死！"他一邊打一邊喊："我就是托伊沃，就是你答應要嫁的那個人！"

公主的肩膀被打得通紅，鞭痕纍纍。她喊："別打啦，讓我給你解釋。我等了你整整三天三夜，說不出的孤單，我以為你肯定是拋棄了我。"托伊沃聽到這些話，便從右邊口袋裏掏出一顆晶瑩的紅草莓，公主用牙一咬，醜怪的角立刻從頭上落下，她面孔變得十分嬌好，像朵新綻開的玫瑰。

托伊沃娶了公主，從此過着幸福美滿的生活。

——J·C·鮑曼與 M·白安科

50 The Husband Who Was to Mind the House
(Norway)

Once upon a time there was a man so surly and cross, he never thought his wife did anything right in the house. So, one evening in hay-making time, he came home, scolding and swearing, and showing his teeth and making a dust.

"Dear love, don't be so angry; there's a good man," said his goody; "to-morrow let's change our work." Yes, the husband thought that would do very well. He was quite willing, he said.

So, early next morning his goody took a scythe over her neck, and went out into the hay-field with the mowers and began to mow; but the man was to mind the house, and do the work at home. First of all he wanted to churn the butter; but when he had churned a while, he got thirsty, and went down to the cellar to tap a barrel of ale. So, just when he had knocked in the bung, and was putting the tap into the cask, he heard overhead the pig come into the kitchen. Then off he ran up the cellar steps, with the tap in his hand, to look after the pig, lest it should upset the churn; but when he got up, and saw that the pig had already knocked the churn over, and the cream was running all over the floor, he got so wild with rage that he quite forgot the ale-barrel, and ran at the pig and gave it such a kick that piggy lay for dead on the spot. Then all at once he remembered he had the tap in his hand; but when he got down to the cellar, every drop of ale had run out of the cask.

Then he went into the dairy and found enough cream left to fill the churn again, and so he began to churn. When he had churned a bit, he remembered that their milking cow was still shut up in the byre, and hadn't had a bit to eat or a

五十　操持家務的丈夫[1]（挪威）

從前有個人脾氣實在暴躁蠻橫，太太在家裏做甚麼他都說做得不好。正當翻曬乾草的季節，一天晚上，他回到家就口出惡言，呲牙咧嘴地鬧得雞飛狗跑。

"親愛的，別發火。好啦，好啦，乖乖聽話！"他的伴兒說，"明天咱們換一下工種。"好啊，丈夫覺得這樣再好不過，便說他願意。

第二天清早，他的伴兒肩上扛着大鐮刀，和割草的莊稼人到牧場去割起草來。男人則留在家做家務。首先，他得攪拌奶油做黃油。可攪了一會兒，渴了，便下到地窖要打一小桶麥酒。他剛敲開桶塞，正要把活嘴子插進大酒桶，就聽見上面豬進了廚房。他拿着活嘴子，三步兩步跑上樓去照看豬，免得它把攪乳器碰翻。可他到了樓上，見豬已經把攪乳器碰得底朝天，奶油流了一地。他氣得發瘋，竟忘記了地窖裏的麥酒桶桶塞開着，他追上小豬，狠狠踢了一腳，豬當場躺在地上，相信是死了。這時，他忽然記起活嘴子還在手裏。可等他跑下地窖，大桶裏的麥酒已經淌得一滴不剩。

他走進乳牛棚，找來剩下的奶油，倒夠裝滿攪乳器的。他又開始攪拌。攪了一會兒，想起奶牛還關在牛棚

1.　選自《挪威民間故事》。

drop to drink all the morning. Then he thought 'twas[1] too far
to take her down to the meadow, so he'd just get her up on
the housetop — for the house was thatched with sods, and a
fine crop of grass was growing there. Now their house lay
close up against a steep down, and he thought if he laid a
plank across to the thatch at the back he'd easily get the cow
up. But still he couldn't leave the churn, for there was his
little babe crawling about on the floor. So he took the churn
on his back, but then he thought he'd better first water the
cow before he turned her out on the thatch; so he took up a
bucket to draw water out of the well; but, as he stooped down
at the well's brink, all the cream ran out of the churn over his
shoulders into the well.

Now it was near dinner-time, and he hadn't even got the
butter yet; so he thought he'd best boil the porridge, and filled
the pot with water, and hung it over the fire. When he had
done that, he thought the cow might perhaps fall off the thatch
and break her legs or her neck. So he got up on the house to
tie her up. One end of the rope he made fast to the cow's
neck, and the other he slipped down the chimney and tied
round his own thigh; and he had to make haste, for the water
now began to boil in the pot, and he had still to grind the
oatmeal. So he began to grind away; but while he was hard
at it, down fell the cow off the housetop after all, and as she
fell, she dragged the man up the chimney by the rope. There
he stuck fast; and as for the cow, she hung halfway down the
wall, swinging between heaven and earth, for she could
neither get down nor up.

---

1. 'twas : = it was 。

裏，整個早上一口未吃，滴水未喝呢。他覺得牽牛去牧場太遠，便想不如把牛牽上房頂——因為這房子是草皮覆蓋的草房頂，上面長着茂盛的青草。他們的房子正好靠着一個陡峭的崗丘，他想要是從崗丘架塊木板搭到屋後草房頂，就容易把牛牽上去了。可他還不能放下攪乳器，因為他的小娃娃正在地上爬呢。他便背起攪乳器。又想還是在把牛牽上房頂之前先餵它一點水吧，便拿起一隻水桶到井裏汲水。可剛在井邊彎下腰，攪乳器裏的奶油全部順着他的肩膀流到井裏。

　　快到吃飯的時候了，可他連黃油還沒做出來呢。他想最好還是煮點麥片粥，就在鍋裏倒上水，把鍋掛在火上。剛做完這些，又想起牛可能會從屋頂掉下，摔斷腿和頸脖，就爬上屋頂把牛拴好。他把繩子一頭繫牢在牛頸上，另一頭順着煙囪吊下去，繫上自己的大腿。得趕快啦，因為鍋裏的水已經開了，他還沒把燕麥磨好呢。他開始快快地磨燕麥，正磨得起勁，牛到底還是一下子從房頂掉下來了。掉下來的時候，繫在腿上的繩子又把他拽上了煙囪。他就這樣緊緊地吊着，塞在煙囪裏。牛呢，也吊在牆半腰，半天半地、上上下下地搖晃，既上不去，也下不來。

And now the goody had waited seven[2] lengths and seven breadths for her husband to come and call them home to dinner; but never a call they had. At last she went home. But when she got there and saw the cow hanging in such an ugly place, she ran up and cut the rope in two with her scythe. But as she did this, down came her husband out of the chimney; and so when his old dame came inside the kitchen, there she found him standing on his head in the porridge-pot.

— translated by Wanda Gag

---

2. seven：常用於比喻很多、十分。

當太太的橫等豎等，七等八等，等着丈夫叫他們回家吃飯，但總也不見人來。最後她走回家。一到家，看見母牛吊在那樣一個尷尬的位置上，她便跑上前用鐮刀割斷了繩子。這樣一來，撲通，他丈夫從煙囪中掉了下來。等到他的太太走進廚房，正看到他頭朝下栽在燕麥粥鍋裏。

—— 萬達 · 蓋格 英譯

Once on a time there was an old widow who had one son, and as she was poorly and weak, her son had to go up into the storehouse to fetch meal for cooking; but when he got outside the storehouse, there came the North Wind, puffing and blowing, caught up the meal, and so away with it through the air. Then the Lad went back into the storehouse for a second and a third time. Every time the same thing happened. At this the Lad got very angry; he decided he'd just look the North Wind up, and ask him to give back his meal. He went a long way and at last he came to the North Wind's house.

"Good day!" said the Lad, "and thank you for coming to see us yesterday."

"GOOD DAY!" answered the North Wind, for his voice was loud and gruff, "AND THANKS FOR COMING TO SEE ME. WHAT DO YOU WANT?"

"Oh!" answered the Lad, "I only wished to ask you to be so good as to let me have back that meal you took from me on the storehouse steps."

"I haven't got your meal," said the North Wind; "but if you are in such need, I'll give you a cloth which will get you everything you want, if you only say, 'Cloth, spread yourself, and serve up all kinds of good dishes!'"

With this the Lad was well content. But, as the way was so long, he couldn't get home in one day, so he turned into an inn on the way; and when they were going to sit down to supper, he laid the cloth on a table which stood in the corner, and said, "Cloth, spread yourself, and serve up all kinds of good dishes." He had scarce said so before the cloth did as it

五十一　上門去找北風的小伙兒[1]（挪威）

從前，一位老寡婦有個兒子。她體弱多病，她兒子便得到倉房去取些玉米渣子、粗麥片之類來做飯。兒子剛走出倉房，呼呼地吹來一陣北風，把糧食捲起飛到天上。小伙兒又回到倉房，去了三次，可每次拿的糧食都被風颳走。小伙兒非常生氣，決定去找北風，向他討回吹走的玉米渣子。他走了一大段路，最後來到北風家。

"您好！"小伙子說，"您昨天去看我們，謝謝啦。"

"你好！"北風答道，他嗓子又粗又大。**"謝謝你來看我，有甚麼事嗎？"**

"哼！"小伙子道，"沒別的，只是麻煩您把在倉房台階上從我手裏拿走的玉米渣子還給我。"

"我沒拿你的玉米渣子呀，"北風說，"可你要是有需要，我給你一塊布吧。你只要說：'布啊布，攤開來，擺上各種好飯菜！'你想要甚麼就都有啦。"

拿到布，小伙子十分滿意。但因為路途遙遠，他一天到不了家，便在半路的一家客店留宿。客人們要坐下吃晚飯時，他把布鋪在屋角一張桌子上，說："布啊布，攤開來，擺上各種好飯菜！"話音剛落，那塊布已經照辦了。

---

1. 選自《挪威民間故事》。

was bid; and all who stood by thought it a fine thing, but most of all the landlord. So, when all were fast asleep, at dead of night, he took the Lad's cloth, and put another in its stead.

So, when the Lad woke, he took his cloth and went off with it, and that day he got home to his mother and told her thus and so. But never a bit of dry bread did the cloth serve up after the Lad said those words the North Wind told him.

"Well," said the Lad, "there's no help for it but to go to the North Wind again." And away he went.

So he came to where the North Wind lived late in the afternoon. "Good evening!" said the Lad. "Good evening!" said the North Wind.

"I want my rights for that meal of ours which you took," said the Lad. "As for that cloth I got, it isn't worth a penny."

"I've got no meal," said the North Wind, "but yonder you have a ram which coins nothing but golden dollars as soon as you say to it, 'Ram, ram, make money!'" So the Lad thought this a fine thing; but this time the very same thing happened as before: his ram was exchanged by the innkeeper. So the Lad went back again to the North Wind, and blew him up and said the ram was worth nothing, and he must have his rights for the meal.

"Well!" said the North Wind, "I've nothing else to give you but that old stick in the corner yonder; but it's a stick of that kind that if you say, 'Stick, stick! lay on!' it lays on till you say, 'Stick, stick! now stop!'"

So as the way was long, the Lad turned in this night too to the landlord; but as he could pretty well guess how things stood as to the cloth and the ram, he lay down at once on the bench and began to snore, as if he were asleep.

Now the landlord, who easily saw that the stick must be worth something, hunted up one which was like it, and when

旁觀的人都覺得這真是件寶物，店主更是心癢難耐。等人們熟睡，夜深人靜時，他拿走了小伙子的布，偷樑換柱放下另一塊。

小伙子一覺醒來，拿着布走了。當天到家後，如此這般地將事情告訴了母親。可他說了北風教他的那些話之後，那塊布連一塊乾麵包也沒有變出來。

小伙子說："咳，沒辦法，我還得去找北風。"說着便走了。

黃昏後他到了北風住的地方。"晚上好！"小伙子說。"晚上好！"北風道。

"您拿走我們的玉米渣子，您得還我個公道。"小伙子說，"說到您給的那塊布嘛，一分錢也不值。"

"我沒拿你的玉米渣子，"北風道，"可你到那邊牽走那頭羊吧，只要你對它說：'羊啊羊，變錢出來！'它不造別的，只給你造金幣。"小伙子想這倒不錯，可和上次一樣，他的羊又被客店主偷換了。小伙子又來找北風，對他大發脾氣，說那羊一文不值，非得要他賠他的玉米渣子不可。

"好吧！"北風道，"我沒別的可給你了，只有靠在那邊牆角的一根舊拐杖，可這拐杖只要你說：'拐杖！拐杖！給我打！'它就打；打到你說：'拐杖！拐杖！停下！'它才停。"

因為路遠，這晚小伙兒仍在那家客棧歇宿。這時他已經八九不離十猜到那布和羊的下落，便馬上在長凳上躺下，打起鼾來裝睡。

那店主一眼便看出這手杖有點名堂，找出一根差不多

he heard the Lad snore, was going to change the two; but just as the landlord was about to take it, the Lad bawled out: "Stick, stick! lay on!" So the stick began to beat the landlord, till he jumped over chairs, and tables, and benches, and yelled and roared, "Oh my! oh my! bid the stick be still, else it will beat me to death, and you shall have back both your cloth and your ram."

When the Lad thought the landlord had got enough, he said, "Stick, stick! now stop!" Then he took the cloth and put it into his pocket, and went home with his stick in his hand, leading the ram by a cord round its horns; and so he got his rights for the meal he had lost.

— translated by Wanda Gag

的，一聽到小伙兒的鼾聲，就想把兩根拐杖調換了。但店主剛要去拿拐杖，小伙子便喊道："拐杖！拐杖！給我打！"拐杖拼命地打起店主來，直打得他在桌椅長凳間上竄下跳，又吼又叫，"哎唷！哎唷！叫拐杖停下吧，快打死我啦，我把布和羊都還給你。"

小伙子覺得打夠了，便說："拐杖！拐杖！停下！"他拿過布放進口袋，手拿拐杖，用繩子拴上羊角，牽着它回了家。這次他討回了丟失玉米渣子的公道。

—— 萬達‧蓋格 英譯

52 The Princess on the Glass Hill (Norway)

Once upon a time there was a man who had a meadow and in the meadow there was a barn in which he stored hay. But every St. John's Eve[1], when the grass was in the height of its vigor, it was all eaten clean up, just as if a flock of sheep had gnawed it down to the ground during the night. This happened once, and it happened twice, but then the man grew tired of losing his crop and said to his sons — he had three of them — that one of them must go and sleep in the barn on St. John's Eve.

The eldest went to the barn and lay down to sleep, but when night was drawing near there was such a rumbling and such an earthquake that the walls and roof shook again, and the lad jumped up and took to his heels and the barn remained empty that year as well. Next St. John's Eve the second son was willing to show what he could do, but when night was drawing near there was a great rumbling, and then an earthquake, which was even worse. When the youth heard it he was terrified and went off, running as if for a wager.

The year after, it was the youngest Cinderlad's[2] turn. He went into the barn and lay down, but in about an hour's time the rumbling and creaking broke out again and again and the earth quaked so that all the hay flew about the boy. Then came a third rumbling and a third earthquake, so violent the

---

1. St. John's Eve：施洗約翰節前夕，又稱仲夏節前夕（Midsummer Eve），為施洗約翰的誕辰。施洗約翰比耶穌早出生六個月，耶穌是由他施洗的。
2. Cinderlad's：cinder，煤灰；lad，小子。

五十二　玻璃山上的公主（挪威）

　　從前一個人有片牧場，牧場上有一座貯存乾草的倉庫。但每到聖約翰節前夜牧草最肥美時，便被吃得精光，好像一夜之間成羣的羊把草地啃得見了地皮。第一年這樣，第二年還是這樣。這人眼見牧草受損，忍無可忍，便吩咐三個兒子說：他們之中有一個在聖約翰節前夜必須到倉庫值夜。

　　老大到倉庫躺下便睡。可夜色降臨時，他聽到一陣隆隆的響聲，地面劇烈地震動，使牆壁屋頂搖搖晃晃，小伙子跳起來沒命地逃跑了。這一年倉庫照舊空空如也。下一個聖約翰節前夜，老二躍躍欲試。黑夜到來，一陣轟轟隆隆的響動之後，又是地震，比去年更劇烈。年輕人聽到這聲音害怕起來，生怕遲了會輸掉賭注似地逃走了。

　　一年以後，輪到小弟辛德萊德（煤灰小子）了。他進了倉房躺下，過了差不多一個小時，隆隆聲、扎扎聲響了又響，劇烈的地震使乾草在小伙子身邊亂飛。接着又是第

boy thought the walls and roof had fallen down, but when that was over everything suddenly grew as still as death around him. He heard something, and stole to the door and found a horse standing eating. It was so big and fat and fine a horse that Cinderlad had never seen one like it before; a saddle and bridle lay upon it, and a complete suit of armor for a knight, and everything was of copper and so bright that it shone again. "Ha, ha! It is you who eat our hay then," said the boy. So he made haste and took out his steel[3] for striking fire and threw it over the horse, and then it had no power to stir from the spot and became so tame the boy could do what he liked with it. So he mounted it and rode away to a place no one knew of but himself, and there he tied it up. When he came home his brothers laughed at him. But they found the grass was all standing just as long and as thick as it had been the night before.

The next and the third St. John's Eve the very same things happened and the boy rode the second and the third horses away to the place where he kept the first before he went home. These two horses were even larger and fatter than the first one he had caught, and everything about them was made of silver and gold and there were two suits of silver and golden armor too.

Now, the king had a daughter he would give to the one who could ride up to the top of a high, high hill of glass, slippery as ice, close to his palace. Upon the very top of this the king's daughter was to sit with three golden apples in her lap, and the man who could ride up and take the three golden apples should marry her and have half the kingdom. The princess was very beautiful, and all who saw her fell in love

---

3. steel：打火鐮，古時用於打擊取火的鐮形鐵器。

三次隆隆作響和地震，猛烈極了，小伙子覺得牆壁房頂已經塌下來。但這之後，突然間一切都停了，四周死一樣地寂靜。他聽到有聲音，便躡手躡腳走到門口，看見一匹馬正在吃草。這馬體健膘肥，辛德萊德從未見過這樣高大壯健的駿馬。馬身上裝有馬鞍、韁繩和一整套騎士盔甲，都是黃銅造的，因此閃閃發光。「哈，哈！原來是你吃了我們的牧草呀！」小伙子道。他匆忙取出打火鐮向馬扔去。於是馬在原地不能動，變得非常馴服，聽任小伙子擺佈。小伙子騎上馬，來到一個除了自己誰也不知道的地方，把馬拴在那裏。回到家裏，他的哥哥嘲笑他。但他們發現牧草一點沒動，像前一天一樣又高又密。

第二和第三年的聖約翰節前夜，完全一樣的事情發生了，小伙子將第二、第三匹馬騎到拴着第一匹馬的地方，就回家了。這兩匹馬比他捉到的第一匹馬更為神駿，身上的馬具全部都是銀製和金製的，也有一套銀的和一套金的盔甲。

且說王宮附近有一座很高的、滑得像冰一樣的玻璃山。國王打算把女兒嫁給一個可以騎馬到山頂的人。公主要坐到山頂上，膝上放着三個金蘋果。誰能騎馬上山拿走金蘋果，就可以娶公主為妻，還得到王國的一半。公主十分美麗，所有見到她的人都身不由己對她一見鍾情。於是

with her, even in spite of themselves. So all the princes and knights came riding and tried to win her and half the kingdom besides.

When the day appointed came, there was such a host of knights and princes under the glass hill, and everyone who could walk or even creep was there to see who won the king's daughter. But no sooner did the horses set foot upon the hill than down they slipped. At length all the horses were so tired they could do no more, and the riders were forced to give up. Suddenly a knight came riding up on so fine a horse that no one had ever seen the like before, and the knight had armor of copper, and his bridle was of copper too, and all his accouterments were so bright that they shone. He rode straight off to the hill, and went up as if it were nothing at all. Thus he rode for a third part of the way up and turned his horse round and rode down again. But the princess thought she had never yet seen so handsome a knight. She threw one of the golden apples down after him, and it rolled into his shoe. But when he had come down from off the hill he rode away so fast no one knew what had become of him.

Next day all the princes and knights began to ride again. Not one could even get so far as a yard up the hill. However, there came a knight riding on a steed and this knight had silver armor and a silver saddle and bridle, and rode straight away to the glass hill. But when he had ridden two thirds of the way up he turned his horse round, and rode down again. When the princess saw him turning back she threw the second apple after him, and it rolled into his shoe.

On the third day everything happened as on the former days. Everyone waited for the knight in silver armor. At last, came a knight riding upon a horse that was such a fine one of unequaled beauty. The knight had golden armor, and the horse a golden saddle and bridle, and these were all so bright they

所有的王子、騎士都騎馬來，想要娶到公主，並贏取王國的一半。

預定的日子到了，許許多多騎士、王子雲集玻璃山下，人們扶老攜幼趕到這裏看看誰能娶得公主。可是這些馬剛踏上山就滑倒，最後都累倒在地，騎手們只好作罷。忽然間，一個騎士騎着一匹前所未見的駿馬來了，他身穿黃銅甲冑、馬勒也是銅的，所有的裝備都熠熠發光。他直接騎向玻璃山，若無其事地上去了。他上到山路三分之一時，掉轉馬頭下了山。公主從未見過這樣英俊的武士，就向他扔下一個金蘋果，蘋果滾進了他的鞋裏。他下了山就飛快地騎走了，無人知道他的去向。

第二天，王子、騎士們又開始上山了，可連一碼高也無人能上得去。這時，一個騎士騎着駿馬來了。他身披銀盔甲，坐在銀馬鞍上，手執銀韁繩，直向玻璃山衝去。但他上了三分之二的路又掉轉馬頭下了山。公主見他回頭，就向他拋出第二個金蘋果，蘋果滾進了他的鞋子。

第三天，和前兩天一樣，人人都在等着銀甲騎士。最後來了一位騎士，騎着一匹神駿無比的馬，他身穿金甲，配備金鞍、金韁，金光閃閃，令人目眩。他騎馬直到玻璃

shone and dazzled everyone. He rode straight away to the glass hill and galloped up as if it were no hill at all. As soon as he had ridden to the top, he took the third golden apple from the lap of the princess, and then turned his horse about and rode down again, and vanished from their sight before anyone was able to say a word to him.

Next day all the knights and princes were to appear before the king and the princess that he who had the golden apple might produce it, but none of them had a golden apple. So the King commanded that everyone in the kingdom should come to the palace, and still no one had the golden apple, and after a long, long time Cinderlad's two brothers came likewise. They were the last of all, so the king inquired of them if there was no one else in the kingdom left to come. "Oh, yes, we have a brother," said the two, "but he never got the golden apple! He never left the cinder heap on any of the three days." "Never mind that," said the king. "As everyone else has come to the palace, let him come too."

So Cinderlad was forced to go to the king's palace. And he took all three apples out of his pocket and with that threw off his sooty rags, and appeared there before them in his bright golden armor.

"You shall have my daughter, and the half of my kingdom, and you have well earned both," said the king.

— *Peter Christen Asbjornsen and Möe*

山下，策馬上山，如履平地。他一到山頂，便從公主膝上拿了第三個金蘋果，掉轉馬頭下了山。沒有人來得及和他說一句話，他就飛馳而去，不見蹤影。

第二天，所有的王子、騎士要到國王和公主駕前出示得到的金蘋果，可是沒有人拿得出。國王命令王國裏所有人都來到王宮，但仍然沒有人有金蘋果。過了很久，辛德萊德的兩個哥哥也來了，他們是最後來的人了。國王問他們王國裏還有沒有人未來。"噢，是的，我們有個弟弟，"兩個哥哥說，"可他不會有金蘋果的。這三天他沒有離開過那爐灰堆。""不管怎樣，"國王道，"每個人都得來王宮，讓他也來。"

於是，辛德萊德被迫來到王宮，他從衣袋裏拿出三個金蘋果，又脫下他那身沾滿爐灰的破舊衣衫，露出閃閃發光的金甲。

"你可以娶我的女兒為妻，還得到半個王國。你完全應份得到的，"國王說。

——彼得·克里斯汀·阿斯布約恩森與穆 [1]

---

1. 阿斯布約恩森（1812—1885），挪威民間傳說搜集者，與其"盟弟"穆合編的《挪威民間故事》是挪威文學史上的里程碑。本文取自該書英譯本。

53 The Little Match Girl (Denmark)

It was late on a bitterly cold, snowy, New Year's Eve. A poor little girl was wandering in the dark cold streets; she was bareheaded and barefooted. She certainly had had slippers on when she left home, but they were not much good, for they were so huge. They had last been worn by her mother, and they fell off the poor little girl's feet when she was running across the street to avoid two carriages that were rolling rapidly by. So the poor little girl had to go on with her little bare feet, which were red and blue with the cold. She carried a quantity of matches in her old apron, and held a packet of them in her hand. Nobody had bought any of her during all the long day; nobody had even given her a copper. The snowflakes fell upon her long yellow hair, which curled so prettily round her face, but she paid no attention to that. Lights were shining from every window, and there was a most delicious odor of roast goose in the streets, for it was New Year's Eve.

She found a corner where one house projected a little beyond the next one, and here she crouched, drawing up her feet under her, but she was colder than ever. She did not dare to go home for she had not sold any matches, and had not earned a single penny. Her father would beat her, besides it was almost as cold at home as it was here. Her little hands were almost dead with cold. Oh, one little match would do some good! Dared she pull one out of the bundle and strike it on the wall to warm her fingers?

She pulled one out, "risch", how it spluttered, how it blazed! It burnt with a bright clear flame, just like a little candle when she held her hand round it. It was a very curious

278

五十三 賣火柴的小女孩（丹麥）

除夕的深夜，天氣寒冷徹骨，雪花紛飛。一個貧窮的小姑娘在又黑又冷的街頭躑躅。她沒有帽子，赤着腳。出家門的時候她還是穿着便鞋的，但鞋太大不合腳，是媽媽穿舊了的；過馬路時，可憐的孩子躲避兩輛飛馳而過的馬車時，把兩隻鞋丟掉了。所以她只好赤着那雙凍得又紅又紫的腳向前走。她的舊圍裙裏裝着許多火柴，手上還拿着一小綑。一整天了，沒有人向她買過一根火柴，也沒有人給她哪怕一個銅板。雪花飄落在她臉龐邊長長的、金黃色的捲髮上，但她已顧不上注意自己美麗的頭髮了。家家戶戶窗口射出明亮的燈光，街上飄散着烤鵝的誘人香味。因為今晚是除夕夜啊。

有一幢房子比相鄰的房子突出一點，小姑娘在這裏一個角落蹲坐下來，把腳縮在身下。但這樣她更冷了。她不敢回家，因為火柴賣不出去，沒掙一分錢，怕挨父親的打。再說，家裏也不比這兒暖多少。她一雙小手快凍僵了。唉，只要點根小小的火柴就會暖和些。敢不敢抽根火柴劃在牆上點着暖暖手？

她抽出一根。嗤的一聲劃着了！多麼明亮！她用手掌攏住火苗，明亮的火焰升起，像枝小蠟燭。真是奇妙的蠟

candle too. The little girl fancied that she was sitting in front of a big stove with polished brass feet and handles. There was a splendid fire blazing in it and warming her so beautifully, but just as she was stretching out her feet to warm them, the blaze went out, the stove vanished, and she was left sitting with the end of the burnt-out match in her hand. She struck a new one, it burnt, it blazed up, and where the light fell upon the wall, it became transparent like gauze, and she could see right through it into the room. The table was spread with a snowy cloth and pretty china; a roast goose stuffed with apples and prunes was steaming on it. It came right up to the poor child, and then — the match went out, and there was nothing to be seen but the thick black wall.

Again, she lit another. This time she was sitting under a lovely Christmas tree. Thousands of lighted candles gleamed upon its branches. The little girl stretched out both her hands toward them — then out went the match. All the Christmas candles rose higher and higher, till she saw that they were only the twinkling stars. One of them fell and made a bright streak of light across the sky. "Some one is dying," thought the little girl; for her old grandmother, the only person who had ever been kind to her, used to say, "When a star falls a soul is going up to God."

Now she struck another match against the wall, and this time it was her grandmother who appeared in the circle of flame. She saw her quite clearly and distinctly, looking so gentle and happy. "Grandmother!" cried the little creature. "Oh, do take me with you! I know you will vanish when the match goes out." She hastily struck a whole bundle of matches, because she longed to keep her grandmother with her. The light of the matches made it as bright as day. Grandmother lifted the little girl up in her arms, and they soared in a halo of light and joy, far, far above the earth,

燭：小姑娘想像自己坐在一個有鋥亮黃銅爐腳和爐架的大火爐前。爐火熊熊，她覺得非常溫暖舒適，但她伸直雙腿想把腿也暖和一下時，火熄滅了，火爐沒有了，只剩下她孤零零地坐着，手裏拿着燒剩的火柴棍。她又擦着一根火柴，火焰升起。在火光照亮牆壁的地方，牆壁變得像薄紗一樣透明，她看得到屋子裏面。鋪着雪白的桌布、擺着漂亮的瓷器的桌子上，有一隻填滿蘋果和李脯的烤鵝，冒着熱氣。烤鵝直向可憐的孩子走過來。但這時火柴又燒完了，眼前只有漆黑的厚牆。

她又點燃了另一枝火柴。這次她仿佛坐在一棵美麗的聖誕樹下，成千上百枝點燃的蠟燭在樹枝上閃耀。女孩向蠟燭伸出雙臂，但這時火柴又點完了，聖誕樹上的蠟燭越升越高，最後她看到它們變成在天空中閃爍的星星。有一顆變成流星，在天空劃出一道亮光。“有個人快要死了，”小姑娘心裏想。因為祖母說過：“當一顆星落下來時，就有一個靈魂飛向上帝的懷抱。”老祖母是這世上唯一疼愛過她的人，但她不在了。

她又在牆上擦亮一根火柴。這一次祖母出現在光暈中。她看得清楚明晰，祖母慈祥、快樂。“祖母！”孩子叫道，“啊，帶我走吧！我知道火柴點完您也就會消失了！”她慌忙把一整綑火柴點着，因為她渴望祖母陪着她。火光將黑夜照耀得如同白晝，祖母把小姑娘抱在懷裏，在一團明亮與歡樂的光暈中高高飛起，遠遠地、遠遠

where there was no more cold, no hunger, no pain, for they were with God.

In the cold morning light the poor little girl sat there, in the corner between the houses, with rosy cheeks and a smile on her face — dead. Frozen to death on the last night of the old year. New Year's Day broke on the little body still sitting with the ends of the burnt out matches in her hand.

— Hans Christian Andersen

地離開塵世。那裏再也沒有寒冷、沒有飢餓、沒有痛苦。因為他們與上帝同在。

　　在寒冷的晨曦中，可憐的小女孩坐在兩座房子之間的角落裏。她兩頰像玫瑰花，臉上帶着微笑，她死了。凍僵在舊年的最後一個夜晚。新年破曉的微光照在她小小的軀體上。她仍然坐在那裏，手中拿着燒剩的火柴棍。

—— 漢斯·克里斯蒂安·安徒生 [1]

---

1. 安徒生(1805—1875)：丹麥人，舉世知名的童話創作大師，還寫過戲劇、小說、詩歌及自傳等。一生著有童話168篇，被譯成一百多種文字。他的故事表現了對善和美必勝的樂觀信念，但有些則非常悲觀，結局極為不幸。這些悲苦的故事往往帶有濃厚的自傳色彩。

54 The Ugly Duckling (1) (Denmark)

The country was lovely just then; it was summer. The wheat was golden and the oats still green. Round about field and meadow lay great woods, in the midst of which were deep lakes. Great dock leaves grew from the walls of a house right down to the water's edge. In amongst the leaves a duck was sitting on her nest. Her little ducklings were just about to be hatched. At last one egg after another began to crack. "Cheep, cheep!" they said. All the chicks were poking their heads out. "Quack! quack!" said the mother duck; and then they all quacked their hardest, and looked about them on all sides. "How big the world is to be sure!" said all the young ones.

The mother got up. "No! I have not got you all yet! The biggest egg is still there; how long is it going to last?" and then she settled herself on the nest again.

At last the big egg cracked, "Cheep, cheep!" said the young one and tumbled out; how big and ugly he was! The duck looked at him.

"That is a monstrous big duckling," she said; "none of the others looked like that; can he be a turkey chick? Well, we shall find that out; into the water he shall go."

Next day was gloriously fine. The mother duck with her whole family went down to the moat around the house. Splash, into the water she sprang. "Quack, quack!" she said, and one duckling plumped in after the other. They were all there, even the big ugly gray one swam about with them. "No, that is no turkey," she said; "see how beautifully he uses his legs and how erect he holds himself: he is my own

五十四　醜小鴨[1]（一）（丹麥）

　　夏天到了；正是鄉村美好的季節。麥田金浪滾滾，燕麥一片蔥綠。田野和草地周圍是　片大樹林，林中有深水湖泊。高大的酸模樹葉子從一間房屋牆壁直長到水邊。酸模樹葉子下，有隻鴨子坐在窩裏，小鴨子快要孵出來了。鴨蛋終於一個接一個地裂開，小鴨"吱吱"地叫，把一個個小腦袋探出蛋殼外。"嘎嘎！"鴨媽媽道。於是所有的小鴨一齊嘎！嘎！地放開嗓門大叫起來，東望望、西看看。"世界可真大呀！"所有的小鴨都説。

　　鴨媽媽站了起來。"不行啊！還未出齊，這最大的鴨蛋還在呢。還得孵多久啊？"鴨媽媽又蹲到窩裏。

　　大鴨蛋終於裂開了。"吱吱！吱吱！"小鴨叫着，一跤跌出蛋殼；他長得多麼大、多麼醜啊！鴨媽媽盯着他看。

　　"這小鴨可真大得嚇人，"鴨媽媽道，"其他小鴨都不是這樣的。別是隻小火雞吧？唔，讓他到水裏去咱們就知道了。"

　　第二天，陽光燦爛，鴨媽媽帶着全家到繞在屋子外的壕溝去。撲通！鴨媽媽一下子跳進水裏。"嘎！嘎！"她喊。小鴨子一隻接一隻地跳了下去，全在水裏了，連那大個兒灰色的醜傢伙也和他們一起游來游去。"不對，他不是火雞，"她説，"瞧他的腿划得多優雅，身子挺得多直。

---

1. 據説這是一篇安徒生把自己的自傳寓意於其中的童話。

chick! Quack, quack! Now come with me and I will take you into the world. But beware of the cat!"

Then they went into the duckyard. There was a fearful uproar going on, for two broods were fighting for the head of an eel, and in the end the cat captured it. "That's how things go in this world," said the mother duck. The other ducks round about looked at them and said, quite loud: "Just look there! Now we are to have that tribe! just as if there were not enough of us already, and, oh dear! how ugly that duckling is, we won't stand him!" and a duck flew at him at once and bit him in the neck. He was bitten, pushed about, and made fun of both by the ducks and the hens. "He is too big," they all said. The poor duckling was at his wit's end, and did not know which way to turn.

So the first day passed, and afterwards matters grew worse and worse. The poor duckling was chased and hustled by all of them, even his brothers and sisters ill-used him; and they were always saying, "If only the cat would get hold of you, you hideous object!" Even his mother said, "I wish to goodness you were miles away."

Then he ran off and flew right over the hedge, where the little birds flew up into the air in a fright. "That is because I am so ugly," thought the poor duckling, shutting his eyes, but he ran on all the same. Then he came to a great marsh where the wild ducks lived; he was so tired and miserable that he stayed there the whole night.

He stayed there two whole days, then two wild geese came, they were not long out of the shell, and therefore rather pert. "I say, comrade," they said, "will you join us and be a bird of passage?" Just at that moment, bang! bang! was heard up above, and both the wild geese fell dead among the reeds, and the water turned blood red. The sportsmen lay hidden round the marsh. The water dogs wandered about in the

他是我的孩子！嘎！嘎！跟我來，我要帶你們去見見世面。可要防着那貓！"

他們來到鴨圈，那裏正吵嚷得厲害，沸沸揚揚，兩羣鴨子正在爭奪一個鰻魚頭。最後，讓一隻貓搶到了手。"這個世道就是這樣，"鴨媽媽道。周圍的鴨子看看他們，大聲叫道："快看呀！又來了這一大家子！好像我們這裏吃飯的人還不夠多！噢，天呀！這隻小鴨多醜，我們受不了，不能放過他！"說着，一隻鴨子馬上撲過去，一口咬住他的脖子。他被雞羣鴨羣推來搡去，啄打取笑。"他個子長得太大了，"他們都說。可憐的小鴨嚇昏了頭，不知往哪裏躲。

第一天就這樣過去了，以後的情況越來越不妙。可憐的小鴨被所有的雞鴨追逐欺侮。甚至他的兄弟姐妹也都不饒他，他們老是說："讓貓抓到你就好了，你這醜東西！"連媽媽也說："但願你離我越遠越好！"

他只好跑開，飛過了樹籬，把小鳥嚇得飛到天空中。"那都是因為我長得太醜，"可憐的小鴨閉上眼睛想道。但他繼續跑啊跑，最後來到了一片野鴨棲息的大沼澤地。他又累又傷心，在那裏過了一夜。

小鴨在這兒呆了整整兩天。兩隻野鵝來了。他們也剛出殼不久，因此冒冒失失的。"我說，朋友，"他們道，"你願意和我們一起當候鳥嗎？"正在這時，砰！砰！天上兩聲槍響，兩隻野鵝都掉到蘆葦中死了，把水染得血紅。原來是獵人藏在沼澤地周圍。諳水的獵犬在沼澤裏到處搜

swamp, splash! splash! It was terribly alarming to the poor duckling. He twisted his head round to get it under his wing and just at that moment a frightful, big dog appeared close beside him. He opened his great chasm of a mouth close to the duckling, showed his sharp teeth—and—splash—went on without touching him.

"Oh, thank Heaven!" sighed the duckling, "I am so ugly that even the dog won't bite me!" Then he lay quite still and waited several hours more before he looked about and then he hurried away from the marsh as fast as he could.

— Hans Christian Andersen

索，把水弄得啪啦啪啦地響。可憐的小鴨嚇壞了，把頭藏在翅膀下。正在這時，一隻可怕的大狗出現在他身旁，張着血盆大口，露出尖利的牙齒逼近小鴨──啪啦啦！──走過去了，沒有碰這小鴨子。

"唉，謝天謝地！"小鴨嘆口氣，道："我醜得褲狗都不咬！"他動也不動地躺着，又等了幾個小時才四面看看，然後拼命地逃出了沼澤地。

── 漢斯·克里斯蒂安·安徒生

55 The Ugly Duckling (2) (Denmark)

Toward night he reached a poor little cottage. An old woman lived there with her cat and her hen. In the morning the strange duckling was discovered.

"What on earth is that!" said the old woman, but her sight was not good and she thought the duckling was a fat duck which had escaped. "This is a capital find[1]," said she; "now I shall have duck's eggs if only it is not a drake!" So she took the duckling on trial[2] for three weeks, but no eggs made their appearance.

Then the duckling began to think of the fresh air and the sunshine, an uncontrollable longing seized him to float on the water, and at last he could not help telling the hen about it. "What on earth possesses you?" she asked, "I think you have gone mad." "You do not understand me," said the duckling. "Don't make a fool of yourself, child, and thank your stars for all the good we have done you! Have you not lived in this warm room, and in such society that you might have learnt something?" "I think I will go out into the wide world," said the duckling.

So away went the duckling, he floated on the water and ducked underneath it, but he was looked askance at by every living creature for his ugliness. Now the autumn came on. The sky looked very cold, and the clouds hung heavy with snow and hail. The poor duckling certainly was in a bad case.

One evening, the sun was just setting in wintry splendor,

---

1. capital find：capital：重大的；find：發現，拾得。
2. on trial：審查。

五十五　醜小鴨（二）（丹麥）

　　黃昏時分他來到一所破舊的小茅屋前，這裏住着一位老婆婆和一隻貓、一隻雞。到了早晨，他們發現了這隻奇怪的小鴨。

　　"天啊，這是個甚麼東西！"老婆婆說。她老眼昏花，還以為是隻走失了的肥鴨呢。"這下可撿到寶啦。"老太太道，"只要不是公鴨，我可有鴨蛋吃了！"這樣，老太太盯了小鴨三個星期，但不見鴨蛋的影子。

　　後來，小鴨開始想念清新的空氣和燦爛的陽光，心裏升起一種抑制不住的渴望，想漂浮在水上。最後，他情不自禁地告訴了母雞。"甚麼使你着魔了？"母雞問，"你一定是瘋了。""你不了解我，"小鴨道。"別傻了，小子，你是吉星高照才能在我們這裏享福哩！你沒看到你住在這暖和和的房間裏，在我們這樣的上流社會中可以學到很多事情嗎？""我還是願意到外面廣闊的世界去。"小鴨道。

　　小鴨走了。他一會兒浮在水面，一會兒潛入水裏，但因為長得醜，誰對他都側目而視。秋天來了，天空看上去很冷冽，帶着雪和冰雹的雲低沉地壓在頭頂。可憐的小鴨自然又陷入了困境。

　　一天晚上，帶着冬日光輝的太陽剛剛下山，一羣美麗

291

when a flock of beautiful large birds appeared out of the bushes; the duckling had never seen anything so beautiful. They were dazzlingly white with long waving necks; they were swans. They spread out their magnificent broad wings and flew away from the cold regions to warmer lands and open seas. They mounted so high, so very high, and the ugly little duckling became strangely uneasy. Oh, he could not forget those beautiful birds, those happy birds!

The winter was so bitterly cold that the duckling was obliged to swim about in the water to keep it from freezing, but every night the hole in which he swam got smaller and smaller. Then it froze so hard that the surface ice cracked, and the duckling had to use his legs all the time, so that the ice should not close in around him; at last he was so weary that he could move no more, and he was frozen fast into the ice.

Early in the morning a peasant came along and saw him; he went out onto the ice and hammered a hole in it and carried the duckling home. There it soon revived and flew away.

It would be too sad to mention all the privation and misery it had to go through during that hard winter. When the sun began to shine warmly again, the duckling was in the marsh, lying among the rushes; the larks were singing and the beautiful spring had come. Then all at once it raised its wings and they flapped with much greater strength than before, and bore him off vigorously. Just in front of him he saw three beautiful white swans advancing toward him. The duckling recognized the majestic birds, and he was overcome by a strange melancholy.

"I will fly to them, the royal birds, and they will hack me to pieces, because I, who am so ugly, venture to approach them! But better be killed by them than be snapped at by the ducks, pecked by the hens."

的大鳥從灌木叢中飛出來。小鴨從未見過這樣美麗的東西。他們白得耀眼，有長長的、彎曲的頸項：這是天鵝。他們展開美麗寬大的翅膀，從這寒冷的地區飛到溫暖的地帶和廣闊的海洋上去，他們飛得很高，高極了，醜小鴨有一種說不出的不安感覺。噢，他忘不了這些美麗的、幸福的鳥兒！

這年冬天天氣寒冷徹骨，小鴨為了不被凍僵只好在水上游來游去。但是他在其中游泳的冰面水洞一夜比一夜小。最後水面的冰凍得裂了開來，小鴨要不斷划動雙腿才不致被周圍的冰凍住。後來他實在太累了，再也不能活動，被牢牢地凍在冰裏。

清晨一位農人走來看到他，便走到冰上，挖開一個洞把小鴨帶回家。不久小鴨甦醒過來便飛走了。

這個嚴冬裏醜小鴨經歷的艱難困苦令人不忍提起。當太陽重新溫暖地照耀着大地時，小鴨正躺在沼澤裏的燈心草叢中。雲雀在歌唱，美麗的春天又來了。忽然間，小鴨舉翅飛起，他的翅膀拍打着，比以前有力多了。小鴨一飛沖天。他看見前面有三隻美麗的白天鵝向他飛來。他認得出這些尊貴的鳥，立刻被一種說不清的憂傷感覺所壓倒。

「我要飛到這些尊貴的鳥兒那邊去，可他們會把我啄成碎片的，因為我這個醜鴨子竟敢接近他們！但讓他們啄死總比被雞鴨咬死好。」

So he flew into the water. The stately swans saw him and darted toward him with ruffled feathers. "Kill me, oh, kill me!" said the poor creature, and bowing his head toward the water. But what did he see reflected in the transparent water? He saw below him his own image, but he was no longer a clumsy dark gray bird, ugly and ungainly, he was himself a swan! It does not matter in the least having been born in a duckyard, if only you come out of a swan's egg!

He felt quite glad of all the misery and tribulation he had gone through; he was the better able to appreciate his good fortune now, and all the beauty which greeted him. Some little children came into the garden and cried out: "There is a new one! and the prettiest." And the old swans bent their heads and did homage before him. He felt quite shy, and hid his head under his wing; he did not know what to think; he was so very happy, but not at all proud; a good heart never becomes proud. And he rustled his feathers and raised his slender neck aloft, saying with exultation in his heart: "I never dreamt of so much happiness when I was the Ugly Duckling!"

— Hans Christian Andersen

於是小鴨飛進水裏。高貴的天鵝看到了他，帶着蓬鬆的羽毛，也向他飛快地游過去。"啄死我吧！唉，啄死我吧！"可憐的小鴨説，把頭低向水面。但是在清澈的水面上他看到了甚麼啊？他看到了自己的影子。但他不再是那笨拙的、暗灰色的醜小鴨了。他是一隻天鵝！如果你是從天鵝蛋裏孵出來的，哪怕你生在鴨圈裏，你還是一隻天鵝！

他十分高興自己經歷過了所有的憂傷磨難，這使他更能珍惜現在的幸運和迎接他的美好的將來。有幾個小孩子跑進花園，叫道："有一隻新來的天鵝！他最漂亮了。"老天鵝彎下頭，向他致意。小鴨覺得有點兒不好意思，把頭藏在翅膀下，不知該怎麼想。他是那麼快樂，卻沒有一絲驕傲。一顆善良的心是不會驕傲的。小鴨抖擻羽毛，高高地伸直細長的脖子，滿懷歡樂地想："當我是一隻醜小鴨時，我從來也不敢奢望過有這樣的幸福啊！"

—— *漢斯·克里斯蒂安·安徒生*

56 The Real Princess (Denmark)

There was once a prince, and he wanted a princess, but then she must be a real princess. He traveled right round the world to find one, but there was always something wrong. There were plenty of princesses, but whether they were real princesses he had great difficulty in discovering; there was always something which was not quite right about them. So at last he had to come home again, and he was very sad because he wanted a real princess so badly.

One evening there was a terrible storm; it thundered and lightened and the rain poured down in torrents; indeed it was a fearful night.

In the middle of the storm somebody knocked at the town gate, and the old king himself went to open it. It was a princess who stood outside, but she was in a terrible state from the rain and the storm. The water streamed out of her hair and her clothes, it ran in at the top of her shoes and out at the heel, but she said that she was a real princess.

"Well, we shall soon see if that is true," thought the old queen, but she said nothing. She went into the bedroom and ordered all the bedclothes to be taken off. Then secretly she laid a pea on the bedstead: then she asked the servants to take twenty mattresses and piled them on the top of the pea, and then twenty feather beds on the top of the mattresses. This was where the princess was to sleep that night. In the morning they asked her how she had slept.

"Oh, terribly badly!" said the princess. "I have hardly closed my eyes the whole night! Heaven knows what was in the bed. I seemed to be lying upon some hard thing, and my whole body is black and blue this morning. It is terrible!"

五十六　真公主（丹麥）

從前有一位王子，想要娶個公主，但他要的是個真正的公主。他走遍天下去尋找，但碰到的總是有點問題。公主倒有的是，但他很難打探清楚她們是不是真真正正的公主，她們總有那麼一點兒不對頭。最後王子只好回家去。他很難過，因為他萬分需要娶到一位真正的公主。

一天晚上，外面狂風暴雨，電閃雷鳴，大雨傾盆而下。這真是一個驚心動魄的夜晚。

就在這暴風雨中，有人在敲城門。老國王親自去開門。一位公主站在門外，但被暴雨淋得狼狽萬分。她的頭髮和衣服濕透，雨水從她的鞋尖流進、鞋跟流出。但她說她是一位真正的公主。

"好吧，過不了多久我們就知道真假了，"老王后想道。但她一聲不響。她走進臥室命人將所有被褥撤去，然後悄悄地在牀板上放下一顆豌豆。她又叫僕人將二十個牀墊放在豌豆上，再在上面加上二十個鴨絨牀墊。他們把公主安置在這裏過夜。早上起來，他們問公主夜裏睡得可好。

"唉，糟糕透了！"公主回答。"我幾乎整夜不曾閉上眼！天曉得牀上有點甚麼東西。我好像躺在甚麼硬的東西上，早晨起來渾身青紫。可怕極了！"

They saw at once that she must be a real princess when she had felt the pea through twenty mattresses and twenty feather beds. Nobody but a real princess could have such a delicate skin.

So the prince took her to be his wife, for now he was sure that he had found a real princess, and the pea was put into the Museum, where it may still be seen if no one has stolen it.

Now this is a true story.

— Hans Christian Andersen

他們立刻看出她一定是位真正的公主，因為她隔着二十層牀墊和二十層羽毛墊還能感到硌着那顆豌豆。除了真正的公主沒有人會有那樣嬌嫩的皮膚。

　　於是王子娶她為妻。因為這時他肯定自己已經找到一位真正的公主了。這粒豌豆便放到博物館裏去。如果沒有被偷走，你還可以看得到。

　　唔，這是個真實的故事。

——*漢斯·克里斯蒂安·安徒生*

57 Children's Prattle (Denmark)

At the merchant's they were having a children's party;
all the children who were attending it had parents who were
either rich or distinguished. The merchant himself was
wealthy and not without learning. He had graduated from
the university. He had both intelligence and a kind heart, but
people did not mention these attributes as often as they did
his great wealth.

People of distinction gathered in his house. Some had
noble blood, others noble spirits; and a few had both, and a
number had neither. But now there was a children's party,
and children have a habit of saying what they think.

There was a very beautiful little girl who was terribly
proud; the servants had kissed that pride into her, for her
parents were really very sensible people. Her father was a
Knight of the Royal Bedchamber and that, the little girl knew,
was something extraordinarily important. "I am a chamber
child," she declared, although she could just as easily have
been a "cellar child," for, after all, we can't choose our
parents. She explained to the other children that she was
"well-born" and that if one was not well-born, then one
couldn't become anything. It didn't matter how hard one
studied, it was being properly "born" that counted.

"And as for those whose names end in *sen*, there is no
hope for them. Nothing can ever become of them," she
explained. "One has to put one's hands on one's waist and
keep these common people with their *sen, sen* names at
elbow's length." And to illustrate what she meant, she put
her pretty little hands on her waist so that her elbows stuck
out sharply. She looked very charming.

五十七　孩子話（丹麥）

　　有個商人家裏正為孩子舉辦一個晚會，全部參加的孩子父母不是富豪便是名人。這位商人自己不但富有而且學問不小，是個大學畢業生。他才德兼備，但人們常說到的是他富有，而少有提及他的才德。

　　這時他家裏高朋滿座。有些有高貴的血統，有些有高尚的人格；少數更是兩者得兼，但很多人卻一樣也沒有。這時孩子們正在開晚會，而孩子們是習慣想到甚麼就說甚麼的。

　　有一個非常美麗但極驕傲的女孩，她被僕人們嬌寵得目空一切，因為她父母是特別講究、十分挑剔的人。父親是王宮寢殿大臣，小姑娘知道那是個要職。她說：“我是宮廷階層的孩子。”殊不知她本來說不好會是個“地窖階層的孩子”呢，因為畢竟父母是由不得人選擇的啊。她對其他孩子們說她的“出身好”，又說，出身不好的人是一事無成的。學習多麼努力也沒用，只有“出身”好才是重要的。

　　她說：“姓名末了是個‘生’字的人是沒有希望的，不會有出息的。對這些名字後面有甚麼‘生、生’的平民百姓，你最好兩手一叉腰，離他們遠遠地。”為了示意，她兩手叉腰，兩個胳膊向外一挺，樣子非常可愛。

But the merchant's daughter got angry. Her father's name was Madsen, and that name, she knew, ended with a *sen*; therefore she said as proudly as she could: "My father can buy a hundred silver marks' worth of candy and throw it in the street, so all the poor children can scramble for it. Can your father do that?"

"But my father," announced the newspaper editor's daughter, "can put your father, and yours too, and all the fathers in the whole town, in the newspaper. And that is why everybody is frightened of him, so my mother says. It is my father who rules the newspaper." And she held her head high as if she were a proper princess with a father who ruled a kingdom.

Behind the door, which stood ajar, was a poor little boy; he was looking in through the crack. The little lad was much too poor to be permitted to go to the party. He had been turning the spit for the cook, and as a reward he had been allowed to stand behind the door and watch the other children play.

"If only I were one of them," he had thought while he listened to everything that was being said; much of it was really not too pleasant for him to hear. The worst of it all was that his father's name ended in *sen*. Nothing could ever become of him! It was very sad.

Now that was that evening.

Years went by, and the years made the children into grownups.

In the center of Copenhagen a palace had been built and it was filled with splendid treasures that everyone wanted to see. People came from far and wide to look at them. Now to which of the children whom we have described did this palace belong? That ought to be an easy question to answer, but it isn't. It belonged to the poor boy, the one who had stood

商人的女兒生氣了。她父親姓麥德生，末尾帶個"生"字。她做出最傲慢的樣子，說："我父親可以買價值一百馬克銀圓的糖，撒在街上，讓窮孩子趴在地上搶。你父親做得到嗎？"

　　一位報紙編輯的千金宣稱："我父親可以讓你的父親，還有你的父親，還有全市鎮孩子的父親見報。所以人人都怕他，我媽媽說的。我爸管着報紙。"她昂起頭，活像有個父親統治着一個王國的真正的公主。

　　在敞開的門背後站着一個窮苦的小男孩，他正從門縫向裏張望。他太窮了，沒資格參加晚會。他給廚子轉動烤肉叉。作為報酬，他們讓他在門背後看看其他的孩子玩耍。

　　"要是我能夠和他們在一起玩，有多好！"他邊聽邊想。他聽到的話可不是很中聽。更難堪的是，他父親的姓末尾正是個"生"字。他不會有甚麼出息了！他很難過。

　　這就是那天晚上的情景。

　　一年年過去了，孩子們都已長大成人。

　　哥本哈根市中心建起一座宮殿，裏面放滿非常貴重的、人人以一睹為快的珍寶。人們從世界各地趕來參觀。這座宮殿是屬於我們上面說到的哪個孩子的呢？這本是個易於解答的問題，但是不然。它屬於那個窮孩子，那站在

behind the door. Something had become of him: he was a
great sculptor, and the palace was a museum for his works.
It had not really mattered that his name ended with *sen*:
Thorvaldsen[1], whose marble statues stand in St. Peter's[2] in
Rome.

What happened to the other children: the offspring of
good family, wealth, and intellectual arrogance? — None of
them could point a finger at[3] any of the others; they had all
been equally silly. — They had become decent and kind
human beings, for they were, in truth, not evil. What they
had thought and said then had only been children's prattle.

— Hans Christian Andersen

---

1. Thorvaldsen：Albert Bertel Thorvaldsen (1768—1844)，丹麥著名
   雕刻家。文中所説博物館亦名 "新古典主義博物館"

2. St. Peter's：聖彼得大教堂：初建於1506年，幾經修繕，內有極珍貴
   的藝術傑作，如米開朗琪羅的《聖母哀悼基督》像，等等。

3. point a finger at：指責。

門背後的孩子。他已經脫穎而出：成為一位偉大的雕塑家。這座宮殿是陳列他作品的博物館，儘管他的姓後面有個"生"字：托瓦爾生。他的大理石雕像陳設在羅馬聖彼得大教堂內。

其他那些出身富貴人家或書香門第的孩子怎樣了呢？他們誰也難責怪誰，都同樣說過些傻話。但他們都成了正派的好人，因為說實在的，他們並不是惡人。他們當時想的、說的，不過是些孩子的閒話罷了。

　　　　　　　　　　　── 漢斯·克里斯蒂安·安徒生

58 The Little Mermaid (1) (Denmark)

Far out at sea the water is as blue as the bluest cornflower, and as clear as the clearest crystal; but it is very deep, too deep for any anchor to reach the bottom; there live the mermen.

Now don't imagine that there are only bare white sands at the bottom; oh no! the most wonderful trees and plants grow there, with such flexible stalks and leaves, that at the slightest motion of the water they move just as if they were alive. All the fish, big and little, glide among the branches just as, up here, birds glide through the air.

The palace of the Merman King lies in the very deepest part. The Merman King had been for many years a widower, but his old mother kept house for him. She was very fond of the little mermaid princesses, her grandchildren. They were six beautiful children, but the youngest was the prettiest of all, her skin was as soft and delicate as a rose leaf, her eyes as blue as the deepest sea, but like all the others she had no feet, and instead of legs she had a fish's tail.

All the livelong day the little princesses used to play in the palace where living flowers grew out of the walls. When the great amber windows were thrown open the fish swam in, right up to the little princesses, ate out of their hands, and allowed themselves to be patted.

The youngest princess was a quiet and thoughtful child, nothing gave her greater pleasure than to hear about the world of human beings up above; she made her old grandmother tell her all that she knew about ships and towns, people and animals. But above all it seemed strangely

五十八　小美人魚（一）（丹麥）

在遠離陸地的海上，海水像最藍的矢車菊般湛藍，像最明亮的水晶般清澈。海水很深，深得沒有船錨能下到海底。那裏住着人魚。

你可別以為海底只是一片白沙。不是的！這裏長着最奇妙的樹木水草，枝葉柔軟，水波最輕微的蕩漾都能使它們隨之搖曳，恰似活潑生動的植物。大魚小魚在樹枝間游來游去，好像鳥兒在空中翱翔一樣。

海底最深處，有一座人魚王的宮殿。人魚王鰥居多年，他母親為他主持家務。她非常鍾愛她的孫女兒人魚小公主。她們是六條美麗的小美人魚，最小的最美麗。她的皮膚像玫瑰花瓣那樣嬌嫩，眼睛像深海海水一樣湛藍；然而和這裏的每條人魚一樣，她沒有腿，身後拖着一條魚尾。

長日無事，小公主們總是在宮殿裏玩耍。宮殿中各種鮮花從牆壁裏長出來。琥珀色的大窗打開的時候，魚兒便從窗口游進宮內，直接向公主們游過去，就在她們手裏吃她們餵食的東西，還讓小公主們輕拍它們、撫摸它們。

小公主是個安靜的、愛思考的孩子，她最愛聽上面人類世界的事了，她纏着祖母把所知道的輪船、城鎮、人和

beautiful to her that up on the earth the flowers were scented, for they were not so at the bottom of the sea; also that the woods were green, and that the fish which were to be seen among the branches could sing so loudly and sweetly that it was a delight to listen to them. You see the grandmother called little birds fish, or the mermaids would not have understood her, as they had never seen a bird.

"When you are fifteen," said the grandmother, "you will be allowed to rise up from the sea." The five princesses, who were fifteen one after another, went up to see the human world and came back very excited. Many an evening the five sisters interlacing their arms would rise above the water together. They had lovely voices, much clearer than any mortal's. These made the youngest all the more filled with longings.

At last her fifteenth birthday came. "Good-by," she said to her grandmother, and mounted as lightly and airily as a bubble through the water.

The sun had just set when her head rose above the water, but the clouds were still lighted up with a rosy and golden splendor, and the evening star[1] sparkled in the soft pink sky, the air was mild and fresh, and the sea as calm as a millpond. A big three-masted ship lay close by. The little mermaid swam right up to the cabin windows, and every time she was lifted by the swell she could see through the transparent panes crowds of gaily dressed people. The handsomest of them all was a young prince with large dark eyes; he could not be much more than sixteen, and all these festivities were in honor of his birthday. Oh! how handsome the prince was, how he laughed and smiled as he greeted his guests, while the music rang out in the quiet night.

---

1. evening star：即金星，在清晨出現時叫啟明星，黃昏出現時有人叫
   "昏星"。我國俗稱太白星。

動物的事講給她聽。小公主認為最最奇妙的是陸地上的花朵有芳香，因為海底下沒有香花；還有綠色的森林，在樹枝間游來游去的魚兒竟會唱出悅耳的歌。你知道，老祖母是把小鳥叫做魚兒的，因為不這樣說小美人魚們就不懂了，因為她們從來未見過小鳥啊。

"等到你們滿十五歲，就讓你們游到海面上去了，"祖母說。五個小公主先後滿了十五歲，都到上面看見了人類世界，很興奮地回來了。許多個夜晚，五個姐姐臂兒挽着臂兒浮上海面，她們美妙的歌聲比人類任何人的聲音更清脆。這些使得最小的公主更滿心嚮往。

終於，她也滿了十五歲！"再見啦！"小公主向祖母道別，輕盈得像個氣泡一樣，浮上了水面。

她的頭露出水面時，太陽已西沉，但雲朵依然披着玫瑰的紅色，霞光滿天。淡紅色的天空閃耀着第一顆晚星。清風徐來，海面平靜得如同一泓池水。一艘大型三桅船就停在附近。小美人魚游近舷窗，海浪輕輕地把她托起時，她就能通過透明的玻璃看到裏面衣著華麗的人羣。其中最俊美的是一位少年王子，長着大大的、漆黑的眼睛，看上去不過十六歲。這裏的歡樂歌舞正是為他慶祝生日。啊，這小王子長得多麼英俊！在寂靜的夜色中弦歌陣陣，小王子的笑聲和對賓客微笑致意的神態多麼飄逸、親切！

It got quite late, but the little mermaid could not take her eyes off the ship and the beautiful prince. The colored lanterns were put out, but deep down in the sea there was a dull murmuring and moaning sound. The waves grew stronger, great clouds gathered, and it lightened in the distance. Oh, there was going to be a fearful storm! The great ship rocked and rolled as she dashed over the angry sea, the black waves rose like mountains, but she dived like a swan through them and rose again and again on their towering crests. The ship creaked and groaned, the mighty timbers bulged and bent under the heavy blows, the water broke over the decks, snapping the mainmast like a reed, she heeled over on her side and the water rushed into the hold.

— *Hans Christian Andersen*

夜已深，但小美人魚的眼光流連在大船和英俊的王子身上，不忍離去。彩燈熄滅了，但海的深處響起沉悶的隆隆聲，海浪漸漸洶湧起來，烏雲低垂，遠處在閃電。一場可怕的暴風雨即將來臨！大船在怒濤中顛簸起伏，比山還高的黑浪捲來。船像一隻天鵝，穿浪而駛，一次又一次升到巨浪尖頂。但大船呻吟了，發出噼啪的破裂聲。在巨浪的衝擊下，粗重的船樑被拗彎、斷裂，海水沖上甲板，主桅像蘆葦一樣倒下。船身傾側，海水湧進船艙。

　　　　　　　　　── 漢斯‧克里斯蒂安‧安徒生

59 The Little Mermaid (2) (Denmark)

Now the little mermaid realized that the ship was in danger. When the lightning flashed it became so light that she could see all on board; and when the ship went down she saw the young prince sink in the deep sea. No! he must not die; so she swam toward him all among the drifting beams and planks, quite forgetting that they might crush her. At last she reached the young prince just as he was becoming unable to swim any farther in the stormy sea. His limbs were numbed, his eyes were closing, and he must have died if the little mermaid had not come to the rescue. She held his head above the water and let the waves drive them whithersoever[1] they would.

By daybreak all the storm was over, the sun rose from the water in radiant brilliance and his rosy beams seemed to cast a glow of life into the prince's cheeks, but his eyes remained closed. The mermaid kissed his fair and lofty brow, and stroked back the dripping hair. At last she saw land in the distance. She swam with him and brought him to the beach. Then she hid behind some rocks to see who would discover the prince. It was not long before a girl came up to him. The mermaid saw that the prince was coming to life, and that he smiled at the girl and not at her, you see he did not know she had saved him. She felt so sad that when he was led away, she dived sorrowfully into the water and made her way home to her father's palace.

Always silent and thoughtful, she became more so now

---

1. whithersoever：〔古〕隨便到甚麼地方。

五十九 小美人魚（二）（丹麥）

這時，小美人魚知道船遇了險。強烈的閃電閃過她把船上的一切看得清清楚楚。船身沉下時，她看見小干子沉到了深海裏。不，不能讓他淹死！於是她在漂滿桅杆、樑木、碎板的海上游過去，忘記了自身被砸死的危險。最後，當小王子在波濤洶湧的海上再也游不動時，她來到他的身旁。他手足已麻木、雙眼緊閉，要不是小美人魚來救他，他一定會淹死了。她把他的頭托出水面，隨着海浪漂流。

破曉時風暴停了。太陽從海面升起，朝霞燦爛。玫瑰色的陽光似乎在王子的面頰上抹上一絲生氣，但他仍緊閉雙眼。小美人魚親吻他美麗的、寬朗的額頭，撫平他的濕髮。最後，她看到了遠處有陸地，就帶着他游到海灘來。她自己藏在大石後，看誰來發現王子。不久就有一位姑娘向他走過來。小美人魚看到王子漸漸甦醒，向着這位姑娘微笑，沒有向小美人魚微笑，因為你想，他並不知道是她救了他啊。她看着姑娘把他帶走，十分難過，黯然潛入水中，游回父親的宮殿去。

她生性沉靜，常默默思索。現在更寡言少語了。多少

than ever. Many an evening and many a morning she would rise to the place where she had left the prince, but she never saw him.

She became fonder and fonder of mankind, and longed more and more to be able to live among them. So she asked her old grandmother, "If men are not drowned, do they live for ever?" The old lady answered, "They have to die too, and their lifetime is even shorter than ours, but they have a soul which lives for ever after the body has become dust; it rises through the clear air, up to the shining stars! to unknown beautiful regions which we shall never see. We may live here for three hundred years, but when we cease to exist, we become mere foam on the water and have no immortal souls."

"I would give all my three hundred years to be a human being for one day," sighed the little mermaid. She decided to go to the sea witch and ask for her help. The sea witch agreed to make her a potion, and told her before sunrise she must swim ashore with it, sit on the beach and drink it; then her tail would divide and shrivel up to what men call legs. But the witch also told her when once she had received a human form, she could never be a mermaid again. And if she did not succeed in winning her lover's love, and being married to him, she will gain no immortal soul. The first morning after his marriage with another, her heart would break, and she would turn into foam of the sea.

"But you will have to pay me, too," added the witch, "and it is no trifle that I demand. You must give me that beautiful voice of yours." So she cut off the tongue of the little mermaid, who was dumb now and could neither sing nor speak, and could never return home. She felt as if her heart would break with grief. She wafted with her hand

個晨昏，她升上海面來到放下王子的地方，但是再也沒有
看到他。

　　她越來越愛人類了，希望能生活在人羣中。於是她問
老祖母："如果人不溺死，他們會長生不老嗎？"老太太
答："人也會死，他們活得比我們還短，但他們死了，身
體化為塵土後，仍有不朽的靈魂；他們的靈魂越過清澈的
天空飛到星星閃耀的地方，飛到我們永遠看不見的、不知
在何處的樂土。我們能在這裏活三百年，可我們死後就變
成大海水面上的泡沫了，我們沒有不朽的靈魂。"

　　小美人魚嘆息道："我願用三百年的生命換取做人類
的一天！"她決心求助於海巫。海巫同意給她配一劑藥，
吩咐她在太陽升起前游到岸邊，在海灘坐下，喝掉它，她
的尾巴就會分開，縮成人腿。但海巫又告訴她，變成人之
後就再也變不回美人魚了。如果不能使她的心上人愛上她
和她結為夫婦，那麼在他和別人成婚後第一個清晨，她的
心便會破碎，她也就變成海洋中的泡沫。

　　海巫又説："可你得給我報酬，我要的報酬不小，你
要把你美麗的聲音給我。"於是她切下小美人魚的舌頭，
小美人魚啞了，不能唱歌，不能説話，也不能回家了。她

countless kisses toward her father's palace, and then rose up through the dark blue water.

The sun had not risen when she came in sight of the prince's palace and landed at the beautiful marble steps. The little mermaid drank the burning, stinging draught, and it was like a sharp, two-edged sword running through her tender frame; she fainted away and lay as if she were dead. When the sun rose on the sea she woke up and became conscious of a sharp pang, but just in front of her stood the handsome young prince, fixing his coal black eyes on her.

— Hans Christian Andersen

心傷欲裂，向父親的宮殿投送無數飛吻，然後穿過深藍色的海水向上游去。

太陽還未升起，王子的宮殿已經在望。小美人魚走上美麗的大理石台階，喝下那火灼般辛辣的魔藥，覺得仿佛有一把雙刃利劍把她嬌柔的身體切開，便昏倒躺在地上，像是已經死去。陽光灑在海面上時，她醒過來，感到一陣劇痛。可是這時英俊的王子就站在面前，用他那雙漆黑的眼睛凝視着她。

— 漢斯·克里斯蒂安·安徒生

60 The Little Mermaid (3) (Denmark)

Her fish's tail was gone, and she had the prettiest little white legs any maiden could desire, but she was quite naked, so she wrapped her long thick hair around her. The prince asked who she was and how she came there, she looked at him tenderly and with a sad expression in her dark blue eyes, but could not speak. Then he took her by the hand and led her into the palace. Every step she took was, as the witch had warned her beforehand, as if she were treading on sharp knives and spikes, but she bore it gladly; led by the prince she moved as lightly as a bubble.

Clothed in the costliest silks and muslins she was the greatest beauty in the palace, but she was dumb and could neither sing nor speak. But she could dance, raising herself on tiptoe and gliding on the floor with a grace which no other dancer could attain. She danced on and on, notwithstanding that every time her feet touched the ground they were like treading on sharp knives.

When at night the others were asleep, she used to go out on to the marble steps; it cooled her burning feet to stand in the cold sea water, and at such times she used to think of those she had left in the deep.

Day by day she became dearer to the prince, he loved her as one loves a good sweet child, but it never entered his head to make her his queen. "Yes, you are the dearest one to me," said the prince, "for you have the best heart of them all. But I was driven on shore by the waves in a shipwreck when a young girl found me on the beach and saved my life. She was the only person I could love in this world, but you are like her, you almost drive her image out of my heart, we will

六十　小美人魚（三）（丹麥）

　　她沒有魚尾巴了，長了一雙每個少女夢想得到的、最美的、雪白的腿。但她赤身裸體，所以她用又長又密的頭髮把身體掩住。王子問她是誰？怎麼來到這裏的？她不能說話，只用那藍色的眼睛深情地、憂鬱地望着他。王子牽着她的手把她帶回宮殿。正如海巫事先警告過她那樣，每走一步，她都像是踏在刀尖槍尖上。可是她甘心忍受。王子領着她，她的步履輕盈得有如氣泡。

　　她穿上最貴重的絲綢衣裙，是全王宮最美的人。但她啞了，不能唱歌也不能說話。可是她能跳舞。她踮着足尖，翩翩起舞，美妙輕盈，舉世無匹。雖然雙腳只要一觸地面，就像踏上了尖刀，然而她還是不住地跳。

　　每當夜闌人靜，她就走下大理石台階，讓那火焰般疼痛的雙腳浸在清涼的海水裏。這時，她就會想念海底深處的親人。

　　日復一日，王子越來越喜歡她，但他對她的愛就像愛個乖孩子，從未想到娶她做王后。他對她說：“你是我最心愛的人，因為你有一顆最善良的心。但在一次海難中，海浪把我沖到岸邊，有個姑娘在海灘上發現我，救了我的性命。在世上我只能愛她一人。但是你長得像她，你在我心目中幾乎代替了她的形象了。我和你永不分離！”

never part!"

Later the prince married the daughter of a neighboring king whom he believed to be the girl who had saved his life on the beach. After the wedding, the bridal pair sailed homeward from the neighboring country. At dusk lanterns of many colors were lighted on board and the sailors danced merrily on deck. The little mermaid could not help thinking of the first time she came up from the sea and saw the same splendor and gaiety; and she now threw herself among the dancers, whirling, as a swallow skims through the air when pursued. The onlookers cheered her in amazement, never had she danced so divinely; her delicate feet pained her as if they were cut with knives, but she did not feel it, for the pain at her heart was much sharper. She knew that it was the last night that she would breathe the same air as he, and would look upon the mighty deep, and the blue starry heavens.

The joy and revelry lasted till long past midnight. All became hushed, only the little mermaid laid her white arms on the gunwale and looked eastwards for the pink tinted dawn; the first sunbeam, she knew, would be her death. An endless night awaited her, who neither had a soul, nor could win one. Then she saw her sisters rise from the water, their beautiful long hair no longer floated on the breeze, for it had been cut off and given to the witch to obtain her help. The witch had given them a knife. Now they told their little sister, "Before the sun rises, you must plunge it into the prince's heart, and when his warm blood sprinkles your feet they will join together and grow into a tail. Quick! Quick! Do you not see the rosy streak in the sky?" Having said this they heaved a deep sigh and sank among the waves.

The little mermaid drew aside the curtain, bent over the sleeping prince and kissed his fair brow, looked at the sky where the dawn was spreading fast; looked at the sharp knife,

後來王子娶了鄰國的公主，以為她就是在海灘中救了他的那個姑娘。婚禮後，新婚夫婦從鄰國乘船回國。暮色降臨，船上彩燈高懸，水手載歌載舞。小美人魚不禁想起她初次升到海面上看到的同樣豪華歡樂的情景。此時她加入跳舞的人羣中，蹁躚起舞、飛旋，像一隻被追逐的燕子。圍觀的人在驚喜中向她歡呼。她從來也沒有像這時跳得那樣神妙。她那纖細嬌嫩的雙腳像刀刺般疼痛，她卻感覺不到，因為她的心比雙腳更要疼痛得多！她知道這是她和王子呼吸同一空氣，看望同一深邃湛藍的星空的最後一夜了。

　　船上歡歌笑語，直到夜闌人散。此時萬籟俱寂，只有小美人魚把雪白的手臂倚在船舷欄杆上，眺望着東方，找尋那微紅的曙色。她知道第一道陽光出現她就要死去。等待她的是無盡的黑夜。她沒有靈魂，也得不到靈魂。這時，她的五個姐姐浮出水面，可是她們美麗的長髮不再在微風中飄動了，她們的頭髮已剪下給海巫以換取她的幫助。海巫給了她們一把刀。現在她們對小妹妹說：“太陽升起前，你一定要把刀插進王子的胸膛。他的熱血濺到你的腳上時，你的腳又會合起來變成魚尾。快！快！沒看見天邊已泛起紅暈嗎？”說完，姐姐們深深地嘆息，沉到波濤下。

　　小美人魚拉開帷幔，彎腰親吻熟睡中王子美麗的前額，又望望曉色迅速來臨的天空。她看了一眼利刀，再看

and looked at the prince again. For a moment the knife quivered in her grasp, then she threw it far out among the waves and dashed overboard and fell, her body dissolving into foam.

Now the sun rose from the sea and above her floated hundreds of beauteous ethereal beings. "We are daughters of the air!" they said. "We do not have an everlasting soul, but we fly to the tropics where mankind is the victim of hot and pestilent winds, there we bring cooling breezes. We diffuse the scent of flowers all around, and bring refreshment and healing in our train. When, for three hundred years, we have labored to do all the good in our power we gain an undying soul. You, poor little mermaid, have with your whole heart struggling for the same thing as we have struggled for. You have suffered and endured, raised yourself to the spirit world of the air; and now, by your own good deeds you may, in the course of three hundred years, work out for yourself an undying soul."

— *Hans Christian Andersen*

一眼王子，有一瞬間，她握着的刀顫抖起來。於是她把刀遠遠地扔到海浪裏，然後縱身躍入海中。她的身體溶解成為泡沫。

這時太陽從海中升起，上空飄動着千百個美麗空靈的形體。"我們是空氣的女兒，"她們說，"我們沒有不朽的靈魂。但是我們飛去熱帶，給受酷熱和瘟風煎熬的人類帶去清涼的微風，我們到處飄送花香，身後給人們留下的是心曠神怡、無病無災。我們在三百年中盡力為善，就能得到永生的靈魂。你，可憐的小美人魚啊，也和我們一樣全心全意地為得到靈魂而奮鬥了。你受苦受難，但勇敢承擔。所以你已經升上空明的精靈世界了。由於你的善行，三百年後你會為自己造就一個永生的靈魂的。"

——漢斯·克里斯蒂安·安徒生

61 The Red Shoes (1) (Denmark)

There was once a little girl named Karen; she was a tiny and delicate little thing, but she always had to go about barefoot in summer, because she was very poor. In winter she only had a pair of heavy wooden shoes. An old mother shoemaker lived in the same village, and she made a pair of little shoes out of some strips of red cloth. They were made with the best intention, for the little girl was to have them.

These shoes were given to her, and she wore them for the first time on the day her mother was buried; they were certainly not mourning, but she had no others. An old lady looked at the little girl, and felt very very sorry for her, so she asked the parson to let her bring up the girl, which he agreed. Karen was well and neatly dressed, and had to learn reading and sewing. People said she was pretty.

The time came when Karen was old enough to be confirmed[1]; she had new clothes, and she was also to have a pair of new shoes. The shop of the shoemaker in the town was full of glass cases of the most charming shoes. Among all the other shoes there was one pair of red shoes Karan liked best. She tried them on. They fitted and were bought; but the old lady's eye sight was very poor, she had not the least idea that they were red[2], or she would never have allowed Karen to wear them for her confirmation. This she did, however.

---

1. confirmed：confirmation（堅信禮），基督教禮儀。初生嬰兒受洗禮，滿七歲受堅信禮，亦稱堅振禮。

2. they were red：堅信禮是一種莊嚴的儀式，應該穿黑色的禮服鞋參加。

六十一 紅舞鞋（一）（丹麥）

從前有個名叫卡琳的小姑娘，生得玲瓏可愛，但是很窮。夏天她光着腳走路，冬天只穿一雙笨重的木鞋。同村住着一位鞋匠老媽媽。她好心好意用紅色的碎布料為那個小姑娘縫了一雙鞋。

小姑娘得到鞋子，她在她媽媽下葬的日子第一次穿上腳。這當然不是送葬的喪服鞋，可是女孩沒有別的鞋子。一位老夫人看着這女孩，十分憐惜她，便請教區牧師允許她撫養這個小女孩，牧師同意了。老太太給卡琳穿上整潔的好衣服，教她唸書和做針黹。人人都讚她漂亮。

卡琳漸漸長大，要受堅信禮了。她有了新衣，還要添置一雙新鞋。鎮上鞋店裏有許多玻璃櫥，裏面擺滿了最美麗的鞋子，卡琳看中了其中的一雙紅鞋，就穿上試試腳。這鞋正合適，老太太便給她買下了。但老太太視力很差，一點也看不到這鞋是紅色的，如果她知道，決不會讓卡琳穿紅鞋去參加堅信禮的。但卡琳還是穿着去了。

Next Sunday there was Holy Communion[3], and Karen was to receive it for the first time. She looked at the black shoes and then at the red ones — then she looked again at the red, and at last put them on. By the church door stood an old soldier, with a crutch; he had a curious long beard. He bent down to the ground and asked the old lady if he might dust her shoes. Karen put out her little foot too. "See, what beautiful dancing shoes!" said the soldier. "Mind you stick fast when you dance," and as he spoke he struck the soles with his hand. When Karen knelt at the altar rails and the chalice was put to her lips, she only thought of the red shoes. She forgot to say the Lord's Prayer.

Now everybody left the church, and the old lady got into her carriage. Karen lifted her foot to get in after her, but just then, the old soldier, who was still standing there, said: "See what pretty dancing shoes!" Karen couldn't help it; she took a few dancing steps, and when she began her feet continued to dance; it was just as if the shoes had a power over them. She danced right round the church; she couldn't stop; the coachman had to run after her and take hold of her, and lift her into the carriage; but her feet continued to dance, so that she kicked the poor lady horribly. At last they got the shoes off, and her feet had a little rest. When they got home the shoes were put away in a cupboard, but Karen could not help going to look at them.

The old lady became very ill; they said she could not live; she had to be carefully nursed and tended, and no one was nearer than Karen to do this. But there was to be a grand

---

3. Holy Communion：聖餐禮，亦稱聖體禮。教徒領受的聖餐（小塊餅和酒）象徵耶穌的血肉，紀念耶穌犧牲生命拯救世人。參加者亦應穿黑色禮服鞋。

第二個星期日要舉行領聖餐儀式，卡琳初次領聖餐。她看看黑鞋，又看看紅鞋，再看看紅鞋，最後還是穿上了。教堂門旁站着一位老兵，脇下支着單撐拐，長着古怪的長鬍子。他彎下腰問老夫人可否為她撣去鞋上的灰塵。卡琳也把小腳伸出去。"看！多美麗的舞鞋！"老兵道。"記住跳舞時貼得緊些，"他用手敲着鞋跟又説。當卡琳在聖壇柵欄前跪下，聖餐杯就在唇邊時，她心裏還是只想着那雙紅舞鞋，忘了唸誦主禱文。

人們都走出教堂了。老夫人上了馬車，卡琳提腳要跟上去；但這時老兵還站在那裏，他說："看，多麼漂亮的舞鞋！"卡琳情不自禁地跳了幾下舞步，但一開始跳，她的腳就停不住了；仿佛鞋有一股控制雙腳的力量。她繞着教堂跳，停不下來。車夫只好去追她，把她抱住，放進馬車裏。可她的腳仍在跳，可憐的老太太被她踢得狼狽萬分。最後，他們把她的鞋脫下，她的腳才歇了下來。她們回家後，把紅鞋藏在衣櫥裏，但卡琳總是禁不住去偷偷看幾眼。

後來，老夫人病重，人們說她將不久於人世，需要細心的照料和看護。卡琳是她最親近的人，這事義不容辭。

ball in the town, and Karen was invited. She looked at the old lady, who after all could not live; she looked at the red shoes. She put on the red shoes after all, then went to the ball and began to dance!

The shoes would not let her do what she liked: when she wanted to go to the right, they danced to the left, when she wanted to dance up the room, the shoes danced down the room, then down the stairs, through the streets and out of the town gate, right away into the dark forest. This frightened her terribly and she wanted to throw them off, but they stuck fast. She tore off her stockings but the shoes had grown fast to her feet, and off she danced, and off she had to dance over fields and meadows, in rain and sunshine, by day and by night. She wanted to sit down, but there was no rest nor repose for her. When she danced toward the open church door, she saw an angel standing there.

— *Hans Christian Andersen*

但鎮上要舉行一個盛大舞會，卡琳也接到了邀請。她看看老夫人，她反正要死了；又看着紅鞋。她到底還是穿上紅鞋，去了舞會，跳起舞來！

　　但她的舞鞋卻不由她；她想向右，鞋子向左，她想進房間，舞鞋卻把她帶出房間，又到了樓下，跳過大街，穿出城門，來到黑沉沉的森林裏。女孩嚇得心驚膽顫，想脫掉舞鞋，但舞鞋緊貼在腳上。她扯下長襪，可舞鞋已經緊緊地長在腳上了。她跳啊跳，不跳不行，穿過田野草地，不管下雨天晴，沒日沒夜，她都在跳。她想坐下，但她不能歇息，無法安眠。當她跳到敞開的教堂門口時，看到一個天使站在那裏。

—— 漢斯・克里斯蒂安・安徒生

"Dance you shall!" said he. "You shall dance in your red shoes till you are a skeleton! You shall dance from door to door, and wherever you find proud vain children, you must knock at the door so that they may see you and fear you. Yea, you shall dance —"

"Mercy!" shrieked Karen, but she did not hear the angel's answer, for the shoes bore her through the gate into the fields over roadways and paths.

One morning she danced past a door she knew well; and a coffin covered with flowers was being carried out. Then she knew that the old lady was dead, and it seemed to her that she was forsaken by all the world, and cursed by the holy angels of God.

At last she danced away till she came to a little lonely house. She knew the executioner lived here. She said, "Come out! come out! I can't come in for I am dancing!" The executioner said, "You can't know who I am? I chop the bad people's heads off." "Don't chop my head off," said Karen, "for then I can never repent of my sins, but pray, pray chop my feet off with the red shoes!" Then she confessed all her sins, and the executioner chopped off her feet with the red shoes, but the shoes danced right away with the little feet into the depths of the forest. Then he made her a pair of wooden legs and crutches, and he taught her a psalm, the one penitents always sing. She kissed the hand which had wielded the ax, and went away.

She went to the parson's house, and begged to be taken into service, if only she might have a roof over her head and live among kind people. The parson's wife was sorry for

六十二 紅舞鞋（二）（丹麥）

　　"你不跳也得跳！"他說。"你要穿着紅鞋一直跳到變成一具骷髏！你要挨門挨戶地跳，路過那些驕縱虛舉的孩子家門時，你要敲敲門，讓他們看見你、害怕你。對，你跳吧！"

　　"可憐可憐我！"卡琳叫道，但她沒有聽到天使回答她，因為紅舞鞋又帶着她跳出城門、跳上田野、穿過大路小徑跳下去了。

　　一天早上，她跳過一家十分熟悉的門口，人們抬着一具撒滿鮮花的靈柩走出來。於是她知道那位老夫人死了。這時，她覺得自己已被全世界的人遺棄，被上帝神聖的天使詛咒。

　　她一直在跳，最後來到一所孤零零的小屋前。她知道劊子手住在這裏。"出來！出來！"她說，"我進不去，因為我得跳舞！"劊子手道："你不知道我是甚麼人吧？我是砍壞人頭顱的人。""不要砍我的頭，"卡琳道，"砍了頭，我就永遠不能悔改了。求求您，砍去我穿着紅鞋的雙腳吧！"她懺悔了自己所有的罪過，劊子手便砍去她穿着紅鞋的雙腳，紅舞鞋帶着小小的斷腳跳進了森林深處。劊子手又為她做了一雙木腳和一副拐杖，還教她唱一首悔罪人常唱的聖歌。她親吻了這雙拿斧頭的手後便離開了。

　　她來到牧師家，請他給她一些工作，只求有個地方遮風蔽雨，和善心人住在一起就行了。牧師的妻子可憐她，

her, and took her into her service; she proved to be very industrious and thoughtful. She sat very still, and listened most attentively in the evening when the parson read the Bible.

Next Sunday they all went to church. But she sat in her little room alone, with her prayer book in her hand. She raised her tear-stained face and said, "Oh, God help me!"

Then the sun shone brightly round her, and the angel whom she had seen on yonder night, at the church door, stood before her. He no longer held the sharp sword in his hand, but a beautiful green branch, covered with roses. He touched the ceiling with it and it rose to a great height, and wherever he touched it a golden star appeared. Then he touched the walls and they spread themselves out: the church itself had come home to the poor girl, in her narrow little chamber, or else she had been taken to it. She found herself on the bench with the other people from the parsonage. And when the hymn had come to an end they looked up and nodded to her and said, "It was a good thing you came after all, little Karen!"

The warm sunshine streamed brightly in through the window, right up to the bench where Karen sat; her heart was so over-filled with the sunshine, with peace, and with joy that it broke. Her soul flew with the sunshine to heaven, and no one there asked about the red shoes.

— *Hans Christian Andersen*

就僱用了她。卡琳工作非常勤快，懂得關心、體貼別人。晚上牧師唸聖經時，卡琳靜靜地坐在一邊，聚精會神地聽着。

到了星期日，家裏人都去了教堂。卡琳卻獨自坐在自己的小房間裏，手裏拿着禱文書。她抬起滿是淚水的臉龐，說道：「啊，上帝，幫助我吧！」

這時，她全身沐浴在明亮的陽光裏，那天夜裏她在教堂門前遇到的天使站在她面前。他手裏不拿利劍了，而是拿着一棵美麗的綠枝，上面長滿玫瑰花。他用這綠枝點了一下天花板，屋頂高聳起來，他每點到一處，就出現一顆金星。他又點了點四壁，房間變得寬大了：是教堂來到了這可憐的小姑娘的陋室？也許是她被帶到了教堂吧？她發現自己和教區的人一起坐在教堂的長凳上。人們唱完讚美詩，都抬起眼，向她點頭，道：「你終於來啦，這真好，小卡琳！」

明媚溫暖的陽光穿過窗子傾瀉進來，一直照到卡琳坐着的凳子。卡琳心裏充滿了陽光，充滿了安謐和快樂，她的心開綻了。她的靈魂隨着陽光飛向天堂，在那裏再沒有人向她提起紅舞鞋的事了。

—— 漢斯·克里斯蒂安·安徒生

63 The Emperor's New Clothes (1) (Denmark)

Many years ago there was an emperor who was so excessively fond of new clothes that he spent all his money on them. He cared nothing about his soldiers nor for driving around except for the sake of showing off his new clothes. He had a costume for every hour in the day, and instead of saying as one does about any other king or emperor, "He is in his council chamber," here one always said, "The emperor is in his dressing room."

One day came two swindlers in town. They gave themselves out as weavers, and said that they knew how to weave the most beautiful stuffs imaginable. Not only were the colors and patterns unusually fine, but the clothes that were made of the stuffs had the peculiar quality of becoming invisible to every person who was not fit for the office he held, or if he was impossibly dull.

"Those must be splendid clothes," thought the emperor. "By wearing them I should be able to discover which men in my kingdom are unfitted for their posts. I shall distinguish the wise men from the fools. Yes, I certainly must order some of that stuff to be woven for me." He paid the two swindlers a lot of money in advance so that they might begin their work at once. They did put up two looms and pretended to weave, but they had nothing whatever upon their shuttles. At the outset they asked for a quantity of the finest silk and the purest gold thread, all of which they put into their own bags while they worked away at the empty looms far into the night.

六十三　皇帝的新衣（一）（丹麥）

許多年以前，有一位皇帝酷愛新衣，所有的錢都花在置衣服上。他不關心士兵；除非是為了眩耀他的新衣，甚至懶得乘車到外面轉轉。他一天中每小時換一次衣服。通常人們都說：「國王或皇帝在會議室議政。」但在這裏臣民都習慣說：「皇帝在更衣室裏。」

一天，城裏來了兩個騙子，自稱是織布匠，織出的衣料要多漂亮有多漂亮，不但色彩鮮艷，款式新穎，而且用這種衣料裁剪出的衣服有一種特質：不稱職守或愚不可及的人是看不見的。

「那種衣服一定很神妙，」皇帝想。「穿上了，我就可以看出我的臣民誰不稱職，還可以分辨出誰聰明誰愚蠢。對，我一定要讓他們給我織些這樣的布！」他預付給兩個騙子許多錢，好讓他們馬上開工。騙子真的安裝上兩台織布機，做出織布的樣子，但織梭上空空如也。一開始，他們就要求給他們大批最好的絲和純金綫，卻全部收進了自己的腰包，只在空織布機上織到半夜。

"I should like to know how those weavers are getting on with the stuff," thought the emperor; but he felt a little queer when he reflected that anyone who was stupid or unfit for his post would not be able to see it. Certainly everyone was anxious to see how stupid his neighbor was.

"I will send my faithful old minister to the weavers," thought the emperor. "For he is a clever man and no one fulfils his duties better than he does!" So the good old minister went into the room where the two swindlers sat working at the empty loom. "Heaven preserve us!" thought the old minister, opening his eyes very wide. "Why, I can't see a thing!" But he took care not to say so. Both the swindlers begged him to be good enough to step a little nearer, and asked if he did not think it a good pattern and beautiful coloring. They pointed to the empty loom, and the poor old minister stared as hard as he could but he could not see anything. "Good heavens!" thought he, "is it possible that I am a fool? Am I not fit for my post? It will never do to say that I cannot see the stuffs."

"Oh, it is beautiful!" said the old minister looking through his spectacles; "I will certainly tell the emperor that the stuff pleases me very much."

Then the swindlers went on to demand more money, more silk, and more gold, to be able to proceed with the weaving; and they put it all into their own pockets, but they went on as before weaving at the empty loom.

The emperor soon sent another faithful official to see how the weaving was getting on, and the same thing happened....

"我想知道他們的布織得怎麼樣了，"皇帝想；但想到誰不稱職或是愚蠢就看不見布料時，心裏有點犯嘀咕。事實上人人都在等着看旁人鬧笑話呢。

　　"派我忠實的老臣到織布匠那裏看看吧，"皇帝想，"因為他是個聰明人，且沒有人比他更稱職。"於是那位忠心的老臣走進了騙子的房間，他們正在空機上織布呢。老臣瞪大了眼睛，想："老天保佑！怎麼，我甚麼也看不見！"但他不敢聲張。兩個騙子請他向織布機走近幾步，問他布料上的花樣和配色是不是很好。他們對空空如也的織布機指指點點，可憐那老臣用力瞪大眼睛，仍然甚麼也看不見。老臣想："天呀，莫非我是個笨蛋？難道我不稱職守？我可絕不能承認看不見他們織出的東西呀。"

　　他戴着眼鏡端詳着說："啊！很漂亮！我肯定要稟告國王我非常喜歡這些布料。"

　　之後，兩個騙子又要了更多錢、更多的絲和金綫，說是用來織布的，卻全都裝進自己口袋裏。他們繼續在空蕩蕩的織布機上織布。

　　皇帝很快又派另一個可靠的官員來視察織布工作，而情況完全一樣。……

Now the emperor thought he would like to see it himself. So, accompanied by a number of selected courtiers, he went to visit the crafty impostors, who were working away as hard as ever they could at the empty loom. "It is magnificent!" said the honest officials. "Only see, Your Majesty, what a design! What colors!" And they pointed to the empty loom, for they thought no doubt the others could see the stuff.

— *Hans Christian Andersen*

這時候，皇帝想親自去看看了，於是選了一批廷臣，由他們陪同去看望那兩個狡詐的騙子。兩個騙子繼續在空織布機上織布，更快、更起勁了。"真是奇觀！"誠實的官員們説，"陛下請看，這圖樣！這顏色！"他們指點着空機，因為他們以為別人肯定都看到了布料。

——漢斯·克里斯蒂安·安徒生

64 The Emperor's New Clothes (2) (Denmark)

"What!" thought the emperor; "I see nothing at all! This is terrible! Am I a fool? Am I not fit to be emperor? Why, nothing worse could happen to me!"

"Oh, it is beautiful!" said the emperor. "It has my highest approval!" and he nodded his satisfaction as he gazed at the empty loom.

The whole suite gazed and gazed, but saw nothing more than all the others. However, they all exclaimed with His Majesty, "It is very beautiful!" and they advised him to wear a suit made of this wonderful cloth on the occasion of a great procession which was just about to take place. The emperor gave each of the rogues an order of knighthood to be worn in their buttonholes and the title of "Gentlemen Weavers".

The swindlers sat up the whole night, before the day on which the procession was to take place. They pretended to take the stuff off the loom. They cut it out in the air with a huge pair of scissors, and they stitched away with needles without any thread in them. At last they said, "Now the emperor's new clothes are ready!"

Both the swindlers raised one arm in the air, as if they were holding something before the emperor and his courtiers and said, "See, these are the trousers, this is the coat, here is the mantle!" and so on. "It is as light as a spider's web. One might think one had nothing on, but that is the very beauty of it!" "Yes!" said all the courtiers, but they could not see anything, for there was nothing to see.

"Will Your Imperial Majesty be graciously pleased to take off your clothes," said the imposters, "so that we may put on the new ones, along here before the great mirror."

六十四　皇帝的新衣（二）（丹麥）

"哎喲！"皇帝想，"我甚麼也看不見啊！不好了！難道我蠢嗎？難道我不配當皇帝？哎呀，真是糟得不能再糟了！"

但是他卻説："嗯，很漂亮！朕十分喜歡！"他一邊滿意地點着頭，一邊盯着空空的織布機。

陪同皇帝前來的人都瞧呀瞧的，誰也沒看見甚麼，卻都異口同聲地隨着皇帝説："很漂亮！"他們又啟請皇帝用這種奇妙的布做一身衣服，穿上參加即將舉行的盛大遊行慶典。皇帝賜給兩個無賴每人一枚佩戴在衣服扣眼上的騎士勳章和"織布紳士"的頭銜。

遊行的前一天，兩個騙子忙了整整一夜。他們假裝將布料從織機上取下，用一把大剪刀在空中裁來剪去，又用沒有穿綫的針不斷地縫。最後，他們説："現在，皇帝的新衣做好了！"

兩個騙子每人舉起一隻胳膊，就像手裏拿着東西似的，對着皇帝和他的大臣説："請看，這是褲子，這是長袍，這是披風！"等等、等等。"這布料像蜘蛛絲一樣輕，穿在身上會覺得輕若無物，但這正是它的妙處。""對啊！"所有的朝臣道。但他們甚麼也沒看見，因為根本就沒有東西可看。

"皇帝陛下，恭請寬衣，"騙子説，"我們好在這面大

The emperor took off all his clothes, and the impostors pretended to give him one article of dress after the other, of the new ones which they had pretended to make. And the emperor turned round and round in front of the mirror. "How well His Majesty looks in the new clothes! How becoming they are!" cried all the people round. "What a design, and what colors!"

Then the emperor walked along in the procession under the gorgeous canopy, and everybody in the streets and at the windows exclaimed, "How beautiful the emperor's new clothes are! What a splendid train! And they fit to perfection!" Nobody would let it appear that he could see nothing, for then he would not be fit for his post, or else he was a fool.

"But he has got nothing on," said a little child.

"Oh, listen to the innocent," said its father; and one person whispered to the other what the child had said. "He has nothing on; a child says he has nothing on!"

"But he has nothing on!" at last cried all the people.

The emperor writhed, for he knew it was true, but he thought "the procession must go on now," so he held himself stiffer than ever, and the chamberlains held up the invisible train.

— *Hans Christian Andersen*

鏡子前給您把新衣穿上。"皇帝脱光了身子，騙子裝腔作勢地給他一件件穿上他們縫的所謂新衣。皇帝在鏡子前來回地照。"皇帝陛下穿上新衣多神氣呀！多合身呀！"左右的人都叫道。"款式設計得多麼好，顏色多麼美！"

之後，皇帝在華麗的御蓋下走在遊行的行列中。街上和路旁窗戶裏看熱鬧的人都喊道："皇帝的新衣多漂亮啊！那下擺多華貴！皇帝穿上多合身啊！"沒有人顯露出他甚麼也看不見，因為那麼一來，他不是不稱職，就是一個笨蛋啦。

"可是，他身上甚麼也沒穿呀！"一個小孩説。

"哎，聽這天真的孩子説甚麼，"小孩的父親道。於是人們竊竊私語，互相傳告這孩子説的話。"他身上甚麼也沒穿，一個小孩説他身上甚麼也沒穿！"

"他沒穿衣服！"最後，大家都叫了起來。

皇帝氣得渾身發抖，因為他知道這是實話。但他想，"現在這遊行是非要進行下去不可了。"於是他比任何時候更挺直身子，而內侍大臣也繼續捧着那並不存在的下擺。

—— *漢斯·克里斯蒂安·安徒生*

65 A Drop of Water (Denmark)

Surely you know what a magnifying glass is. It looks like one of the round glasses in a pair of spectacles; but it is much stronger, and can make things appear a hundred times larger than they are. If you look at a drop of water from a pond through it, a thousand tiny animals appear that you cannot see with the naked eye; but they are there and they are real. They look like a plate of live shrimps jumping and crowding each other. They are all so ferocious that they tear each other's arms and legs off, without seeming to care. I suppose that is their way of life, and they are happy and content with it.

Now there once was an old man whom everybody called Wiggle-waggle, because that happened to be his name. He always made the best of things; and when he couldn't, he used magic. One day when he looked through his magnifying glass at a drop of ditch water he was shocked at what he saw. How those creatures wiggled and waggled: hopping, jumping, pulling, pushing, and eating each other up — yes, they were cannibals.

"It is a revolting sight!" exclaimed old Wiggle-waggle. "Can't one do anything to make them live in peace, and each mind his own business?" He thought and thought, and when he couldn't find an answer, he decided to use magic. "I'll give them a bit of color; then they will be easier to study," he decided. He let a drop of something that looked like red wine fall into the ditch water — but it wasn't red wine, it was witch's blood of the very finest type, the one that costs two shillings a drop. All the little creatures immediately turned pink. Now they looked like a whole town of naked savages.

六十五　一滴水（丹麥）

　　你一定知道放大鏡是甚麼。它看上去像塊眼鏡上的圓鏡片，可強度大得多，可以把東西放大一百倍。如果你用放大鏡看一滴池塘裏的水，就會顯出你肉眼看不到的上千種微小動物。它們在那裏，真實地存在，看上去像一盤鮮蝦，亂蹦亂跳，你擁我擠。它們個個兇猛異常，把對方撕扯得斷腿折臂，卻毫不在意。我想這就是它們的生活方式，它們心滿意足，樂此不疲。

　　從前有個老頭子，人人都叫他扭扭擺，因為他恰好就姓扭名扭擺。他做事總要做到最好，如果做不到，就用魔術。一天，他用放大鏡觀察一滴陰溝裏的水，為眼前所見大吃一驚。那些小生物怎麼扭來擺去得這麼厲害：蹦蹦跳跳、拉拉扯扯、推推碰碰，你擁我擠，互相吞噬。真的，他們是些吃同類的動物。

　　"直叫人反胃！"扭扭擺老頭兒叫起來，"難道就不能用甚麼法子讓他們和平共處，不去招惹別人嗎？"他絞盡腦汁也想不出對策，他決定動用魔術。"我給他們上點顏色吧，這樣就容易研究了。"他把一滴像紅葡萄酒般的東西加到那滴陰溝水裏——可不是紅葡萄酒，是一種最上乘的女巫血，一滴就值兩先令那種。所有的小生物立刻變成粉紅色，現在他們看上去就像滿城赤身露體的野人。

"What have you got there?" asked an old troll[1] who had come visiting. "If you can guess what it is," replied Wiggle-waggle, "then I will make you a present of it."

The troll looked through the magnifying glass. What he saw looked like a city with all the inhabitants running around naked. It was a disgusting sight, but even more disgusting to see was the way people behaved. They kicked and cuffed each other; they beat and bit and shoved; those who were on the bottom strove to get to the top, and those on the top struggled to be on the bottom. "Look, his leg is longer than mine! I will bite it off! Away with you!" "Look, he has a lump behind his ear. It is small but it embarrasses him and gives him pain. We will really make him suffer!" And they pushed and pulled him; and finally they ate him up, all because he had had a little lump behind his ear. One little creature sat still, all by herself in a corner, like a modest, sensitive little maiden. She wanted peace and quiet. But she was dragged out of her corner, mistreated, and finally she was eaten up.

"It is most instructive and amusing," said the troll.

"But what do you think it is?" asked Wiggle-waggle. "Have you figured it out?"

"That is easy," answered the troll. "It's Copenhagen[2] or some other big city, they are all alike."

"It's ditch water," said Wiggle-waggle.

— *Hans Christian Andersen*

---

1. troll：北歐神話中人物。
2. Copenhagen：丹麥首都。

"你手裏是甚麼呀？"一個愛惡作劇的老侏儒來串門，問道。"要是你猜得出，"扭扭擺回答，"我就把它送給你。"

老侏儒往放大鏡裏一看，看到的就像一座城，滿城的居民赤裸着身體到處亂跑。這就夠噁心了，但更令人反胃的是這些人的行徑。他們互相拳打腳踢，毆打撕咬，壓在底層的拚命想爬上來，上面的又掙扎着擠下水底。"瞧，他的腿比我的長！我要把它咬下來！滾吧！""看，他耳朵後面有個包，包雖小，可也是個累贅，還挺痛，咱們來給他吃點苦頭！"他們把他推過來搡過去，最後把他整個吃掉，就因為他耳朵後長了個小包。一個小東西獨自靜靜地坐在一個角落裏，就像個謙恭和善、多愁善感的少女。她需要和平安靜，可是她被拖出角落，百般虐待，最後也被吃掉。

侏儒說："看了這很受教益，也很有趣。"

"可你知道這是甚麼嗎？"扭扭擺問，"你想出來了嗎？"

"這還不容易？"侏儒答，"這是哥本哈根呀，要不就是別的甚麼大城市。個個都一樣。"

"這是一滴陰溝裏的水。"扭扭擺說。

——漢斯·克里斯蒂安·安徒生

66 The Merman (Iceland)

Long ago a farmer lived at Vogar, who was a mighty fisherman, and, of all the farms round about, not one was so well situated with regard to the fisheries as his.

One day, according to custom, he had gone out fishing, and having cast down his line from the boat, and waited awhile, found it very hard to pull up again, as if there were something very heavy at the end of it. Imagine his astonishment when he found that what he had caught was a great fish, with a man's head and body! When he saw that this creature was alive, he addressed it and said, " Who and whence[1] are you?"

"A merman from the bottom of the sea," was the reply.

The farmer then asked him what he had been doing when the hook caught his flesh. The other replied, "I was turning the cowl of my mother's chimney-pot, to suit it to the wind. So let me go again, will you?"

"Not for the present," said the fisherman. "You shall serve me awhile first." So without more words he dragged him into the boat and rowed to shore with him.

When they got to the boat-house, the fisherman's dog came to him and greeted him joyfully, barking and fawning on him, and wagging his tail. But his master's temper being none of the best, he struck the poor animal; whereupon the merman laughed for the first time.

Having fastened the boat, he went toward his house, dragging his prize with him, over the fields, and stumbling

---

1. whence：〔古〕= from where。

348

六十六　人魚（冰島）

　　很久以前，在沃加爾住着一位農夫，他還是個非常能幹的漁人。而且這一帶所有農場中，沒有一個農場有他的農場這樣好的捕魚位置和條件了。

　　一天，他和往常一樣外出打魚。他把釣鈎投出船外，等了一下，發現釣鈎拉不動，好像鈎住了很重的東西。拉起釣鈎，他發現釣到的竟是一條人頭人身的大魚！你可以想像出他是怎樣的驚駭萬狀！他看到這怪物還活着，便招呼他說："你是誰呀？從哪裏來的？"

　　回答是："海底下的人魚。"

　　農夫問他被釣着的時候他在做甚麼。人魚回答："我正在轉動我母親煙囱頂上的通風罩，讓它順着風向。放了我吧，好嗎？"

　　"現在放還不行，你得先給我做點事。"漁人說。於是他不多說話就把人魚拉上船，帶着他把船划到岸邊。

　　他們回到停貯船的小屋時，漁夫的狗汪汪吠着、搖着尾巴高興地來迎接他，像在討好他。可是主人心緒不佳，可憐的小狗挨了打。這時人魚第一次笑了一聲。

　　漁夫繫好船，拖着他捕獲的人魚，穿過田野，向他家

over a hillock, which lay in his way, cursed it heartily; whereupon the merman laughed for the second time.

When the fisherman arrived at the farm, his wife came out to receive him, and embraced him affectionately, and he received her salutations with pleasure; whereupon the merman laughed for the third time.

Then said the farmer to the merman, "You have laughed three times, and I am curious to know why you have laughed. Tell me, therefore." "Never will I tell you," replied the merman, "unless you promise to take me to the same place in the sea wherefrom you caught me, and there to let me go free again." So the farmer made him the promise.

"Well," said the merman, "I laughed the first time because you struck your dog, whose joy at meeting you was real and sincere. The second time, because you cursed the mound over which you stumbled, which is full of golden ducats. And the third time, because you received with pleasure your wife's empty and flattering embrace, who is faithless to you and a hypocrite. And now be an honest man and take me out to the sea whence you have brought me."

The farmer replied: "Two things that you have told me I have no means of proving, namely, the faithfulness of my dog and the faithlessness of my wife. But of the third I will try the truth, and if the hillock contain gold, then I will believe the rest."

Accordingly he went to the hillock, and having dug it up, found therein a great treasure of golden ducats, as the merman had told him. After this the farmer took the merman down to the boat, and to that place in the sea whence he had caught him. Before he put him in, the latter said to him: "Farmer, you have been an honest man, and I will reward you for restoring me to my mother."

走去。路上有個小山丘，他走過時絆了一下，便連聲咒罵，這時人魚第二次笑出聲。

　　漁夫回到農場，妻子出來迎接，親熱地擁抱他，他對她的親熱擁抱很高興。人魚又笑了，這是第三次。

　　於是農夫對人魚說：「你笑了三次，我很奇怪你為甚麼笑，你告訴我為甚麼吧。」「我決不會告訴你的，除非你答應把我送到海上，回到捉住我的地方，把我放了。」農人答應了。

　　「好，」人魚說，「我第一次笑是因為你打了你的狗，可你的狗歡迎你時，它的快樂是真誠的。第二次你絆倒在土丘上，你痛罵土丘，可這土丘下埋滿了金幣啊。第三次你妻子的擁抱是虛情假意的，她對你不忠，是個虛偽婦人，可你卻很高興。好了，做個守信用的人，把我送回原來捉住我的地方吧。」

　　農夫回答：「你說的兩件事我無法證實，一件是狗的忠誠，一件是妻子不忠。但第三件我可以看看真相。如果土丘下埋滿金幣，我就相信其餘兩件事。」

　　於是他到土丘那裏，挖開土丘，發現大量金幣在裏面，正如人魚所說。之後農夫把人魚放到船上，到了捉住他的海面。他把人魚放回水裏之前，人魚說：「農夫，你是個守信用的人，你把我放回去和母親團聚，我會報答你的。」

Then the farmer put the merman into the sea, and he sank out of sight.

It happened that not long after, seven sea-grey cows were seen on the beach, close to the farmer's land. These cows appeared to be very unruly, and ran away directly the farmer approached them. So he took a stick and ran after them. He contrived to hit out the bladder on the nose of one cow, which then became so tame that he could easily catch it, while the others leaped into the sea and disappeared. The farmer was convinced that this was the gift of the merman. And a very useful gift it was, for a better cow was never seen nor milked in all the land, and she was the mother of the race of grey cows so much esteemed now.

— Jon Arnason

於是農夫把人魚放進海裏，人魚沉到水下不見了。

　　其後不久，農夫看到有七條像海水般灰色的母牛來到他田地附近的海灘上。這些牛看上去野性難馴，農夫一走近，它們就馬上跑開。農夫拿了一根棍子追趕牛羣。他好容易才把一條牛鼻子上一個小囊泡敲掉，這牛就變得很馴服，不費力就把它捉住了。其餘的牛跳進海裏消失了。農夫深信這就是人魚送給他的禮物。這禮物確實不錯，因為這一帶再也沒有比它更好、產奶更多的母牛了。這條牛就是現在人們評價很高的灰色母牛種的始祖。

　　　　　　　　　　　　　　　　—— 喬恩·阿納森 [1]

---

1. 喬恩·阿納森，搜集冰島民間傳說的作家，有“冰島格林”之稱。本篇選自《冰島民間傳說》。

American Tales

美洲童話

67 Rip Van Winkle (1) (U.S.A.)

Whoever has made a voyage up the Hudson must remember the Kaatskill[1] mountains. At the foot of these fairy mountains, the voyager may have descried the light smoke curling up from a village, whose shingle-roofs gleam among the trees, just where the blue tints of the upland melt away into the fresh green of the nearer landscape. It is a little village of great antiquity, having been founded by some of the Dutch colonists.

In that same village, and in one of these very houses, there lived many years since a simple good-natured fellow of the name of Rip Van Winkle. He was, moreover, a kind neighbor, and an obedient hen-pecked husband.

The children of the village would shout with joy whenever he approached. He assisted at their sports, made their playthings, taught them to fly kites and shoot marbles, and told them long stories of ghosts, witches, and Indians. Whenever he went dodging about the village, he was surrounded by a troop of them, hanging on his skirts, clambering on his back, and not a dog would bark at him throughout the neighborhood.

The great error in Rip's composition was an insuperable aversion to all kinds of profitable labor. He declared it was of no use to work on his farm; it was the most pestilent little piece of ground in the whole country; every thing about it went wrong, and would go wrong, in spite of him. His

---

1. Kaatskill：此山在紐約州東南。

六十七　山中方一夜（一）（美國）

　　無論是誰，只要曾經沿着哈德孫河溯流而上，都會記得那卡茲基爾羣山。在這仙境般羣山的山麓，旅行人會看到有座飄着裊裊輕煙的村莊．這座村莊正座落在遠處一片高地與近處碧綠的山景漸漸融為一體的地方，村莊的點點木瓦屋頂隱現在樹叢深處。這是一座年代久遠的小山村，為荷蘭殖民者所建。

　　就是在這個村落，就是在村落的一所房子裏，許多年來住着一個憨厚質樸的人，名叫瑞普・凡・溫克爾。他脾氣好，和鄰睦里，對妻子的管束責罵逆來順受。

　　只要他一走近，村裏的孩子就快活得又喊又鬧。孩子們遊戲玩耍，他在一旁助陣，他給他們造各種玩具，教他們放風箏、彈石子，還給他們講長長的故事，有惡鬼，有巫婆，有印第安土人。不管他在村裏怎麼躲躲藏藏，他總還是被一羣孩子圍着，牽衣爬背。連鄰近的狗也沒有一隻見了他會向他吠叫一聲。

　　瑞普秉性中最大的毛病莫如對所有有益有用的勞動一概深惡痛絕了。他有一塊這一帶最小最貧瘠的田地。他口口聲聲說在田裏耕種沒有用，說過去這塊地種甚麼不長甚麼，將來也好不了，他種了也是白費氣力。他的孩子也穿

children, too, were as ragged and wild as if they belonged to nobody.

Rip Van Winkle, however, was one of those happy mortals, who take the world easy, eat white bread or brown, whichever can be got with least thought or trouble, and would rather starve on a penny than work for a pound. If left to himself, he would have whistled life away in perfect contentment; but his wife kept continually dinning in his ears about his idleness, his carelessness, and the ruin he was bringing on his family. Morning, noon, and night, her tongue was incessantly going, and everything he said or did was sure to produce a torrent of household eloquence. Rip had but one way of replying to all lectures of the kind, and that, by frequent use, had grown into a habit. He shrugged his shoulders, shook his head, cast up his eyes, but said nothing. This, however, always provoked a fresh volley from his wife; so that he was fain[2] to draw off his forces, and take to the outside of the house.

Rip's sole domestic adherent was his dog Wolf, who was as much hen-pecked as his master; for Dame Van Winkle regarded them as companions in idleness, and even looked upon Wolf with an evil eye, as the cause of his master's going so often astray. True it is, in all points of spirit befitting an honorable dog, he was as courageous an animal as ever scoured the woods — but what courage can withstand the ever-during and all-besetting terrors of a woman's tongue?

— *Washington Irving*

---

2. fain：〔古〕=have to，只得。

得破破爛爛，像是沒爹沒娘的野孩子。

可瑞普活得無憂無慮，他屬於芸芸眾生中快樂的一員，他事事聽其自然，與世無爭；只要不費腦筋、沒有麻煩，他才不在乎吃白麵包還是黑麵包呢！他情願餓着只吃一分錢的東西，也不願為掙一塊錢去花氣力！要是聽任他自由自在，不受管束，他會無所作為，終其一生，心滿意足。問題是他的太太整天在他耳邊嘮叨，數說他懶散、萬事不管，要把這家敗了才算。她從早到晚喋喋不休，不管他說甚麼、做甚麼都會招來一頓劈頭蓋腦的痛罵。她這種訓斥，瑞普只有一種對策，久而久之，便成了習慣：他聳聳肩、搖搖頭、翻翻白眼、一言不發。但卻總是引來又一排責罵的砲火；他只好全綫潰退，跑出家門。

瑞普在家唯一的追隨者就是他那名叫狼兒的一條狗。它和主人一樣事事受管制。因為它的女主人凡‧溫克爾太太把他們看做一對懶惰閒散的難兄難弟。她把它主人不務正業遷怒於它，對它目露兇光。確實，不管從哪一點看，它都是一條忠心耿耿的狗，在樹林裏搜尋獵物時，和別的狗一樣勇猛。可是有甚麼樣的勇氣膽量能頂得住曠日持久的、逃不脫擺不開的、可怕的女人舌頭呢？

—— 華盛頓‧歐文 [1]

---

1. 歐文 (1783—1859)， 美國作家。有 "美國文學之父" 之稱。最偉大的著作為《見面札記》（*The Sketch Book*)，本篇選自該集。

68 Rip Van Winkle (2) (U.S.A.)

Poor Rip was at last reduced almost to despair; and his only alternative, to escape from the labor of the farm and clamor of his wife, was to take gun in hand and stroll away into the woods. Here he would sometimes seat himself at the foot of a tree, and share the contents of his wallet[1] with Wolf, with whom he sympathized as a fellow-sufferer in persecution.

In a long ramble of the kind on a fine autumnal day, Rip had unconsciously scrambled to one of the highest parts of the Kaatskill mountains. He saw at a distance the lordly Hudson, far, far below him, moving on its silent but majestic course. For some time Rip lay musing on this scene; evening was gradually advancing; the mountains began to throw their long blue shadows over the valleys.

As he was about to descend, he heard a voice from a distance, hallooing, "Rip Van Winkle! Rip Van Winkle!" He looked round, but could see nothing but a crow winging its solitary flight across the mountain. He thought his fancy must have deceived him, and turned again to descend, when he heard the same cry ring through the still evening air, "Rip Van Winkle! Rip Van Winkle!"—at the same time Wolf bristled up his back, and giving a low growl, skulked to his master's side, looking fearfully down into the glen. Rip looked anxiously in the same direction, and perceived a strange figure slowly toiling up the rocks, and bending under the weight of something he carried on his back.

---

1. wallet：knapsack，行囊。

六十八 山中方一夜（二）（美國）

可憐的瑞普最後幾乎絕望了。他從農業勞動和老婆的吵鬧聲中脫身的唯一出路就是拿起獵槍逛到樹林裏。他有時坐在樹下和狼兒分吃行囊中的食物——他把狼兒當作同受迫害的難友。

有一次，在一個晴朗的秋日裏，瑞普像上述情況，又閒逛了很久，不知不覺爬上了卡茲基爾山的一座高峰。他極目遠眺，看到遠處氣象恢宏的哈德孫河。河水靜靜地在山下流淌，莊嚴瑰麗。面對這景色，瑞普躺着，久久地陷入了沉思遐想。暮色漸漸降臨，羣山將長長的青色山影投向山谷。

他剛要下山，卻聽到遠處傳來一陣叫喊聲："瑞普·凡·溫克爾！瑞普·凡·溫克爾！"他四下望望，甚麼也沒有，只有一隻烏鴉孤零零地在山間飛着。他想是自己聽錯了，轉身又要下山，卻又聽到同樣的叫聲在寂靜的暮色中回蕩。"瑞普·凡·溫克爾！瑞普·凡·溫克爾！"——就在這時，狼兒拱起背，低低地咆哮了一聲，悄悄地走到主人身旁，驚恐地望着下面的峽谷。瑞普也緊張地看着那個方向，只見一個奇怪的身形吃力地慢慢爬上巖石，背上揹着的東西把他壓彎了腰。

On nearer approach Rip was still more surprised at the singularity of the stranger's appearance. He was a short square-built old fellow, with thick bushy hair, and a grizzled beard. His dress was of the antique Dutch fashion. He bore on his shoulder a stout keg, that seemed full of liquor, and made signs for Rip to approach and assist him with the load. As they ascended, Rip every now and then heard long rolling peals, like distant thunder, that seemed to issue out of a deep ravine, toward which their rugged path conducted. Passing through the ravine, they came to a hollow, like a small amphitheatre, surrounded by perpendicular precipices.

On entering the amphitheatre, new objects of wonder presented themselves. On a level spot in the centre was a company of odd-looking personages playing at nine-pins[2]. They were dressed in a quaint outlandish fashion; and most of them had enormous breeches, of similar style with that of the guide's. They all had beards, of various shapes and colors. The whole group reminded Rip of the figures in an old Flemish painting[3], in the parlor of Dominie[4] Van Shaick, the village parson. What seemed particularly odd to Rip was, that though these folks were evidently amusing themselves, yet they maintained the gravest faces, the most mysterious silence. Nothing interrupted the stillness of the scene but the noise of the balls, which, whenever they were rolled, echoed along the mountains like rumbling peals of thunder.

— Washington Irving

---

2. nine-pins：九柱地滾球戲，可能起源於歐洲大陸。球柱為木質，佈成方陣，一角向着球員，球員用地滾球擊球柱。

3. old Flemish painting：一般指15至17世紀初佛蘭德斯（今法國、比利時及荷蘭的一部分）的繪畫。

4. Dominie：Pastor，即牧師。

再走近些，那陌生人的怪模樣使瑞普大吃一驚。他是個身材矮而寬的老頭，長着亂草般的濃密頭髮，灰白的鬍鬚，一身裝束是古代荷蘭式的。他肩上扛着一個結實的桶，裏面像是裝滿液體。他打手勢讓瑞普過來幫他抬這桶。他們向上爬去，瑞普時不時聽到一陣陣隆隆聲，像是遠處的雷鳴，從一條深谷中發出來。他們走着的崎嶇小路正是通向這深谷的。穿過深谷，他們來到一個窪地，像是個被垂直的峭壁環繞的小型圓形競技場。

　　走進這競技場，又出現了一些怪異的東西。競技場中央一塊平地上，有一羣形狀奇怪的人正在玩九柱戲。他們穿着奇怪的、異國情調的古裝，中間許多人都穿着大馬褲，和剛才一路來的那個人的一樣。他們都留着鬍鬚，只是各人的式樣和顏色不同罷了。這羣人讓瑞普想起本村教區牧師凡·賽厄克客廳裏那幅荷蘭古畫上的人物。使瑞普最驚異的是，雖然這些人顯而易見玩得饒有興致，卻一個個繃着臉，一語不發，令人感到神秘莫測。除了球滾在地上時，沿着山脈發出沉雷似的隆隆回聲之外，沒有一點聲音打破這裏的靜寂。

—— 華盛頓·歐文

69 Rip Van Winkle (3) (U.S.A.)

As Rip and his companion approached them, they suddenly desisted from their play, and stared at him with such fixed statue-like gaze, and such strange, uncouth, lacklustre countenances, that his heart turned within him, and his knees smote together. His companion now emptied the contents of the keg into large flagons[1], and made signs to him to wait upon the company. He obeyed with fear and trembling. By degrees Rip's awe and apprehension subsided. He even ventured, when no eye was fixed upon him, to taste the beverage, which he found had much of the flavor of excellent Hollands[2]. He was naturally a thirsty soul, and was soon tempted to repeat the draught. One taste provoked another; and he reiterated his visits to the flagon so often that at length his senses were overpowered, his eyes swam in his head, his head gradually declined, and he fell into a deep sleep.

On waking, he found himself on the green knoll whence he had first seen the old man of the glen. He rubbed his eyes—it was a bright sunny morning. He recalled the occurrences before he fell asleep. He looked round for his gun, but in place of the clean well-oiled fowling-piece, he found an old firelock lying by him, the barrel incrusted with rust, the lock falling off, and the stock worm-eaten. He now suspected that the grave roisterers of the mountain had put a track upon

---

1. flagons：= bottles。
2. Hollands：荷蘭酒。

六十九　山中方一夜（三）（美國）

　　當瑞普和他的同伴走近時，他們突然停下球戲，一個
個像泥雕木塑般盯住他，表情怪異、呆滯，盯得他心裏不
斷打轉，盯得他雙膝抖個不停。這時他的同伴將桶裏的東
西倒進一些大酒瓶裏，向他打手勢讓他侍候這些人飲酒。
他嚇得戰戰兢兢地照辦了。漸漸地，瑞普的恐懼害怕一點
點消失。他甚至趁沒有人盯着他的時候，壯着膽子嚐了一
口酒，發現竟像上等荷蘭杜松子酒的味道。他天生就是個
嗜酒的人，禁不住喝了一口又一口，越喝越想喝。他一次
次地往大酒瓶那邊跑，到最後醉得糊糊塗塗，醉眼昏花，
頭也慢慢垂下，倒身沉沉睡去。

　　一覺醒來，他發現自己睡在一座翠綠的小山崗上，正
是在這裏，他最初看到了峽谷中的那個老頭。他揉揉眼睛
——是早晨，陽光明媚。他想起了他睡着之前發生的事。他
四處顧望找他的獵槍，可在他身旁明明該是放着一把用油
擦得槍膛鋥亮的獵槍，現在卻放着一把舊火槍。槍管生滿
了銹，槍拴掉了下來，槍托被蟲蛀了。他懷疑是不是山裏

him[3] and, having dosed him with liquor, had robbed him of his gun. Wolf, too, had disappeared, but he might have strayed away after a squirrel or partridge. He whistled after him and shouted his name, but all in vain; the echoes repeated his whistle and shout, but no dog was to be seen.

What was to be done? The morning was passing away, and Rip felt famished for want of his breakfast. He grieved to give up his dog and gun; he dreaded to meet his wife; but it would not do to starve among the mountains. He shook his head, shouldered the rusty firelock and, with a heart full of trouble and anxiety, turned his steps homeward.

As he approached the village he met a number of people, but none whom he knew, which somewhat surprised him, for he had thought himself acquainted with every one in the country round. Their dress, too, was of a different fashion from that to which he was accustomed. They all stared at him with equal marks of surprise, and whenever they cast their eyes upon him, invariably stroked their chins. The constant recurrence of this gesture induced Rip, involuntarily to do the same, when, to his astonishment, he found his beard had grown a foot long!

He had now entered the skirts of the village. The very village was altered; it was larger and more populous. There were rows of houses which he had never seen before, and those which had been his familiar haunts had disappeared. Strange names were over the doors—strange faces at the windows—every thing was strange. His mind now misgave him: he began to doubt whether both he and the world around him were not bewitched.

---

3. put a track upon him：跟蹤他。

那些沉着臉打球飲酒的人在他後面盯梢，用酒把他醉倒，奪了他的槍。狼兒也不見蹤影了，可說不定它是追松鼠啦、松雞啦去了吧。他打口哨呼喚它，喊它的名字。沒有用。只有口哨聲和喊聲的回音，狗卻無影無蹤。

怎麼辦呢？一個上午過去了。瑞普飢腸轆轆，想吃早飯。丟了狗和槍，他已經很傷心了，又怕回去見老婆。可不能在山裏等着餓死啊。他搖搖頭，扛上綉跡斑斑的火槍，憂心忡忡地轉身回家。

走近村子，他碰到許多人，可一個也不認識，他覺得有些驚訝，因為他自認為在這周圍農村裏他是無人不識的呢。他們的服飾和他見慣的也不同。他們也都同樣吃驚地望着他，一見到他，又都摸摸下巴。一來二去，這種手勢使瑞普不由自主地也摸摸自己的下巴。這一摸，使他大吃一驚——他發現自己的鬍鬚竟長了一尺長！

這時，他已走到村邊。村子變得面目全非：村子大了，人更多了。有一排排他從來未見到過的房子，而那些他熟悉的、常去的地方卻不見了。房屋門上標着的名字很陌生——窗戶裏露出的臉也很陌生 —— 一切都是陌生的。他心裏疑惑起來，開始懷疑是不是他和周圍的世界都中了妖術。

It was with some difficulty that he found the way to his own house, which he approached with silent awe, expecting every moment to hear the shrill voice of Dame Van Winkle. He found the house gone to decay—the roof fallen in, the windows shattered, and the doors off the hinges.

— *Washington Irving*

瑞普好不容易才找到了回家的路。走近家門，他心中懍懍然，不敢做聲，準備隨時聽到凡‧溫克爾太太的尖聲叫罵。可是他看到他的房子已經破敗不堪，屋頂塌了，窗戶散了，門也脫卸了。

　　　　　　　　　　　　　　—— 華盛頓‧歐文

He entered the house. It was empty, forlorn, and apparently abandoned. He called loudly for his wife and children—the lonely chambers rang for a moment with his voice, and then all again was silence.

He now hurried forth, and hastened to his old resort, the village inn—but it too was gone. A large rickety wooden building stood in its place. All this was strange and incomprehensible. He recognized on the sign, however, the ruby face of King George[1], but even this was singularly metamorphosed. The red coat was changed for one of blue and buff[2], a sword was held in the hand instead of a sceptre, the head was decorated with a cocked hat, and underneath was painted in large characters, *GENERAL WASHINGTON*.

There was, as usual, a crowd of folk about the door, but none that Rip recollected. The very character of the people seemed changed. There was a busy, bustling, disputatious tone about it, instead of the accustomed phlegm and drowsy tranquillity.

The appearance of Rip, and an army of women and children at his heels, soon attracted the attention of the tavern politicians. They crowded round him, eyeing him from head to foot with great curiosity. The orator bustled up to him,

---

1. King George：指喬治三世（1738 —— 1820），1776 年美國獨立戰爭時期的英王。

2. blue and buff：美國獨立戰爭時軍隊制服的顏色。

七十　山中方一夜（四）（美國）

他走進屋子。裏面空蕩蕩，不見人影。顯然沒有人住了。他大聲叫喊他的妻兒。空屋裏面響着他的叫聲，然後又恢復了靜寂。

瑞普急急向前，又走到以往他常在裏面消磨時光的鄉村客店。但客店亦已不復存在。原址上是一座不很牢固的大木屋。這一切都透着奇怪，讓人無法理解。可他確實又在招牌上認出了喬治國王那張紅噴噴的臉。但這喬治王也變得莫名其妙：原來的紅色外衣變成藍色和暗黃色相間的了，手裏拿着的王杖變成了一把劍，頭上還戴着一頂三角帽。招牌漆着大字：華盛頓將軍。

店門口像往常一樣聚着一羣人，可瑞普一個也想不起來是誰了，就連人的性格似乎也變了。人人都顯得匆匆忙忙、吵吵鬧鬧的，再也不是以前那樣散漫隨和、悠然自得的了。

瑞普出現，加上他身後大隊女人孩子，很快引起了正在酒店裏的政治家們的注意。他們把他團團圍住，好奇地從頭到腳打量着他。一個正在長篇大論說話的人連忙過來

and inquired on which side he voted. Rip stared in vacant stupidity. Another short but busy little fellow pulled him by the arm, and rising on tiptoe, inquired in his ear whether he was Federal or Democrat[3]. Rip was equally at a loss to comprehend the question. "Alas! gentlemen," cried Rip, somewhat dismayed, "I am a poor quiet man, a native of the place, and a loyal subject of the king, God bless him!"

Here a general shout burst from the bystanders—"A tory! a tory! a spy! a refugee! hustle him! away with him!" It was with great difficulty that the self-important man in the cocked hat restored order. Rip humbly assured him that he meant no harm, but merely came there in search of some of his neighbors, who used to keep about the tavern.

"Well—who are they?—name them."

Rip bethought[4] himself a moment, and inquired, "Where's Nicholas Vedder?" There was a silence for a little while, when an old man replied, "Nicholas Vedder! why, he is dead and gone these eighteen years!"

"Where's Brom Dutcher?" "Oh, he went off to the army in the beginning of the war; he never came back again."

"Where's Van Bummel, the schoolmaster?" "He went off to the wars too, was a great militia general, and is now in congress."

Rip cried out in despair, "Does nobody here know Rip Van Winkle?" "Oh, Rip Van Winkle!" exclaimed two or three, "Oh, to be sure! that's Rip Van Winkle yonder, leaning against the tree."

— *Washington Irving*

---

3. Federal or Democrat：在政治觀點上是屬於聯邦派（保守的）還是民主共和派（自由主義的）的。

4. bethought：〔古〕bethink 的過去式，細想，使自己想起。

問他投的是哪邊的票。瑞普茫然地瞪着他，露出一副傻相。有個愛管閒事的矮個子拉拉瑞普的胳臂，踮起腳尖對着他的耳朵問，他是聯邦派還是民主派。瑞普還是聽不懂他在問甚麼，他暗自心驚，叫道："哎喲！先生們，我是個安分守己的人，在這個地方土生土長，是國王的忠實子民啊。願上帝保佑他！"

圍觀的人聽到這話哄然大叫："保皇黨！保皇黨！奸細！逃亡貴族！揍他！轟走他！"那個頭戴三角帽、自覺有身份的人費了九牛二虎之力才使眾人安靜下來。瑞普低聲下氣一再向他保證他沒有惡意，只是到這裏來找幾位常在酒店附近的鄰居。

"那麼他們是誰？叫甚麼名字？"

瑞普想了一想，問："尼古拉·維德在哪兒？"靜了片刻，一個老頭子答："尼古拉·維德！天啊，他去世十八年了啊！"

"布諾姆·達特徹呢？""噢，戰爭一爆發他就參軍了。一去不返。"

"凡·布梅爾呢？就是那個小學校長。""他也去參戰了，是個民團將軍。現在當上國會議員啦！"

瑞普絕望了，他喊起來："那麼這裏難道就沒有人認識瑞普·凡·溫克爾了嗎？""啊，瑞普·凡·溫克爾！"有兩三個人同時喊起來："哎呀，當然認識呀，那邊那個不就是瑞普嗎？靠着棵樹呢！"

—— 華盛頓·歐文

71 Rip Van Winkle (5) (U.S.A.)

Rip looked, and beheld a precise counterpart of himself, as he went up the mountain: apparently as lazy, and certainly as ragged. The poor fellow was now completely confounded.

"God knows," exclaimed he, at his wit's end; "I'm not myself—I'm somebody else—that's me yonder—no—that's somebody else got into my shoes—I was myself last night, but I fell asleep on the mountain, and they've changed my gun, and every thing's changed, and I'm changed, and I can't tell what's my name, or who I am!"

At this critical moment a fresh comely woman pressed through the throng to get a peep at the gray-bearded man. She had a chubby child in her arms, which, frightened at his looks, began to cry. "Hush, Rip," cried she, "hush." The name of the child, the air and the tone of her voice, all awakened a train of recollections in his mind.

"What is your name, my good woman?" asked he.

"Judith Gardenier."

"And your father's name?"

"Ah, poor man, Rip Van Winkle was his name, but it's twenty years since he went away from home with his gun, and never has been heard of since—his dog came home without him."

"Where's your mother?"

"Oh, she too had died but a short time since."

七十一　山中方一夜（五）（美國）

　　瑞普看過去，見到一個人，和他上山時一模一樣，恰似從一個模子裏造出來！顯然也是那樣懶散，一點不錯，也同樣穿得破破爛爛。可憐的瑞普這下完全糊塗了。

　　他不知所措，喊道：“天曉得！我不是我啦！我成了別人了！那邊那個才是我——不對——是別人變成了我，昨晚我還是我自己呢。可我在山上睡了一覺，他們就換了我的槍，又把甚麼都換了，把我也換了。我不知道我叫甚麼名字，也不知道我是誰了！”

　　正不可開交，一個精神奕奕、俏麗可人的女人擠進人羣，要看一眼這個鬍子花白的男人。她懷中抱着一個小臉紅撲撲的孩子。孩子看到瑞普的樣子，嚇哭了。“別哭啦，瑞普，”女人大聲説：“別哭。”孩子的名字及她那神態語調一下子喚起了他腦中一連串的回憶。

　　“你叫甚麼名字啊，好心的太太？”他問。

　　“朱迪斯·加德尼爾。”

　　“那你父親叫甚麼？”

　　“哎，可憐的，他名字叫瑞普·凡·溫克爾。可他帶着槍離家出走已經二十年了，從此杳無音信——只有他的狗倒獨自回來了。”

　　“你媽呢？”

　　“哎，他走後不久她也去世了。”

The honest man could contain himself no longer. He caught his daughter and her child in his arms. "I am your father!" cried he— "Young Rip Van Winkle once—old Rip Van Winkle now!—Does nobody know poor Rip Van Winkle?"

All stood amazed, until an old woman put her hand to her brow, and peering under it in his face for a moment, exclaimed, "Sure enough! it is Rip Van Winkle—it is himself! Why, where have you been these twenty long years?"

Rip's story was soon told, for the whole twenty years had been to him but as one night.

To make a long story short, the company broke up, and returned to the more important concerns of the election. Rip's daughter took him home to live with her; she had a snug, well-furnished house, and a stout cheery farmer for a husband. As to Rip's son and heir, who was the ditto of himself, seen leaning against the tree, he was employed to work on the farm; but evinced an hereditary disposition to attend to any thing else but his business.

— Washington Irving

這時這老實人再也控制不住自己。他一把抱住女兒和她的孩子。"我就是你父親啊！"他喊道："我就是從前那個年青的瑞普·凡·溫克爾，現在的老頭子瑞普·凡·溫克爾啊！難道就沒有人認識可憐的瑞普·凡·溫克爾了嗎？"

所有的人都站在那裏目瞪口呆了。一個老婆婆用手遮在眼眉上，覰着眼端詳了他的臉好一會兒，喊道："千真萬確！這是瑞普·凡·溫克爾！就是他！哎呀，二十年這麼長的時間你都在甚麼地方呀？"

瑞普很快就把故事講完了，因為這整整二十年他只是過了一夜。

長話短說，人羣散去，又去忙他們所關心的更重要的選舉話題去了。瑞普的女兒帶他回家住在一起。她有一幢溫暖舒適、裝飾很好的房子，丈夫是個結結實實、快快活活的農場主。至於瑞普的兒子兼繼承人呢，就是那個他看見靠在樹旁的他的模子。這兒子在農場裏幹活兒，他繼承了他的脾氣：除了自己正經該幹的事，事事關心。

—— 華盛頓·歐文

72 The Three Brothers (U.S.A.)

There was once a man who had three sons, but no fortune except the house he lived in. Now, each of them wanted to have the house after his death; but their father did not know how to treat them all fairly. He did not want to sell the house, because it had belonged to his forefathers. At last he said to his sons: "Go out into the world, and each learn a trade, and when you come home, the one who makes best use of his handicraft shall have the house."

The sons were quite content with this plan, and the eldest decided to be a farrier, the second a barber, and the third a fencing master. They fixed a time when they would all meet at home again, and then they set off. It so happened that they each found a ciever master with whom they learned their business thoroughly. The farrier shod the king's horses, and he thought, "I shall certainly be the one to have the house." The barber shaved nobody but grand gentlemen, so he thought it would fall to him. The fencing master got many blows, but he set his teeth, and would not let himself be put out, because he thought, "If I am afraid of a blow, I shall never get the house."

Now, when the given time had passed, they all went home together to their father; but they did not know how to get a good opportunity of showing off their powers, and sat down to discuss the matter.

Suddenly a hare came running over the field. "Ah!" cried the barber, "she comes just in the nick of time." He took up his bowl and his soap, and got his lather by the time the hare

七十二 三兄弟（美國）

從前一個人有三個兒子。這人除了住房以外沒有任何財產。三個兒子都想在他死後得到這幢房子，父親不知怎樣才能不偏不倚地對待他們。因為是祖屋，他不想賣掉。最後，他對兒子們説：“去外面闖闖吧，每個人學門手藝，等你們回來，誰的手藝最好，這幢房子就歸誰。”

兒子們對這安排挺滿意。大兒子打算做個釘馬蹄鐵的工匠，二兒子想當理髮師，三兒子想做個劍術教練。他們約好在家再聚的時間便出發了。説來也巧，他們每個人都找到了好師傅，又將師傅的全套本事學到了手。馬蹄鐵匠給國王的馬打掌，他想：“房子肯定是我的啦。”理髮師給理髮的全是王公大臣，他也想房子他準能到手。劍術教練練劍時挨了不少打，可他咬緊牙關，不讓自己半途而廢，因為他想：“要是我怕挨打，我就永遠得不到那房子。”

這時，約定的時間到了，他們都回到家一起來見父親，可誰也不知道怎樣找個好機會顯顯自己的本事，便坐下來商量。

忽然一隻野兔跑過田間。“噢！”剃頭師叫起來，“來得正好。”他拿出水碗肥皂，預備皂沫，等野兔跑近便給

came quite close, then he soaped her in full career[1], and shaved her as she raced along, without giving her a cut or missing a single hair. His father, astonished, said: "If the others don't look out, the house will be yours."

Before long a gentleman came along in his carriage at full gallop. "Now, father, you shall see what I can do," said the farrier, and he ran after the carriage and tore the four shoes off the horse as he galloped along, then, without stopping a second, shod him with new ones. His father said: "You know your business as well as your brother. I don't know which I shall give the house to at this rate."

Then the third one said: "Let me have a chance, too, father." As it was beginning to rain, he drew his sword and swirled it round and round his head, so that not a drop fell on him. Even when the rain grew heavier, so heavy that it seemed as if it was being poured from the sky out of buckets, he swung the sword faster and faster, and remained as dry as if he had been under a roof. His father was amazed, and said: "You have done the best; the house is yours."

Both the other brothers were quite satisfied with this decision, and as they were all so devoted to one another, they lived together in the house, and carried on their trades, by which they made plenty of money, since they were so perfect in them. They lived happily together to a good old age.

— edited by Kate Wiggin & Nora Smith

---

1. in full career：全速，猛衝。

她飛快地塗上，又在兔子飛奔時給她剃好鬍鬚，沒有割傷一點兒或碰掉一根毛。父親看得目瞪口呆，說：「要是那兩個不小心些，這房子就會是你的了。」

不久，一位紳士駕車疾馳而來。「好，父親，這回看我的吧。」馬蹄鐵匠說着，追上那車，趁馬飛跑時拆下四個舊馬蹄鐵，又一分一秒不停地釘上新的。父親說：「你的手藝和你哥哥的一樣熟練。照這樣，我真不知道這房子該給誰了。」

這時，小兒子說：「父親，也給我一個機會吧。」正說着，天下起雨來，他拔出劍在頭上一圈圈舞了起來，結果一滴雨也沒有落到他身上。後來雨越下越大，好像一桶一桶的水從天上傾瀉下來，他的劍也越舞越快，身上乾乾爽爽，就像站在屋頂下一樣。他父親吃驚了，說，「你的本事最高強，房子給你啦。」

兩個哥哥對這個決定心悅誠服。因為他們兄弟相親相愛，便一起住在這房屋裏，各自幹着自己的行業。他們的手藝都是臻善至美，所以賺了許多錢。他們一直愉快地生活，活到很老。

——*凱特·威金 與 諾拉·史密斯 編*

73 Electricity (U.S.A.)

Ben never thereafter mentioned my little adventure in printing, so I tried to be somewhat more lenient about his maxims. Trying though they were, however, they were nothing compared to an enthusiasm which beset him about this time. This was the study of what he called "Electricity".

It all started with some glass tubes and a book of instructions sent him by a London friend. These tubes he would rub with a piece of silk or fur, thereby producing many strange and, to me, unpleasant effects. When a tube was sufficiently rubbed, small bits of paper would spring from the table and cling to it, or crackling sparks leap from it to the finger of anyone foolish enough to approach. Ben derived great amusement from rubbing a tube and touching it to the tip of my tail. Thereupon a terrible shock would run through my body, every hair and whisker would stand on end. This was bad enough, but my final rebellion did not come until he, in his enthusiasm, used the fur cap to rub the tube. And *I* was in the cap.

"Ben," said I, "this has gone far enough. From now on, kindly omit me from these experiments."

"I fear that you are not a person of vision, Amos," said he. "I shall tear the lightning from the skies[1], and harness it to do the bidding of man." Nothing I could say, though, served to dampen Ben's enthusiasm.

---

1. I shall tear the lightning from the skies：法國經濟學家杜爾哥(Anne-Robert-Jacques Turgot)曾頌揚富蘭克林說："他從天空捕捉雷電，從專制統治者手中奪回權力。"

七十三 電的故事[1]（美國）

　　本後來再也沒有提到我在那次印刷實驗中闖下的禍，所以我也就努力嘗試多少接受了他定下的那些規矩。這些東西雖然夠要命的，可是和那時他做研究的那股熱勁比起來，就微不足道了。他那時研究的東西叫做"電"。

　　這事兒都是從幾根玻璃管鬧起的，還有倫敦一個朋友送給他的說明書。他用一塊絲綢或毛皮來回擦那幾根管子，就產生了一些奇怪的、對我來說是不愉快的效果。把一根管子擦到了火候兒，桌上一塊塊小紙片就會跳起黏在管子上面。哪個傻瓜要是用手指靠近管子，就會有火花噼啪地跳到手指上。本最喜歡摩擦玻璃管、用它來碰我的尾巴尖兒。管子一碰，我全身就會猛地一震，每根毛和鬍都直豎起來。這就夠倒霉的了，可我也就忍了，直到他的熱勁兒上來，用皮帽子去摩擦管子——而我，就在這帽子裏。這我最後就要抗議了。

　　"本，"我說，"你做得夠過份了，從現在起，發發善心，別用我做這種實驗了吧。"

　　"恐怕你不是個有遠見的人啊，阿莫斯，"他說，"我要從天空捕捉雷電，駕馭它，用它造福人類。"不管我說甚麼，還是沒法給本的熱情潑冷水。

---

1. 此篇以本傑明・富蘭克林的寵物，一隻老鼠的口吻述說富蘭克林研究電的故事。本・富蘭克林（1706 — 1790），美國著名政治家、發明家。本是本傑明的暱稱。

Soon he received an elaborate machine that could produce much greater currents than the glass tubes. It was wcrked by a crank which he ground at happily for hours. After he had played with the new apparatus for a few weeks and had it working well, Ben decided to give an exhibition of his achievements in this field. A large hall had been secured for the occasion.

Frankly, I was bored by the whole affair, but since Ben seemed rather hurt by my attitude I tried to take a little interest. I read his speech and the descriptions of all the various experiments. By noon I understood everything quite thoroughly.

In the afternoon he went to have his hair curled, leaving me in the hall, where I went on with my research. Determined that no errors should mar this performance, I carefully went over each wire and piece of apparatus, comparing them with his diagrams and descriptions. I discovered that he had apparently made several grave mistakes, for not a few of the wires were connected in a manner that seemed to me obviously incorrect. There were so many of these errors to rectify that I was kept quite busy all afternoon. My corrected arrangements seemed to leave several loose wires and copper plates with no place to go, so I just left them in one of the chairs on the stage. I was barely able to finish before Ben arrived from the hairdresser's .

When we arrived back at the hall in the evening the brilliantly lit auditorium was crowded. Seated in chairs on the stage were the Governor and his Lady; the Mayor; several of the clergy; and the Chief of the Volunteer Fire Brigade holding his silver trumpet. Ben made his speech, and then stepped to the new apparatus and signaled to a young apprentice from the print shop who was stationed at the crank. The lad turned with a will, and a loud humming sound came

不久，他收到了一台複雜的儀器，這儀器靠搖一根曲柄來發電，可以發出比玻璃管強得多的電流。本興緻勃勃地一搖就是幾小時。他擺弄了這新儀器幾個星期，把它調好以後，決定開個展覽會展示他在這一領域的成就。為此還訂下一個大廳。

　　老實說，我覺得整個兒這件事非常無聊，但我的態度似乎傷了本的心，我就做出有點兒興趣的樣子。我讀了他的演說詞和對所有各種實驗的說明，到了中午就差不多全都懂了。

　　下午他出去捲捲髮，把我留在大廳，我繼續進行巡視。為了確保這次展覽不出差錯，我仔細檢查了每根電綫和每件儀器，把它們和圖解及說明相比較。我發現他明顯地犯了一些嚴重錯誤，因為相當多的電綫依我看顯然是連接錯了。糾正這樣多的錯誤讓我忙了整整一個下午。這些錯誤改過來之後，多出來一些電綫頭和銅片沒處連接，我就把它們放在講台的一張椅子上。我剛完工，本就從理髮師那裏回來了。

　　傍晚我們回到大廳時，燈火輝煌的禮堂裏人頭攢動。台上就座的有州長、州長夫人、市長和幾位牧師，還有手裏拿着銀號筒的志願消防隊隊長。本作了演講，然後走向那新儀器，對站在曲柄旁邊的印刷廠小學徒打了個手勢。小伙子便用力搖動曲柄，轉動着的輪子發出巨大的嗡嗡

from the whirling wheel while blue sparks cracked about it.

"And now, my friends," said Ben proudly, "when I turn this knob you shall see a manifestation of electrical force never before witnessed on this continent."

They did.

As Ben turned the knob the Governor rose straight in the air in much the same manner that I used to when Ben applied the spark to my tail. His hair stood out just as my fur did. His second leap was higher and his hair even straighter. There was a noticeable odor of burning cloth. On his third rising the copper plate flew from the chair, landing, unfortunately, in his Lady's lap. Her shriek, while slightly muffled by her wig, was, nevertheless, noteworthy. The Fire Chief, gallantly advancing to their aid, inadvertently touched one of the wires with his silver trumpet. This at once became enveloped in a most unusual blue flame and gave off a strange clanging sound.

Ben sprang at the apprentice, who was still grinding merrily. The lad, not an admirer of the Governor, ceased his efforts with some reluctance. The Governor was stiff and white in his chair, his Lady moaned faintly under her wig, the Fire Chief stared dazedly at his tarnished trumpet, and the audience was in an uproar.

"Never mind, Ben," I consoled him as we walked home, "I feel certain that we'll succeed next time."

"Succeed!" shouted Ben. "SUCCEED! Why, Amos, don't you realize that I have just made the most successful, the most momentous experiment of the century? I have discovered the effects produced by applying strong electric shocks to human beings."

"Granted the Governor *is* one," I said, "we surely did."

— *Robert Lawson*

聲，周圍閃着藍色火花，噼啪作響。

"注意了，朋友們，"本驕傲地説，"我一撳這按鈕，你們就會看到有電力顯示出來，這是全美洲大陸從來沒有過的。"

他們確實看到了。

本一撳按鈕，州長一下子離地跳了起來，就像本在我尾巴上通電流時我彈起一樣。他的頭髮也像我的毛一樣豎起來了。第二下他跳得更高，頭髮也豎得更直了，還發出一股人人聞得到的衣服燒焦的氣味。他跳到第三次時，銅片從椅子上飛起來，不幸落到他太太的膝蓋上。她尖叫一聲，雖然被掉下來的假髮捂住了嘴，聲音輕了些，仍然驚動了眾人。消防隊長勇敢地上前幫一把，不小心銀喇叭碰到一根電綫頭，喇叭周圍立刻升起一團最罕見的藍色火燄，發出奇怪的嘟嘟聲。

本撲向學徒，他還興沖沖地搖着曲柄呢。這小伙子對州長沒有尊敬之感，不太願意地住了手。州長面色蒼白、直挺挺地坐在椅子上；他太太的臉捂在假髮裏，發出虛弱的呻吟聲；消防隊長目光恍惚地看着他那變了色的喇叭。觀眾嘩然。

"別往心裏去，本，"在回家路上我安慰他，"下次咱們肯定會成功的。"

"成功！"本大聲叫道，"成功！天啊，阿莫斯，你難道不明白我已經做出本世紀最成功、最重要的實驗了嗎？我發現了強電擊對人體造成的效果了呀。"

"如果州長就是一例，"我説，"我們確實成功了。"

——羅伯特·勞森

74 About Elizabeth Eliza's Piano
(U.S.A.)

Elizabeth Eliza had a present of a piano, and she was to take lessons of the postmaster's daughter. They decided to have the piano set across the window in the parlor, and the carters brought it in, and went away. After they had gone the family all came in to look at the piano; but they found the carters had placed it with its back turned towards the middle of the room, standing close against the window.

How could Elizabeth open it? How could she reach the keys to play upon it? Solomon John proposed that they should open the window, which Agamemnon[1] could do with his long arms. Then Elizabeth should go round upon the piazza[2], and open the piano. Then she could have her music-stool on the piazza, and play upon the piano there.

So they tried this; and they all thought it was a very pretty sight to see Elizabeth playing on the piano, while she sat on the piazza, with the honeysuckle vines behind her. It was very pleasant, too, moonlight evenings. Mr. Peterkin liked to take a doze on his sofa in the room; but the rest of the family liked to sit on the piazza. So did Elizabeth, only she had to have her back to the moon.

All this did very well through the summer; but, when the fall came, Mr. Peterkin thought the air was too cold from the open window, and the family did not want to sit out on

---

1. Solomon John ... Agamemnon：所羅門‧約翰和阿加梅農都是這家的大男孩子。
2. piazza：陽台（美），柱廊（英），廣場（義）。

七十四　伊麗莎白·愛麗沙的鋼琴[1]（美國）

　　伊麗莎白·愛麗沙收到一件禮物，是架鋼琴，她要跟郵政局長的女兒上鋼琴課。家人決定將鋼琴放在客廳窗前。送貨人將鋼琴抬進來就走了。他們走後全家人都進來看看鋼琴，卻發現送貨的人把鋼琴緊貼窗戶放下，琴背朝着房間中央。

　　那伊麗莎白怎麼打開琴蓋呀？她怎麼才能伸手摸到琴鍵彈琴呢？所羅門·約翰建議先把窗戶打開，阿加梅農胳膊長，夠得到開窗戶。然後伊麗莎白可以繞到窗外陽台，打開琴蓋，再把琴凳放在陽台上，就在那兒彈鋼琴好啦。

　　他們試了這個辦法，大家都覺得伊麗莎白坐在陽台上彈鋼琴，背後襯着忍冬藤，樣子很好看。夜晚在月色下，這情景也很賞心悅目。彼特金先生喜歡在房間裏的沙發上打盹兒；但家裏其他人喜歡坐在陽台上。伊麗莎白也喜歡坐在陽台上，可她只能背對月亮。

　　整個夏天這個安排順順當當。但秋天來了，彼特金先生覺得敞開窗戶房間裏太冷，家人也都不願再坐在外面的

1.　本篇選自 *The Peterkin Paper*。

the piazza. Elizabeth practised in the mornings with her cloak on; but she was obliged to give up her music in the evenings the family shivered so.

One day, when she was talking with the lady from Philadelphia, she spoke of this trouble. The lady from Philadelphia looked surprised, and then said, "But why don't you turn the piano round[3]?" One of the little boys pertly said, "It is a square piano[4]." But Elizabeth went home directly, and, with the help of Agamemnon and Solomon, turned the piano round.

"Why did we not think of that before?" said Mrs. Peterkin. "What shall we do when the lady from Philadelphia goes home again?"

— Lucretia Hale

---

3. turn the piano round：費城太太說 "turn round" 有轉圓圈的意思，而小孩誤以為是把鋼琴變成（turn）圓形（round）。

4. a square piano：方形（正式應該是長方盒形）的鋼琴在十九世紀頗流行於英美。

陽台上了。伊麗莎白早晨披着斗篷練琴；可晚上她只好不練，因為家人都冷得發抖呢。

　　一天，她和費城來的太太閒談，說起這件麻煩事，那太太覺得很奇怪。她道："那你們為甚麼不把鋼琴轉過來呢？"一個小男孩愣頭愣腦地說："那可是個方形的鋼琴啊。"但伊麗莎白馬上跑回家，讓阿加梅農和所羅門幫忙把鋼琴轉了過來。

　　"咱們自己以前怎麼就沒有想到呢？"彼特金太太說，"費城來的太太要是回家去，咱們可怎麼辦呀？"

——露克麗西婭·黑爾

75 Pooh Goes Visiting and Gets into a Tight Place (U.S.A.)

Edward Bear, known to his friends as Winnie-the-Pooh, or Pooh for short, was walking through the forest one day, humming proudly to himself, when suddenly he came to a sandy bank, and in the bank was a large hole.

"Aha!" said Pooh. "If I know anything about anything, that hole means Rabbit," he said, "and Rabbit means Company," he said, "and Company means Food." So he bent down, put his head into the hole, and called out: "Is anybody at home?"

"No!" said a voice; and then added, "You needn't shout so loud. I heard you quite well." "Bother!" said Pooh. "Isn't there anybody here at all?" "Nobody."

Winnie-the-Pooh took his head out of the hole, and he thought to himself, "There must be somebody there, because somebody must have *said* 'Nobody.'" So he put his head back in the hole, and said: "Hallo, Rabbit, isn't that you?" "No," said Rabbit, in a different sort of voice this time.

"But isn't that Rabbit's voice?" "I don't *think* so," said Rabbit.

"Well, could you very kindly tell me where Rabbit is?" "He has gone to see his friend Pooh Bear, who is a great friend of his."

"But this *is* Me!" said Bear, very much surprised. "What sort of Me?" "Pooh Bear." "Oh, well, then, come in."

So Pooh pushed and pushed and pushed his way through the hole, and at last he got in.

"You were quite right," said Rabbit, looking at him all over. "It is you. What about a mouthful of something?" Pooh was very glad to see Rabbit getting out the plates and mugs;

七十五　饞嘴熊阿噗（美國）

　　狗熊愛德華，朋友們叫他溫尼-阿噗，或者簡稱阿噗。一天，他正穿過一片樹林得意地哼着小調。忽然間他走到一片沙堤上，上面有個大洞。

　　"啊哈！"阿噗説："要是我沒猜錯的話，有洞就有兔子，有兔子就有伴兒，有伴兒就有吃的。"他彎下腰，把頭探進洞裏，叫道："有人在家嗎？"

　　"沒人！"一個聲音答，接着又説："你用不着喊得這麼響，我聽得見！""討厭！"阿噗説，"真的一個人都沒有？""沒有。"

　　溫尼-阿噗把頭伸出洞外，暗想："一定有人，因為一定得有人説'沒人'呀。"所以他又把頭伸回到洞裏説："嗨，兔子，是你吧？""不是。"兔子這回換了一種聲音説。

　　"可這不就是兔子的聲音嗎？""不見得。"兔子説。

　　"好吧，那麼勞駕告訴我兔子在哪兒。""他去看他的朋友溫尼 - 阿噗啦，那可是他的好朋友。"

　　"可溫尼 - 阿噗就是我呀！"熊十分驚奇，説道。"哪個我？""狗熊阿噗呀！""噢，是嗎？那麼進來吧。"

　　阿噗左推右拱終於擠進了洞。

　　"你説得對，"兔子從頭到腳打量了他一番，説，"還真是你，吃點東西怎麼樣？"阿噗見兔子拿出杯杯盤盤

and when Rabbit said, "Honey or condensed milk with your bread?" he was so excited that he said, "Both."

And for a long time after that he said nothing ... until at last, humming to himself in a rather sticky voice, he got up, shook Rabbit lovingly by the paw, and said that he must be going on. So he started to climb out of the hole. He pulled with his front paws, and pushed with his back paws, and in a little while his nose was out in the open again ... and then his ears ... and then his front paws ... and then his shoulders ... and then —

"Oh, help!" said Pooh. "I'd better go back. Oh, bother! I shall have to go on. I can't do either! Oh, help *and* bother!"

Now by this time Rabbit wanted to go for a walk too, and finding the front door full, he went out by the back door, and came round to Pooh, and looked at him.

"Hallo, are you stuck?" he asked.

"N-no," said Pooh carelessly. "Just resting and thinking and humming to myself."

"Here, give us a paw." Pooh Bear stretched out a paw, and Rabbit pulled and pulled and pulled. ...

"*Ow!*" cried Pooh. "You're hurting!" "The fact is," said Rabbit, "you're stuck." "It all comes," said Pooh crossly, "of not having front doors big enough." "It all comes," said Rabbit sternly, "of eating too much. Well, well, I shall go and fetch Christopher Robin."

Christopher Robin lived at the other end of the Forest, and when he came back with Rabbit, and saw the front half of Pooh, he said, "Silly old Bear," in such a loving voice that everybody felt quite hopeful again.

"I was just beginning to think," said Bear, sniffing slightly, "that Rabbit might never be able to use his front

的，十分高興。兔子問："你麵包上想抹蜂蜜還是濃縮奶？"阿噗聽到這話很興奮，便説："都要！"

很久很久他都沒有説話……直到最後嘴裏還含着食物，哼着歌，站起身來，親熱地握握兔子的爪子，説他得走了。阿噗開始向洞外爬去，他用前爪爬，後爪推，不一會兒，他的鼻子鑽出了洞，然後是耳朵，然後是前爪，然後是肩膀，然後——

"噢，幫個忙！"阿噗説，"我還是退回去吧。咳，討厭！還得往前爬。我進不行也退不得啦！哎喲，幫幫忙吧！要命！"

這時，兔子也想出去散散步了。他發現前門堵上，就從後門走了出去，繞到阿噗身前看看。

"嗨，你堵住了吧？"他問。

"沒，沒有，"阿噗滿不在乎地説，"不過就是歇一會兒，想點事兒，再哼隻小曲兒罷咧。"

"來吧，把爪子給咱。"狗熊阿噗伸出一隻爪子，兔子拉啊拉啊拉啊。……

"哎喲！你拉痛我啦！"阿噗喊。兔子説，"你真堵在這兒了。""都怪你不弄個大點的前門，"阿噗生氣地説。"都怪你吃得太多，"兔子冷冷地説。"好啦，好啦，我去把克里托弗·羅賓叫來吧。"

羅賓住在林子的另一邊，他和兔子一起來了，見到阿噗的上半身，就説："我的傻老熊啊。"聲音親善，各人聽了都覺得事情還有希望。

狗熊輕輕吸着氣説："我剛才在想，兔子這前門恐怕

door again." "Of course he'll use his front door again," said Christopher Robin. "If we can't pull you out, Pooh, we might push you back." "You mean I'd *never* get out?" said Pooh.

"I mean," said Rabbit, "we shall have to wait for you to get thin again." "How long does getting thin take?" asked Pooh anxiously. "About a week, I should think." "But I can't stay here for a *week*!"

"We'll read to you," said Rabbit cheerfully. "Do you mind if I use your back legs as a towel-horse?"

"A week!" said Pooh gloomily. "*What about meals?*" "I'm afraid no meals," said Christopher Robin, "because of getting thin quicker."

Bear began to sigh, and then found he couldn't because he was so tightly stuck; and a tear rolled down his eye, as he said: "Then would you read a Sustaining Book, such as would help and comfort a Wedged Bear in Great Tightness?"

So for a week Christopher Robin read that sort of book at the North end of Pooh, and Rabbit hung his washing on the South end ... and in between Bear felt himself getting slenderer and slenderer. And at the end of the week Christopher Robin said, "*Now!*"

So he took hold of Pooh's front paws and Rabbit took hold of Christopher Robin, and all Rabbit's friends and relations took hold of Rabbit, and they all pulled together.... And for a long time Pooh only said "*Ow!*" ... And "*Oh!*"...

And then, all of a sudden, he said "*Pop!*" just as if a cork were coming out of a bottle. Out came Winnie-the-Pooh — free!

So, with a nod of thanks to his friends, he went on with his walk through the forest, humming proudly to himself.

— *A. A. Milne*

再也用不上了。"羅賓説，"他當然還用得上。如果我們不能把你拉出來。就把你推回去。""你的意思是我再也出不去了？"阿噗問。

"我的意思是，"兔子説，"我們只好等你變瘦了。""要多長時間才能變瘦呀？"阿噗着急地問。"我想差不多個星期吧。""叫我不能在這兒呆一個星期啊！"

"我們會給你唸點書的，"兔子高高興興地説。"我把你的腿當毛巾架用用，你不介意嗎？"

"一個星期！"阿噗發愁地説，"那我吃甚麼啊？""恐怕沒有吃的了，這樣瘦得快些，"羅賓説。

阿噗嘆起氣來。可發現連嘆氣也不行，因為塞得緊。一滴眼淚滾落下來，他説："那你們能唸本養生活命的書嗎？就要那幫助和安慰一隻被夾在洞裏脱不得身的熊的那種書。"

於是，一個星期來，羅賓在阿噗的北邊唸着這類書，兔子在南邊晾起洗濕的衣物，狗熊夾在中間感到自己漸漸苗條起來。一個星期過後，羅賓説："來吧！"

他握着阿噗的前爪，兔子抱住羅賓，兔子的親朋好友又都抱住兔子。大家一起一拉……阿噗"哎喲""噢"地叫了半天。

突然間，他叫了一聲"砰！"就像一隻瓶塞跳出瓶口一樣，蹦了出來。溫尼-阿噗出來了，自由了！

他向朋友們點頭致謝，又得意地哼着小曲兒穿過樹林走了。

—— *A·A·米爾恩*

76 Pecos Bill and His Bouncing Bride
(U.S.A.)

The story of Bill's love, Slue-Foot[1] Sue, is a long one. It began with the tale of the Perpetual Motion Ranch. Bill had bought a mountain. It looked to him like a perfect mountain for a ranch. It was shaped like a cone, with smooth sides covered with grassy meadows. At the top it was always winter. At the bottom it was always summer. In between it was always spring and fall. The sun always shone on one side; the other was always in shade. The cattle could have any climate they wished.

Bill had to breed a special kind of steer for his ranch. These had two short legs on one side and two long legs on the other. By traveling in one direction around the mountain, they were able to stand up straight on the steep sides. The novelty wore off, however, and at last Bill sold the Perpetual Motion Ranch to an English duke. The day that the boys moved out, the lord moved in. He brought with him trainload after trainload of fancy English things. The cowboys laughed themselves almost sick when they saw these dude things being brought to a cattle ranch.

Pecos Bill didn't laugh. He didn't even notice the fancy things. All he could see was the English duke's beautiful daughter. She was as pretty as the sun and moon combined. She was the loveliest creature he had ever seen. She was as lively and gay as she was pretty. Bill discovered that Slue-Foot Sue was a girl of talent. He soon lost all his interest in cowpunching. He spent his afternoons at the Perpetual Motion

---

1. Slue-Foot：〔美俚〕偵探。

七十六　皮科斯·比爾和他上下彈跳的新娘[1]（美國）

　　提起比爾的情人探子阿蘇的故事，説來話長。這還得從“永動牧場”説起。比爾買下了一座山，覺得這山做牧場再合適不過。山呈圓錐形，平滑的山坡長滿牧草。山頂終年積雪，山腳夏日炎炎，山腰卻是春、秋常駐；山的一面經年陽光燦爛，一面永遠不見太陽。牛羣在山上要甚麼樣的氣候就有甚麼樣的氣候。

　　比爾得要為牧場培養一種特種牛，牛一邊的兩條腿長，一邊兩條腿短；這樣朝一個方向繞山走時，在陡峭的山坡上可以站直。可是這種荒唐主意終成泡影，比爾最後只好將“永動牧場”賣給了一位英國公爵。牧場的小伙子們遷出當天，公爵搬了進來，帶來一節節車廂的英國高級玩藝兒。牛仔們見把這些講究的東西運到一個牧牛場，幾乎笑岔了氣。

　　比爾沒有笑，他連那些講究的東西都沒有看到，眼裏只有英國公爵美麗的女兒。她美得與日月爭輝，是比爾見到過的最漂亮的人兒。她不僅好看，還快樂活潑。比爾還發現她是個天份很高的姑娘。他很快就對牧牛完全失去興趣，每天下午都泡在“永動牧場”，教公爵小姐阿蘇馴服

---

1. 本篇是一種具有特殊風格的美國童話。這類童話多數是西部牛仔故事，所謂“大話故事（tall tales）”，即將情節、內容誇大至不可信的地步。這類故事本書還選了“火伕短工的獵犬‘快無比’”。

Ranch, teaching Sue to ride a broncho. After several months of Bill's lessons, she put on a show. She jumped onto the back of a huge catfish in the Rio Grande River[2] and rode all the way to the Gulf of Mexico, bare-back. Bill was proud of her.

Sue's mother was terribly upset by her daughter's behavior. She didn't care much for Bill. She was very proper. It was her fondest hope that Sue would stop being a tomboy and marry an earl or a member of Parliament. As soon as she realized that her daughter was falling in love with a cowboy, she was nearly heart-broken. There was nothing she could do about it, however. Slue-Foot Sue was a headstrong girl who always had her own way. At last the duchess relented. She invited Bill to tea and began to lecture him on English manners. She taught him how to balance a teacup and how to bow from the waist.

When the boys from the Ranch saw what was going on they were disgusted. Here was their boss, their brave, big, cyclone-riding Pecos Bill, mooning around in love like a sick puppy. The thought of losing Bill to a woman was too much. Even worse was the thought that Bill might get married and bring a woman home to live with them. That was awful.

In spite of their teasing and the duchess's lessons, Bill asked Slue-Foot Sue to marry him. She accepted before he could back out.

On his wedding day Pecos Bill shone like the sun in his new clothes. His boys were dressed in their finest chaps[3] and boots for the occasion. Half of them were going to be

---

2. Rio Grande River：美國德克薩斯州與墨西哥的界河，流入墨西哥灣。

3. chaps：chaparajos的簡寫，原為墨西哥西班牙語，穿此褲便於在美國西部的荆棘叢（chaparral）中行走，故名。

野馬。教了幾個月，阿蘇就露了一手。她光着背跳上格蘭德河一條大鯰魚背上，騎着魚一直到了墨西哥灣。比爾以她為榮。

　　阿蘇的媽媽對女兒的舉止懊惱非常，她不大喜歡比爾。她是個很講規矩的人，最大的希望就是阿蘇別再像個野小子，好好地嫁個伯爵或者國會議員就得了。一知道女兒愛上個牛仔，她那份傷心就別提了。可她毫無辦法，阿蘇是個很倔強的姑娘，一向我行我素。最後公爵夫人也心軟了，她請比爾來喝茶，開始教他英國的規矩，教他怎樣端好茶杯，怎麼彎腰深深鞠躬。

　　可是牧場的小伙子們見到這情景覺得噁心。他們的頭兒，那勇敢的大個子、飛馬旋風的比爾被愛情弄得暈暈乎乎，像隻小病狗。把比爾拱手讓給一個女人的念頭使他們受不了。想到比爾還要結婚，把一個女人帶回家和他們住在一起，就更膩味了。

　　不管他們嘲笑也好，公爵夫人訓話也好，比爾到底向探子阿蘇求婚了。沒等他來得及收回成命，阿蘇就接受了。

　　結婚那天，比爾一身新衣，神采飛揚。他的夥伴們也都為參加婚禮穿上最好的皮套褲和靴子。一半人做男儐

groomsmen. The other half were going to be bridesmen. They rode to the Perpetual Motion Ranch in a fine procession, Bill at the head on Widow-Maker. At the ranch house waited the rest of the wedding party.

Down the stairs came the bride. She was a vision of beauty. Pecos Bill lost his head. He leapt down from Widow-Maker and ran to meet her. "You are lovely," he murmured. "I promise to grant you every wish you make." That was a mistake. For months she had been begging Bill to let her ride Widow-Maker. Bill, of course, had always refused because he had promised the pony no other human would ever sit in his saddle.

Now Sue saw her chance. Before she allowed the wedding to proceed, she demanded that Bill give her one ride on his white mustang. "No, no!" cried Pecos Bill. Before he could stop her Sue dashed down the drive and placed her dainty foot into the stirrup. The duchess screamed. The bishop turned pale. Widow-Maker gave an angry snort. He lifted his four feet off the ground and arched his back. Up, up, up shot Slue-Foot Sue. She disappeared into the clouds.

"Catch her, catch her!" roared Bill at the boys. They spread themselves out into a wide circle. Then from the sky came a scream like a siren. Down, down, down fell Sue. She hit the earth with terrible force. She landed on her bustle. The wire acted as a spring. It bounced. Up again she flew. Up and down, up and down between the earth and sky Sue bounced like a rubber ball. This went on for a week. When at last she came back to earth to stay, she was completely changed. She no longer loved Pecos Bill.

Now Pecos was the unhappiest man Texas had ever seen. At last he called his hands together and made a long speech. He told them that the days of real cowpunching were over.

相，另一半人做女儐相，組成整齊的行列，浩浩蕩蕩地奔向永動牧場。比爾騎着誰騎誰摔死的"喪門星"走在前頭。參加婚禮的其他人都在牧場的房子裏等候。

新娘走下樓梯，美極了。比爾看傻了，他跳下"喪門星"卯卜夫。"你真可愛，"他低聲道，"我答應，你要甚麼我就給你甚麼。"這裏他犯了個錯誤。幾個月來阿蘇一直求比爾讓她騎"喪門星"，比爾當然每次都拒絕了，因為他答應過這馬，不許任何人騎它。

這回阿蘇看到機會來了。她要比爾在婚禮舉行之前讓她騎一次這白色野馬。"不行、不行！"比爾喊起來。可他還未來得及阻止，阿蘇已衝下車道，把纖足踏上馬蹬。公爵夫人尖叫起來，主教變了臉色。"喪門星"憤怒地噴了下鼻子，揚起四蹄，弓起脊背，阿蘇被拋了起來，飛，飛，飛，高高地拋向天空，消失在雲端裏。

"接住她！接住她！"比爾向小伙子們大喊，他們散開成一個大圓圈。這時，只聽得空中傳來汽笛般的一聲尖叫，阿蘇掉下來，掉下來，重重地摔在地上。着地的是裙撐，裙撐架就像彈簧，反彈起來，阿蘇又飛向高空。就這樣，阿蘇像個皮球，在天上地下來回地反彈，整整彈了一個星期。最後她終於落在地面上，人整個兒變了。她不再愛比爾了。

這時比爾成了整個德克薩斯州有史以來最不幸的男人。他把夥計們叫到一起，講了長長的一席話，告訴他們

He was going to sell his herd. He divided the cows and calves among his boys. He himself mounted Widow-Maker and rode away. None of them ever saw him again.

— *James C. Bowmen*

真正的牛仔生活過去了，他要賣掉牛羣。他把母牛和小牛分給小伙子們，自己騎上"喪門星"走了。從此人們再也沒有見到過他。

—— 詹姆斯·C·鮑曼

77 The Boomer Fireman's Fast Sooner Hound (U.S.A.)

One day when a Boomer[1] fireman pulled into[2] the roadmaster's office looking for a job, there was that Sooner[3] hound of his loping after him. Not that a rabbit would have any chance if the Sooner really wanted to nail him, but that crazy hound dog didn't like to do anything but run and he was the fastest thing on four legs.

"I might use you," said the roadmaster. "Can you get a boarding place for the dog?" "Oh, he goes along with me," said the Boomer. "I raised him from a pup just like a mother or father and he ain't never spent a night or a day or even an hour far away from me."

"Well, I don't see how that would work out," said the roadmaster. "It's against the rules of the road to allow a passenger in the cab, man or beast." "Why he ain't no trouble," said the Boomer. "He just runs alongside."

"Oh, is that so? Well, don't try to tell that yarn[4] around here," said the roadmaster. "I'll lay my first paycheck against a fin[5] that he'll be fresh as a daisy[6] when we pull into the junction." "It's a bet," said the roadmaster.

On the first run the Sooner moved in what was a slow walk for him. He kept looking up into the cab where the Boomer was shoveling in the coal. The roadmaster was so

---

1. boomer：流動性的工人、短工。
2. pull into：（車）駛入。
3. Sooner：捷足者。
4. yarn：故事。
5. fin：五元紙幣。
6. as fresh as a daisy：表示很新鮮的樣子。

406

七十七　火伕短工的獵犬"快無比"（美國）

一天，一個燒火的短工闖進鐵路站長的辦公室，想要找份工作，他那獵狗"快無比"跑跑跳跳，跟在身後，要是這"快無比"真要釘住隻兔子，這兔子就別想逃得脫了。可是這怪狗除了跑，甚麼都不喜歡，他是四條腿的動物中跑得最快的。

"我可以僱用你，"站長說，"你能找個人家寄養這狗嗎？""哦，他跟着我就行，"短工說，"我就像他爹媽一樣把他養大，他沒有一天、一夜，甚至一個鐘頭離開過我。"

"是嗎？我看那樣只怕不行，"站長說，"讓個乘客——不管是人還是動物——在司機室，都是違反鐵路章程的。""哦，他不惹麻煩，跟着車跑就是了，"短工說。

"哦，真的？可別在這兒吹牛呀，"局長說。短工說："我拿我第一次收到的工資單賭你五塊錢，等火車到站，他的氣色肯定還像朵剛開的小野菊。""一言為定，"局長說。

跑第一趟車，"快無比"跟着就像慢慢散步。他一直邊跑邊抬頭望着司機室，短工在那兒鏟煤燒火。賭輸了這

sore at losing the bet that he transferred the Boomer to a local passenger run[7] and doubled the stakes. The Sooner speeded up to a slow trot, but he had to kill a lot of time, at that, not to get too far ahead of the engine.

Then the roadmaster got mad enough to bite off a drawbar. People got to watching the Sooner trotting alongside the train and began thinking it must be a mighty slow road. Of course, the trains were keeping up their schedules the same as usual, but that's the way it looked to people who saw a no-good mangy Sooner hound beating all the trains without his tongue hanging out an inch or letting out the least little pant. The roadmaster would have fired the Boomer but he was stubborn from the word go and hated worse than anything to own up he was licked.

"I'll fix that Sooner," said the roadmaster. "I'll slap the Boomer into the cab of the Cannon Ball, and if anything on four legs can keep up with the fastest thing on wheels I'd admire to see it."

The word got around that the Sooner was going to try to keep up with the Cannon Ball. Farmers left off plowing, hitched up, and drove to the right of way[8] to see the sight. It was like a circus day or the county fair. The schools all dismissed the pupils, and not a factory could keep enough men to make a wheel turn.

The roadmaster got right in the cab so that the Boomer couldn't soldier on the job to let the Sooner keep up. You couldn't see a thing for[9] steam, cinders and smoke, and the rails sang like a violin for a half hour after the Cannon Ball passed into the next county. Every valve was popping off

---

7. run：一趟路程，一班車。
8. right of way：鐵路用地。
9. for：= because of。

局，站長十分惱火，他把短工轉到短途客車上，又將賭注加倍。"快無比"加快步伐，變成慢步小跑，但他為了不比火車超前太遠，還得磨磨蹭蹭打發不少時間。

這下站長氣得咬牙切齒，可以一口咬斷列車掛鈎。人們跑來看到"快無比"在列車旁溜溜地慢跑，開始想，這路車實在太慢了。當然啦，火車像往常一樣準時到站。但人們看到一條這麼不起眼的癩皮狗把所有列車毫不費力地甩在後面，大氣不喘一口，舌頭不吐出一吋，就會有火車太慢的感覺。站長本想解僱短工算了，可他是個嘴硬的人，最恨的是認輸。

"我非得治治那條'快無比'，"站長說，"我把短工放在'砲彈'列車車頭上，倒想看看哪個四條腿的能跑過輪子上的最快的傢伙！"

"快無比"跑得過"砲彈"列車的消息傳開來，農夫扔下耕犁，趕上牛車馬車，到鐵路邊來看熱鬧。這天活像是馬戲團演出日或是縣裏的集市廟會。學校放了假，工廠也沒人開機器了。

站長登上車頭，怕短工為了幫"快無比"趕上車而偷工減料。除了蒸汽、煤灰和煙，甚麼都看不見了。列車駛進鄰縣後，鐵軌還像小提琴般歡奏了半個小時，所有汽門

and the wheels three feet in the air above the roadbed. The Boomer was so sure the Sooner would keep up that he didn't stint[10] the elbow grease[11].

The roadmaster stuck his head out of the cab window, and—whosh!—off went his hat and almost his head. But he let out a whoop of joy. "THE SOONER! THE SOONER!" he yelled. "He's gone! Ain't *nowhere* in sight!"

Then the Cannon Ball was puffing into the station at the end of the run. Before the wheels had stopped rolling, the roadmaster jumped nimbly to the ground. A mighty cheer was heard from a group of people nearby. The roadmaster beamed as he drew near them. "Here I am!" he shouted. "Do you want to take my picture in the cab?"

"Go way back and sit down!" a man shouted as he turned briefly toward the railroad official. "You might as well scrap that Cannon Ball. The Sooner has been here a good half hour. Look at him!" The Sooner was loping easily around a tree.

— *Jack Conroy*

---

10. stint：停止，節省。
11. elbow grease：苦幹，重活。

呼呼地排氣、車輪離路基三呎高。短工有把握"快無比"一定會趕上火車，所以他不停加油猛幹。

站長把頭探出司機室窗戶，呼，一陣風吹走了帽子，險些連頭也吹掉！可他大聲歡呼："'快無比'！'快無比'！他落後了，連影子也看不到啦！"

這時"砲彈"列車跑完全程，駛進了車站。車還沒停穩，站長便輕巧地跳下車，只聽得附近的人羣歡聲雷動。站長走近人羣時，滿臉笑容。"我到啦！"他喊，"要不要拍一張我在司機室裏的照片？"

"到一邊去坐下吧！"一個男人很快轉過身對着這鐵路站長喝道，"把你那'砲彈'列車報廢算了，'快無比'早半個鐘頭都到啦。你看他！""快無比"正慢悠悠地繞着棵樹轉呢。

——傑克·康羅依

78 The Wonderful Tar-Baby Story (U.S.A.)

Brer[1] Fox was always fixing some way to catch Brer Rabbit so, one day Brer Fox went to work and got him some tar, and mixed it with turpentine, and fixed up a contraption that he called a Tar-Baby. He took this here Tar-Baby and sat her in the big road, and then he laid off in the bushes for to see what the news was going to be. He didn't have to wait long, neither[2], for by and by here came Brer Rabbit pacing down the road — lippity-clippity, clippity-lippity — just as sassy[3] as a jay-bird, till he spied the Tar Baby and then he fetched up on his hind legs like he was astonished.

"Morning!" says Brer Rabbit, says he. Tar-Baby says nothing, and Brer Fox, he lay low, winked his eye slow, and lay low. "How you come on[4], then? Are you deaf?" says Brer Rabbit, says he. Tar-Baby stay still, and Brer Fox he lay low.

"You're stuck up, that's what you are," says Brer Rabbit, says he, "and I'm going to cure you." Brer Fox, he sort of chuckled in his stomach.

"I'm going to learn[5] you how to talk to respectable folks if it's my last act," says Brer Rabbit, says he. "If you don't take off that hat and tell me howdy[6], I'm going to bust you

---

1. Brer：= Brother，美國南方方言。
2. neither：either 的誤用。
3. sassy：〔美式英語〕= saucy：愉快、活潑；冒失、莽撞。
4. How you come on：= how do you get along。
5. to learn：to teach 的誤用。
6. tell me howdy：say "How do you do" to me。

七十八　柏油娃娃的妙用（美國）

　　狐狸大哥常常佈下陷阱想捉住兔小弟。一天，狐狸大哥找來些柏油，拌上松脂，做出個新玩意兒，起名叫柏油娃娃。他拿這柏油娃娃放在大路中間坐着，自己走開藏到灌木叢中等着看新鮮事兒。沒等多久，兔小弟就像隻松雞那樣莽莽撞撞地順着大路過來了。看到柏油娃娃，他一愣，用後腿站起，一副驚訝的樣子。

　　"早上好！"兔小弟他説。柏油娃娃一聲不響。狐狸大哥呢，他伏得低低的，他慢慢地眨眨眼睛，伏得低低的。"那你到底怎麼啦，你聾了嗎？"兔小弟他説。柏油娃娃一動不動，狐狸大哥他伏得低低的。

　　"你嘴巴黏上了是不是？我看你就是嘴巴黏住了，"兔小弟他説，"我來給你治一治！"狐狸大哥他肚裏呵呵暗笑。

　　"我只好拿出最後一招，教訓教訓你對有身份的人説話應該是甚麼樣子，"兔小弟他説。"你再不脱下你那帽子，對我問聲好，我一拳把你打開膛，"他説。兔小弟這裏不

wide open," says he. Brer Rabbit keeps on asking, and the Tar-Baby, she keep on saying nothing, till presently Brer Rabbit draw back with his fist, he did, and *blip* he took her on the side of the head. His fist stuck, and he can't pull loose. The tar held him.

"If you don't let me loose, I'll knock you again," says Brer Rabbit, says he, and with that he fetched a swipe with the other hand, and that stuck fast. "Turn me loose, before I kick the natural stuffing out of you," says Brer Rabbit, says he, but Tar-Baby, she say nothing. She just held on, and then Brer Rabbit lose the use of his two feet the same way. Then Brer Rabbit squall out that if the Tar-Baby don't turn him loose, he'll butt her cranksided. And then he butted, and his head got stuck. And there he was.

And Brer Fox he sauntered forth looking just as innocent as a mocking-bird. "Howdy, Brer Rabbit," says Brer Fox, says he. "You look sort of stuck up this morning," says he, and then he rolled on the ground and he laughed and laughed till he couldn't laugh any more. "Well, I 'spect[7] I got you this time, Brer Rabbit," says he; "You've been running round here sassing me for a mighty long time but I 'spect you've come to the end of the row[8]. And there's where you are, and there you'll stay, till I fix up a brush pile and fires her up, 'cause I'm going to barbecue you this day, sure."

Then Brer Rabbit talked mighty humble. "I don't care what you do with me, Brer Fox," says he, "just so you don't fling me in that brier-patch. Roast me, Brer Fox." "It's so much trouble for to kindle a fire," says Brer Fox, says he, "that I 'spect I'll have to drown you."

---

7. 'spect：= suspect。

8. end of the row：at the end of one's row 為美國俚語，意為淪落不堪。

停地問，柏油娃娃那裏照樣一聲不吭。最後兔小弟掄起拳頭，噗的一聲照她頭側打去。他的拳頭被柏油黏住，收不回來了。

　　"你再不放開我，我還要打，"兔小弟他說。說着他用另外一隻手又一巴掌打過去。這隻手也緊緊地黏住了。"放開我，別叫我把你的五臟六腑踢出來，"兔小弟他說。可柏油娃娃她還是不說話，就這樣黏着他。接着兔小弟又用腳踢，兩隻腳也都黏住了。這時兔小弟大喊大叫，說要是柏油娃娃不放開他，他就要用頭把她撞歪撞倒。於是他用頭撞過去，頭也黏上了。他黏在那裏。

　　這時狐狸大哥悠悠閒閒走出來，一副清白無辜的樣子。"你好啊，兔老弟，"狐狸大哥他說，"今兒早上看樣子你是讓黏住了啦。"說着，笑得在地上打滾。他笑個不停，等到笑不動了，才說，"好啦，兔老弟，我看這回我大概是逮住你了。你在這裏跑來跑去盡跟我搗亂，時間夠長的了。我看你這下山窮水盡了吧。你黏住在這兒了，好好呆着吧。等我去弄個柴堆點着火。因為我今天要把你烤來吃。肯定要吃掉你了。"

　　這時兔小弟說話低聲下氣了。"你拿我怎麼樣都不要緊，狐狸大哥，"他說，"只千萬別把我扔到那荊棘叢裏就行。把我烤了吧，狐狸哥。""生火太費事，"狐狸大哥他說，"我看還是把你淹死算了。"

"Drown me just as deep as you please, Brer Fox," says Brer Rabbit, says he, "but don't fling me in that brier-patch." "There ain't any water nearby," says Brer Fox, says he, "and now I 'spect I'll have to skin you."

"Skin me, Brer Fox," says Brer Rabbit, says he, "but please, Brer Fox, please don't fling me in that brier-patch," says he.

Of course Brer Fox wanted to hurt Brer Rabbit as bad as he could so he caught him by the hind legs and slung him right in the middle of the brier-patch. There was a considerable flutter where Brer Rabbit struck the bushes, and Brer Fox sort of hung around[9] to see what was going to happen. By and by he heard someone call him, way up the hill, and he saw Brer Rabbit sitting cross-legged on a chinkapin log combing the pitch out of his hair with a chip. Then Brer Fox knew he'd been fooled mighty bad. And Brer Rabbit was obliged to fling back some of his sass, so he hollered out: "Bred and born in the brier-patch, Brer Fox — bred and born in the brier-patch!" and with that he skipped out as lively as a cricket[10] in the embers[11].

— *Joel Chandler Harris*

---

9. hung around：hanging around。
10. as lively as a cricket：非常快樂、活潑。
11. embers：ember days，四季節，天主教會和基督教聖公會的節日。

416

"你要把我淹多深就淹多深吧，狐狸哥，可就是別扔我到荊棘叢裏去，"兔小弟他説。"可近處沒有水。我看乾脆把你剝了皮得了。"狐大哥他説。

　　"剝吧，狐狸哥。可是求你啦，求你別把我扔到荊棘叢裏，"兔小弟他説。

　　當然啦，狐狸大哥要把兔小弟害得愈苦愈好，於是他抓起兔小弟兩隻後腿，一下把他扔到荊棘叢的正中央。兔小弟掉下去的地方沙沙地好一陣響動，狐狸大哥在周圍轉了轉想看看兔小弟怎樣了。過了一會兒，他聽到有人叫他，在山上。他抬頭一看，兔小弟蹺着二郎腿坐在一截栗木矮樁上，正用塊木片刮去毛上的柏油呢。狐狸哥知道自己上了大當，兔小弟當然又要説回點風涼話啦。這不，只聽他喊："狐狸哥呀，我生在荊棘叢，長在荊棘叢哩！"説着，高高興興一蹦一跳地走了。

　　　　　　　　　　　　——*喬爾·錢德勒·哈里斯*[1]

---

1. 哈里斯（1848—1908），美國作家，熟悉黑人的傳説和方言。本篇選自《雷默斯大叔的歌和話》（*Uncle Remus, His Songs and His Sayings*）。此書由黑人口述，哈里斯整理記錄而成。"柏油娃娃"發表後，曾在美國掀起方言文學熱潮，本文由 M. H. Arbuthnot 改寫成規範英語，但文中多處仍保留不規範英語，如 she keep、his fist stuck、she say nothing 等等，不一一指出。

79 The Hungry Peasant, God, and Death
(Mexico)

Not far from the city of Zacatecas[1] there lived a poor peasant, whose harvest was never sufficient to keep hunger away from himself, his wife and children. Every year his harvests grew worse, his family more numerous. Thus as time passed, the man had less and less to eat for himself, since he sacrificed a part of his own rations on behalf of his wife and children.

One day, tired of so much privation, the peasant stole a chicken with the determination to go far away, very far, to eat it, where no one could see him and expect him to share it. He took a pot and climbed up the most broken side of a nearby mountain. Upon finding a suitable spot. he made a fire, cleaned his chicken, and put it to cook with herbs. When it was ready, he took the pot off the fire and waited impatiently for it to cool off. As he was about to eat it, he saw a man coming along one of the paths in his direction. The peasant hurriedly hid the pot in the bushes and said to himself, "Curse the luck! Not even here in the mountains is one permitted to eat in peace."

At this moment the stranger approached and greeted, "Good morning, friend!"

"May God grant you a good morning," he answered.

"What are you doing here, friend?"

"Well, nothing, señor[2], just resting. And, Your Grace, where are you going?"

---

1. Zacatecas：墨西哥同名州的首府，在墨西哥中部偏北。

2. señor：〔西班牙語〕先生。墨西哥原為西班牙殖民地，西班牙語為通用語言。

七十九 飢餓的農夫、上帝與死神
（墨西哥）

離薩卡台卡斯市不遠，住着個窮苦的農夫，莊稼的收成總是不足維持他和妻兒的溫飽。收成一年比一年少，家裏人口卻一年比一年多。因此年復一年，農夫吃的越來越少了，因為他把自己的那份口糧分出一些給妻兒了。

一天，迫於如此貧困艱辛，農夫偷了一隻雞，決心拿到遠遠的、沒人見也沒人跟他分的地方吃掉。他拿了一隻鍋到附近一座山下，從最巉巖的一面爬上去。他找到一塊合適的地方，生個火，宰好雞，加些野菜便放在鍋裏煮起來。雞煮好後，他把鍋從火上端開，急不可待地等着雞涼下來。他正要吃的時候，看見一個人沿着一條小路朝他這個方向走。農夫急忙將鍋藏進樹叢，自言自語道：“倒霉！連在大山裏安靜地吃口飯都不行！”

正說着，陌生人過來和他打招呼，“朋友，早上好！”

“願上帝保佑你，早上好！”農夫答。

“朋友，你在這兒做甚麼？”

“哎，沒做甚麼，先生，就是歇歇腳。閣下呢？您去哪兒啊？”

"Oh, I was just passing by and stopped to see if you could give me something to eat."

"No, señor, I haven't anything."

"How's that, when you have a fire burning?"

"Oh, this little fire; that's just for warming myself."

"Don't tell me that. Haven't you a pot hidden in the bushes? Even from here I can smell the cooked hen."

"Well yes, señor, I have some chicken but I shall not give you any; I would not even give any to my own children. I came way up here because for once in my life I wanted to eat my fill."

"Come friend, don't be unkind. Give me just a little of it!"

"No, señor, I shall not give you any."

"Yes, you will as soon as I tell you who I am."

"Well then, who are you?"

"I am God, your Lord."

"Uh, hm, now less than ever shall I share my food with you. You are very bad to the poor. You only give to those whom you like. To some you give haciendas, palaces, trains, carriages, horses; to others, like me, nothing. You have never even given me enough to eat."

God continued arguing with him, but the man would not even give Him a mouthful of broth, so He went His way.

When the peasant was about to eat his chicken, another stranger came along; this one was very thin and pale. "Good morning, friend!" he said. "Haven't you anything there you can give me to eat?"

"No, señor, nothing."

"哦，我是路過，停下來看看你能不能給我點兒吃的。"

　　"不行，先生，我甚麼吃的也沒有。"

　　"怎麼可能呢，你正燒着火呀。"

　　"哦，這點火；只是取暖用的。"

　　"別跟我說這話，你不是藏了隻鍋在樹叢裏嗎？我在這兒都聞得到煮熟的雞的香味啦。"

　　"啊，是的，先生，我是有點雞，可一點兒也不能給你，我連自己的孩子都一點也沒有給呢。我老遠上這兒來就為的想這輩子自己吃一頓飽飯。"

　　"哎，朋友，別這麼小氣啊，就給我一點兒吧！"

　　"不，先生，我一點兒也不給你。"

　　"你會給的。我一告訴你我是誰，你就會給了。"

　　"那好吧，你是誰？"

　　"我是上帝，你的主。"

　　"呃，嗯，這回我更不能把雞給你了，你對窮苦人太刻薄，你只把恩惠賜給你喜歡的人。有些人你給他們莊園、宮殿、火車、馬車和駿馬，可對另外的人，像我這樣的，你甚麼也不給，你從來沒有讓我吃飽過。"

　　上帝繼續和他爭論，可那人一口雞湯也不給他，他只好走自己的路。

　　農夫剛要吃雞，又來了一個陌生人，這人十分瘦削蒼白。"朋友，早上好，"他說，"你這兒有甚麼東西能給我吃嗎？"

　　"沒有，先生，甚麼也沒有。"

"Come, don't be a bad fellow! Give me a little piece of that chicken you're hiding."

"No, señor, I shall not give you any."

"Oh yes, you will. You refuse me now because you don't know who I am."

"Who can you be? God, Our Lord Himself, just left and not even to Him would I give anything, less to you."

"But you will, when you know who I am."

"All right; tell me then who you are."

"I am Death!"

"You were right. To you I shall give some chicken, because you are just. You, yes, you take away the fat and thin ones, old and young, poor and rich. You make no distinctions nor show any favoritism. To you, yes, I shall give some of my chicken!"

— Frances Toor

"哎，別那麼不夠朋友！把你藏着的那雞給我一小塊吧。"

"不，先生，我一點也不給你。"

"噢，你會給的。你不給是因為你不知道我是誰。"

"你還能是誰？我們的主，上帝本人剛走，連他我都一點也沒給，別説是你了。"

"可你一知道我是誰，你就會給了。"

"好吧，那告訴我你是誰。"

"我是死神！"

"你説對了。我真要給你點雞，因為你是公平的。是的，你不分肥瘦、老幼、貧富，一律把他們帶走。你一視同仁，沒有偏愛。是的，對你我要給一些雞！"

—— 弗蘭西斯·杜爾

80 Carried Off by the Moon
(Netsilik Eskimo)

Kukiaq was a great shaman[1] who lived not too long ago. Originally, he was from a far place, but after his family died, he moved to Netsilik land, and lived most often around Kingait.

Once he was standing by a breathing-hole[2], waiting to catch a seal. It was a fine midwinter evening, no wind, and the moon was full. He had his face turned directly toward the moon, and the moon seemed near. He gazed steadily at it and before he knew it, the moon really was coming closer and closer, until it hovered overhead! And then he saw a phantom sledge and a man driving it. There was a team of dogs, and as they approached Kukiaq, he saw that the moon itself was the driver! The dogs were eager to get close to Kukiaq, and the moon had trouble reining them in. At last, the moon stopped and gestured to Kukiaq to come with him. Kukiaq ran over to him. The moon, a big, angry man, stood with his back to Kukiaq near his sledge, which was made of four whale jawbones tied together.

"Close your eyes and sit on my sledge," the moon said. Kukiaq sat down. At once the sledge began to move. Kukiaq could feel the swish and the wind of its speed around him; they were sweeping along. Kukiaq wanted to see where they were going, but could only peek through his eyelids, the wind was so strong. He looked into a tremendous abyss, and almost fell off the sledge. Thoroughly frightened, Kukiaq closed his

---

1. shamon：薩滿是一種宗教；薩滿僧尼是被認為能治病及通鬼神的人。
2. breathing hole：北極冰下水棲動物借以升起呼吸之孔。

八十　被月亮帶走的人[1]
（涅特希利克愛斯基摩）

　　庫基亞克倒也不是個古人，他是個有很大法力的薩滿僧。他原來住在遠處，家人死後，他便搬到涅特希利克一帶，大部分時間住在金蓋特附近。

　　一次他正站在一個冰上通氣孔旁，守候着想抓隻海豹。這是隆冬季節，個晴朗無風的夜晚，月亮正圓。他舉頭望月，月亮仿佛很近。他目不轉睛地盯着月亮，不知不覺月亮竟真的冉冉下降，最後懸掛在頭頂！這時他看見有個人駕着輛幻影般的雪橇，還有一羣狗。等他們走近，庫基亞克看到駕雪橇的竟是月亮本身！那羣狗要向庫基亞克奔過來，月亮險些勒不住它們。最後，月亮停下了，對庫基亞克打個手勢讓他跟他走。庫基亞克向他跑過去。月亮是個魁梧的人，滿面怒容站在雪橇旁，背朝庫基亞克。雪橇是用四塊鯨的頷骨縛在一起造成的。

　　"閉上眼睛坐到我的雪橇上來，"月亮說。庫基亞克坐下。雪橇立刻滑動起來，庫基亞克只覺得耳邊風聲呼呼，一路風馳電掣。庫基亞克想看看究竟去哪兒，但風太大了，只能把眼睛睜開一條縫。他向下看到一道令人毛骨悚然的深淵，幾乎摔下了雪橇。庫基亞克嚇得又緊緊閉上雙

---

1. 此篇為涅特希利克愛斯基摩人的傳說。

eyes tightly again. They drove on, and he heard from the resounding noise of the sledge that they were on new ice, bare of snow. In a while the sledge stopped and Kukiaq opened his eyes. He saw before him a large village, many houses, many people: suddenly two of his friends ran up and struck him with their fists! He was in the Land of the Dead, up in the sky!

Now the moon wanted to take Kukiaq to his house. They walked to the entrance together. In the passage lay a big dog, so they had to step on it in order to get through. The dog growled, but that was all. The inside of the house was moving in and out, like tent walls flapping in the wind; the walls of the passage moved like a mouth chewing. But they got through safely. The house had two rooms, and in one sat a young, pretty woman holding a child. Her lamp was burning with such a big flame that Kukiaq's neckband became scorched simply by glancing at her. She was the sun! She waved at Kukiaq and made room for him on her platform, but he was afraid he would forget to go home again, and he hurried away, letting himself slide down from the house of the moon towards the earth again. He fell and fell, and he ended up right back at the very breathing-hole where the moon found him before.

Kukiaq is the last of our shamans who has been up with the sun and the moon.

— *Kund Rasmussen*

眼。他們繼續前行，聽到雪橇下面的軋軋聲，他知道走上了另一塊還未被雪覆蓋的新凍結的冰上。不一會兒，雪橇停住了，庫基亞克睜開雙眼，看到有一片大村落，裏面有許多房子和許多人。忽然他的兩個朋友跑上前來，用拳頭捶打他！原來他到了天上的死亡之鄉！

這會兒，月亮想帶庫基亞克去他的房子。他們一起走到門口，過道裏躺着一條大狗，他們只好踩在狗身上過去。狗咆哮了幾聲也就算了。屋子裏的牆一會兒向內、一會兒向外翻動，活像帳篷在風中飄動；過道牆壁像一張正在嚼東西的嘴。但他們平安無事進了屋。屋子裏有兩個房間，一間裏面坐着個美貌少婦，懷中抱着個孩子。她的燈吐出巨大的火舌，庫基亞克只瞟了她一眼，衣領便燒焦了。啊，原來她是太陽！她向庫基亞克招招手，在她坐的台子上為他騰了點地方，可是他怕這樣一來忘了回家，便慌忙離開了。他從月亮的房子一直滑向地面，滑啊滑啊，正好停住在先前月亮找到他的那個冰上通氣孔旁。

庫基亞克是我們薩滿人中最後一個上天見到太陽和月亮的人。

—— 昆德·拉斯穆森 [2]

---

2. 拉斯穆森（1879 — 1933），丹麥探險家和人種學專家，精通愛斯基摩語，曾在極地生活，有大量著作。

81 Little Burnt-Face (Red Indian)

Once upon a time, in a large Indian village on the border of a lake, there lived an old man who was a widower. He had three daughters. The eldest was jealous, cruel, and ugly; the second was vain; but the youngest of all was very gentle and lovely. Now, when the father was out hunting in the forest, the eldest daughter used to beat the youngest girl, and burn her face with hot coals; yes, and even scar her pretty body. So the people called her "Little Burnt-Face". When the father came home from hunting he would ask why she was so scarred, and the eldest would answer quickly: "She is a good-for-nothing! She was forbidden to go near the fire, and she disobeyed and fell in." Then the father would scold Little Burnt-Face and she would creep away crying to bed.

By the lake, at the end of the village, there was a beautiful wigwam. And in that wigwam lived a Great Chief and his sister. The Great Chief was invisible; no one had ever seen him but his sister. Now, one Spring, his sister made known that her brother, the Great Chief, would marry any girl who could see him. Then all the girls from the village — except Little Burnt-Face and her sisters — and all the girls for miles around hastened to the wigwam, and when they entered, his sister told them not to take the seat next to the door, for that was where her brother sat. But they never saw the Chief, though many of them stayed all night.

One day Little Burnt-Face's two sisters put on their finest blankets and brightest strings of beads and started out to see the Great Chief. As soon as they were gone, Little Burnt-

八十一　小焦臉兒[1]（紅印第安）

從前，湖畔一個印第安大村落裏住着一位年老的鰥夫，他有三個女兒。大女兒嫉妒成性，又兇又醜，二女兒庸俗虛榮，只有小妹妹非常溫雅可愛。父親去森林裏打獵時，大女兒總要打小妹妹，還用燒紅的煤烙她的面孔，甚至把她美麗的軀體也折磨得傷痕纍纍。所以人們都叫她"小焦臉兒"。父親打獵回來問她怎麼會渾身是傷，大女兒搶着答道："她是個廢物，不讓她靠近火爐，她就是不聽，這不，跌進火裏了。"父親大罵了小焦臉兒一頓，她只好悄悄哭着上牀了。

湖畔村頭有座美麗的小窩棚，裏面住着大酋長和他的姐姐。大酋長是隱身人，除了他姐姐誰也沒有見過他。這一年的春天，大酋長的姐姐告訴大夥兒，哪個姑娘能見到她弟弟，他就娶她為妻。於是，村裏的姑娘——除了小焦臉兒和她兩個姐姐——和住在方圓許多里內的姑娘都趕到小窩棚來。她們走進去後，大酋長姐姐告訴她們別坐在門邊的那把椅子，因為那是她弟弟的座位。雖然許多姑娘在那裏呆了一整夜，可誰也沒看見大酋長。

一天，小焦臉兒的兩個姐姐披上她們最好看的毛毯，戴上最鮮亮的串珠，出門去看大酋長。她們剛走，小焦臉

---

1. 選自《紅印第安人童話》，是關於米克馬克族印第安人的故事。美洲印第安人的故事一般冗長而結構鬆散，但本篇條理清晰，語言通暢，故選入。

Face dressed herself in her birch-bark clothes and put her father's moccasins on her bare feet. Then she, too, started out to visit the wigwam. Poor Little Burnt-Face! She was a sorry sight! For her hair was singed off, and her little face was as full of burns and scars as a sieve is full of holes. And as she passed through the village the boys and girls hissed, yelled, and hooted. And when she reached the lake, her sisters saw her coming, and they tried to shame her, and told her to go home. But the Great Chief's sister received her kindly, and bade her stay, for she saw how sweet and gentle Little Burnt-Face really was.

Then as evening was coming on, the Great Chief's sister took all three girls walking beside the lake, and the sky grew dark, and they knew the Great Chief had come. And his sister asked the two elder girls, "Do you see my brother?" And they said, "Yes."

"Of what is his shoulder-strap made?"

"Of a strip of rawhide."

"And with what does he draw his sled?"

"With a green withe."

Then his sister turned to Little Burnt-Face and asked, "Do you see him?"

"I do! I do!" said Little Burnt-Face with awe. "And he is wonderful!"

"And of what is his sled-string made?" asked his sister gently.

"It is a beautiful Rainbow!" cried Little Burnt-Face.

"But, my sister, of what is his bow-string made?"

"His bow-string," replied Little Burnt-Face, "is the Milky Way!" Then the Great Chief's sister smiled with delight, and taking Little Burnt-Face by the hand, she said, "You have surely seen him."

兒便穿上她的樺樹皮衣服，赤腳套上父親的鹿皮靴，也去了那窩棚。可憐的小焦臉兒！她的樣子實在不好看！她的頭髮是燒焦的，小臉上滿是灼傷的疤痕和麻斑，像個篩子。她穿過村子時，姑娘、小伙兒都噓她，怪叫着對她起哄。她走到湖邊，兩個姐姐見她來，也想羞辱她，趕她回家。但是大酋長的姐姐親切地接待她，請她留下，因為她看得出小焦臉兒真是十分溫文爾雅。

傍晚時分，大酋長的姐姐帶着姐妹三人走在湖邊，天色漸晚，她們知道大酋長已經來了。大酋長姐姐問兩個姐姐：“你們見到我弟弟了嗎？”她們說：“見到了。”

“他的肩帶是甚麼做的？”

“用條生牛皮做的。”

“他用甚麼拉滑撬？”

“用根綠柳條。”

接着大酋長姐姐又轉身問小焦臉兒：“你看見他了嗎？”

“看見了！看見了！”小焦臉兒敬畏地說，“他神妙極了！”

“他的滑撬繩是用甚麼做的？”大酋長的姐姐柔聲問。

“是一道美麗的彩虹！”小焦臉叫道。

“那麼好妹妹，他的弓弦是甚麼做的呢？”

小焦臉兒答：“他的弓弦是銀河啊！”這時大酋長姐姐高興地笑了。她拉着小焦臉兒的手說：“你確實看見他了。”

She led the little girl to the wigwam, and bathed her with dew until the burns and scars all disappeared from her body and face. Her skin became soft and lovely again. Her hair grew long and dark like the Blackbird's wing. Her eyes were like stars. Then his sister brought from her treasures a wedding-garment, and she dressed Little Burnt-Face in it. After all this was done, his sister led the little girl to the seat next to the door, saying, "This is the Bride's seat," and made her sit down. And then the Great Chief, no longer invisible, entered, terrible and beautiful. And when he saw Little Burnt-Face, he smiled and said gently, "So we have found each other!"

And she answered, "Yes."

— *Frances J. Olcott*

她領着小姑娘走進窩棚，用露水給她洗澡洗臉，直到把全身和臉上的燒痕傷疤全洗掉。她的皮膚又變得細嫩美麗了，頭髮也長長了，像畫眉鳥的翅膀那樣黑，眼睛像天上的星星。大酋長姐姐從她的寶物中拿出一套結婚禮服給小焦臉兒穿上。之後，她領着小焦臉兒走到門邊的座位前，讓她坐下，説："這是新娘的座位。"這時，大酋長不再隱形了，他走進來，威武英俊。他一見到小焦臉兒，就微笑着柔聲道："我們到底有緣相聚了！"

　　她回答："你説的是。"

—— *弗朗西·J·奧爾科特*

82 Manabozho and His Toe
(North American Indian)

Manabozho, the great wizard of the Indians, was so powerful that he began to think there was nothing he could not do. Very wonderful were many of his feats, and he grew more conceited day by day. Now, it chanced that one day he was walking about amusing himself by exercising his extraordinary powers, and at length he came to an encampment where one of the first things he noticed was a child lying in the sunshine, curled up with its toe in its mouth.

Manabozho looked at the child for some time, and wondered at its extraordinary posture.

"I have never seen a child before lie like that," said he to himself, "but I could lie like it."

So saying, he put himself down beside the child, and, taking his right foot in his hand, drew it toward his mouth. When he had brought it as near as he could, it was yet a considerable distance away from his lips.

"I will try the left foot," said Manabozho. He did so, and found that he was no better off; neither of his feet could he get to his mouth. He curled and twisted, and bent his large limbs, and gnashed his teeth in rage to find that he could not get his toe to his mouth. All, however, was vain.

At length he rose, worn out with his exertions and passion, and walked slowly away in a very ill humor, which was not lessened by the sound of the child's laughter, for Manabozho's efforts had awakened it.

"Ah, ah!" said Manabozho, "shall I be mocked by a child?"

八十二　曼納博茲霍和他的腳趾
（北美印第安）

曼納博茲霍是印第安人的大魔術師。他法力無邊，竟以為自己無所不能了。他有許多神奇的本領，於是日益自負。好，有一天他碰巧到處走走，施展施展非凡的法術，以此自娛。最後他來到一座帳營前，第一眼看到的是個小娃娃躺在陽光下，跷曲起身體，把小腳趾放到嘴裏吮。

曼納博茲霍對着娃娃看了好一會兒，覺得這孩子的姿勢怎麼這樣特別。

"我從來沒有見過一個孩子是這樣躺着的。"他自言自言地說，"可是我也能像他那樣躺着。"

說着，他在孩子身邊躺下，用手拿着右腳伸向嘴巴。他盡力拉，但離嘴唇還是有相當一段距離。

"我試試用左腳吧，"曼納博茲霍說。他又用左腳，但也不比右腳好，兩隻腳都彎不到嘴巴的地方。他跷曲起身體，扭彎了又扭彎，又去扳大腿，發現還是無法把腳趾送進嘴裏。他氣惱得咬牙切齒。但這些都沒有用。

最後他站起來。由於過度用力和氣惱，他筋疲力竭。他滿心不高興地慢慢走開。娃娃被他吵醒了，咭咭地笑，使他心情更壞了。

"唉！唉！"曼納博茲霍說，"我竟落到被個小娃娃笑話的下場嗎？！"

He did not, however, revenge himself on his victor, but on his way homeward, meeting a boy who did not treat him with proper respect, he transformed him into a cedar-tree. "At least," said Manabozho, "I can do something."

— *edited by Kate Wiggin & Nora Smith*

他倒也沒有拿他的勝利者出氣，而是在回家時把在路上碰到的一個男孩子變成一棵杉樹了，因為這男孩沒有對他表示應有的尊敬。

"至少我還能做點事情，"曼納博茲霍説。

——凱特·威金 與 諾拉·史密斯 編

Asian Tales

亞洲童話

83 The Banyan Deer (India)

There was once a Deer the color of gold. His eyes were like round jewels, his horns were white as silver, his mouth was red like a flower, his hoofs were bright and hard. He had a large body and a fine tail. He lived in a forest and was king of a herd of five hundred Banyan Deer. Near by lived another herd of Deer, called the Monkey Deer. They, too, had a king.

The king of that country was fond of hunting the Deer and eating deer meat. He did not like to go alone so he called the people of his town to go with him, day after day. The townspeople did not like this for while they were gone no one did their work. So they decided to make a park and drive the Deer into it. Then the king could go into the park and hunt and they could go on with their daily work.

They made a park, planted grass in it and provided water for the Deer, built a fence all around it and drove the Deer into it. Then they shut the gate and went to the king to tell him that in the park near by he could find all the Deer he wanted. The king went at once to look at the Deer. First he saw there the two Deer kings, and granted them their lives. Then he looked at their great herds. Some days the king would go to hunt the Deer, sometimes his cook would go. As soon as any of the Deer saw them they would shake with fear and run. But when they had been hit once or twice they would drop down dead.

八十三　印度榕樹鹿[1]（印度）

從前有一頭金色的鹿，長着寶石般的圓眼睛、白銀般的鹿角、花朵般的紅嘴，走路四蹄輕快穩健。他身體壯碩，還有一條漂亮的尾巴。金鹿住在一座森林裏，是五百頭榕樹鹿的鹿王。附近住着另一個鹿羣名叫猴鹿，也有一個鹿王。

這個國家的國王喜歡打鹿吃鹿肉。他不願獨自一人去打獵，天天叫上鎮裏的人和他一起去。可是這些人都不願去，因為他們去了沒有人替他們幹活兒。於是他們決定建造一個獵場，把鹿趕進場裏，這樣國王就可以去獵場打獵，而他們可以各自做日常工作了。

他們建造起一個獵場，在裏面種上草，又給鹿引進水源，還在四周圍上籬笆，之後把鹿羣趕了進去。他們把大門關上，就去稟告國王，他想要甚麼鹿都可以在附近那個獵場裏找到了。國王立刻前往視察，他首先看到兩頭鹿王，便免他們一死。接着他又看了他們的鹿羣。有幾天國王去獵鹿，有時派他的廚師去。哪頭鹿見到他們，都嚇得簌簌發抖，飛奔而逃。可是若被打中一、兩下，就倒地死去。

---

1. 本篇選自《本生經》（印度古巴利文《小部》中一部經典）的英譯本《本生經故事》(*Jātaka Tales*)。《本生經》以的寓言故事的方式敍述佛陀前生曾為國王、商人、象、猴等所行的善業功德，闡發佛教的基本教義。故事中的榕樹鹿王即為佛陀。佛陀又號釋迦牟尼。

The King of the Banyan Deer sent for the King of the Monkey Deer and said, "Friend, many of the Deer are being killed. Many are wounded besides those who are killed. After this suppose one from my herd goes up to be killed one day, and the next day let one from your herd go up. Fewer Deer will be lost this way." The Monkey Deer agreed. Each day the Deer whose turn it was would go and lie down, placing its head on the block. The cook would come and carry off the one he found lying there.

One day the lot fell to a mother Deer who had a young baby. She went to her king and said, "O King of the Monkey Deer, let the turn pass me by until my baby is old enough to get along without me. Then I will go and put my head on the block." But the king told her that if the lot had fallen to her she must die. Then she went to the King of the Banyan Deer and asked him to save her. "Go back to your herd. I will go in your place," said he.

The next day the cook found the King of the Banyan Deer lying with his head on the block. The cook went to the king, who came himself to find out about this. "King of the Banyan Deer! did I not grant you your life? Why are you lying here?" "O great King!" said the King of the Banyan Deer, "a mother came with her young baby and told me that the lot had fallen to her. I could not ask any one else to take her place, so I came myself."

"King of the Banyan Deer! I never saw such kindness and mercy. Rise up. I grant your life and hers. Nor will I hunt any more the Deer in either park or forest."

— *translated by Ellen C. Babbitt*

於是印度榕樹鹿的鹿王命人把猴鹿王請來，說，"朋友，許多鹿都被打死了，此外還有許多受了傷。以後是不是輪着來，今天我們的鹿羣出一頭讓他打死，明天你們的鹿羣出一頭，這樣我們可以少犧牲一些。"猴鹿王同意了。每天輪到哪頭鹿，這鹿就出去躺下，把頭靠到台墩上。廚師來了就把躺在那裏的鹿扛走。

一天，抽籤輪到一頭帶着幼兒的母鹿。她去見鹿王，說："猴鹿王陛下啊，放過我這回吧。等我的小鹿長到可以離了我，我再去把頭放到台墩上。"可是鹿王告訴她，抽到了籤就只有去死。於是她又去見印度榕樹鹿王，求他救救她。"回到你的鹿羣裏去吧。我來替你。"他說。

第二天，廚師看到榕樹鹿王把頭放在台墩上躺着。廚師去見國王，國王親自來看是怎麼回事。"榕樹鹿王啊，我不是免你一死了嗎？你為甚麼躺在這裏？"國王問。"大王陛下啊，"榕樹鹿王說，"有頭母鹿帶着幼兒來告訴我，抽籤抽到她。我不能叫別人代替她，所以我自己來了。"

"榕樹鹿王啊！我從來沒有見到過這樣慈悲的心懷。起來吧。我赦免你，也赦免她。從此我再也不在獵場、也不在森林獵鹿了，"國王說。

—— 艾倫 · C · 巴比特 英譯

84 The Monkey and the Crocodile
(India)

A monkey lived in a great tree on a riverbank. In the river there were many crocodiles.

A crocodile watched the monkeys for a long time, and one day she said to her son, "My son, get one of those monkeys for me. I want the heart of a monkey to eat."

"How am I to catch a monkey?" asked the little crocodile. "I do not travel on land, and the monkey does not go into the water."

"Put your wits to work, and you'll find a way," said the mother.

And the little crocodile thought and thought.

At last he said to himself, "I know what I'll do. I'll get that monkey that lives in a big tree on the riverbank. He wishes to go across the river to the island where the fruit is so ripe."

So the crocodile swam to the tree where the monkey lived. But he was a stupid crocodile.

"Oh, monkey," he called, "come with me over to the island where the fruit is so ripe."

"How can I go with you?" asked the monkey. "I do not swim."

"No — but I do. I will take you over on my back," said the crocodile.

The monkey was greedy, and wanted the ripe fruit, so he jumped down on the crocodile's back.

"Off we go!" said the crocodile.

"This is a fine ride you are giving me!" said the monkey.

八十四　猴子與鱷魚（印度）

一隻猴子住在河邊的一棵大樹上，河裏有許多鱷魚。

一條鱷魚觀察了猴子很長一段時間，有一天，她對兒子說：“我的兒，去給我捉一隻猴子來，我想吃猴子心。”

“我怎能捉得住猴子呢？”小鱷魚問，“我不能在陸地上走，猴子也不會到水裏來。”

“動動腦筋，你就會找到辦法了，”母親說。

小鱷魚想啊想的。

最後他自言自語：“我知道怎麼辦了。我要捉到住在河邊大樹上那隻猴子。他想過河到島上去，那裏的果子熟透了。”

於是鱷魚游到猴子住着的樹旁。可是他是一條笨鱷魚。

“哎，猴子，”他喊道，“跟我過河到小島上去吧，那裏的果子熟透啦。”

“我怎能跟你去呀？”猴子說，“我又不會游泳。”

“你不會——可我會呀。我背你過去吧。”鱷魚說。

猴子饞嘴，想吃熟果子，便跳下到鱷魚背上。

“走囉！”鱷魚說。

“你帶我這趟路真讓我愜意啊！”猴子道。

"Do you think so? Well, how do you like this?" asked the crocodile, diving.

"Oh, don't!" cried the monkey, as he went under the water. He was afraid to let go, and he did not know what to do under the water.

When the crocodile came up, the monkey sputtered and choked. "Why did you take me under water, crocodile?" he asked.

"I am going to kill you by keeping you under water," answered the crocodile. "My mother wants monkey heart to eat, and I'm going to take yours to her."

"I wish you had told me you wanted my heart," said the monkey, "then I might have brought it with me."

"How queer!" said the stupid crocodile. "Do you mean to say that you left your heart back there in the tree?"

"That is what I mean," said the monkey. "If you want my heart, we must go back to the tree and get it. But we are so near the island where the ripe fruit is, please take me there first."

"No, monkey," said the crocodile, "I'll take you straight back to your tree. Never mind the ripe fruit. Get your heart and bring it to me at once. Then we'll see about going to the island."

"Very well," said the monkey.

But no sooner had he jumped onto the bank of the river than—whisk! he ran into the tree.

From the topmost branches he called down to the crocodile in the water below:

"My heart is way up here! If you want it, come for it, come for it!"

— *translated by Ellen C. Babbitt*

446

"愜意嗎？唔，你喜歡這樣吧？"鱷魚問着潛下了水底。

"哎，別呀！"猴子喊起來，身子已經沉到水裏去了。他不敢放開鱷魚，也不會潛水。

鱷魚浮上水面，猴子吐着口沫，嗆噎着説："鱷魚，你怎麼把我沉到水裏去呢？"

"我要把你淹死在水裏，"鱷魚答。"我媽想吃猴子心，我要把你的心拿給她。"

"你怎麼不早告訴我你想要我的心呢？"猴子説，"那我就可以把我的心帶來了。"

傻鱷魚説："奇怪！你是説你把心留在那樹上了嗎？"

"正是呀，"猴子説，"如果你想要我的心，咱們就得回樹上去拿。可我們離那長着熟果子的島已經這樣近了，還是請你先把我送到島上去吧。"

"不行，猴子，"鱷魚説，"我要直接送你回樹上去，管他熟果子不熟果子的。馬上把你的心拿給我，然後咱們再説去島上的事。"

"好吧，"猴子説。

可是他一從鱷魚背跳到河岸，就嗖的一聲，爬到樹上去了。

他從樹頂的樹枝上向下對水裏的鱷魚喊道：
"我的心就在這兒哪！你想要就來拿呀！來呀！"

—— 艾倫·C·巴比特 英譯

85 The Story of Little Black Mingo
(India)

Once upon a time there was a little black girl, and her name was Little Black Mingo. She had no father and mother, so she had to live with a horrid cross old woman called Black Noggy, who used to scold her every day, and sometimes beat her with a stick.

One day Black Noggy called her, and said: "Take this chatty down to the river and fill it with water." So Little Black Mingo took the chatty and ran down to the river as fast as she could, and while she was filling it a mugger came creeping softly down behind her and caught her by the leg in his great cruel mouth and swam away with her to an island in the middle of the river, and set her down beside a huge pile of eggs. He said, "To-morrow little muggers will come out and then we will have a great feast, and we will eat you up." Then he waddled off to catch fish for himself.

Little Black Mingo sat down on a big stone and hid her face in her hands, and cried bitterly. Presently she heard a queer little squeaky noise. "Oh, Little Black Mingo, help me, or I shall be drowned." She got up and saw a bush coming floating down the river with a mongoose[1] wriggling and scrambling about in it. So she waded out and caught hold of the bush and pulled it in, and carried the mongoose to shore.

The mongoose saw the pile of muggers' eggs. He sat down and began to crack the eggs, and eat the little muggers as they came out. He was hungry, and he ate so many that the pile got much smaller, and when the old mugger came

---

1. mongoose：學名為　　，靈貓科小型食肉動物。

八十五　小黑明戈的故事（印度）

　　從前有個黑人小姑娘叫小黑明戈，她無父無母，只好和一個脾氣暴戾的惡老太婆住在一起。這老太婆叫黑樹椿，每天都呵斥責罵小明戈，有時還用棍子打她。

　　一天黑樹椿叫來小明戈，說：「拿這桶到河邊打滿滿桶水來。」小黑明戈拿起桶飛跑到河濱，正在打水時，一隻可怕的大鱷魚偷偷爬到她身後，用那可怕的大嘴一下咬住她的腿，拖着她游到河心的一個小島上，放在一大堆鱷魚蛋旁。他說：「明天小鱷魚就要出殼了，我們要好好吃一頓，到時就把你吃掉。」說完，就搖搖擺擺游開去抓魚吃了。

　　小黑明戈坐在一塊大石頭上，雙手掩臉哭得非常傷心。這時，她聽到一絲古怪的微弱吱吱叫聲，說：「唉，小黑明戈，救救我啊，我要淹死啦。」她站起身來，看見一叢灌木樹枝漂在河裏順流而下，有隻貓鼬在上面掙扎爬動。她趟下河去，拉住樹枝，把貓鼬拖上岸來。

　　貓鼬看見了那堆鱷魚蛋，便坐下，把蛋敲碎，小鱷魚一爬出來就把他們吃掉。他真餓了，吃了那麼多，那堆蛋眼看小了下去。老鱷魚一回來就發現有人動了他的蛋，哎

back he saw at once that some one had been meddling with them. Oh! what a rage he was in, for there were only six eggs left! So he swam across to the shore, and fetched the big chatty, and covered the eggs with it. And he went off quite proud and happy.

By and by the mongoose came back, and he was terribly disappointed when he found the eggs all covered with the big chatty. So he ran off to Little Black Mingo, and asked her to help him, and Little Black Mingo came and took the big chatty off the eggs, and the mongoose ate them, every one. Little Black Mingo said, "The mugger will eat me all."

"No, he won't," said the mongoose. So he climbed on to the edge of the chatty, and Little Black Mingo pushed the chatty out into the water, and then she clambered into it and paddled with her two hands as hard as she could, and the big chatty just sailed beautifully. So they got across safely, and Little Black Mingo filled the chatty half-full of water and took it on her head, and they went up the bank together.

But when the mugger came back, and found only empty egg-shells, he was fearfully angry. He roared and he raged, till the whole island shook, and his tears ran down his cheeks and pattered on the sand like rain. So he started to chase Little Black Mingo and the mongoose. He raced after them, but they ran, and just before he caught them they got into the house, and banged the door in his face. So he hid behind the back of the house and waited.

Now, Black Noggy was just coming home from the bazaar[2] with a tin of kerosene on her head and a box of matches in her hand. And when he saw her the mugger rushed out and gobbled her up, kerosene tin, matches, and all!!!

---

2. Lazaar：古代波斯（今伊朗）的集市，此名稱後傳入印度、土耳其及北非等地。

呀，他發的脾氣可大了，因為只剩下六個蛋啦！他游到對岸拿來大水桶，罩在剩餘的蛋上，放心得意地走了。

後來貓鼬又來了，見到鱷魚蛋都蓋在大桶下，失望極了。他跑去找小黑明戈，請她幫忙。小黑明戈走過來把桶掀開，貓鼬一個一個把蛋吃得乾乾淨淨。小黑明戈說：“鱷魚會把我整個吃掉的。”

“不會的，他吃不了你。”貓鼬說。他爬上桶邊，小黑明戈把桶推到水裏，也爬了進去，兩隻手拚命划起來。水桶悠悠地漂航起來。於是，他們平安無事過了河，小黑明戈打了半桶水，頂在頭上和貓鼬一起走上堤岸。

鱷魚回來發現只剩下些空蛋殼，氣得七竅生煙。他暴跳如雷，連吼帶叫，整個島都震顫起來。他的眼淚順着腮幫子雨點似的滴落在沙灘上。他起身去追小黑明戈和貓鼬。他在後面猛追，他們在前面跑。他剛要抓住他們，他們已經鑽進屋裏，砰地對着他的臉把門關上。鱷魚便藏在屋後等着。

這時，黑樹椿頭上頂着一罐煤油，手裏拿着一盒火柴，從集市回來。一見到她，鱷魚撲上去，三口兩口便把她、連煤油罐和火柴整個兒都吞下肚去！

When Black Noggy found herself in the mugger's dark inside, so she felt for the match-box, and took out a match and lit it. But the mugger's teeth had made holes in the kerosene tin, so that the flame of the match caught the kerosene, and BANG!! the kerosene exploded, and blew the old mugger and Black Noggy into little bits. So Little Black Mingo and the mongoose got the nice little house for their very own, and there they lived happily ever after.

— *Helen Bannerman*

黑樹樁發現自己在漆黑的鱷魚肚裏，便摸索到火柴盒，抽出一根火柴劃着了，誰知鱷魚的利齒把煤油罐戳出許多洞來，火柴便點着了煤油，砰地一聲，煤油爆炸，將老鱷魚和黑樹樁炸得粉碎。於是小黑明戈和貓鼬把舒適的小屋據為己有，從此幸福生活。

——海倫‧班那曼

86 The Shell Maiden (China)

Long ago there lived a poor fisher youth who was a
devoted son. During the life-time of his parents, he did
everything he could to make them happy and comfortable.
When summer came and mosquitoes were greedy, he would
go to bed early each night, so that they could satisfy their
hunger upon him before his parents came to their rest. When
they died successively, as the young man had no money, he
sold all his belongings in order to give his parents' spirits a
proper start on their journey to the World of Shadows. He
bought paper gowns, paper shoes and even a small paper
house. He burned these as offerings so that they should go
along with the spirits to the Shadowy World. And he laid
their coffins in a neat grave mound which he planted with
grass and tended with care.

Every morning the young fisherman, who now lived
alone, went out in his boat to catch fish from the sea. One
day, not long after the funeral, when he drew in his net he
found in it a huge shell shaped like a horn. With its creamy
outside and its lining of rose, he thought the shell so pretty
that he carried it home.

The next evening when he returned from his fishing he
saw to his surprise that his house had been dusted and the
floor had been swept. Bowls of steaming white rice and spicy
salt turnips were set out on the table.

"Who can have done this for me?" he asked himself.
But the next evening also, his hut was swept clean and his
dinner was cooked. As the same thing happened day after
day, the fisher youth grew more and more curious.

八十六　螺殼女（中國）

　　很久以前，有個窮苦的年青打漁人是個孝子。父母在世時，他盡力供養他們，使他們舒適快樂，暑夏時節蚊蟲猖獗，他每晚先上牀讓蚊子叮他吃飽，好讓父母安歇。後來，父母相繼去世。年青人身無分文，為了送父母亡靈體面地到陰間去，他變賣了所有的什物，用賣得的錢買了紙袍、紙鞋，甚至還有一幢小紙屋。他焚燒了這些東西作為祭品，好讓它們伴隨父母的亡靈到陰間。他又將父母的靈柩合葬在一個整潔的墓穴裏，在墓上種上草，精心守墳掃墓。

　　這時，年青的漁夫孤身一人。每日清晨，他乘船出海捕魚。父母下葬後不久，有一天，他撒網撈上來一個牛角形的巨螺。螺殼外表奶油似地光潤，裏面是玫瑰色的。他看這個大螺十分美麗，便帶了回家。

　　第二天，他打漁回來，吃了一驚，因為看到房間打掃得乾乾淨淨，桌上擺好冒着熱氣的白米飯和椒鹽腌蘿蔔。

　　“這是誰給我做的呢？”他心裏想。第二天傍晚，他的小屋又打掃得整齊潔淨，晚飯也做好了。日復一日，天天如此，年青的漁夫也愈發覺得奇怪了。

One morning he hid outside his hut and peeked in at the window. All was quiet inside. Suddenly he saw a figure rise from the pink-and-white shell. It was a maiden so fair that the room seemed as light as though a hundred candles were burning. For a long time the young fisherman watched the maiden busy herself with setting the place in order. Then at last he stepped inside the door.

"O Shining Shell Maiden," he said, "how come you here in my poor humble hut?"

"I come from the Heavenly Kingdom, Excellent Young Sir," the Shell Maiden replied. "The Emperor of the Gods was pleased with your unselfishness. As a reward for your respect for your parents he has sent me to care for your house and cook for you."

Well, of course it was not long before the young fisherman married the lovely Shell Maiden. And he had many sons who cared for him in his old age just as kindly as he had cared for his own parents.

— *Gan Bao*

一天早上，他藏在屋外，從窗戶向裏偷看。屋裏靜悄悄的。突然間他看見一個人影從粉紅潔白的螺殼裏走出來。這是個姑娘。她美麗極了，頓時使茅屋如同亮起百支蠟燭，變得耀眼生輝。年青的漁夫久久地望着這姑娘忙碌地收拾房間。最後，他走進門去。

　　"光艷照人的螺殼姑娘啊，"他說，"你怎會屈駕到寒舍來的？"

　　"相公，我是從天上下凡來的，"螺殼女道，"玉皇大帝喜歡你憨厚無私，為了獎賞你對父母的孝心，他讓我來為你料理家務、給你燒飯。"

　　當然啦，過了不久，年青漁夫便娶了這美麗的螺殼女為妻。他有許多兒子，兒子們在他的晚年孝敬他，就像他當初孝敬自己的父母一樣。

—— 干寶[1]

---

1. 干寶：中國東晉（約公元 4 世紀）史學家、文學家，著《晉紀》，稱良史，又編集神怪靈異故事為《搜神記》。原書已佚，今存本為後人輯錄，本篇選自此書，有刪改。

87 The Daughter of the Dragon King
(China)

In a certain part of our land there was long, long ago a young man named, Liu Ye, who had studied and studied to prepare for the examinations that were held every year. He hoped, when he had passed them, to receive a government position. But in spite of the days and nights which poor Liu Ye spent in the examination cell, he did not pass. This young man turned his face sadly toward home, and as he walked he came upon a young woman who was tending her goats on the banks of the River Ching[1]. Now this young woman was poorly dressed, but her face was as fair as a plum blossom in spring, and her body was as slender as a willow branch. Liu Ye halted to speak to her.

The young woman told him, "I am the youngest daughter of the Dragon King who lives in the Lake of Tung Ting. Not long ago my father gave me in marriage to the son of the dragon who lives in this river. His servants were jealous when I entered his palace. They told lies about me and my husband believed them. He put me outside his courts and forced me to tend the goats."

Tears rolled down the pale cheeks of the fair young woman, and the heart of Liu Ye was touched by her misery. "What can I do to help you, O Daughter of the Dragon King?" he asked.

Then the young woman begged him to deliver a letter to her father, saying, "On the northern bank of the Lake of Tung Ting there stands a giant orange tree. Strike it thrice with

---

1. River Ching：涇川，渭河支流，在陝西省中部。

八十七　龍女（中國）

　　古時候我國某個地方有個年青人叫柳毅。他苦讀詩書準備一年一度的考試，希望榜上有名，求得一官半職。不料在考場日夜辛苦，最後卻名落孫山。他怏怏地回家，路過涇川碰到一個少婦在岸邊牧羊。他雖然衣衫襤褸，卻桃腮柳腰，美麗非常。柳毅住腳和她攀談。

　　她告訴他：“我乃洞庭湖龍君幼女，不久前家父將我嫁與涇川龍之子。我入宮遭僕婢所忌，丈夫聽信僕婢讒言，將我趕出宮外，逼我在此牧羊。”

　　美麗的少婦淚流滿臉，柳毅動了惻隱之心。他問：“龍君的千金，我能幫你做點甚麼呢？”

　　於是少婦請他給她父親帶封信去。她說，“洞庭湖北

your belt and there will come a messenger to guide you to the Dragon King's palace."

Liu Ye took the letter and did what she said. At once there rose from the lake a young man dressed in armor and carrying a shining sword in his hand. Liu greeted him with these words, "I bear a message for the Dragon King who · lives in the Lake of Tung Ting. I would go to his palace."

The young man in armor thrust his sword into the lake. The waters parted and he led Liu Ye safely to the palace of the Dragon King. What splendid sights the young man saw there! The Dragon King's palace was made of bright-colored stones. Liu was led through one crystal door after another. At last in one splendid courtyard he came upon the great Dragon King himself. He had the form of a man dressed in robes of bright purple.

"I come from your daughter, O Dragon King," Liu Ye said, kowtowing before him. "I live in the neighboring kingdom of Wu. I was returning from the Examination Halls when I saw your fair daughter, tending her goats upon the banks of the River Ching. Her clothes were in tatters. Her shoes were worn through. She gave me this letter to deliver to your majesty." When the Dragon King read the letter from his beloved daughter, the tears flowed from his eyes. His attendants who stood near him began to weep and to wail.

"Stop that noise!" cried the Dragon King. "Chien Tang will hear."

"Who is Chien Tang?" asked Liu Ye.

"He is my younger brother," the Dragon King answered. "Ai, he has a temper, a terrible temper." The Dragon King had scarcely had time to tell Liu Ye about Chien Tang when there arose a clattering sound. A red dragon so large that it darkened the sky flew through the air and disappeared in the clouds. Soon the shining beast reappeared before their eyes.

460

岸有棵大橘樹，你用衣帶擊樹三下便會有人帶你去龍君宮殿了。"

柳毅拿了信依言去做。湖中立刻升起一個身穿盔甲手持利劍的年輕人。柳毅對他說，"我有一封給洞庭湖龍君的信。我想去龍宮見他。"

武士將劍插入湖中，湖水中分，他帶着柳毅平安到達龍宮。柳毅只見眼前景色壯麗，龍宮由各色寶玉砌成。武士引着他走過一重重的水晶門，最後在一個豪華的庭院中謁見龍君。他身為人形，穿着光燦燦的紫袍。

柳毅跪下叩拜說，"龍君陛下，我從令媛那裏來。我是鄰近吳郡人，從試院回家時碰見令媛，她衣履破舊，在涇川之畔牧羊。這是她讓我帶給陛下的信。"龍君讀了愛女的信，淚落如雨，左右侍臣都陪着哭泣。

這時龍君道，"別哭了！小心錢塘聽到。"

柳毅問，"錢塘是誰？"

龍君答："他是我的弟弟。唉，他的脾氣很暴烈。"龍君正告訴柳毅關於錢塘的情況，話未說完，只聽到一聲霹靂，一條赤色巨龍騰空飛起，遮天蔽日，穿雲而去。不久，這渾身閃閃發光的巨龍又從天而降，出現在他們眼

A lovely young woman rode on his back as he flew down from the heavens. It is the young woman who tended the goats!

"Ai, I found her in a sad plight," the Red Dragon said, "but I have punished her wicked husband."

The beautiful daughter of the Dragon King was so grateful to Liu Ye that she persuaded her father to offer her hand to him in marriage. But the young man was troubled, because they have just killed her first husband. And so he refused.

"I only wished to reward you, O Excellent Youth," the Dragon King's daughter said as she bade Liu Ye good-by. "But perhaps the lucky hour has not yet arrived. We shall wait a while."

The youth went home. In time his family arranged a marriage for him with a daughter of the Chang family. But scarcely had they eaten the wedding rice when the bride died. Liu Ye's second marriage with a daughter of a family named Han was no more successful, for again the bride flew away to the Shadowy World. Then one day a go-between came and said, "I know of a beautiful young widow, and since she is so young her mother is anxious that she should marry again." Well, it all ended in Liu Ye's marrying the young widow.

For more than a year they lived happily together, and when the gods sent them a son, the woman said to her husband, "This blessing from heaven binds us together forever. Now I can tell you that I am the daughter of the Dragon King of Lake Tung Ting, the woman you saved from her misery on the banks of the River Ching. I made a vow I would reward you. I wished to marry you then, but you refused. But I never stopped wishing that the day might come when I should be your wife." Then Liu Ye and the Dragon

前。一位美麗的少婦騎在他背上，正是那個牧羊女！

赤龍說：「唉，我看到她的境況實在悲慘，但是我也懲罰過她的惡丈夫了。」

龍女感柳毅之恩，要她父親把她許配給他。但柳毅因他們剛殺了她丈夫，於心不安，便拒絕了。

龍女向柳毅道別時，說：「啊，公子，我不過是想報答大恩罷了。但是也許時機未到。我們就等一等吧。」

柳毅回家後，家人給他娶來張家女兒，但合巹禮剛成，新娘便死了。又娶韓家女，新婦同樣一命歸西。一天，有個媒人來說：「我認識一個年輕貌美的寡婦，因為她年輕，她母親堅持要她再嫁。」結果柳毅娶了她。

他們很恩愛，過了一年多，生了一個兒子。這時少婦對丈夫說：「上天已賜下麟兒，把我們永遠結合在一起，現在我可以告訴你了：我就是當時在涇川之畔受難，被你救回來的洞庭龍君之女。我誓願要報答你，本想當時就嫁給你，但遭你拒絕。然而我一直希望有朝一日成為你的妻

King's daughter went to live in a splendid palace in the Lake of Tung Ting and in time the fortunate youth became a dragon himself.

— *Li Chao-wei*

子。"於是柳毅和龍女回到洞庭湖，住在豪華的龍宮裏。後來柳毅很幸運也化身成龍了。

——李朝威 [1]

1. 李朝威，中唐（約8、9世紀）時人，生平不可考。本篇見於《太平廣記》卷419，原題"柳毅傳"。

88 The King of the Monkeys (China)

Every three thousand years Si Wang Mu's peach tree blossoms. And it is three thousand years more before its fruit is ripe. As soon as the peaches are ready the Royal Mother of the West celebrates her birthday with a great banquet. She spreads her table beside a fountain which drips shining jewels, on the shores of the Gem Lake. What food she brings forth! Rich meat, rare fruits, the peaches-of-long-life! Bears' tongues, dragon livers, and phoenix eggs! Only once was it spoiled, and that was because of the wicked King of the Monkeys.

Well, that Monkey King was a mischievous creature. This monkey was born on the rocky side of a mountain, far to the east. He soon became King of the Monkeys. He was so powerful that with one jump he could travel from one end of the earth to the other, and he could fly even as high as the Jade Emperor's palace in the Heavenly Kingdom. People called him Sun Wu Kung.

Now at just about this time it so happened that the fruit-of-long-life on the peach tree in the Kun Lun Mountains was ready for eating, and Si Wang Mu was preparing for her great birthday banquet. To her Feast of the Peaches the Western Empress invited all the gods and the goddesses who lived in the Heavenly Kingdom. But she did not invite Sun, the wicked King of the Monkeys.

When he heard of the feast Sun grew very angry. In a fury he set forth for the mountains of Kun Lun, with the magic rod in hand he cast a spell on everyone present in the feast. Then he ate all the fairy peaches and all the best foods. He

八十八 猴王孫悟空（中國）

　　話説西王母的桃樹三千年一開花，又三千多年一結果。仙桃一熟，西王母便大排筵席慶賀生日。席設瑤池旁一道噴珠撒玉的仙泉邊，待客的盡是佳餚珍果——吃了長生不老的仙桃！熊舌、龍肝、鳳卵，琳瑯滿席！可是有一次盛宴被那可惡的猴王弄得不歡而散。

　　説起來這猴王真是個愛惡作劇的傢伙，他是東方遠處一座山邊的巖石裏生出來的，很快便成了眾猴之王。他神通廣大，一個筋斗能從天涯翻到地角，還能飛到玉皇大帝的天宮。這就是人説的孫悟空。

　　事情發生在崑崙山上仙桃成熟可食的時候。西王母大備壽筵，邀請天上各路男女神仙前來赴蟠桃宴，卻沒有邀請刁鑽的猴王孫悟空。

　　孫悟空聞訊大發雷霆。一怒之下，他拿着金剛棒直奔崑崙山，向赴宴各人施魔法。接着他飽餐一頓仙桃，把佳

drank the best wines. So much did he eat and drink that he could not think clearly, and on his way back to heaven he took the wrong turning. Somehow or other he came to the palace of the great teacher, Lao Chun, who had in his keeping some of the heavenly pills which, like the peaches of Kun Lun, will make men live forever. the King of the Monkeys found those pills-of-long-life hidden in a gourd. He gulped down one just as he had eaten the peach-of-long-life at the birthday feast of Si Wang Mu.

How angry the gods were when they heard of these deeds of the wicked King of the Monkeys! The Jade Emperor summoned his warriors, and Sun called to his aid all the troops of his monkey army. The gods spread a net across the broad heavens. But Sun was not taken. By the aid of his iron rod he had changed himself into a cloud and floated safely away.

Each time Sun was captured he would make his magic rod small and hide it behind his ear. He could always change his shape in seventy-two ways and escape. Then too, nothing could kill him, neither sword, fire, nor lightning because he had eaten the peach and swallowed the pill. At last, in despair, the Jade Emperor called upon the greatest god of them all, Buddha.

"How dare you think of yourself as the Ruler of Heaven?" Buddha said to the Monkey King.

"I have power enough. I cannot die. I can ride on the winds and walk through the sea. In one jump I can travel from one end of the earth to the other."

"And yet," Buddha said, "you cannot go further than the palm of my hand." The Monkey King made a mighty leap. Before you could blink your eyes, he had flown to the other end of the earth. There on the red pillar that holds up the heavens he wrote his name so as to show he had really been there. Then he returned to face Buddha.

餚吃盡，又痛飲美酒。他酒足飯飽，醺醺然中，在回天府時走錯了路，誤闖進太上老君的宮殿。老君殿裏藏着一些仙丹，像崑崙仙桃一樣，吃了長生不老。猴王找到藏在葫蘆裏的長生藥，又像吃西王母壽筵上的仙桃一樣吞下一粒。

聽到猴王如此胡作非為，眾天神大怒。玉皇大帝調兵遣將，孫悟空也喚來麾下的猴兵猴將做幫手。眾天神佈下天羅地網，卻奈何不了孫悟空。他手中有金剛棒，幫他化作一朵白雲，安然脫身。

每逢孫悟空被捉到，他便把金剛棒變小，藏在耳後，他有七十二變，總能逃脫。此外，他刀槍不入，也不怕火燒雷劈，因為他吃了仙桃，吞了長生藥。最後，玉皇大帝無奈只好去請法力最高的如來佛。

如來佛喝問猴王，"你好大膽，竟敢以為天上是唯你獨尊嗎？"

猴王答："我無所不能，也不會死，我能騰雲駕霧，踏波入海。我一個筋斗可從天邊翻到地角。"

如來佛道："但你翻不出我的掌心。"猴王盡力一跳，眨眼間便已到了天邊，那裏有一根赤柱擎天，猴王在上面留名以示到此一行，然後便回去面見如來佛。

"Now make me the Ruler of Heaven," the Monkey King cried.

"No, Foolish One," Buddha said, "You have not yet left the palm of my hand."

"How can that be?" the Monkey King cried. "I set down my name on the red pillar of heaven at the other end of the earth."

"Still, the words that you wrote are here on my hand," Buddha said as he held up his forefinger. Sun grew weak and trembled, for he saw that the name he had written on the red pillar of heaven was, indeed, there before him on the finger of Buddha.

Then Buddha drove the Monkey King out of the Heavenly Kingdom and put him in prison under the five rocky mountains.

— *Wu Cheng-en*

"現在天上可以任我獨尊了吧，"猴王喊道。

"蠢猴，你還未跳出我的掌心呢。"如來佛道。

"焉有此理！"猴王大叫，"我已在天邊的擎天赤柱上留名啦。"

"你寫的字就在我手上，"如來佛舉起食指道。猴王看見他寫在擎天赤柱上的名字確實就在他眼前如來佛的手指上，便氣餒了，發抖了。

後來如來佛將猴王逐出天宮囚押在五指山下。

—— 吳承恩[1]

<hr>

1. 吳承恩（1500—1582），中國明代小說家，著有《西遊記》，本篇編
自該書。

89 Lily and the Wooden Bowl (Japan)

Long, Long ago there lived an old woman and her beautiful granddaughter named Lily. They were very, very poor. Presently the old woman was very ill. Sadly she bade the girl to come to her and gave her a large lacquered bowl. Then gently she touched the girl's cheek and said: "Dear child, now I am gone and you will be left alone in the world. Your face must be concealed to hide your beauty from the eyes of evil men who will spoil your innocence." She made Lily promise that she would never remove the wooden bowl from her head, and died.

Then Lily had to work in the rice fields for a rich farmer to earn her living. With her back bending she worked all day long in the fields. Her hands were cracked and bleeding but the wooden bowl shaded her snow white face against the sun. One day the rich farmer came and asked Lily to attend on his wife who was ill. Now the man was kind-hearted but his wife was cruel. She despised Lily from the moment she laid eyes upon her. Looking at her elegant figure she became very jealous and made up her mind to drive the girl from the house.

Now the farmer's son Kumaso had finished his studies in the city and returned home. He was a kind and handsome boy. He couldn't understand why the servant girl Lily always had her head covered with a bowl. So he asked his mother about that. She told him: "Her face is badly scarred. She suffered from smallpox when she was a child. So she wanted to wear that bowl to hide it." But Kumaso didn't believe what his mother said because, as he watched Lily, he found

八十九　百合子和木碗（日本）

　　很久很久以前，有一個老婦人，和她美麗的孫女百合子一起過活，她們很窮很窮。後來老人病重，她悲傷地把姑娘叫到跟前，交給她一個上漆的大木碗。她輕輕地摸着姑娘的臉説：“親愛的孩子，我要去了，剩下你孤苦零丁地在世上。你要把臉遮起來，別讓壞男人看到你美麗的容貌，玷污你的清白。”她讓百合子答應把木碗戴在頭上，永遠不拿下來。然後她就死了。

　　百合子只好到一個富有的農夫的稻田裏種田，以維持生計。她終日在田裏彎着腰工作，雙手開裂、流血，但木碗遮着她雪白的臉，太陽曬不到。有一天這有錢的農人來叫她去侍候他生病的太太。農人心腸慈善，但太太是個狠毒的人。她一見百合子優美的身段就心生嫉妒，決心把她趕出她家門。

　　這時農人的兒子熊襲從城裏學成回家。他是個仁慈而俊美的青年。他不明白這個女僕百合子為甚麼頭上總帶着一個碗，便去問他母親。她告訴他：“她滿臉麻子，因為小時得了天花。所以戴個大碗把臉遮住。”但是熊襲看到百合子的身材那麼苗條，舉止那麼溫柔端莊，他不相信母

her figure was so slender, her manners so gentle and graceful. His curiosity soon turned to love. Almost every day he went to meet Lily secretly. Yet their happiness was spoiled since Kumaso could not persuade Lily to take off the wooden bowl from her head. At any rate she would not break the promise she had given to her grandmother.

One day when they met again, being impatient, Kumaso removed the bowl without warning. Lily ran away and wept. Although the bowl remained where it were, the young man did catch a glimpse under the bowl and the sight of Lily's face had taken his breath away. Never before had a man seen such rare beauty. He went to his parents and announced that he would have Lily for his wife. His father was glad but the mother was in great anger and said: "No! You have been deceived. The bowl is a trick!" But Kumaso stood firm and would marry no other woman.

So before midnight the cruel woman entered Lily's room, holding a heavy bamboo stick and said: "Now leave this house of mine at once, before my son sees you!" "But what have I done?" asked the poor girl. "Go, I said!" she raised the bamboo stick above Lily's head and she, crouching at the corner of the room, ready to receive the blow. At this moment, came running the father and son who heard the noise. "What's going on here?" the father demanded, snatching the stick from his wife's hand. The wicked woman said with gnashing teeth: "Send her away! or I go!"

As both husband and son showed no sympathy for her, the woman left the house and never came back.

The wedding was held next day. When the bride appeared in her wedding gown, and with the wooden bowl still on her head, the guests began to whisper and giggle. But Kumaso was determined, he took Lily by her hand and said gently: "Don't worry. With or without the bowl, you will be my

親的話。不久，他的好奇心變成了愛情。他幾乎每天都悄悄地去和她相會。但是相會雖然歡愉，卻因百合子不肯順從他的意思摘下木碗而使他不悅。因為無論如何她也不肯違反對祖母的承諾。

有一天他們又相會了，熊襲忍耐不住，出其不意把木碗揭起。百合子哭着跑開了。雖然木碗沒有揭下，但一刹那間熊襲已經瞥到木碗下百合子的臉，他簡直透不過氣來。從沒有人看過這樣絕世的俊美。他去見他父母，説要娶百合子為妻。他父親很高興，但母親勃然大怒，説：“不行！你受騙了。那木碗是騙人的東西！”但熊襲的心意已定，決不另娶。

半夜裏，那狠毒的女人進入百合子的房間，手裏拿着一根粗竹棍，説：“馬上給我滾出我家門，別讓我兒子看到你！”“我做錯甚麼事了嗎？”可憐的姑娘問。“我説，出去！”她把竹棍舉到百合子頭上，百合子縮到房間角落裏，準備挨打。這時父親和兒子聽見吵鬧聲，跑了進來。“你們在幹甚麼？”父親問着，從妻子手裏奪過竹棍。那惡婦咬牙切齒地説：“把她趕出去！不然我就走！”

父子倆人都不同情她。惡婦走了，再也沒有回來。

次日他們舉行婚禮。當新娘子身上穿着吉服，頭上戴着木碗出來時，賓客開始竊竊議論和嗤嗤發笑。但熊襲不為所動。他握着百合子的手溫柔地説：“別難過，不管你

dear wife." And they drank their lucky cup of wine that meant they were made man and wife. As Lily's lips touched the cup, suddenly the wooden bowl split and fell onto the ground. The astonishing beauty of the bride revealed for the first time to the eyes of the world! Because now no one could do her any harm as she was protected by her dear husband.

— *Japanese Folk Tale*

頭上戴不戴木碗，你都是我的愛妻。"他們飲過交杯酒，便成為夫婦了。但百合子的唇一沾到酒杯，木碗忽然裂開，掉到地上。於是百合子令人驚嘆的絕代容顏第一次顯露在世人面前！因為現在有丈夫保護，別人傷害不了她，木碗就不再需要了。

—— 日本民間故事

90 How Many Donkeys? (Turkey)

There was the tinkle of tiny bells, the sharp clip of small hoofs, the throaty drone of a solitary singer. Nasr-ed-Din Hodja was bringing the donkeys back from the mill, their saddlebags filled with freshly ground wheat. The hot Turkish sun beat down on his turbaned head. The staccato trot of his donkey jiggled him back and forth. But Nasr-ed-Din Hodja was too pleased to be uncomfortable.

He chuckled. "They gave me plenty of advice about taking care of their donkeys and their wheat. As though I did not know more about donkeys than any man in Ak Shehir[1]."

His eyes rested lazily on the road ahead. "Just over that hill," he mused contentedly, "is Ak Shehir, where they are waiting for their donkeys. There is not a scratch or a bruise on one of the little creatures. No donkeys in all Turkey have had better treatment today than these nine."

Idly he began counting them. "What?" he gasped. "Eight donkeys?" He jumped from his donkey and ran hither and yon, looking behind rocks and over hilltops, but no stray donkey could he see. At last he stood beside the donkeys and counted again. This time there were nine. With a sigh of relief he climbed onto his own donkey and went swinging along the road.

Passing through a cluster of trees he thought it time to count the donkeys again.

"One—two—three—" and up to eight he counted, but

---

1. Ak Shehir：土耳其地名。

九十　到底有幾頭毛驢？[1]（土耳其）

　　小鈴叮噹，蹄聲得得，伴着一個孤獨人低沉沙啞的歌聲。納斯爾·丁·霍加把毛驢從磨坊趕回來，鞍上褡褳裏裝滿剛磨好的麥子。土耳其熱辣辣的太陽直射在他纏着頭巾的頭上。毛驢跑跑停停，顛得他前後搖晃。但納斯爾·丁·霍加心中歡喜，一點兒也不感到不舒服。

　　他呵呵一笑："還囉哩囉嗦教我怎麼看管毛驢、怎麼照顧麥子哩，不知道我管毛驢是阿克謝希爾的第一把手嗎？"

　　他眼光懶懶地望着前頭的路，心滿意足地思忖："翻過這座山，就是阿克謝希爾了。驢主們還在那邊等着他們的毛驢呢。這羣乖乖的小牲口身上一塊皮也沒碰破，今兒整個土耳其也沒有一頭毛驢照顧得比我這九頭更好啦。"

　　閒極無聊，他數起毛驢來。"哎呀！"他倒吸一口冷氣，"怎麼只有八頭？"他從毛驢背上跳下來，跑前跑後，看看巖石後又望望山頂，那走失的毛驢蹤跡全無。最後，他站在驢羣邊又數了一遍，這次數出九頭。他如釋重負，嘆口氣，騎上驢背又搖搖晃晃地上路了。

　　穿過一叢樹，他覺得又該數數毛驢了。

　　"一、二、三、"他數到八，卻沒有第九頭。他從驢背

1.　選自《從前有個霍加》，這個納斯爾·丁·霍加又憨又風趣，在土耳其，甚至在中東，是個家喻戶曉的故事人物。霍加是一種種姓，也是對穆斯林學校教師的稱呼。

no ninth donkey was to be seen. Down from his donkey's back he came. Behind all the trees he peered. Not a hair of a donkey could he find. Again he counted, standing beside his donkeys. There they all were—nine mild little donkeys waiting for orders to move on. Nasr-ed-Din Hodja scratched his poor head in bewilderment. Was he losing his mind or were the donkeys all bewitched? Again he counted. Yes, surely there were nine.

As he rode on, he looked about him for the evil spirits which must be playing tricks on him. Each donkey wore the blue beads[2] which should drive away the evil spirits. He was glad to see a friend coming toward him down the road.

"Oh, Mustapha Effendi[3]," he cried. "Have you seen one of these donkeys? I have lost a donkey and yet I have not lost it."

"What can you mean, Hodja Effendi?" asked Mustapha.

"I left the mill with nine donkeys," explained the Hodja. "Part of the way home there have been nine and part of the way there have been eight. Oh, I am bewitched! Help me! Help me!"

Mustapha was used to the queer ways of the Hodja, but he was surprised. He counted the donkeys silently. "Let me see you count the donkeys," he ordered the Hodja.

"One—two—three," began the Hodja, pointing at each one as he counted up to eight. As he said the last number, he stopped and looked at his friend with a face full of helplessness and terror. His terror turned to amazement as Mustapha slapped his knee and laughed until he almost fell from his donkey.

---

2. blue beads：藍色的玻璃珠，土耳其人普遍用作辟邪物帶在身上。
3. Effendi：「閣下」、「老爺」；土耳其人對人的尊稱，現已廢去不用。

上跳下，探頭把一棵棵樹背後都看過，連一根驢毛也找不到。站在驢羣邊他又數了一遍，全都在呀──九頭乖乖的小毛驢正等着他命令繼續走呢。納斯爾‧丁‧霍加着慌了，抓抓他那可憐的腦袋。是他神智不清，還是這些毛驢受了妖法？他又數一遍。對呀，確實是九頭呀。

他繼續騎驢趕路，一邊東張西望，找那作弄他的、有邪術的妖精。每頭毛驢都帶着藍色珠子，應該可驅鬼避邪的呀。他一眼看見有個朋友順着大路向他走來，很高興。

"哎，穆斯塔發大爺，"，他喊道："你看見一頭毛驢了嗎？我丟了一頭驢，可又沒丟。"

"你這是甚麼意思啊，霍加大爺？"穆斯塔發問。

"我從磨坊出來的時候趕了九頭毛驢，"這位霍加解釋道，"可回家的路上，走一路是九頭，走一路又成了八頭。哎，我中了邪了，幫我一把吧！幫我一把吧！"

穆斯塔發對這位霍加的怪誕行為已習以為常，可還是十分驚訝。他一聲不吭地數了數毛驢。"讓我看看你怎麼數毛驢的，"他對這霍加說。

"一、二、三、"霍加數了起來，點着毛驢一直數到八。他說到八時停住了，一臉無可奈何、一臉恐懼地望着他的朋友。他見穆斯塔發拍着膝蓋，笑得幾乎要從毛驢上滾下來，他的恐懼變成了驚異。

"What is so funny?" asked the Hodja.

"Oh, Hodja Effendi!" Mustapha laughed. "When you are counting your brothers, why, oh why, do you not count the brother on whom you are riding?"

Nasr-ed-Din Hodja was silent for a moment to think through this discovery. Then he kissed the hand of his deliverer, pressed it to his forehead[4] and thanked him a thousand times for his help. He rode, singing, on to Ak Shehir to deliver the donkeys to their owners.

— Alice Geer Kelsey

---

4. pressed it to his forehead：土耳其人對人表示尊敬的方式。

"甚麼事這樣好笑？"霍加問。

"我的霍加大爺啊！"穆斯塔發笑着，"你數你的毛驢哥們兒的時候，唉，唉，到底為甚麼不數你自己騎的那頭呀？為甚麼呀？"

納斯爾‧丁‧霍加不做聲，把這發現從頭到尾想了一遍。然後，他親吻了這救苦救難的人的手，又把這手放在自己的前額上，對他的幫助千謝萬謝。於是騎上毛驢，唱着歌兒，繼續向阿克謝希爾走去，把毛驢歸還給驢主。

——*愛麗斯‧吉爾‧凱爾西*

91 Nasr-ed-Din Hodja in the Pulpit
(Turkey)

Nasr-ed-Din Hodja[1] one day addressed his congregation from the pulpit in the following words: "I beseech you to tell me truly, O brethren! O true believers! if what I am going to say to you is already known to you."

And the answer came, as in one voice, from his congregation, that they did not know, and that it was not possible for them to know, what the Hodja was going to say to them. "Then," quoth[2] the preacher, "of what use to you or to me is an unknown subject?" And he descended from the pulpit and left the mosque.

On the following Friday his congregation, instead of having decreased, had greatly increased, and their anxiety to hear what he was going to say was felt in the very atmosphere.

The Hodja ascended the pulpit and said, "O brethren! O true believers! I beseech you to tell me truly if what I am going to say to you is already known to you."

The answer that came to the Hodja was so spontaneous as to suggest prearrangement. They all shouted, "Yes, Hodja, we do know what you are going to say to us."

"That being the case," quoth the Hodja, "there is no need either of you wasting your time or of me wasting my time." And, descending from the pulpit, he left the mosque. His congregation, having prayed, also left gradually, one by one and in groups.

---

1. Hodja：霍加是對穆斯林學校教師的稱呼，另見上篇註。
2. quoth：〔古〕= said。

九十一　納斯爾·丁·霍加在佈道壇上
（土耳其）

　　有一天納斯爾·丁·霍加在佈道壇上對他的會眾説：
"教友們啊，真誠的信徒啊！我請求你們對我説實話：我將
要給你們宣講的內容你們是不是已經知道了？"

　　他的會眾回答了，齊聲説他們並不知道，他們也不可
能知道，霍加要對他們説些甚麼，於是佈道人説："那
麼，講一個人家都不知道的話題，無論對你們還是對我來
説，有甚麼用處呢？"説着他走下佈道壇，出了清真寺。

　　下一個星期五佈道日，聽講的會眾不但沒有減少反而
增加了。整個會場洋溢着一種氣氛：人人焦急地等着要聽
他説些甚麼。

　　霍加登上講壇，説："教友們啊，真誠的信徒啊！我
請求你們對我説實話：我將要給你們宣講的內容你們是不
是已經知道了？"

　　會眾異口同聲回答了，看得出很可能是事先商量好了
的。他們一同大聲説："是的，霍加。我們確實知道您要
給我們説甚麼。"

　　"既然這樣，"霍加説，"那就沒有必要既浪費你們的
時間，又浪費我的時間了。"於是他走下佈道壇，出了清
真寺。他的會眾做過祈禱後也就一個一個或三五成羣地陸
續散去。

On the following Friday Nasr-ed-Din Hodja again mounted the pulpit, and saw that his mosque was so crowded that not a nook or corner in it was empty. He addressed his congregation in exactly the same manner. "O brethren! O true believers!" said he, " I ask you to tell me truly if what I am going to say is already known to you?"

And again the answer of his numerous congregation had evidently been'prepared beforehand, for one half of them rose and said, "Yes, Hodja, we do know what you are going to say to us," and the other half rose and said, "O Hodja effendi, how could we poor ignorant people know what you intend to say to us?"

The Hodja answered. "It is well said; and now if the half that knows what I am going to say would explain to the other half what it is, I would be deeply grateful, for, of course, it will be unnecessary for me to say anything."

Whereupon he descended from the pulpit and left the mosque.

— Allan Ramsay & Francis McCullagh

下一個星期五，納斯爾·丁·霍加又上了佈道壇，看到清真寺內教友擠得滿滿地，連每個角落裏都是人。他完全照樣對教友說：“教友們啊，真誠的信徒啊！請你們實實在在告訴我，我要向你們說的話，你們是不是已經知道了？”

　　這次眾多教友們的回答顯而易見是事先商量好的：一半人站起來說：“是的，霍加。我們確實知道你要向我們說甚麼。”而另一半人卻站起來說：“霍加老爺，我們這些無知無識的可憐人怎麼會知道你想對我們說甚麼呢？”

　　霍加回答道：“說得好。那麼如果已經知道我要說甚麼的這一半人向不知道的那一半人宣講宣講，我就感激不盡了。因為我當然也就不需要再說甚麼啦。”

　　說着，他走下佈道壇，出了清真寺。

　　　　　　　　——阿倫·拉姆齊 與 弗朗西斯·麥卡拉

92 The Happiest Man in the World
(Turkey)

A man who was living in comfortable enough circumstances went one day to see a certain sage, reputed to have all knowledge. He said to him: "Great Sage, I have no material problems, and yet I am always unsettled. For years I have tried to be happy, to find an answer to my inner thoughts, to come to terms with the world. Please advise me as to how I can be cured of this malaise."

The sage answered: "My friend, what is apparent to some is hidden to others. I have the answer to your ailment, though it is no ordinary medication. You must set out on you travels, seeking the happiest man in the world. As soon as you find him, you must ask him for his shirt, and put it on."

This seeker thereupon restlessly started looking for happy men. After travelling through one country after another for many days, he found the wood in which everyone said lived the happiest man in the world.

He heard the sound of laughter coming from among the trees, and quickened his step until he came upon a man sitting in a glade. "Are you the happiest man in the world, as people say?" he asked. "Certainly I am," said the other man. "My name is so-and-so, my condition is such-and-such, and my remedy, ordered by the treatest[1] sage, is to wear your shirt. Please give it to me, I will give you anything I have in exchange."

The happiest man looked at him closely, and he laughed. He laughed and he laughed and he laughed. When he had

---

1. treatest：在口語中有極好的東西之意。

488

九十二　世上最幸福的人[1]（土耳其）

　　有個人過着豐衣足食、居處舒適的生活。一天，他去見一個以無所不知聞名的聖人，對他説：“偉大的聖人啊，我物質生活沒有問題，佪總是心神不寧。多少年了，我一直想使自己快樂，想對縈繞心頭的問題尋求一答案，並想與世界相協調，請告訴我，我怎樣才能治好這毛病呢？”

　　聖人回答：“朋友，有的道理對一些人很明顯，對另一些人卻很隱晦。我有個法子治你的毛病，可它並非是尋常藥方。你得走出家門，去找世上最幸福的人。找到後，請他把他的襯衫給你穿在身上。”

　　這人便開始孜孜不倦地尋找幸福的人。日復一日，他走過一個又一個國家，最後找到一片樹林，人人都説裏面住着世上最幸福的人。

　　他聽見林中傳來笑聲，便加快了腳步，來到一個正坐在林中空地上的人面前。“你就是那位人稱世上最幸福的人嗎？”他問。“當然是啦，”那人説。這人便道：“我名叫某某，我的情況是如此這般，最會治病的聖人給我開的方子是穿上你的襯衫。請給我吧。我願把我所有的任何東西給你作交換。”

　　那最幸福的人湊近端詳了他，笑了。他哈哈大笑，笑

---

1. 這是在許多國家都有的民間傳説，本篇選自一土耳其版本。

quietened down a little, the restless man, rather annoyed at this reaction, said: "Are you unhinged, that you laugh at such a serious request?" "Perhaps," said the happiest man, "but if you had only taken the trouble to look, you would have seen that I do not possess a shirt." "What, then, am I to do now?"

"You will now be cured. Striving for something unattainable provides the exercise to achieve that which is needed: as when a man gathers all his strength to jump across a stream as if it were far wider than it is. He gets across the stream."

The happiest man in the world then took off the turban whose end had concealed his face. The restless man saw that he was none other than the great sage who had originally advised him.

"But why did you not tell me all this years ago, when I came to see you?" the restless man asked in puzzlement.

"Because you were not ready then to understand. You needed certain experiences, and they had to be given to you in a manner which would ensure that you went through them."

— *Turkish Folk Tale*

個不停。等他稍歇時，那不倦地尋找幸福的人對這反應有點不高興，說："你可是瘋了？怎麼對這樣一個嚴肅的請求發笑呢？""也許是吧，"最幸福的人說，"可是只要你費神看一看，就會發現我連一件襯衫也沒有啊。""那麼，我怎麼辦呢？"

"現在你的病要治好了。努力追求一件不可得的東西，可以使人受到為達到此目的所需的鍛煉，就好比一個人用盡全力跳越一條事實上比想中窄得多的溪流，他輕而易舉就跳過溪了。"

世上最幸福的人說着，摘下纏頭巾，被頭巾一端遮住的臉露了出來。這人看到他不是別人，正是那原先勸告過他的聖哲。

"可是你怎麼不把這些在幾年前我去看你的時候就告訴我呢？"這孜孜不倦尋找幸福的人大惑不解地問。

"因為你那時還不具備理解的條件，你需要一定的經歷、體驗，我要以確保你能貫徹始終去做的方式把這些經驗給予你。"

—— 土耳其民間傳説

Other Tales
其他童話

93 The Eagle (Babylon)

The eagle was regarded as a symbol of the sun-god in Babylon. He once quarrelled with the serpent and incurred the reptile's hatred. Feeling hungry he resolved to eat the serpent's young, and communicated his intention to his own family. One of his children advised him not to devour the serpent's brood, because if he did so he would incur the enmity of the god Shamash[1]. But the eagle did not hearken[2] to his offspring, and swooping down from heaven sought out the serpent's nest and devoured his young. On his arrival at home the serpent discovered his loss, and at once repaired in great indignation to Shamash, to whom he appealed for justice. His nest, he told the god, was set in a tree, and the eagle had swooped upon it, destroying it with his mighty wings and devouring the little serpents as they fell from it.

"Help, O Shamash!" cried the serpent. "Thy net is like unto[3] the broad earth, thy snare is like unto the distant heaven in wideness. Who can escape thee?"

Shamash, hearkening to his appeal, described to him how he might succeed in obtaining vengeance upon the eagle.

"Take the road," said he, "and go into the mountain and hide thyself in the dead body of a wild ox. Tear open its body, and all the birds of heaven shall swoop down upon it. The eagle shall come with the rest, and when he seeks for the best parts of the carcase, do thou seize him by his wing, tear

---

1. Shamash：美索不達米亞（Mesopotamia）宗教信奉的太陽神，是正義之神和宇宙的主宰。
2. hearken：＝ harken，傾聽。
3. unto：＝ to 或 until。這裏是個虛詞，沒有特別意義。

九十三　鷹（巴比倫）

在巴比倫，鷹被看作太陽神的象徵。有一次他和大蛇爭吵，引起蛇對他的仇恨。鷹餓了，決定去吃蛇的幼兒，便把這打算和家人商量。一個孩子勸他別吃幼蛇，因為吃了幼蛇會得罪沙瑪什神的。可是鷹不聽從孩子的勸告，從天上飛撲下去，找到大蛇的窩，把小蛇吞噬了。大蛇回家發現幼蛇被食，立刻懷着極大悲憤訴於沙瑪什之前，請求得到公道。他告訴這位神祇，他的巢築在樹上，被老鷹巨大有力的翅膀掀翻了，幼蛇跌出巢外時被鷹吞噬掉。

"沙瑪什啊，幫助我吧！"大蛇喊道，"您的羅網像大地一樣遼闊，您的絆索上至高遠的天庭，誰能逃出您的掌握呢？"

沙瑪什側耳傾聽他的懇求，便告訴他怎樣才能得向老鷹復仇。

"上路吧，"他說，"進到山裏，藏身在一頭野牛屍體中。把牛屍撕開，天上的飛鳥都會飛落到牛屍上，老鷹也會去的。等到他在找牛屍最好吃的部位時，你去抓住他的

off his wings, his pinions, and his claws, pull him in pieces and cast him into a pit. There may he die a death from hunger and thirst."

The serpent did as Shamash had bidden him. He soon came upon the body of a wild ox, into which he glided after opening up the carcase. Shortly afterward he heard the beating of the wings of numberless birds, all of which swooped down and ate of the flesh. But the eagle suspected the purpose of the serpent and did not come with the rest, until greed and hunger prompted him to share in the feast.

"Come," said he to his children, "let us swoop down and let us also eat of the flesh of this wild ox."

Now the young eagle who had before dissuaded his father from devouring the serpent's young, again begged him to desist from his purpose.

"Have a care, O my father," he said, "for I am certain that the serpent lurks in yonder carcase for the purpose of destroying you."

But the eagle did not hearken to the warning of his child, but swooped on to the carcase of the wild ox. He so far obeyed the injunctions of his offspring, however, as closely to examine the dead ox for the purpose of discovering whether any trap lurked near it. Satisfied that all was well he commenced to feed upon it, when suddenly the serpent seized upon him and held him fast. The eagle at once began to plead for mercy, but the enraged reptile told him that an appeal to Shamash was irrevocable, and that if he did not punish the king of birds he himself would be punished by the god, and despite the eagle's further protests he tore off his wings and pinions, pulled him to pieces, and finally cast him into a pit, where he perished miserably as the god had decreed.

— *Lewis Spence*

翅膀，撕下翅膀，拔下翅上的羽毛，折斷他的爪子，把他撕成片片，投入一個深坑裏。他在坑裏將飢渴而死。"

大蛇照沙瑪什吩咐的去做。不久爬到一條死野牛身體上，把牛屍撕開，蜿蜒爬進體腔裏。其後不久他便聽到無數飛鳥的擊翅聲，這些鳥全都是撲下來吃死牛肉的。但是老鷹疑心這是蛇有意佈下的陷阱，沒有和別的鳥一起來。直到飢餓難忍，饞涎欲滴，才來分享這頓美餐。

"來吧，"他對孩子們說，"咱們也飛下去，咱們也去吃這野牛肉吧。"

這時上次勸父親不要吃幼蛇的小鷹又求他不要貪嘴。

"父親啊，還是小心為妙，"他說，"我敢肯定那條蛇一定藏在那牛屍裏要害死你。"

但是老鷹不聽孩子的忠告，飛落到野牛屍上。這時他也還聽從孩子的告誡，仔細察看牛屍，找找屍體附近有沒有陷阱。見到一切正常，他就開始吃起來。大蛇突然把他纏住，纏得緊緊的。老鷹馬上求饒，但被激怒的蛇對他說：向沙瑪什的控告豈能改變、撤回？如果他不懲罰這鳥中之王，他自己將受到神的懲罰。儘管老鷹還在抵抗爭辯，蛇還是撕斷他的雙翅，拔去羽毛，把他撕成片片，最後投入深坑裏。他在那裏按照神的旨諭悲慘地死去。

—— 劉易斯·斯彭斯

94 The Rabbi[1] and the Inquisitor[2] (Israel)

The city of Seville[3] was seething with excitement. A Christian boy had been found dead, and the Jews were falsely accused by their enemies of having murdered him in order to use his blood ritually in the baking of matzos[4] for Passover[5]. So the rabbi was brought before the Grand Inquisitor to stand trial as head of the Jewish community.

The Grand Inquisitor hated the rabbi, but, despite all his efforts to prove that the crime had been committed by the Jews, the rabbi succeeded in disproving the charge. Seeing that he had been bested in argument, the inquisitor turned his eyes piously to Heaven and said:

"We will leave the judgment of this matter to God. Let there be a drawing of lots. I shall deposit two pieces of paper in a box. On one I shall write the word 'guilty' — the other will have no writing on it. If the Jew draws the first, it will be a sign from Heaven that the Jews are guilty, and we'll have him burned at the stake. If he draws the second, on which there is no writing, it will be divine proof of the Jews' innocence, so we'll let him go."

---

1. rabbi：受過正規宗教教育、擔任猶太人社會或猶太教會眾精神領袖或導師之人。
2. inquisitor："異端裁判所"（Inquisition）的法官、庭長。"異端裁判所"為中世紀天主教教廷的司法機構，使用酷刑、抄家等手段鎮壓包括猶太人在內的"異端分子"。
3. Seville：西班牙同名省省會。
4. the baking of matzos：遵照耶和華的吩咐，猶太人在逾越節那天要宰殺羊羔，用血塗在薄餅上烤焙。
5. Passover：逾越節，猶太人的節日，見《舊約·出埃及記》第12章。

九十四　拉比與宗教法庭庭長（以色列）

塞維利亞全城沸沸揚揚、激動不安。人們發現一個基督教徒男孩死了。猶太人被仇人誣指為殺人兇手，說他們要在逾越節烤薄餅時塗上男孩的鮮血獻祭。因此拉比作為猶太社區的領袖就被傳到宗教大法庭庭長面前受審。

大法庭庭長仇恨這位拉比。可是，雖然他費盡心機想證明是猶太人犯的罪，拉比卻一一使他的指控無法成立。看到自己在辯論中吃了敗仗，庭長假惺惺地抬眼望天，說：

"我們把這件事交給上帝裁決吧。咱們來抽簽。我把兩張紙放到一個盒子裏。一張我寫上'有罪'，另一張不寫字。如果這個猶太人抽到第一張，就是上天降下猶太人有罪的信號，我們就要把他燒死在火刑柱上。要是他抽到第二張沒有字的，那就是神證明猶太人無罪，我們便放他走。"

Now the Grand Inquisitor was a cunning fellow. He was anxious to burn the Jew, and since he knew that no one would ever find out about it, he decided to write the word "guilty" on both pieces of paper. The rabbi suspected he was going to do just this. Therefore, when he put his hand into the box and drew forth a piece of paper he quickly put it into his mouth and swallowed it.

"What is the meaning of this, Jew?" raged the inquisitor. "How do you expect us to know which paper you drew now that you've swallowed it?"

"Very simple," replied the rabbi. "You have only to look at the paper in the box."

So they took out the piece of paper still in the box.

"There!" cried the rabbi triumphantly. "This paper says 'guilty', therefore the one I swallowed must have been blank. Now, you must release me!"

And they had to let him go.

— Nathan Ausubel

這大法庭庭長是個非常狡猾的傢伙，他一心想燒死這個猶太人。他自認為無人會得知，便決定在兩張紙上都寫上"有罪"。拉比料想他會出此策，因此他把手伸進盒子抽出一張紙後，便飛快地放進嘴裏把紙嚥了下去。

　　"猶太人，你這是甚麼意思？"庭長勃然大怒說，"你把紙嚥下，我們還能知道你抽的是哪張紙嗎？"

　　"很簡單，"拉比回答，"你只要看看盒子裏那張紙就行啦。"

　　於是他們拿出還在盒子裏的那張紙。

　　"看吧！"拉比勝利地喊道，"這張紙上寫着'有罪'，所以我嚥下的那張一定是白紙了。現在你得放我走了！"

　　他們只好放了他。

——納森·奧休貝爾

95 The Conceited Spider (West Africa)

In the olden days all the stories which men told were stories of Nyankupon, the chief of the Gods. Spider, who was very conceited, wanted the stories to be told about him.

Accordingly, one day he went to Nyankupon and asked that, in future, all tales told by men might be Anansi stories[1], instead of Nyankupon stories. Nyankupon agreed, on one condition. He told Spider (or Anansi) that he must bring him three things: the first was a jar full of live bees, the second was a boa-constrictor, and the third a tiger. Spider gave his promise.

He took an earthen vessel and set out for a place where he knew were numbers of bees. When he came in sight of the bees he began saying to himself, "They will not be able to fill this jar."—"Yes, they will be able."—"No, they will not be able," until the bees came up to him and said, "What are you talking about, Mr. Anansi?" He thereupon explained to them that Nyankupon and he had had a great dispute. Nyankupon had said the bees could not fly into the jar — Anansi had said they could. The bees immediately declared that of course they could fly into the jar — which they at once did. As soon as they were safely inside, Anansi sealed up the jar and sent it off to Nyankupon.

Next day he took a long stick and set out in search of a boa-constrictor. When he arrived at the place where one lived he began speaking to himself again. "He will be just as long as this stick."—"No, he will not be so long as this."—"Yes,

---

1. Anansi stories：Anansi(阿難西)是蜘蛛的名字，非洲(尤其是西非)的許多民間傳説都是以蜘蛛阿難西為主人公。

九十五　自負的蜘蛛（西非）

　　古時，人們講的故事都是關於尼安庫潘的，他是諸神中的主神。蜘蛛非常狂妄自負，他要讓人講他的故事。

　　一天，他去到尼安庫潘之前，要求以後人們講故事不講尼安庫潘的，而要講他阿難西的。尼安庫潘同意了，只提出一個條件：他讓蜘蛛阿難西給他拿來三件東西：第一是裝滿蜜蜂的一個罐，第二是一條蟒蛇，第三是一隻老虎。蜘蛛也應允了。

　　他拿起一隻瓦罐出發到一個地方去，他知道那裏有不少蜜蜂。等他走到看見了蜜蜂的地方，他開始自言自語："這些蜜蜂裝不滿這個罐。"——"不對，裝得滿。"——"對了，裝不滿。"説來説去，蜜蜂便過來對他説："阿難西先生，你説甚麼呀？"他趁勢對蜜蜂解釋他怎樣怎樣和尼安庫潘爭得不可開交：尼安庫潘説蜜蜂飛不進罐裏，阿難西説飛得進去。蜜蜂馬上宣稱他們當然飛得進——而且立刻飛進去了。等到他們全都飛了進去，阿難西馬上把罐口封上，送去給尼安庫潘。

　　第二天，阿難西拿了一根長棍出發去找蟒蛇。他走到有條蟒蛇棲息的地方，又自言自語："他就和這根棍子一樣長。"——"不對，他沒有這根棍子長。"——"對呀，

he will be as long as this."

These words he repeated several times, till the boa came out and asked him what was the matter. "Oh, we have been having a dispute in Nyankupon's town about you. Nyankupon's people say you are not as long as this stick. I say you are. Please let me measure you by it." The boa innocently laid himself out straight, and Spider lost no time in tying him on to the stick from end to end. He then sent him to Nyankupon.

The third day he took a needle and thread and sewed up his eye. He then set out for a den where he knew a tiger lived. As he approached the place he began to shout and sing so loudly that the tiger came out to see what was the matter. "Can you not see?" said Spider. "My eye is sewn up and now I can see such wonderful things that I must sing about them." "Sew up my eyes," said the tiger, "then I too can see these surprising sights." Spider immediately did so. Having thus made the tiger helpless, he led him straight to Nyankupon's house. Nyankupon was amazed at Spider's cleverness in fulfilling the three conditions. He immediately gave him permission for the future to call all the old tales Anansi tales.

— *W. H. Barker & C. Sinclair*

504

他和棍子一樣長。"

　　他反反覆覆地說了許多遍，直到蟒蛇出來了，問他是怎麼回事兒。"哦，關於你，我在尼安庫潘的鎮上和他們爭吵了一場。那裏的人說你沒有這根棍子長，我說你和棍子一樣長。請你讓我用這棍子把你量一量吧。"這沒有心計的蟒蛇伸直身子躺下，蜘蛛連忙不失時機地把蛇從頭到尾縛在棍子上。然後把他送去給尼安庫潘。

　　第三天他用針綫把一邊眼皮縫起來，又出發去一個地方。他知道那裏有個虎穴。走近虎穴，他開始高聲又唱又喊，喊得老虎出來問怎麼回事兒。"你沒看見嗎？"蜘蛛說。"我把眼皮縫起來，看見許多妙不可言的事，非唱出來不可。""把我兩個眼皮縫起來吧，"老虎說，"那我也看得到這些稀奇的景物了。"蜘蛛立即把他雙眼眼皮縫上。這樣一來，老虎只能聽人擺佈了。蜘蛛把他直接領到尼安庫潘的家。尼安庫潘見蜘蛛這樣聰明，居然做成了這三件事，十分驚異，他立刻允許蜘蛛：以後把所有古時的故事都叫做阿難西故事。

　　　　　　　　　　　　——W·H·巴克 與 C·辛克萊

96 Goolahwilleel, the Topknot Pigeons (Australia)

Young Goolahwilleel used to go out hunting every day. His mother and sisters always expected that he would bring home kangaroo and emu[1] for them. But each day he came home without any meat at all. They asked him what he did in the bush, as he evidently did not hunt. He said that he did hunt.

"Then why," said they, "do you bring us nothing home?"

"I cannot catch and kill what I follow," he said. "You hear me cry out when I find kangaroo or emu; is it not so?"

"Yes; each day we hear you call when you find something, and each day we get ready the fire, expecting you to bring home the spoils of the chase, but you bring nothing."

"To-morrow," he said, "you shall not be disappointed. I will bring you a kangaroo."

Every day, instead of hunting, Goolahwilleel had been gathering wattle-gum[2], and with this he had been modelling a kangaroo — a perfect model of one, tail, ears, and all complete. So the next day he came towards the camp carrying this kangaroo made of gum. Seeing him coming, and also seeing that he was carrying the promised kangaroo, his mother and sisters said: "Ah, Goolahwilleel spoke truly. He has kept his word, and now brings us a kangaroo. Pile up the fire. To-night we shall eat meat."

---

1. emu：鴯鶓形似鴕鳥，產於澳洲森林，善走不能飛。
2. wattle-gum：金合歡樹樹膠，產於澳洲的樹的樹脂。

九十六　羽冠鴿古拉威利爾（澳洲）

　　小古拉威利爾往常每天出外覓食。他的媽媽和姐妹總望着他會帶些甚麼小袋鼠啦、鴯鶓啦的回家給她們吃。可每天他一點肉類都沒有帶回來。她們說，他顯然沒去獵食，到灌木叢裏都幹些甚麼啦？他說他真的獵食去了。

　　“那你怎麼甚麼也沒給我們帶回家來？”她們問。

　　“我又追又趕的，可抓不到、殺不死這些東西，”他說，“我找着小袋鼠和鴯鶓的時候，你們不是聽到我喊叫了嗎？”

　　“是的呀，每天你找到這些東西，我們都聽見你喊，我們就把火生好，指望你把抓到的東西拿回來，可你總是兩手空空的。”

　　“明天吧，”他說，“明天我準不會叫你們失望了。我給你們帶回一隻小袋鼠吧。”

　　其實古拉威利爾每天並沒有去獵食，卻在搜集金合歡樹的樹膠，用來做成一隻袋鼠形的東西 —— 一模一樣，有尾巴，有耳朵，甚麼都有。第二天他拿着樹膠做的袋鼠向他們的住處走去。他媽媽和姐姐妹妹看到他帶着答應帶來的袋鼠，便說，“噯，古拉威利爾沒撒謊，他說到做到，給我們帶隻袋鼠來啦。堆起生火的柴吧。今晚咱們有肉吃了。”

About a hundred yards away from the camp Goolahwilleel put down his model, and came on without it. His mother called out: "Where is the kangaroo you brought home?"

"Oh, over there." And he pointed toward where he had left it.

The sisters ran to get it, but came back, saying: "Where is it? We cannot see it."

"Over there," he said, pointing again.

"But there is only a great figure of gum there."

"Well, did I say it was anything else? Did I not say it was gum?"

"No, you did not. You said it was a kangaroo."

"And so it is a kangaroo. A beautiful kangaroo that I made all by myself." And he smiled quite proudly to think what a fine kangaroo he had made.

But his mother and sisters did not smile. They seized him, and gave him a good beating for deceiving them. They told him he should never go out alone again, for he only played instead of hunting, though he knew they starved for meat. They would always in the future go with him.

And so forever the Goolahwilleels went in flocks, nevermore singly, in search of food.

— *Mrs. Llangloh Parker*

508

古拉威利爾在離家大約一百碼的地方把他的袋鼠模型放下，自己走過去。他媽媽喊道："你帶來家的袋鼠在哪兒呀？"

"噢，在那邊呢。"他指着放樹膠袋鼠的地方。

姐妹們跑過去拿，可又回來了，說："哪兒呀？沒看見。"

"就在那邊，"他又指着說。

"可那邊只有一大塊樹膠捏成的東西呀。"

"對呀，我說過是別的了嗎？我沒說是樹膠嗎？"

"你沒說啊，你說是隻袋鼠。"

"是袋鼠呀。一隻漂亮的袋鼠，完全是我自己做的。"他驕傲地笑着，想想自己做了多麼好的一隻袋鼠。

可他媽媽和姐妹沒有笑。她們抓住他，為他騙了她們，把他好好打了一頓。她們對他說，再也不讓他單獨出去了，只因他明明知道她們特別想吃肉，卻光貪玩不去覓食。往後她們要和他一起出去。

因此，羽冠鴿永遠是成羣地去覓食，再也不見單獨外出了。

——蘭格洛·帕克夫人

97 The Fox and the Cat

It happened once that the cat met Mr. Fox in the wood, and because she thought he was clever and experienced in all the ways of the world, she addressed him in a friendly manner.

"Good-morning, dear Mr. Fox! how are you, and how do you get along in these hard times?"

The fox, full of pride, looked at the cat from head to foot for some time, hardly knowing whether he would deign to answer or not. At last he said:

"Oh, you poor whisker-wiper, you silly piebald, you starveling mouse-hunter! what has come into your head? How dare you ask me how I am getting on? What sort of education have you had? How many arts are you master of?"

"Only one," said the cat meekly.

"And what might that one be?" asked the fox.

"When the dogs run after me, I can jump into a tree and save myself."

"Is that all?" said the fox. "I am master of a hundred arts, and I have a sackful of cunning tricks in addition. But I pity you. Come with me, and I will teach you how to escape from the dogs."

Just then a huntsman came along with four hounds. The cat sprang trembling into a tree, and crept stealthily up to the topmost branch, where she was entirely hidden by twigs and leaves.

"Open your sack, Mr. Fox! open your sack!" cried the cat, but the dogs had gripped him, and held him fast.

九十七　狐狸和貓

　　從前有一隻貓在樹林裏遇見狐狸先生。貓想這位狐狸很聰明，對一切人情世故通曉達練，便友好地和他打招呼。

　　"早呀，親愛的狐狸先生！你好嗎？眼前日子難過，你怎麼樣？"

　　狐狸趾高氣揚，盯着貓從頭到腳看了半天，簡直拿不準該不該紆尊降貴回一句話。最後他説：

　　"哼，你這可憐巴巴的蠢斑貓，只知道用爪子去蹭蹭鬍子，餓得半死去捉老鼠吃！你那腦袋裏在轉些甚麼？好大的膽，敢問我日子過得怎樣，你受過甚麼教育嗎？你精通幾門技巧？"

　　"只有一種，"貓逆來順受地説。

　　"你那一種是甚麼？"狐狸問。

　　"狗來追的時候，我會上樹逃命。"

　　"就這個？"狐狸説，"我精通上百種技藝，還有一袋子錦囊妙計。可是我可憐你，跟我來吧，讓我教你被狗追時怎樣脱身。"

　　正在這時，來了一個獵人帶着四條獵犬。貓哆哆嗦嗦跳上一棵樹，不聲不響爬到樹頂的枝子上，身子完全藏在枝葉間。

　　"把你的錦囊打開來吧，狐狸先生！把錦囊打開來！"貓喊道。但幾條獵犬已經撲到他身上，把他緊緊抓住了。

"Oh, Mr. Fox!" cried the cat, "you with your hundred arts, and your sackful of tricks, are held fast, while I, with my one, am safe. Had you been able to creep up here, you would not have lost your life."

— *Folk Tale*

"喂，狐狸先生！"貓喊道，"你有一百種技藝，又有一袋子錦囊妙計，可還是被抓住了。我呢只有一種，卻安全脫身。你要是能夠爬到這裏來，也就不會丟了性命了。"

—— 民間故事

98 The Nail

A tradesman had once transacted a good day's business
at a fair, disposed of all his goods, and filled his purse with
gold and silver. He prepared afterward to return, in order to
reach home by the evening so he strapped his portmanteau,
with the money in it, upon his horse's back, and rode off. At
noon he baited in a small town, and as he was about to set
out again, the stable-boy who brought his horse said to him:
"Sir, a nail is wanting in the shoe on the left hind foot of
your animal."

"Let it be wanting," replied the tradesman; "I am in a
hurry and the iron will doubtless hold the six hours I have
yet to travel."

Late in the afternoon he had to dismount again, and feed
his horse, and at this place also the boy came and told him
that a nail was wanting in one of the shoes, and asked him
whether he should take the horse to a farrier. "No, no, let it
be!" replied the master; "it will last out the couple of hours
that I have now to travel; I am in haste." So saying he rode
off; but his horse soon began to limp, and from limping it
came to stumbling, and presently the beast fell down and
broke its leg. Thereupon the tradesman had to leave his
unfortunate horse lying on the road, to unbuckle the
portmanteau, and to walk home with it upon his shoulder,
where he arrived at last late at night.

"And all this misfortune," said he to himself, "is owing
to the want of a nail. More haste, the less speed!"

— *Folk Tale*

九十八　一顆釘子

　　有一次，一個商人在集市做買賣，生意興隆，所有貨物全部賣出，錢包裹裝滿金幣銀幣，然後他便準備回家。為了趕在黃昏前到家，他把錢裝在行李包裹，把行李包綑在馬背上，騎上馬走了。午間他在一個小鎮上吃過飯、餵過馬，正要出發，牽馬的馬僮對他說，"先生，您的馬左後蹄的馬掌缺了一顆釘子。"

　　"缺就缺吧，"商人說；"我急着趕路呢。剩下六個鐘頭的路程馬掌能挺得住的，沒問題。"

　　接近黃昏的時候，他又得下馬、餵馬。在這裏馬僮又來告訴他馬掌少了一顆釘子，問他要不要把馬送到打馬掌的鐵匠那裏。"不用，不用，讓它去！"主人回答；"我還要走的這兩三個鐘頭的路，馬掌還壞不了；我還要趕路呢。"說着他又上馬走了。但是不久他的馬就瘸了腿，後來甚至失蹄，終於倒下把一條腿摔斷。商人無法，只好留下那倒霉的馬躺在路上。他解下行李包，扛在肩上走回家。到家時已經深夜了。

　　"出了這件倒霉事，"商人自言自語說，"都只為缺了一顆釘子。真是欲速則不達啊！"

—— 民間故事

99 A Good Lesson

It was Sunday. The trains were crowded. A gentleman was walking along the platform looking for a place. In one of the cars he saw a vacant seat. But a small suit-case was lying on it and a stout gentleman was sitting next to it.

"Is this seat vacant?" asked the gentleman.

"No, it is my friend's," answered the gentleman. "He is just coming—this is his suit-case."

"Well," said the gentleman, "I'll sit here till he comes." Five minutes later the train started, but nobody came.

"Your friend is late," said the gentleman. "He has missed his train, but he need not lose his suit-case." And with these words he took the suit-case and threw it out of the window.

The stout gentleman got up and tried to catch the suit-case, but it was too late. It was his suit-case and he had taken a second seat for his own comfort.

— Folk Tale

九十九 一個好教訓

這天是星期日，火車上人羣擁擠。一位紳士在站台上
走着，想找個位子。他在一個車廂裏看到一個空座位，但
座位上卻放着一隻小提箱，旁邊位子上坐着一位身粗體壯
的先生。

"這位子是空的嗎？"紳士問道。

"不空，這是我朋友的座位，"那人回答，"他一會兒
就來——這是他的箱子。"

"好吧，"紳士說，"我先坐着等他來吧。"五分鐘後，
火車開動，但沒有人來。

"你的朋友晚到了，"紳士說，"他誤了火車了，可他
不必丟掉箱子。"說着，他拿起箱子，扔到窗外。

那位身材粗壯的先生站起來想接住箱子，可是來不及
了。其實這是他的箱子。他為圖自己舒服，用箱子佔了一
個空位。

—— 民間故事

100 Honesty Is the Best Policy

A woodman was once working on the bank of a deep river. Suddenly his axe slipped from his hand and dropped into the water.

"Oh! I have lost my axe," he cried. "What shall I do? The water is very deep and I am afraid to dive into it. What shall I do? Who can help me?"

Mercury[1] heard the poor man's cries and appeared before him.

"What is the matter, poor woodman?" he asked. "What has happened that you are so sad and unhappy?"

Mercury listened to the man's story and then said: "Perhaps I can help you." He dived into the river and brought up a golden axe. "Is this yours?" he asked. "No, that is not mine," was the answer. Mercury dived a second time and this time brought up a silver axe. "Is this yours?" he asked. Again the answer was "No". So Mercury dived a third time and this time brought up the very axe, that the woodman had lost. "That is my axe," cried the man. "Yes, that is my own good axe. Now I can work again."

Mercury was so pleased with the fellow's honesty that he at once made him a present of the other two axes and disappeared before the fellow could even say "Thank you".

The woodman went home very pleased with his good luck. He told his friends all about it and one of them decided to try his luck. So he went to the same place, dropped his axe

---

1. Mercury：水星，另一義為古羅馬宗教信奉的神。

一百　誠實最明智

　　有一次，一個砍柴人在一條很深的河的岸邊幹活。忽然間，他失手把斧頭掉進河裏。

　　"哎呀，我把斧頭丟失了，"他喊起來，"怎麼辦呢？水這樣深，我不敢潛到水下。怎麼辦呢？有誰能幫忙呀？"

　　墨丘利聽到這可憐人的叫喊，出現在他面前。

　　"甚麼事情呀，可憐的砍柴人？"他問："出了甚麼事啦，讓你這樣悲傷難過？"

　　墨丘利聽了樵夫敘述事情經過後，說："也許我能助你一臂之力。"他潛下河底拿上來一把金斧。"這是你的嗎？"他問。"不是，那不是我的，"樵夫回答。墨丘利又潛下水底，這次拿上來一把銀斧。"這是你的嗎？"他問。樵夫又答："不是。"墨丘利第三次潛下水底，這次拿上來的正是樵夫丟失的斧頭。"這是我的斧頭，"樵夫喊起來了。"是的，這正是我的斧頭。現在我可以再用它幹活兒了。"

　　墨丘利十分喜歡這人的誠實正直，便立刻把另外兩把斧頭作為禮物送給他，沒等他說聲"謝謝"便消失了。

　　樵夫回家去，對自己的好運氣很高興。他把事情經過全部告訴了他的朋友們。其中有個朋友想去試試運氣。他去到樵夫丟斧頭的地方，把他的斧頭扔到河裏，喊道：

into the river, and cried out: "Oh! I have lost my axe. What shall I do? Who can help me?"

Mercury appeared as before, and when he learnt that the man had lost his axe, he dived into the river. Again he brought up a golden axe. "Is this yours?" he asked.

"Yes, it is," said the second woodman. "You are not telling me the truth," said Mercury. "You shall neither have this axe nor the one that you so foolishly dropped into the water."

— Folk Tale

"哎呀！我把斧頭丟了。我怎麼辦呢？誰能幫幫我的忙呀？"

墨丘利和上次一樣出現了。他聽說那人丟了斧頭，就潛入河水中。他又拿上來一把金斧。"這是你的嗎？"他問。

"是啊，是我的，"這個樵夫回答。"你沒有對我說實話，"墨丘利説。"你得不到這把斧頭，也得不到你自己那麼愚蠢地扔到水裏去的那把了。"

——*民間故事*

一百叢書 30

世界童話精選一百段
100 PASSAGES FROM THE WORLD'S BEST CHILDREN'S STORIES

編譯者◆石幼珊　謝山

發行人◆王學哲

總編輯◆施嘉明

責任編輯◆金堅

出版發行：臺灣商務印書館股份有限公司

台北市重慶南路一段三十七號

電話：(02)2371-3712

讀者服務專線：0800056196

郵撥：0000165-1

網路書店：www.cptw.com.tw

E-mail：cptw@cptw.com.tw

網址：www.cptw.com.tw

局版北市業字第 993 號

香港初版：1999 年 2 月

臺灣初版一刷：1999 年 7 月

臺灣初版三刷：2005 年 9 月

定價：新台幣 450 元

本書經商務印書館（香港）有限公司授權出版

ISBN 957-05-1596-1
版權所有　翻印必究

世界童話精選一百段＝100 passages from the
world's best children's stories ／ 石幼珊,
謝山編譯. --臺灣初版. --臺北市：臺灣商
務，1999〔民88〕
　　面 ； 公分.-（一百叢書：30）

ISBN 957-05-1596-1（平裝）

815.9　　　　　　　　　　　　　88008006

一百叢書   100 SERIES

英漢 · 漢英對照

讀者回函卡

感謝您對本館的支持，為加強對您的服務，請填妥此卡，免付郵資寄回，可隨時收到本館最新出版訊息，及享受各種優惠。

姓名：＿＿＿＿＿＿＿＿＿＿＿＿＿＿　　性別：□男 □女

出生日期：＿＿年＿＿月＿＿日

職業：□學生 □公務（含軍警） □家管 □服務 □金融 □製造
　　　□資訊 □大眾傳播 □自由業 □農漁牧 □退休 □其他

學歷：□高中以下（含高中） □大專 □研究所（含以上）

地址：□□□＿＿＿＿＿＿＿＿＿＿＿＿＿＿＿＿
　　　＿＿＿＿＿＿＿＿＿＿＿＿＿＿＿＿＿＿＿

電話：（H）＿＿＿＿＿＿＿＿＿（O）＿＿＿＿＿＿＿＿

購買書名：＿＿＿＿＿＿＿＿＿＿＿＿＿＿＿＿＿＿＿

您從何處得知本書？

　　　□書店 □報紙廣告 □報紙專欄 □雜誌廣告 □DM廣告
　　　□傳單 □親友介紹 □電視廣播 □其他

您對本書的意見？ （A/滿意 B/尚可 C/需改進）

　　　內容＿＿＿ 編輯＿＿＿ 校對＿＿＿ 翻譯＿＿＿
　　　封面設計＿＿＿ 價格＿＿＿ 其他＿＿＿＿＿＿

您的建議：＿＿＿＿＿＿＿＿＿＿＿＿＿＿＿＿＿＿＿
　　　　　＿＿＿＿＿＿＿＿＿＿＿＿＿＿＿＿＿＿＿
　　　　　＿＿＿＿＿＿＿＿＿＿＿＿＿＿＿＿＿＿＿

臺灣商務印書館

台北市重慶南路一段三十七號　電話：（02）23116118・23115538
讀者服務專線：080056196　傳真：（02）23710274
郵撥：0000165-1號　E-mail：cptw＠ms12.hinet.net

廣 告 回 信
台灣北區郵政管理局登記證
第 6 5 4 0 號

100臺北市重慶南路一段37號

臺灣商務印書館 收

對摺寄回，謝謝！

傳統現代　並翼而翔

Flying with the wings of tradition and modernity.